The Bardic Isles Series

Master of Music
Cry of the Kestrel
Rider of the Wind (to be released in 2025)

I0781014

Author's Note

This is not a stand-alone novel, but rather the second book in The Bardic Isles Series. Reading or listening to the first book is highly recommended for a better understanding of the workings of this unique, musical world, and the relationships of the people who live there, who will never be merely characters to me. Those things, while touched on in this book, are not fully explained because the author has a dislike of books in a series that spend an entire chapter or two rehashing what came before. So, onward we go!

Praise for book 1, *Master of Music*

"Himeda employs realistic dialogue and a clear, immersive tone that moves the action effortlessly forward as characters develop. She's creatively crafted a fantasy novel in which magic comes from music itself. A brisk, expertly crafted tale."
— *Kirkus Reviews*

"Music is magic in this charming, richly written apprenticeship fantasy. Himeda writes lush, engaging scenes of travel and music-making, in exacting and evocative prose."
— *BookLife Reviews*

"A magical, musical fantasy world that's both beautiful and unique. Himeda's prose is like music itself—lyrical, sweeping, and, at times, building toward an unknown crescendo. (The author's) love and knowledge of music shines through on every page, the writing's cadence making *Master of Music* a joy to read."
— *The BookLife Prize*

"Filled with stunning descriptions and wonderful details, *Master of Music* is a superb first book in this series. The story is incredible, the characters simply remarkable."
— *Kathy Stickles for Reader Views*

"The (audiobook's) flawless narration by the talented Will Hahn was interlaced with awesome musical compositions. What started as short flute, harp, and pipe melodies culminated in amazing, fully-fledged songs, all composed by Marla Himeda. It made me feel as if I were watching an exhilarating stage play. This is a brilliant fantasy that offers both children and adults a lot to enjoy and will appeal to everyone who likes fantasy and music."
— *Olga Markova for Readers' Favorite*

Praise for Book 2, *Cry of the Kestrel*

"Himeda once again constructs a world with unique musical magic and three-dimensional characters who immediately endear themselves to readers. Kaelin's coming-of-age story is a genuine pleasure to follow as he grapples with right and wrong in an increasingly muddled world. Himeda's depiction of music as a magical force for change will likely inspire budding musicians of all ages. A sharply-written, moving tale that weaves together epic adventure and genuine heart in equal measure."

– *Kirkus Reviews*

"This sequel offers enthralling world-building, lush accounts of music and magic-making, and an ending that is truly suspenseful. Vivid prose and surprising magic will please lovers of any thoughtful fantasy."

– *BookLife Reviews*

"A worthy sequel that stays true to the skillful writing that debuted with young Kaelin. The authenticity of the characters and the exquisite capture of emotions create a relationship that pulls at our heartstrings. Beautifully depicted and thoroughly engaging. A complete joy to read."

– *The B.R.A.G. Medallion*

"A riveting fantasy story that I would highly recommend to every reader, young and old. You will laugh and cry, and just feel delighted as you delve into Kaelin's world of music. Readers can be assured they will feel as if they are right there experiencing every moment along with the characters. The author has created a story that has surpassed the first one ... I adored every page."

– *Kathy Stickles for Reader Views*

Cry of the Kestrel

Book Two of The Bardic Isles Series

Marla Himeda

print ISBN: 978-1-959900-03-0
.mobi ISBN: 978-1-959900-04-7
.epub ISBN: 978-1-959900-05-4
audiobook ISBN: 978-1-959900-06-1
Library of Congress Control Number: 2024908891

Published in Kaneohe, HI, USA

*For Michiko, the Master in my life who so freely shared
her knowledge and wisdom, and who ignited
a love of music that has lasted a lifetime*

*And for the readers who are continuing this journey with
Kaelin through the Bardic Isles, as he meets the Masters in
his own life and is forever changed by each of them*

Contents

(continued)

The Bardic Isles

Eyrie
Braelach
Riona Springs
Shoal
Kyria
Skye
Loryn
Zephyr
Loch Lyon
Mt Tiern
Aille
Rilla
Oriel
Elba
Mt Carag
Glyn
Shay
Caer Wynd
Rhys
Loch Senan
Lyssa
Wyndle
Ciara
Lyra

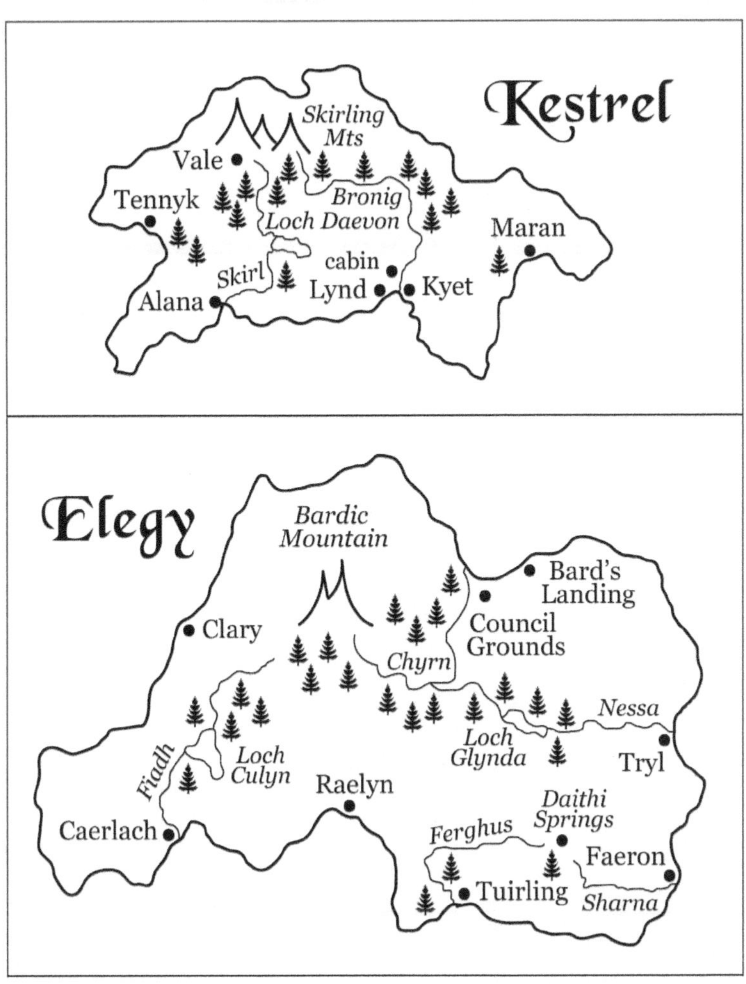

Kestrel
Skirling Mts
Vale
Tennyk
Bronig
Loch Daevon
Maran
cabin
Skirl
Lynd
Kyet
Alana

Elegy
Bardic Mountain
Clary
Bard's Landing
Council Grounds
Chyrn
Nessa
Fiadh
Loch Culyn
Loch Glynda
Tryl
Raelyn
Daithi Springs
Caerlach
Ferghus
Faeron
Tuirling
Sharna

Movement One

The Instrument Master

Chapter 1

On a chilly morning in mid-spring, Kaelin stood at the stern of a Bardic ship, watching the island of Kestrel fade into the distance. Swirling threads of fog rose from the water, capriciously robbing him of his view and restoring it by turns. It made little difference. His eyes were blurred with a mist of their own, for he was leaving his island for the island of Eyrie. And, for the first time in his life, he was alone.

The cycles pass slowly for the young, or so his Master was fond of saying, but Kaelin reflected moodily that this past one had been far too short for his liking. Nearly a cycle ago he had stood on this same ship when his Master had taken him to the Spring Council on Elegy. In a bid to have Kaelin accepted as his apprentice, Master Bergid had pledged his robe and rank on Kaelin successfully playing for the Council. And play Kaelin had, wresting control of his instrument from the mountain, whose powerful music sought to release itself through the only person in the Bardic Isles who could hear it. He had delivered a stunning performance that swept his audience into experiencing for themselves the pain of his repressed gift and the release of it under the guidance of the Master he loved. The apprentice had returned to Kyet with his Master for ten wonderful months of further training in composition and instrumental playing.

Kaelin stared longingly at the receding coast of Kestrel, thinking of his Master, Darryk, and Laena. His brows creased in worry at the thought of his sister. It had only been a month since the accident. Laena's husband, Donal, had been late returning from Kyet after a delivery there during a storm. Kaelin shuddered, remembering the frantic search. The horses were found on the bank of a flooded stream not far from Lynd, still harnessed to the overturned wagon. Donal was trapped under it, drowned. Laena could not sleep for nights afterward unless Kaelin played his harp or flute for her. Then she would be lulled to sleep, her mind filled with musical visions of the mountains and kestrels. Kaelin had not wanted to leave her, but Laena had insisted that he go, and Master Bergid had assured him that she would be looked after.

"She has friends who are taking turns staying with her, and I'm sure Darryk will help in any way he can since he's currently assigned to the Southeast Territory," his Master said. "Go ahead with the plans we've set in place."

The plans he referred to had been for Kaelin to spend a cycle with the other four Masters, three months with each. It had taken the combined efforts of Master Bergid and Darryk to persuade Kaelin to increase his knowledge in a way that no one else, of any Bardic rank, had ever had the chance to.

"Think of it, Kaelin!" Darryk said persuasively. "All four Masters have agreed to personally train you in the area of their expertise! It's a chance you must *not* pass up."

Kaelin said nothing, stubbornly unconvinced that any Master could possibly compare to his own.

"Of course," Darryk continued, "if that doesn't tempt you, perhaps the thought of pipes..." He shrugged when the scowl on his young friend's face silently accused him of not fighting fair. "Well, it *is* your chance to make them, under the supervision of the Instrument Master of the Bardic Isles himself. Why, you're liable to come back with a better set than Master Bergid's!"

Kaelin's scowl deepened. He bit his lip and glanced anxiously up at his Master. "Who's going to take care of you, sir? All the chores ... and your meals! You already stay up so late, working..."

"I'll have someone come in twice a week to help me, just as I did before you came along," his Master promised. "And I can always have a meal delivered from the inn if I get too busy to fix it myself." He smiled when his apprentice's expression didn't clear. "I'll be just fine, Kaelin. The cycle will pass quickly, and you'll be back before you know it. You know that your place beside me will always be here, waiting."

Kaelin slowly nodded, persuaded more by his awareness that it was his Master's wish than by any temptations of acquired knowledge or new pipes. And so it was decided. He would go first to the island of Eyrie and Master Talan.

"He's been working on improving stringed instruments lately," Master Bergid said, "especially the lute. And the last time I spoke with him he hinted at an improvement he had in mind for the harp." The Master frowned. "Which he perversely refused to divulge. Perhaps you could wheedle it out of him."

After three months with Master Talan, Kaelin would depart for the island of Zephyr and Master Marek. "He can help you in two ways," Bergid said. "The first being your flute technique." At Kaelin's look of surprise, he continued dryly. "Well, he *is* the Master Flutist of the Bardic Isles, and for very good reason. Much as I hate to admit it, his playing is a bit better than mine, and I'm sure he'll have a few pointers for you that you can then," he cleared his throat, "discreetly pass on to me."

Kaelin laughed. "What's the second way he can help me?"

"I'll leave you to discover that for yourself, lad," Master Bergid had responded, leaving his apprentice madly curious.

From Zephyr he would travel to Lyra and Voice Master Rial. Kaelin was told that, although he might be a bit stiff-mannered, there was nothing inflexible about Master Rial's voice. "Indeed," his Master told him, "you might find it difficult to do with your flute what Master Rial can with his voice. The closest I've heard to it is Fenadal's, but even he has much to learn to approach Master Rial's level of expertise. Learn all you can about vocal development from him. I have waited for your voice to change before sending you to him for that reason."

"And don't forget to get plenty of rest while you're there," Darryk advised. "You'll need it for your next stop."

"Ah, yes," his Master said thoughtfully. "I must agree with Darryk that you'll be on your toes the entire time you spend with Master Grened." He frowned slightly. "I almost wish I could spare you the trip to Elegy, but there is much you can learn from our Master Harpist. Besides being irrefutably the best Harpist in the Bardic Isles, there are those dyes you want to replenish and learn to produce. There is no one else to learn that from, not if you want dyes of that quality for your woodwork."

"Just watch your step with him, Kaelin," warned Darryk. "Master Grened will not hesitate to punish the slightest misstep."

The Master turned a droll eye upon Darryk. "I don't suppose you have any firsthand knowledge of that, do you?"

There was no answering humor in Darryk's eyes. "Yes, sir, I do, as a witness to the minor infraction of another Bard." He looked at Kaelin. "Many things that your Master takes humorously, as they're intended, Master Grened will see as insolence and punish accordingly. He has no tolerance for mistakes, either, however honest they may be. So please be careful, Kaelin."

The Master's humor vanished. "Surely Master Grened would not be so severe with a youngster," he said with a frown. "Kaelin will not come of age for over two cycles."

Darryk's silence made clear his opinion that Kaelin's lack of cycles would not stay the Master Harpist's hand. The frown directed toward him deepened. "I was not aware that Master

Grened's reputation had slid so drastically."

"Forgive me, sir, if my words implied criticism," the Bard said quietly. "I have the highest regard for Master Grened's abilities and am grateful for what I learned from him on the instrument I love most. My words were intended only as a warning to my young friend to be careful."

The Master cocked a brow at Kaelin. "Well, then, lad, I suggest you take Darryk's advice and tread softly on Elegy."

"I will, sir!" A week later, he had boarded a ship for Eyrie.

As the island of Kestrel disappeared from view, Kaelin blinked away threatening tears and turned from the rail. With favorable winds, it would be late afternoon before they reached their destination, and he'd best take his packs to his cabin.

A series of staccatos, all of a single pitch, came from above, and the apprentice glanced up. High above the mast of the ship, a large kestrel flew. Kaelin watched it with interest, certain he'd seen this same bird several times in the vicinity of his Master's home. He liked to think it was the same kestrel he had seen in the woods of Vale, looking down on him from the branch of a twisted oak. He had heard the beautiful, wild music coming from the bird, the inherent music of the creature that no one else could hear but him. Later he'd played a variation of it, unaware that not far off, a Master sat motionless at a small campfire, listening and experiencing the same glorious freedom of flight that he was. The kestrel's song had brought his Master to him, and Kaelin longed to take up his flute and play it once again, to soar effortlessly into the sky and fly back to the Master he had not wished to leave.

The kestrel sent a barrage of scolding staccatos down upon the ship and flew back toward Kyet. Kaelin watched him enviously, then was surprised when the bird suddenly changed direction and flew back to the ship. Once again a spate of notes sounded above, and once again the bird flew back toward Kyet. When the ship ignored the clear avian imperative to return to the port it had just left, the kestrel returned for the third time and circled the ship. Wondering at the bird's unusual behavior, Kaelin watched it for a moment before reluctantly turning away. He had promised his Master not to listen to the song of any living thing until he came of age. The kestrel issued a final outburst as though strongly disapproving of this, then flew off in the direction they were headed, toward Eyrie.

Kaelin went below deck and found his quarters small but comfortable. He listened for a moment to sounds of the ocean waves as the ship sliced a path through them, then reached for his harp. Perhaps he couldn't play the song of the kestrel, but there were other ways to release his melancholy. Nor was he worried about sweeping the sailors above into his music, leaving the ship unmanned. When his Master had told him that he was the first person to be born gifted in over two hundred cycles, and his music had the power to transport his listeners into his own experience of it, the apprentice had been hesitant to play in anyone's hearing. Though his inhibited gift had been freed, and he now understood that his music had not caused anyone harm, Kaelin had still worried it could inadvertently do so, especially if they happened to be doing something that demanded their full attention. But then, just last season, he'd unexpectedly discovered a way to block others from that pull.

He had written a short composition for pipes, musically describing the darkness of night on the lowest pipes, then gradually rising higher to experience the dawn of a new day. When he played it for his Master, Bergid was astonished, telling him that, for the first time, Kaelin's music had not pulled his own senses into it. He suggested that Kaelin play the same opening of darkness, then segue into one of his other compositions. When Kaelin did so, the Master remained unaffected.

"Do it again," Bergid said, "but this time, don't play the darkness. Just imagine it filling your mind and play."

Kaelin did so, and his Master nodded in satisfaction. "I think you've just found a way to keep others from being pulled into your music! Simply cloak your mind in darkness before you play."

Now, in his cabin below deck, Kaelin closed his eyes, letting darkness fall over his mind like a barrier. Then he allowed the roll of the ship and the sound of the sea to become the theme from which he skillfully wove his music.

The crew and other passengers paused, listening. The rhythmic swells of the sea sprang to life with the vivid imagery of the harpist. Though the music didn't pull their senses into the experience, none of them ever forgot that voyage to Eyrie or the music of the young apprentice who sailed with them. Always they would hear the faint whisper of Kaelin's music through the sounds of the sea.

They spied the eastern coast of Eyrie late that day and soon approached the rocky coastline. Sailors busily adjusted the sails, sending the ship skimming southward toward Skye, the main seaport on the southeast coast. Kaelin looked curiously at the passing scenery. It was easy to see why most of the wool and leather used in the Bardic Isles came from Eyrie. Wide vistas of grassland stretched inland from the coast to the low hills of the interior. He shivered slightly; such open space was unnerving to one accustomed to the rugged mountains and forests of Kestrel.

The ship rounded the southern point and tacked northward into the wind toward Skye, situated in the most sheltered spot within the bay. As they approached the wharf, Kaelin shouldered his packs, surprised to see Master Talan waiting for him at the end of the dock. He had assumed one of the eighteen Bards assigned to Eyrie, or someone of much lower rank, would have been sent to fetch him. The ship slid smoothly alongside the dock, and the crew hurried to man the ropes and secure the gangplank. As Kaelin walked across it, the crew slapped their hands rhythmically against the rail, startling him so badly he nearly tripped as he stepped onto the dock. The voice of the Captain boomed suddenly from the deck.

"It may be an apprentice robe ye wear, lad, but it's a Master's berth ye'll always have on *my* ship! Such music as that was a rare treat."

Kaelin was taken aback by the unexpected praise. "Thank you, Captain," he managed to say, then was startled a second time by a voice speaking directly behind him.

"An impressive farewell, Kaelin. Perhaps I'd better warn Master Bergid that his berth is in danger of being reserved for your use!"

Kaelin flushed deeply as he turned to face the Master Bard of Eyrie and gave him a deep bow. "Master Talan. I'm honored to meet you, sir. I'm sorry if I—"

The Master raised a hand, the creases around his eyes deepening with amusement. "I'm only teasing, lad. It's a privilege to witness such a tribute to an apprentice of the Bardic Order. Come along, now, we've a bit of a walk ahead of us."

The Instrument Master was tall and lean, with a muscular build. His light brown hair was streaked with grey, his eyes the color of cinnamon tea. He swung one of Kaelin's packs over his own shoulder, waving aside the apprentice's frantic objection, and headed west. The smoothly cobbled streets were filled with merchants and crewmen, who greeted the Master cheerfully and glanced curiously at his young companion. Now and then the Master paused for brief conversations with shopkeepers who hailed him at their doors. As they moved past the business section and came to streets with small homes and meticulously kept gardens, a young child burst from a doorway, crying and clutching something in her arms. She ran wailing straight to the Master, who immediately stooped down and steadied her.

"Now then, Terra, what dreadful thing has happened?"

The little girl gasped out her tale of woe. "It was Collin!" she cried accusingly. "He took Mirra from me—and wouldn't give her back!—and he ... he *killed* her!" She held out a bedraggled wooden doll for the Master's inspection.

"Hmm, let's have a look, then." The Master examined the doll. "Mirra just has a broken arm, and fortunately I have exactly what she needs." He set down Kaelin's pack and rummaged for a moment in one of the many pockets of his robe.

"Ah, here it is." The Master withdrew a small jar, scooped a tiny amount of a clear substance with a small pick that seemed to magically appear in his hand, then worked the substance into both halves of the dangling wooden arm. He held it firmly together with one hand while his other dove into another pocket and produced a strip of cloth. He bound the doll's arm tightly, then handed her back to the delighted child. He held up a warning finger as Terra shyly thanked him.

"Mirra's had quite a shock," he told her gravely, "and is going to need some time to recover. Keep the bandage on until tomorrow, child. Until then, she's going to need music to help her heal." He sighed. "If only someone could sing to her..."

"*I* can sing, Master Talan!" Terra announced proudly.

"Excellent!" the Master said approvingly. "You sing to her, then, take the bandage off tomorrow, and she'll be fine."

Terra cuddled her doll.

"Tell Collin that Mirra has been successfully treated by the Master Bard, who will not be pleased to repeat his work."

"I'll tell him." With a triumphant gleam in her eye, Terra walked away, crooning softly to her doll.

The Master straightened, swung Kaelin's pack over his shoulder, and strode on as though nothing unusual had occurred. Kaelin grinned and hurried alongside him, his spirits lifting. Any Master who would take the time to stop and save the life of a doll, he decided, was someone he'd be happy to learn from.

Chapter 2

Master Talan and Kaelin soon left Skye behind and took a narrow road that led along the bay. "I'm afraid there's no mountains here, but that has its advantages," the Master told him. "For one thing, it's much easier to travel about. And there's a splendid variety of plants I've never seen anywhere else. I've quite grown to love it here."

"You're not from Eyrie?"

The Master shook his head. "I grew up in the woods of Kestrel, just as you did, though not in such a remote location as Vale. So, I understand the scenic shock you're undergoing." The light brown eyes danced into his. "If you'd like to crawl under my desk to feel more at home, I'll have no objections. I cleaned it out especially for you."

Kaelin laughed. Their path turned northward up a grassy slope. At the top stood the Master's home, commanding a fine view of the ocean and the craggy, windswept coast behind them. The Master turned and surveyed the scenery for a moment, filling his lungs with enormous quantities of air. "A bit windy up here, perhaps, but the view more than compensates, don't you think?"

Kaelin, looking around in appreciation, agreed. When he followed the Master into his home, however, the scenery underwent an abrupt change. If the underside of Master Talan's desk was free of clutter, it was the only part of the room that was. Clothes, dishes, and scrolls lay strewn with careless abandon, as though an enormous hand had stirred the room like a pot of stew.

Apparently unaware of the chaos, Master Talan gestured toward an open door near the fireplace. "The guest room is through there," he said absentmindedly. "You can clear away whatever you need to make room for your things."

I guess he doesn't have visitors very often, Kaelin thought as he worked his way into the guest room. He cleared space for his packs, then unburdened the bed and rolled his bedroll out on top of it, since there was no bedding. Then he navigated his way back to the Master. *How does he ever get any work done here?*

He hurried to help Master Talan with the meal he was heating up over the kitchen fire. The leftover stew looked anything but appetizing, and Kaelin shuddered as he ladled grey meat and limp carrots and potatoes into two bowls. *Worse than the worst I ever made. Darryk would be horrified.* He grinned to himself, remembering that Darryk had finished his rotation here the previous cycle, so he must be well aware of the Instrument Master's culinary shortcomings. Master Talan ate his stew quickly, but Kaelin barely managed half a bowlful.

"I'm afraid I'm not much of a cook." The Master smiled ruefully. "Too busy making instruments to bother learning how."

"I'd be happy to take care of all the cooking while I'm here, sir," Kaelin quickly offered.

"You'll hear no objections from me on that score, lad." The Master pushed his bowl aside and headed toward the door. "Come now, I've something to show you."

Kaelin followed him around to the back of the house to where a second building stood, only slightly smaller than the Master's home. Master Talan opened the door and lit a lantern standing on a table next to it. Kaelin drew a sharp breath as the enormous room was bathed in light. Whatever the state of Master Talan's home, there was nothing disorderly about his workshop. Gleaming tools hung on the walls in precise rows. Workbenches and tables were spotlessly clean. Many types of instruments, in various stages of completion, hung or lay in careful order. Wood shavings and sawdust were neatly swept into a receptacle.

"This is the most amazing workshop I've ever seen!" the apprentice exclaimed, looking around in awe.

The creases in the Master's weathered face deepened. He walked over to one of three large cabinets and opened one of its many drawers. It was filled with wooden screws, sorted into cubicles by size. "These cabinets contain all the parts needed in the making and repairing of instruments," the Master said. He stirred a few of the piles with absorbed interest, then opened another drawer. This one held jars of resins and stains. A third contained various types of strings. "My Bards must first learn how to make these items before they're allowed to use them." The Master opened drawer after drawer, exhibiting all the small items needed to produce the beautiful instruments used in the Bardic Isles.

"Are you really going to teach me how to make all this, Master Talan?" Kaelin asked eagerly.

"I'll certainly try," the Master replied dryly.

"When can we start?"

"Well, *I* generally work here at all hours, but I would hardly expect you to," the Master told him. "It's getting late, and if you're tired from your journey—"

"I could *never* be tired in a workshop like this!" The apprentice flushed. "Forgive me for interrupting you, sir."

Master Talan chuckled. "I believe you and I are going to get along well, lad. Quite well, indeed. Go on then, fetch your instruments and I'll have a look at them."

A few minutes later, Kaelin presented him with his two instruments. The Master took his flute and examined it from all angles. "An extremely well-made instrument." The flush of pleasure that spread over the apprentice's face did not escape his notice. "Ah ... you made it yourself, then?"

"With help from my Master."

"Well, I would expect nothing but the best from someone under Master Bergid's instruction. He's a superb craftsman of instruments in his own right, but *this*," he scanned the length of the flute with an appreciative eye, "tells me he either outdid himself as a teacher, or he had an exceptionally gifted student to work with." He glanced at Kaelin inquiringly.

"My Master is an excellent teacher," Kaelin said loyally.

Talan smiled. "Given the fact that he gave you rosewood to work with, I suspect both are true. It's a rare wood, brought here from Gaul, which I imagine a boy from Vale would know."

Kaelin nodded, and the Master quirked a brow. "You might not know, however, that the merchants of Gaul import it from far more southern climates, making it impressively expensive. Your Master would not have given such precious material to a novice in woodcraft." He nodded approvingly at Kaelin's flute. "And his trust was quite justified, for this is a finely crafted instrument that could hold its own next to any Master's. I thought as much at the last Spring Council but didn't have the opportunity to inspect it for myself." He tapped the headjoint. "I have, however, a suggestion for improving this that might interest you." He rummaged around in one of his drawers. "Let's see now, where did I put it? I just finished it the other day, with you in mind..." He smiled triumphantly. "Ah, here it is."

The Master drew out a curved wooden ring and a flute headjoint. He lifted the headjoint and blew a clear note on it. Then he placed the wooden ring over the headjoint hole. It fit perfectly, making a platform all around, yet leaving the hole free. Kaelin watched as the Master carefully secured it to the headjoint with an adhesive substance from one of his many jars. Then he cocked an eyebrow at Kaelin and placed the flute to his lips again. The tone he produced this time was markedly clearer and more resonant. He chuckled at Kaelin's dumbfounded expression.

"As I'm sure you know," the Master lectured, "the sound of a wind instrument like your flute is produced by vibrating air. The size of the stream you direct into it and the precision of its entrance through the headjoint directly affect the tone. Now," he indicated the headjoint on Kaelin's flute, "with a hole like that one, your lip rests against it too closely to direct the air efficiently. He tapped the headjoint lying on the table. "With a platform around the hole, your lip rests further above it, enabling you to control your air stream with far greater accuracy. That, in turn, improves the tone ... with a bit of practice." He handed the headjoint with the platform to Kaelin. "Give it a try."

Kaelin quickly switched his headjoint for the Master's and rested his lower lip against the platform. It felt strange at first, but as he experimented with it, he immediately felt the difference in control he had over the tone. "Would you teach me to make one for my flute?" he asked eagerly.

Master Talan smiled with satisfaction. "Now, that's what I like about young people. Show them an improvement and they're off and running with it. No ridiculous attachments to old ways." He folded his arms and looked at the apprentice appraisingly. "Perhaps you and I can strike a bargain. I'll give you a piece of rosewood to make a platform for your flute headjoint. Then, once you're satisfied with it, I want you to demonstrate its effectiveness to the other Masters you'll be staying with. Your Master and Master Marek will be easily persuaded, but Masters Rial and Grened might be a bit difficult." A wry smile crossed the Master's face. "They consider me something of a rebel, constantly tinkering with tradition. However, if someone whose flute playing commanded their greatest respect was enthusiastic about one of my unorthodox improvements..."

"If you think I can be of help, sir, it's a bargain!"

"Oh, I don't just *think* so," the Master returned dryly. "I heard you play, remember, and although it was nearly a cycle ago, I've not forgotten. Neither, I'm sure, have they. The link you forged with your music, enabling us to experience what *you* were experiencing, was unprecedented. With the help of such a performer as that," he continued, not seeming to notice Kaelin's discomfiture, "there should be a platform on the headjoint of every flute in the Bardic Order before the end of this cycle. You've no idea how much time, trouble, and sheer aggravation you'll be saving me." He put the headjoint away with an air of immense satisfaction, then turned a keen glance upon the apprentice.

"I believe Master Bergid has allowed you to perform for the Bards of Kestrel this cycle, has he not?"

"Yes, sir," Kaelin replied, "but I'm not allowed to play for anyone outside the Order, with the exception of my sister, unless I place a block first. My Master has also forbidden his Bards from discussing my gift with anyone outside the Order."

"A wise precaution," the Master said. "Your playing will command quite enough attention without adding to it a gift that will have a line of villagers stretching from your Master's door to Kyet, clamoring to hear you play. He told us about the block you discovered and asked us to put our Bards under the same restriction upon your arrival. Have you discovered anything more about your gift this cycle?"

"My Master has forbidden me to explore my gift any further until I come of age, the earliest he will lift the restriction."

If Master Talan realized the apprentice had not quite answered the question put to him, he made no sign of it. "Another wise precaution," he murmured. "And," he added, "speaking of your Master, I'd like to thank you for what you did that day, following him and redeeming his pledge when it was clearly a far more dangerous thing for you to do than any of us could have known. What you did for him," he said warmly, "you did for us all. Not one of us had any desire to take your Master's robe. We would have grieved the loss of our colleague, and the Council would not have been the same without him around to..." he smiled whimsically, "spice things up!"

Kaelin laughed, and the Master's gaze turned to the other instrument the apprentice had brought with him. "Now, let's have a look at that harp of yours," he said. "I believe Darryk instructed you in its making?"

Kaelin nodded and handed him his harp.

The Instrument Master's eyes widened. "So, *this* is where my order of seasoned rosewood went!" he exclaimed. "Of all the underhanded, conniving Masters in Bardic history, lad," he said with admiration, "I believe yours heads the list. I was waiting for an order of rare woods that was due to arrive from Tryl after the Spring Council last cycle. When it came, everything was there except the seasoned rosewood. When I complained to the merchant, I was told that a Master had sent a message to him, commandeering it for his own use and promising him ten percent more in payment than I had. He refused to tell me which Master it was, claiming he was under oath not to." Master Talan shook his head in exasperation. "One of my own colleagues ... and I'm Cathal's best customer! I believe I'll have several choice words for both of them, when next we meet."

Kaelin grinned. "Yes, sir."

The Instrument Master inspected Kaelin's harp with the same absorbed interest he had given his flute. "Hmm, yes ... well, my wood could scarcely have been put to better use. The column and neck are very well made, indeed. The woods you used for the body provide a nice contrast to the rosewood and are beautifully fitted. Tell me about them." He turned a keen eye upon the apprentice.

"The larger piece is spruce," Kaelin said promptly, "and is the soundboard for the harp."

"Which does what?"

"It amplifies the sound."

"Why spruce?"

"Because it's light and strong, and it has an even grain."

"And the smaller strip inset here?" The Master indicated a strip of wood running the length of the soundboard.

"That's beech. It's used because it's tough enough to bear the tension of the strings."

The Instrument Master smiled as he continued his inspection of the harp. "I'm glad to see that Darryk has as much talent as a teacher as he had as a student. He spent his last rotation here, most of it pestering me with detailed questions about harp making." He glanced up. "Not that I minded. Thanks to him and your devious Master, not to mention your own woodworking talent, you have a harp here that not even our Master Harpist will be able to find fault with."

Kaelin's face lit. "Thank you, sir."

"I can easily see why carved tuning pegs have become all the rage this cycle, and your carvings on the frame are exquisite." The Master looked admiringly at the carving of Bardic Mountain at the base of the harp's frame and the kestrel in flight at the top. "Elegy and Kestrel?"

"Those are the only two islands I've been to. I'm hoping to find symbols for the other three during my travels this cycle."

The Master nodded, then rummaged through another drawer. He took out a package and emptied it on the table. Thin wooden crooks fell out, each with a small screw protruding from the lower edge of one side. Then he took a small lap harp from the wall and drilled a hole a short distance below a tuning peg. He screwed one of the crooks into the hole, so that it stood close to the string and firmly plucked it. Then, with a conspiratorial smile, he pushed the piece of wood against the string and plucked it again. The pitch of the string was a half step higher. Kaelin, quick to see the significance of this, grinned broadly and applauded.

The Instrument Master bowed with a flourish to his enthusiastic audience of one. "Except for my Bards, you're the first to see my latest little device." He waved his hand expressively. "As you're obviously aware, the problem with the lap harp is its restriction to one major and relative minor key." He tapped the little wedge of wood. "But with these little crooks placed next to each string, a harpist can play in any key he likes. Raising every F and C string will make the key of D major and B minor available and so forth." He chuckled. "You won't need to talk Master Grened into using these, lad. The dictates of tradition are unlikely to prevent him from improving his *own* instrument!"

They laughed together and then the Master gave the apprentice an appraising glance. "What, exactly, would you like to learn from me?"

"Oh, *everything,* sir!"

The Master's mouth quirked in amusement. "That would require more cycles than you're probably willing to spend away from your Master, lad. If you could be a bit more specific?"

Kaelin looked at him hopefully. "Pipes? I have the use of my Master's, and it's a fine set, of course, but, well..."

Master Talan chuckled. "An instrument isn't really yours unless you've made it yourself, is that it? No one understands that better than I do. Making a set of pipes can certainly be arranged, for I have seasoned wood ready for such use. I assume you've been using a partial set of twelve pipes?"

Kaelin shook his head. "I've been using my Master's full set of seventeen."

Talan's eyes widened. "At the last Spring Council, your Master told us that you'd reached an advanced level on three instruments. We assumed he was referring to flute, lyre, and lute, an impressive feat for an apprentice." He glanced at Kaelin's harp. "Am I now to understand that he was referring to the three *primary* Bardic instruments? Harp, flute, and pipes?"

Kaelin nodded. "I've begun studying lyre and lute as well but haven't reached the advanced forms on those yet."

The Master cleared his throat. "Well, then, a full set of seventeen pipes it is. You'll need to draw a detailed set of plans for their construction first, as you undoubtedly did for your harp. There are precise formulas to calculate the length of each pipe, depending on its width and what diameter the bore should be to produce the desired pitch and timbre of the tone. Perhaps I can assess your drawing and cyphering skills in the morning. If they pass my inspection, you can begin those calculations." He indicated Kaelin's flute and harp. "There's no need to assess your skills in woodworking, though I'll expect you to demonstrate your ability to make anything your pipes will require from my cabinet before you begin its construction. In the afternoon, I'll teach you how to make the platform for your flute and the crooks for your harp. You should also learn the basics of other types of instrument-making as well, as time permits." He lifted his brows inquiringly at Kaelin. "Would that suit you?"

"Oh, yes, sir! Thank you, Master Talan!" He hesitated. "I hope I'm not going to keep you from your other work."

"Oh, don't bother about that. All of us have agreed to give you three months of our time, during which the Bards assigned to us can keep things running smoothly." He chuckled. "Good experience for them and a welcome change for me. Gives me the chance to work on a few more radical ideas I've been mulling over as well. Your Master and Marek are no longer any fun, but I make it a point to shock Rial and Grened at least twice a cycle ... if only to keep their hearts in good working order." He rose to put away his tools, and the apprentice hurried to sweep up the tiny curls of wood shavings from the table, using a small hand broom and receptacle he had spotted hanging from underneath it.

The Master's eyes glinted with approval. "The table over there will be your workbench," he said, nodding toward it. "Now or in the morning, you can study the pipes prototype hanging on the wall over there, then make a detailed list of every small construction piece you will need to make a set of your own. Collect those parts from my cabinets, taking the time to familiarize yourself with their contents, then arrange the parts on your workbench and come fetch me. If it's not too late by then, you can show me which of the parts you'll require my instruction to make."

"Yes, sir!" Kaelin eagerly headed toward the wall of prototypes. The Master chuckled and was soon absorbed in his own work.

The apprentice studied the pipes, made his list, then opened every drawer in the Master's cabinets and collected what he would need to construct his pipes. It wasn't long before he was standing before the Instrument Master's work desk.

Talan looked up in surprise. "Finished already?"

"Yes, sir."

"I believe I also asked you to familiarize yourself with my cabinets' contents," the Master said pointedly.

Kaelin nodded. "I did, sir."

"Indeed! Tell me, then, what is inside them."

"The top left drawer of the cabinet on the left has pegs," Kaelin promptly replied, "a quarter size, with each drawer across the top increasing that size by an eighth."

The Master blinked. "And the drawers beneath that?"

"They have smooth dowel pins in them, also arranged in increasing size. The third row has fluted pins, the fourth has spirals." Kaelin continued reciting the contents of the cabinet in order, then, when the Master made no comment, he moved on to the second cabinet's contents and from that to the third.

"I may have looked like I was oblivious to what you were doing, lad," Talan said dryly, "but I'm quite aware that you looked through those contents but once." He gave Kaelin an approving nod, then rose and headed toward the apprentice's work desk, where neatly assorted piles were awaiting his inspection.

Late that night, Kaelin lay awake, thinking. His Master and Darryk had been right, he decided. There was much to be learned from the other Masters, and for the first time since leaving, he was excited about doing so. Nevertheless, his heart still ached to be back home again. Master Talan was a wonderful Master, but he wasn't *his*. Kaelin rolled over and thought about what fun it would be to show his own Master the flute platform and harp crooks ... and his new set of pipes. *My own Bardic pipes!* Hugging the thought closely to himself, he fell sound asleep.

Chapter 3

Master Talan shook his head in disbelief. Surely no Bard had ever worked as hard as this apprentice of Bergid's did. *Must be the third time this week I've gotten up to find the guest room door left open in the middle of the night and the guest mysteriously missing.* Without bothering to light a lamp, he walked carefully to the front door, then remembered the floor was no longer an obstacle course. He shook his head again. *A clean home for the first time in twenty cycles, decent food to eat ... clearly Bergid knew what he was about. I might just take on an apprentice myself and give the Council another good shock.*

He pushed open the door of his workshop, not surprised to find Kaelin busily hollowing out another pipe, his construction plans spread out on the table.

The boy looked up at the Master's entrance and flushed. "I hope I haven't disturbed your sleep, sir."

The Master waved aside his apology and pulled up a stool. "How is it coming?"

"I'm just finishing the last pipe." The apprentice held it out to the Master. "Is it all right?"

Master Talan checked it over thoroughly. "It's as well done as all the others. However, you can't continue this sort of pace and still expect to do your best work."

Kaelin's smile faded at the mild rebuke. "I'm sorry, sir."

"I rather doubt that," the Master replied, "but you should be. Having an apprentice spend more hours in my workshop than I do myself is liable to damage my reputation. Now, I've decided on an appropriate punishment for putting me at such risk, and," he warned, "I'll tolerate no argument about it. You are strictly forbidden to enter my workshop for a week, starting now."

Kaelin was rendered momentarily speechless.

"You and I are going to do some traveling," Master Talan continued. "How do you expect to find an appropriate symbol for Eyrie if all you ever see of it is the inside of my workshop?"

Kaelin grinned. "I'd like the chance to see Eyrie."

"Then perhaps we should get some sleep. We'll leave in the morning." The Master rose and started for the door.

"Sir?"

Talan turned to see Kaelin lift his pipe entreatingly. He chuckled. "Oh, very well. Finish that pipe first. I suppose you couldn't sleep anyway, knowing one pipe was left unfinished."

They spent the next several days roaming the hills of Eyrie at their leisure, heading west to Loryn, then angling north through the sparse woods toward Riona Springs. Kaelin discovered that the coastal regions were mostly grassland, sectioned off for the grazing of livestock, and the rolling hills of the interior were primarily farmland. They passed clusters of small businesses involved in the processing of meat, dairy products, and leather, with scattered homesteads surrounding them. Wherever they went, everyone greeted the arrival of the Master with broad smiles. It was easy to see why, for the Master Bard always had time for everyone, down to the smallest child shyly asking his help in carving a whistle. He kept a special bag in his pack filled with an endless supply of chimes, miniature drums, and whistles that he dispensed freely to all the youngsters who tagged after him. He regaled the older population with tales of Bardic history, accompanying himself skillfully on any available instrument, which the villagers practically fell over themselves to offer. After playing, the Master glanced appraisingly at the borrowed instrument and dug into seemingly unlimited pockets to fish out whatever he felt would improve it. Then, after a brief flurry of tools, he handed the instrument back to its delighted owner. As he had observed with his own Master, Kaelin saw that the position of Master Bard involved much more than skilled musicianship. It required a genuine interest in all those under his charge, a giving of time and energy, and a deep desire to teach them their heritage so that none would ever forget.

On their long walks over the hills, Master Talan showed Kaelin many rare varieties of plants not found on the mountainous isles and taught him their uses. One afternoon, the Master's discourse was interrupted by a spate of staccatos.

"A kestrel is a rare sight on Eyrie," Talan said, following its flight twice around their heads before it flew off, "and I doubt Master Marek sees any of them, either. They much prefer the woods of Elegy, Lyra, and, of course, Kestrel."

The third time this happened, the Master looked speculatively at Kaelin. "I don't suppose *you* have anything to do with this kestrel's visit to my island, do you?"

"I recognize him," the apprentice admitted, "and he seems to have followed me here, but I've done nothing I know of that would cause him to do that."

Master Talan nodded thoughtfully as he watched the kestrel depart, then resumed his instruction. "This is wild clary," he told the apprentice, pointing to a plant with hairy stems and paired leaves along its branches. "It will bloom in early summer into beautiful pyramids of purple flowers, which are delicious in salads. Let's pick some of the leaves to make tea ... good for the digestion. And, if you ever get anything in your eyes that flushing with water can't remove, moisten the seeds from this plant and place them under your eyelids." He chuckled at the apprentice's horrified expression. "Leave them there until they fall out on their own, and they'll clear your eyes of the irritant."

"That's because my eyeballs would fall out with them," the apprentice muttered, and the Master laughed. "Who would even *think* of doing something like that?" Kaelin wondered, staring incredulously at the plant. "I've got something in my eye ... hmm, I know, I'll grab some seeds out of that hairy plant over there, stuff a few of them in my irritated eye and see what happens!" He shook his head. "There's some strange people in the world, sir."

"Perhaps that's a good thing for the rest of us," The Master said with a chuckle. "You'll find this plant only on Eyrie, for it loves the grasslands. The healers cultivate it and send the dried seeds to their colleagues on the other islands."

At night, they spread their bedrolls over the heather and slept under a spectacular display of stars. Master Talan pointed out the constellations and described their outlines so vividly that the apprentice could see the pictures they made in the sky as clearly as if an artist had brushed them across the heavenly canvas. In the morning, Kaelin was surprised to find the heather unharmed by his weight during the night, the graceful stems soon swaying in the breeze once again. The Master told him they would splash the hillsides with pink and purple blooms from mid to late summer.

Each of them had chosen one instrument to bring with them. Kaelin had his flute, the Master his harp, and they played together every night before going to sleep, adapting duets from the flute forms. The Master improvised effortlessly with flute solos as well, even when the apprentice tried to trick him by modulating into a spontaneous composition of his own. The Master simply arched a brow in his direction and continued weaving his accompaniment with the flute's melody, regardless of where Kaelin sent it. When at last the youngster broke off with a grin of admiration, the Master continued on, improvising on Kaelin's melody with skillful fingers. The apprentice quickly rejoined him, accompanying the harp's improvisation with the ease of someone who had been thoroughly schooled by the Composition Master of the Bardic Isles. When they finished, Master Talan laughed and offered him his harp, Kaelin traded his flute for it, and off they went again, playing until the fire had burned low and needed to be banked for the night.

They spent a pleasant day at Riona Springs, a series of three beautiful warm-water pools they enjoyed soaking themselves in. Then they followed the Kyrial River back to Skye. When they finally returned to the Master's home, Kaelin cast an eager glance toward the workshop, but the Master fixed him with a stern eye. "I trust my punishment has been effective, and you've learned to mix work with pleasure now and then. You will find your work all the better for it."

Kaelin's eyes danced with mischief. "If I ever forget, sir, I won't hesitate to come to you for further punishment!"

A week later, Kaelin had finished his pipes. They were a full set of seventeen, securely bound together near the top, with a second row of binding a handspan lower. Across the bottom, a wooden frame curved upwards to fit the graduated pipe lengths. This not only stabilized them but gave Kaelin a splendid place for carving. Finished, the pipes curved toward him as though begging him to blow across their gleaming tops and produce the rich, mellow tones the well-made instrument was capable of.

The Master's workshop was often a lively place, with Bards coming and going, working on projects for the Master or discussing the business of their assigned territories. Kaelin himself spent hours with Master Talan, learning how to construct a lute, a lyre, and a kithara.

"There are seven Bardic instruments, the harp, lap harp, flute, pipes, lute, lyre, and kithara," Master Talan told him. "Though some would have us list eight," he added with a frown. "Every one of them is a special field of its own. Each has its own style, its own personality, and its own limitations. You simply can't understand any of them properly without making each intricate part, until every detail is known. An instrument that can't be designed or taken apart," and the Master's frown deepened, "is simply not an instrument at all ... at least, not a *Bardic* instrument." What the eighth instrument was that failed to meet this criteria and so irritated the Master, Kaelin could not guess. Observing the Master's expression, however, he decided it was better not to ask.

Kaelin did not forget Master Talan's lesson and no longer worked such late hours in the workshop. Instead, he spent most evenings playing his instruments for an ever-increasing audience. Of the seventeen Bards assigned to Eyrie, all eventually came to the Master's home to see this youngster who had been acknowledged by the Council as the Master Bard of Kestrel's apprentice. Curiosity brought them once; Kaelin's music brought them back again and again, especially Brent, who was delighted to finally hear Kaelin play.

"We weren't *allowed* to hear you on Kestrel, and you resisted all our efforts to hear you on Elegy," the Bard grumbled. "And now I find our apprentice giving nightly concerts on Eyrie without my knowledge under my very nose! The only thing that will appease me is if you play a second song."

Kaelin laughed and began a second piece. He was at ease with playing for a Bardic audience now, thanks to what his Master had told him on the voyage back to Kyet from Bard's Landing.

You have my permission to play for those in the Bardic Order upon our return, and I'm expecting you to do so. After cycles of being afraid to play for anyone else, you might well feel nervous at first. If so, remember that your music takes your listeners to the place you're describing. Describe it well, then, and let your music carry both you and your listeners off to enjoy the experience together. It's the music that matters. When Kaelin made no reply, the Master indicated the billowing sails above them. *Do the sails of a ship stiffen the moment they are observed and refuse to be filled with the wind? And if they did, wouldn't we all sit here, unable to go anywhere? So must you allow yourself to be filled with your music without regard to your audience. Your gift will be useless if you refuse its expression to others.*

So Kaelin had begun to play with increasing freedom at his Master's home for Bards that sat spellbound. Indeed, the apprentice's music swept their senses into experiences so vivid that most found it difficult to rouse themselves afterwards. Word had traveled from Bard to Bard across Kestrel about the Master's apprentice, who could sweep his audience up into the skies to see the island of Kestrel from above, or take them deep into the woods of Vale, or off exploring the banks of the Bronig ... whatever, it seemed, the young prodigy was musically describing. Discovering that the Bards of Eyrie had also heard rumors of his gift was a bit disconcerting to Kaelin, but Master Talan, who had begun nightly ensemble sessions in his newly cleared and cleaned home, had asked him to play for them afterwards. The reaction of the listening Bards had been as thunderstruck as his first performances on Kestrel had been, and they had immediately petitioned the Master to make it a permanent feature. The Instrument Master had readily agreed.

Here on Eyrie, Kaelin was aware of growing in a way that staying with his Master would have made difficult, if not impossible, to do. He was so accustomed to playing for his Master, shaping his phrases in ways he knew would please the Composition Master, that now, playing so far from his presence ... *I play only for myself.* And that, he decided, was not such a bad thing, and, he realized intuitively, was perhaps one of the reasons his Master had sent him away.

His first month with Master Talan disappeared more quickly than the apprentice would have thought possible, and in the second week of the following month Kaelin turned thirteen. He told no one it was his birthday, preferring to remember the wonderful one his Master had given him the previous cycle. Moreover, Master Talan was busy leaving instructions for his Bards and packing for the trip he was taking the following morning to Elegy for the Spring Council.

"I'm sorry to leave you like this," the Master told him. "But you have plenty of work to keep you busy. Brent will be staying with you while I'm away, and he'll be hosting several Bards here for ensemble playing, a few of whom you haven't met. Brent is adept at making each of the instruments you'll be working on, and he will also be handling my affairs while I'm away."

Kaelin nodded. "I have a letter for my Master," he said hopefully, "if you wouldn't mind..."

"I'll be happy to deliver your letter for you."

"Thank you, sir." He stood chewing on his bottom lip for a few moments, and the Master smiled.

"And I'll tell him how much you miss him."

Two weeks later, Master Talan returned in the evening to find his home resonating with music. He paused at the open door, observing the scene before him. A lively trio was in progress, music the Master did not recognize. Kaelin alone was not looking at his music, and Talan smiled, knowing he had just identified its composer. None of the performers were playing their primary instrument. Kaelin was playing his harp, while Bards Tyrel and Gryndl were on flute and pipes. The Master stood still, curious to see if Brent would notice the imbalance between two of the players, and if so, how he would handle it. The flute danced its way upward, Kaelin following with firmly plucked notes that gradually slowed, then brought the trio to a beautifully strummed ending.

Brent nodded to the apprentice. "A delightful trio, Kaelin. Thank you for composing it for us."

"It was my pleasure, sir," the apprentice said with a smile, and Brent turned to the piper.

"An excellent job, Gryndl, setting a steady foundation for the flute and harp, despite the fact that they seemed to be having a problem communicating." He frowned at Tyrel. "In the main theme, your triplet pattern connects with the first and third notes of Kaelin's, yet you played them consistently late, like you didn't want them to touch his. Is there some reason for that?"

The lean Bard glanced at Kaelin and shrugged. "Is it my fault he can't play compound rhythms evenly? Maybe he should find someone of his own rank to practice with."

Kaelin flushed and lowered his eyes, Gryndl rolled his, and Brent's narrowed. "Kaelin's rhythm is sterling," Brent said evenly. "You're the one lacking rhythmic precision, not to mention basic courtesy." He nodded toward the apprentice, who was studiously inspecting the settings of his harp crooks. "You owe him an apology," he told Tyrel.

"You're not Master Talan, to lecture me about my playing or my courtesy." Tyrel glared at Brent. "I'm here to play ensembles, not to cater to someone who's—" He bit the sentence off.

"Just an apprentice?" Brent asked coldly.

Silence fell over the room, broken by an unexpected voice coming from the doorway.

"While I'm away," the Master said in a steely voice, "the Bard I leave in charge speaks for me and will be obeyed implicitly by all of you." He looked meaningfully at Tyrel. "You will apologize for your rudeness."

There was a moment's silence. "Yes, Master Talan," Tyrel said submissively. "I apologize, Brent, for my unthinking words."

"Apology accepted," Brent said.

The Master nodded toward the apprentice. "You will also deliver the apology you owe Kaelin."

Tyrel glanced at the apprentice and frowned.

"An apprentice is as worthy of your respect as any other Bardian, of any rank, age, or occupation," the Master told him sternly. "If you have not yet learned that, then you do not deserve the robe you wear. You will deliver your apology, or you'll leave my island and await the next Bardic rotation two cycles from now to see if any other Master will have you. The choice is yours."

Brent and Gryndl glanced at each other, startled, and Tyrel's face paled. A Bard without a posting had no status or stipend in the Bardic Order, light blue robe and silver cord notwithstanding. Until another Master marked his name, he would have nowhere to go except back to his own family, if he had one.

Tyrel glanced at the Master's unyielding expression and turned to Kaelin. "I also apologize to you," he said stiffly.

Kaelin looked up into a pair of dark, resentful eyes. "I took no offense, sir," he said.

"Now, if you don't mind," the Master said, "I would like to receive Brent's report, then get a little extra sleep tonight."

"Certainly, Master Talan," Gryndl said, rising immediately. "And welcome home, sir! We'll be off, then ... assuming," he added with a sour glance at Tyrel, "you'll tolerate my company, since I'm not 'just an apprentice.'" Not waiting for a response, he turned to the others. "Thanks for an instructive rehearsal, Brent. And thank you, Kaelin, for your composition and participation. These pipes you've made are beautiful, and it was a pleasure to play them. Thank you for loaning them to me."

"You're always welcome to their use, sir," Kaelin said, his expression lighting up at the Bard's words of praise for his new instrument. "It was wonderful to play with all of you," he added, including Tyrel in his glance, but the Bard refused to meet his gaze. The apprentice took up his polish cloth and began applying it to his harp. The two Bards gathered their packs, bowed to the Master and left.

The Instrument Master shook his head as he set down his pack and instruments. "Please tell me, Brent, that this isn't an example of what's been going on during my absence."

"It isn't … at least, not with anyone else. I've held ensembles in the evening, as you requested, and they've gone well. Everyone's been improving, especially with the inspiration provided by that talented young rascal over there." Brent grinned at Kaelin. "Everyone except for Tyrel, that is," he amended, "whose first attendance was tonight."

The Master frowned. "He refused your summons?"

"He couldn't come until the dispute between two Holders in Braelach was resolved, one of whom had sown his wheat field over the boundary line between their holdings. For the record, he did a good job resolving it." The Bard shrugged. "I've no idea where his resentment of Kaelin comes from, considering he only just met him today. He's been given no cause that I know of."

At the Master's inquiring look, the apprentice shook his head. "I haven't spoken with Bard Tyrel, sir," he said, "except to greet him when he came in tonight and respond to his apology."

The Master frowned again but said no more on the subject. He answered Brent's questions concerning the Spring Council, then told Kaelin his Master had sent him a letter, which the apprentice eagerly received. "Now," he said, glancing at Brent, "perhaps you can give me your report on Kaelin's progress. Then, while he's busily devouring that letter of his, you can catch me up on how my island has been faring under your guidance."

Brent nodded and gave a glowing report of Kaelin's progress, then shook his head in mild exasperation. "The only complaint I have of him is that, unlike any other apprentice I've ever known, he apparently will not stop working until he's ordered to do so. You might have warned me, sir," the Bard said reproachfully. "He treats your workshop as though its shelves and drawers were filled with confections from the sweet shop! I had to stop myself from opening a few of them to check for myself."

The Master chuckled and Brent continued. "I had to order him to stay in bed as well, to prevent him from sneaking back out and spending half the night there. After that, he obediently waited until the crack of dawn. Aside from that failing, if failing it is, our apprentice is a pleasure to work with, and to play with, and I'll happily babysit him again whenever you wish."

Kaelin looked up indignantly, and the Master laughed. "A good report, indeed," he said approvingly. "Now go read that letter before you worry it to shreds."

Kaelin quickly put away his harp and pipes, then went to his room to open his Master's letter. All thoughts of the unfriendly Bard left him as he immersed himself in news of home, of Darryk's prowess at mediating disputes between the craft and trade Guilds, of Fenadal's singing astounding the townsfolk of Kyet, and of the Master's latest compositions for the new pipes he was sure his apprentice would be returning with and could hardly wait to see. The missive ended with assurances that Laena was being well looked after and never left alone. At last, his letter still clasped in one hand, Kaelin drifted off to sleep.

Chapter 4

In a cabin a few furlongs east of Skye, Tyrel sat in front of his untouched supper, brooding over his encounter with Master Bergid's apprentice. Master Talan and Brent had assumed his attitude had stemmed from Kaelin's low rank, but Tyrel had nothing whatever against apprentices. Only *this* apprentice, a boy he had reason to believe had infiltrated the Bardic Order and could well bring about its destruction. And that, Tyrel would not allow. They had paid a high enough price for this safe haven Master Cyral had found for them. It would not be lost because of some Druidic brat posing as a Bardic apprentice. Being forced to apologize to him in front of the Master had been galling.

Of course, Tyrel admitted, he wasn't sure yet about the boy's duplicity. If Kaelin was what he appeared to be, then Tyrel owed him that apology. But if he wasn't, then the boy had done a sterling job of duping Masters and Bards into thinking he had the Bardic gift Master Cyral himself had possessed. It was outrageous, and Tyrel was not about to let this youthful snake bring down the Order he loved.

The Bard absentmindedly pushed vegetables and meat around his plate, thinking of the secret not even the Masters knew. Everyone assumed the Bards left behind in Eire had all been killed or assimilated by the Druidic Order. Was it not taught in every schoolhouse and sung by every Bard, himself included? He alone knew the truth, that there still remained Bards in Eire living in hiding. Tyrel had become privy to this information a few months after passing his Bard tests nearly two cycles ago.

He had been sitting in front of his fire, wishing the Spring Council wasn't still six months away. All new Bards were required to attend it, whether or not it was a rotation cycle, for assignment to their first island. Until then, they continued teaching the students they had taught as an Instrumentalist, and they reported to the Master they'd taken their tests under, which for Tyrel was Master Grened. This turned out to be a requirement Tyrel dreaded, for the Master Harpist insisted on his presence once a week, discoursing at length on the duties a Bard was expected to perform and giving him tasks to complete that were, in Tyrel's mind, more suited to an apprentice. He was sent to fetch reports from the Bards of Elegy, bring ordered supplies from the merchants in Tryl, and see to the shipment of the Master's many scrolls to Caer Wynd for recording and archiving. And try though he might, satisfying the Master Harpist was nearly impossible. Nothing was ever done quite well enough, and when it was, a gruff "well enough" was all he received for his pains. Despite this, Tyrel had persevered, faithfully carrying out every task the irascible Master gave him, and devoutly hoping his first rotation placed him anywhere but Elegy.

Exhausted from his weekly session with the Master that morning and teaching all afternoon, the Bard had almost drowsed off by his fire when a loud popping sound startled him. He reached for the poker and was stirring the flames to new life when one of them captured his attention. Unlike the others, this one didn't flicker. It stood motionless, with regal indifference, as though the other flames existed only to pay homage to it. And in the center of the flame was ... *a hole?* He stared at it, mystified. *I must be dreaming. This can't be real.*

Yet, real or not, the flame pulled him slowly but surely toward it. Alarmed, he tried to wrench himself away but could not. And then the flame, or whatever was in the empty center of the flame, spoke.

Ah ... a Bard, I see. How fortunate!

Tyrel leapt from his chair so abruptly that it upended behind him. "What ... who—" he sputtered. "I don't understand!"

Obviously, the voice said with some amusement. *Perhaps we can begin with introductions. You are?*

"Er ... I'm Bard Tyrel," came the faint response.

Bard Tyrel. I am Prime Belek of the Bardic Order.

"Prime ... you mean the Senior Master of the Council? That's Master Bergid. I've never even heard of you!"

The highest position in the Bardic Order may be the Senior Master of the Council where you are, but here in Eire, it's still the Prime of the Council, determined by strength in the gift.

Tyrel was thunderstruck. "You're in ... Eire?"

Of course. The voice paused for a moment. *When you look into the flame, what do you see?*

"I see a ... dark hole in a flame that doesn't move."

An ungifted Bard, then. Well, perhaps that's for the best.

"Ungifted?" Tyrel asked, an edge to his voice at hearing yet another Master speak to him disparagingly.

I meant no offense. A Bard is either born gifted or he is not.

Tyrel nearly laughed. "Born *gifted?* With the gift that Master Cyral had?" He shook his head. "No one's been born with such a gift since the days of the Master himself."

No one at all? Belek exclaimed. *Not even the Masters?*

"No," Tyrel said with certainty.

After a long silence, Belek spoke as though to himself. *So ... a Council of ungifted Masters...*

Tyrel frowned and the voice continued.

It's fortunate, then, that you're the one I've met. You're exactly who we need to help us escape the misery our Order has suffered since Master Cyral took the majority of us away. To think that, at long last, we may soon join our brethren!

The Bard was astounded. "You want to come here, to the Bardic Isles?"

Ah ... so it's islands Cyral found? Of course, we wish to join you! Are the Isles not as much our birthright as yours? Did Cyral not wish to save us all? He took those he could to a new land, to live in peace and freedom. But those left behind were not so fortunate. We live in hiding, unable to openly wear the robes we have earned, afraid of anyone finding out that we are more than the wandering minstrels we appear to be. We need to escape this place and be reunited with our brethren. Nor will we come empty-handed. We will bring the gift of old within us, to infuse the Bardic Isles with its power and help keep it from discovery. Will you help us? Will you be our spokesperson and advocate?

For a moment, the smoothly spoken words fairly lit Tyrel's mind with possibilities. What an amazing opportunity, to be the intermediary between the Council of Masters and the Bards of their homeland ... and to bring back the gift Master Cyral himself had possessed!

Then tendrils of doubt dispelled the image. "Why me? Why didn't you use this power to contact the Council directly?"

I can't just roam the islands at will, connecting with whomever I choose! That's not how the gift works.

"Then how *does* it work?" Tyrel asked curiously. "How did you find me?"

I haven't the time it would take to give you elementary lessons in the gift, Belek said. *Traveling through fire to an unknown place of such distance took cycles to learn and requires a great deal of skill and energy. Now that it's taken me to you, I can direct it to take me back, provided you're near the element. And that,* he said flatly, *will have to be enough to satisfy your curiosity for now.*

"So, you found me by mere chance?" Tyrel asked, astonished.

In essence, yes.

"You should be talking with a Master, then, not a Bard in his first cycle. I'll go get Master Gren—"

Not yet! If you do that, there will be nothing here for him to see. So go right ahead … if you think he'll believe you.

Tyrel was silent. Master Grened, he knew, would not believe a word of this. Far more likely he'd send his delusional Bard straight to a healer. "If you don't trust one of our Masters," he said slowly, "then why should I trust you?"

For a long moment only the crackling of the fire disturbed the stillness. *What if I told you that your Order is in as much peril as ours?*

"What do you mean?"

There is a traitor among you. Someone likely posing as a member of the Bardic Order. Someone born with great power, but not of Bardic origin. It's the power of the Druids he wields, a power that could bring about the destruction of your land. Is that what you want?

The Bard frowned. "Why would someone with Druidic power join the Bardic Order? He has no need of musical training."

Because he won't be a fool! If he wields his power without an instrument, he'll be known immediately for what he truly is. When Tyrel made no response to this, Belek groaned. *Has the knowledge of the Bardic and Druidic gifts been so lost to your people that you no longer even know the difference?*

"How would we know?" Tyrel retorted defensively. "It's not like anyone left a detailed description!"

No, of course they didn't, the voice said soothingly.

Knowledge of the gift was shrouded in secrecy long before the exodus from Eire. My apologies.

"So, then, what *is* the difference?" Tyrel demanded. "If I go looking for this imposter, as I assume you're asking me to do, how am I to know if I've found someone with the Druidic or the Bardic gift, if either one will be using Bardic instruments?"

The Bardic gift is the mastery of sound and can be used for communication within an element, as I am doing now. But I'm in the element of fire, not in your mind. The Druidic gift is the mastery of the energy fields that surround us, which gives a Druid access to a listener's mind. Look for one who can transport your senses, seemingly with his music, and if he looks directly at you, gain mastery of your mind.

Tyrel recoiled. What a horrible thing, to have one's mind invaded and taken over by a Druid!

I didn't travel the element of fire such a distance on a whim, Belek continued. *For cycles after the exodus, our Ovates watched for the hint of anyone gifted, finally assuming that you had traveled too far for the gift to be detected. But lately they've insisted that someone strongly gifted in the Druidic arts has arisen in the west, beyond the horizon's edge. What if, we wondered, this land was home to the Bards who took ship from Aille-Mara, never to be seen again? A refuge we desperately need ... yet harboring a deadly snake. Who knows how many cycles this Druid's gift has been growing until it was strong enough for our seers to detect? Certainly, he would be old enough by now to have become a Bard, for the gift usually emerges between fifteen and twenty cycles of age. Your Council is ungifted and has no protection against such a person. He will set his sights on ingratiating himself with the Masters, intent on acceptance by those who have the sole power to induct another member of the Council. The Masters will believe what they want to believe ... that after all these cycles, the Bardic gift has blossomed anew in this single individual. Do you see now why I do not wish to speak to one of your Masters yet? I must assume this imposter has already gained their trust. And even if he has not yet infiltrated their minds, they will not be disposed to believe they've been duped by one of their own.*

Tyrel nodded slowly. He did not yet know the other four Masters, but he couldn't imagine Master Grened believing he had ever been wrong about anything. And the Master's unpredictable, often irrational behavior ... *could it possibly be?* He blanched at the thought that the Master's mind might have been infiltrated. That a cunning Druid was clearing the way for an opening on the Council, one that he would humbly accept.

You, however, I can trust, Belek said. *You are a Bard with a quick, impartial mind, able to understand that someone who wields the ancient power of the Druids must be stopped now before he grows any stronger. Once he has established himself on your Council, he will quickly be made Prime, citing Bardic Law that states the Prime must be decided by strength in the gift. And then he'll be free to focus on his real goal ... the destruction of the Bardic Order.*

"That could never happen!" Tyrel protested.

You think not? If I was able to find and communicate with you, this Druid in your land may be able to communicate with one of his own here! And if he tells them the precise location of the Bardic Isles, I think you know exactly what you can expect to find arriving on your shores. The carnage at Aille-Mara will be revisited throughout your land, and we'll lose our chance of finding the refuge we need. He is a great danger to us both!

The horrific vision of warrior ships arriving in the Bardic Isles, of warriors pillaging villages and spilling the blood of defenseless Bardians with every step they took, robbed Tyrel of speech.

You must search for him, Belek implored. *He will appear to be an honest soul, for how else could he fool the Masters? And he'll have special abilities that others do not, abilities that seem truly marvelous. When you find him—and find him you must before he attains Master eligibility!—do not believe what you see and hear, for he'll be an artist in deception. Can I count on you to do this? Can I count on you to save the Order we both love?*

Righteous resolve rose in Tyrel like a flame, melting the threads of doubt in his mind. "I'll look for him," he promised. "And when I've found him, I'll stop him."

The Bard came back to the present with a start, his fork falling from his hand and clattering to the floor. He picked it up and pushed his uneaten meal aside. Filled with the zeal of a new convert, he had obeyed Belek's instructions to look and listen for any rumor of a Bard whose music had unusual power. The upcoming Spring Council, fortuitously coming in a rotation cycle, had been the perfect place and time to do so. Tyrel grimaced, thinking of all the hours he'd spent trudging from camp to camp, listening to conversation after conversation, discouraged when all anyone wanted to talk about was the apprentice who had arrived with Master Bergid, and the Master's cord that had been pledged to the Council. Though he'd listened closely, no one had said anything about the apprentice's musical abilities, and why would they? An apprentice, especially an underaged one like Kaelin, could hardly have known much about instrumental playing. Certainly, the Bards of Kestrel would have known if the Master's apprentice had shown any signs of the ancient power of Cyral. And not a single one of them had said anything of the sort. Regardless, the boy was too young ... why, he would have been a mere child when the gift emerged! Tyrel had been forced to admit defeat and tell Belek that the one he was looking for must not have rotated this cycle. The Prime had not been pleased.

Upon receiving his posting, Tyrel had taken ship to Eyrie and continued his search there, checking every Bard that hadn't passed his rotation and therefore had not attended the Spring Council. After all, possessing the Druidic power of old didn't necessarily make one proficient in the making of Bardic Instruments. His efforts had produced no results, however, much to Belek's displeasure. But then rumors began drifting over from Kestrel of the incredible music of the Master's apprentice, music that could transport his listener's senses into whatever scene or memory he was musically describing. This had commanded the Bard's immediate attention, especially when Master Talan let it be known that no Bard was to speak of this outside the Order. Could it be possible, he wondered, that the one Belek was searching for was a mere boy, not yet of age? It would certainly explain why Master Bergid had risked his position in the Bardic Order for him, and why the other four Masters had allowed him to stay. One didn't summarily shoo away the first person in over two centuries to be born with such power as that, underaged or not.

Tyrel had not told Belek about the youngster, not even when Kaelin arrived to spend three months with Master Talan, and none of Tyrel's colleagues could talk of anything else. For the Prime had a temper, he had discovered, and it was best if Tyrel assessed the boy's abilities for himself before revealing his identity. *I'll find out if Kaelin's the threat Belek is warning of. If he is, I'll stop him, as I told Belek I would. Then he'll let me tell the Masters and we can arrange for the reunification of our Order!*

The first thing he would need to do, Tyrel decided, was listen to one of the apprentice's performances and ascertain his ability. The boy was admittedly a fine harpist, disturbingly better than he himself was, but nothing remarkable had happened during the ensemble rehearsal that would lead him to believe the boy had special powers, Druidic or otherwise. Nevertheless, the respect the other two Bards had given the apprentice had irritated Tyrel, ultimately resulting in his imprudent outburst. Here was an underaged apprentice—likely armed with Druidic skills of persuasion—basking in the open approval of Masters and Bards while he, a full-fledged Bard, burned with a vital secret no one even knew about.

He would need to be more careful. If it became necessary to move against the boy, no one must suspect he was responsible for it. And if he was wrong about the apprentice, Tyrel promised himself he would make it up to him. He would apologize sincerely for his attitude and unkind words, and he would do it in front of Master Talan. And that, he thought, was likely going to happen, because it was difficult to believe someone so young could be gifted with the power of old. When Tyrel had said as much to Gryndl after leaving the Master's home, however, the Bard had told him that ensembles were a conversation—as if Tyrel himself were the apprentice, unaware of such things!—and that one had to hear one of Kaelin's solo performances to be swept away.

Fine. Tyrel banked his fire for the night, nervously keeping his eyes averted from the flames. *I'll go hear him for myself in a few days and settle the matter.*

Chapter 5

For the next few days, Master Talan was busy in the evenings with Bards who came to hear about the Spring Council and demonstrate their improved ensemble skills to the Instrument Master. Kaelin was happy to be included, for as much as he loved solos, he'd grown to love the interaction of ensembles even more, weaving his part in a stimulating musical conversation with Bards who were excellent musicians.

One evening, after two quartets had received the Master's praise and critique, Brent asked if Kaelin would play his flute for them. The apprentice obliged, filling his music with the hills of Eyrie and the places he and Master Talan had visited. When Kaelin was finished playing, he laid his flute aside. The Bards were silent, their eyes closed upon the peaceful coastal scenes of Eyrie Kaelin's music had just described. All, that is, except Tyrel. Kaelin had felt the Bard's hostile eyes upon him more than once that evening, but to look up from his playing directly into their probing scrutiny was disconcerting. Clearly, one listener had not forgotten the performer.

The others stirred, their enthusiastic response and lively talk about what it would be like if everyone had such a gift turning aside Kaelin's uneasiness. Horrified at the overheard comment that Master Bergid's apprentice ought to get himself joined the moment he came of age and begin producing little gifted musicians without delay, he took up his harp, closed his eyes and began to idly strum a few arpeggios, letting the sweet sound soothe him. *If only the wind could somehow take me away!*

As if the wish itself had music of its own, Kaelin heard a faint song that seemed to spring from nowhere, the notes capricious and unpredictable. Entranced, he listened for a moment, then, not wishing to disturb the conversations that had sprung up around the room, he set a block in his mind and began to softly play the notes he heard, notes that lifted him without warning high above the Master's home.

He caught his breath as the very air around him shimmered with color, a kaleidoscope of paths swirling toward him from all directions. Music came from each of them. Though he ached with the desire to follow the path that stretched toward the island of Kestrel, Kaelin hesitated. For what if his music took him where he longed to be? Might he see his Master as clearly as if they were together?

Impossible, he told himself uneasily. *And what if I could see him, but he couldn't see me?*

Repelled by the thought of spying on his Master, he stopped playing, and his eyes opened directly into Tyrel's. Kaelin shuddered, all thoughts of his Master forgotten. What was in the Bard's expression that turned him cold? *You're being ridiculous,* he told himself sternly. *For whatever reason, he just doesn't like apprentices, and there's nothing you can do about that except stay away from him.*

Nevertheless, he could not pull his eyes away from the Bard's unnerving regard, and for a moment he heard music that was utterly different than what he had just been playing. The turbulent notes invaded Kaelin's mind, and without conscious thought, he began to play them. Closing his eyes to shut out the Bard's attention, Kaelin was captivated by the scene that unfolded in his mind, wondering whether what he was seeing was real, or the fragment of an unremembered dream.

He was sitting by a fire in a small room, his attention fixed on flames that danced in rhythm to his music. Flickering shades of orange and yellow ... except for one. One flame did not dance with the others, standing motionless in the center of the miniature inferno. He stared entranced, filled with dread as he realized that the flame was speaking.

"There is a traitor—"

A resounding crash brought an abrupt end to both Kaelin's playing and the conversations in the room. The apprentice shook his head, confused at finding himself transported back without warning, then gripped the frame of his harp as a wave of dizziness and nausea nearly overwhelmed him. Tyrel was on his knees, broken shards of pottery scattered around him.

For a long moment no one moved. Then Tyrel shook his head slightly and spoke as though dazed. "I'm terr ... terribly sorry, sir," he apologized to Master Talan. "So careless of me! I got up and lost my balance for a moment and must have knocked your vase off the table."

"That's quite all right," the Master told him. "Accidents happen to us all."

"I'll replace it, sir," Tyrel promised, then busied himself cleaning up the mess. He did not look at Kaelin again, nor did anyone notice that the apprentice still sat with his harp clutched tightly, his face pale. The room soon filled once again with conversation.

Kaelin stirred and put his instruments away, his hands shaking. When he dared to look again in Tyrel's direction, he was relieved to see the Bard looking over a music score with one of the other Bards and paying him no attention at all.

What just happened? Kaelin frowned, trying to make sense of what his music had shown him ... the unmoving flame, the voice that spoke from it. *What traitor?* None of it made any sense.

Deciding some fresh air would soothe his aching head, he went out to the workshop to check on the leather he had set to soak. Master Talan was teaching him how to make a drum, the frame of which already stood finished on his workbench. Now the apprentice was softening the hide to be stretched over it. As Kaelin manipulated the smooth skin in the cold water, he smiled in anticipation of finishing his drum in the morning.

When the apprentice returned to the house, he glanced around the room warily, but didn't spot Tyrel. Kaelin walked quickly over to where the Master and Brent were discussing the interpretation of one of the ensembles that had been played earlier and listened with interest. The next time he glanced around the room, he saw Tyrel standing with a few of his colleagues. *There he is ... must have missed him before*. Then Master Talan asked him a question, and he pushed aside all thought of the unfriendly Bard and joined the discussion.

The Bards stayed well into the evening, enjoying a few more ensembles before packing up their instruments and preparing to leave. Tyrel, about to slide his lap harp into his pack, suddenly uttered an exclamation of dismay and began searching the floor.

"Have you lost something?" Brent inquired.

"Yes," Tyrel said distractedly. "One of my tuning pegs is missing. I can't imagine how it could have come off..."

The other Bards obligingly searched the floor with him, but it could not be found.

"I have a spare one you can have," Master Talan said.

"Oh, I couldn't impose on you, sir," Tyrel said quickly. "I'm sure it will turn up. And if not, I can make myself a new one."

"It's no bother," the Master assured him. "I'll just be a moment."

The Bards finished packing up, then waited for the Master's return, talking together by the door with their packs slung over their shoulders. When Master Talan finally came in, looking grave, all conversation died.

"Is something wrong, Master Talan?" Brent asked quietly.

"Yes," the Master replied. "I'm afraid there is." He handed a tuning peg to Tyrel, then waited for them all to be seated. "I would like to know who was in my workshop this evening."

Kaelin stood up. "I was, Master Talan. I went there to turn the hide for my drum."

"You didn't happen to notice my tuning fork while you were there, did you?"

"Yes, sir, I did. It was sitting on your work desk."

"Did you move it?"

"No, sir. I had no need to use it."

The Master frowned. "Did anyone else go into the workshop after Kaelin returned?"

The Bards uniformly shook their heads.

"Was anyone else seen leaving the house?"

Once again only head shakes answered the Master.

"Is your tuning fork missing, sir?" Brent asked in concern. The Master's tuning fork was made of solid silver, a rare and valuable metal in the Bardic Isles.

"Yes, it is, and a thorough search of my workshop has not brought it to light." The Master sighed heavily. "I'm certain I left it on my work desk, just as Kaelin said. It's not there now, nor is it anywhere else in my workshop. I apologize for delaying your departure tonight, but I must ask all of you to empty your packs."

The Bards immediately began unslinging their packs and emptying them. Kaelin went to get his own pack while the Master quickly ascertained that his tuning fork was not in any Bard's pack.

"Thank you, and my apologies for needing to ask such a thing. Kaelin?"

The apprentice sat down and opened his pack. He removed several articles of clothing, a considerable pile of music manuscript and exercises, miscellaneous items for travel, his small flute, and, at the bottom of his pack, a slim, hard object that was cold and unfamiliar to his hand. Slowly, he pulled the silver tuning fork of the Master Bard of Eyrie out into the firelight.

The Bards stared dumbfounded at Kaelin, except for Brent, whose eyes were fixed on the tuning fork in as much disbelief as Kaelin's were. He thought back to the day on Kestrel when he and five other Bards had unanimously dubbed Kaelin "our apprentice," and the many evenings he'd spent with Kaelin at Darryk's camp a cycle ago on Elegy. He thought of Kaelin's friendship with Darryk, of the apprentice pledging his robe for the sake of his Master, who had pledged his for Kaelin. He could not believe such a boy capable of theft.

The expression on Master Talan's face mirrored that of the Bard's. *Kaelin ... a thief? Surely not! Why on earth would he do such a thing?* For if there was one thing he knew about this boy who played music that transported one's senses to wondrous places, it was that he loved his Master above everything else. There was no surer way to lose that Master than to commit an act of theft. And, he knew, the boy would lose far more than that. By the expression on Kaelin's face, the apprentice knew it, too.

Talan groaned inwardly. He had developed an attachment to this eager young apprentice that was going to make his next action extremely difficult. For Bardic Law was specific in cases of theft where the stolen property was found in the possession of one who had no alibi. And in this case, Kaelin had openly admitted to being alone in the Master's workshop. Opportunity and evidence combined gave Talan no choice.

"Bring the fork to me, Kaelin." The Master spoke gently, but Kaelin flinched as though struck. He stumbled to his feet and handed the tuning fork to the Master as though it were made of lead.

Master Talan took the silver tool in troubled silence. He had seen the apprentice's shocked expression when he felt the tuning fork in his pack, had seen the color drain from his face when he pulled it out. Yet Kaelin had exhibited no nervousness when asked to empty his pack. The Master stood still for a moment, his mind and emotions in conflict.

You know perfectly well this boy wouldn't steal a single wood shaving from you! But Talan also knew he had been wrong before. Cycles ago, he had hired a boy from a poor family to clean his workshop. Leon had been as guileless as Kaelin appeared to be, and yet he had stolen expensive wood from Talan's supplies ... a few pieces here, a few there. The Master had hesitated to charge him with theft, and because of that, many others had suffered from the boy's thievery before he was finally caught and brought before the Guild his family belonged to.

That was different. You know Kaelin far better than you knew Leon.

Talan thought he did, but did he trust himself so well that he would set aside Bardic Law?

This is not a villager under Guild Law, he told himself sternly. *However young, Kaelin is a full member of the Bardic Order under Bardic Law, and you are a Master of that Law. Do what you're sworn to do!*

Talan looked at the apprentice's pale face and his heart twisted. "Have you learned enough of Bardic Law, Kaelin, to understand what I must do?"

"Yes, sir." The apprentice's voice was a bare whisper.

"Very well, then. I charge you with theft, an extremely serious charge. If you admit your guilt openly now, I must take your apprentice robe and Bardic instruments from you. For one cycle you will be forbidden to interact or speak to anyone of Bardic rank, except in response to a direct question. You will return to Kestrel, where Master Bergid will be responsible for seeing that you're escorted directly to your family, either by himself or by one of his Bards. You will remain there, your actions closely monitored by our

Order until the cycle is over, at which time you may go where you will as any free Bardian. Or, if you wish, you may appear before the Council and enter a plea to be reinstated to our Order and regain your robe and instruments." He paused, then added, "For an admitted crime of theft, it is customary to inflict punishment with a strap as well, but this I decline to do. You are not yet of age, so I will leave that to the discretion of your own Master."

Kaelin's heart hammered inside his chest like a berserk drum. Surely this was a dream, a twisted nightmare worse than any Bardic Mountain or the sense deprivation test had ever inflicted. He dug his nails into his palms, but the sting made no difference. The Bards still stared aghast; the Master still stood silently waiting for his response. Kaelin swallowed hard, unsure if his voice would work or if it, too, would disappear as surely as his Bardic apprenticeship just had. "And if ... if I admit no guilt, sir?" He did not recognize his own voice.

"Unless you are truly innocent, that would not be wise," the Master said gravely. "If you admit no guilt, you will keep your robe and bear a token of the contested charge around your neck until you stand before the Council to plead your case. Until then you will be restricted from your instruments, except when under instruction by a Bard or Master. If the Council exonerates you, you will regain their full use and your position as Master Bergid's apprentice. If the Council decides against you, the punishment will be the same as if you admitted your guilt now, but," he sternly warned, "it will be made permanent, with no chance of reinstatement, and all five Masters will have the right to inflict punishment with a strap as well." Seeing Kaelin's stricken expression, his voice softened.

"A severe punishment, but we can never allow a thief and liar Bardic rank. His robe would give him authority that could harm those we are sworn to protect. The balance of our society depends heavily on the Bardic Order not abusing its position, so we hold our members to the highest of standards. If you are guilty of theft,

Kaelin, it would be far better to admit it now. If you need time to think before you answer, you may have it."

The apprentice was silent for only a moment, long enough for five words to ring clearly through his mind. The first promise he ever gave to his Master.

I will never lie again.

He lifted his chin. "Thank you, sir, but I need no time. I have not spent two cycles with the Master Bard of Kestrel without learning to value the truth. I admit no guilt." He looked steadily into the Master's eyes. "I did not take your tuning fork, Master Talan, nor have I ever touched it before finding it in my pack."

"Do you know then, how it came to be there?"

Kaelin hesitated. "I know how it might have, but I don't know for certain. I only know that I didn't place it there."

Tearing his eyes away from the clear amber eyes looking into his, the Master walked over to a wooden chest and removed a chain from which a large black medallion hung. Engraved on the medallion were two narrow bars of yellow inlay, slanting downwards from left to right across the shining black surface. The Master placed the chain around Kaelin's neck. Not having been made for anyone so young, the medallion fell low and heavy against his chest.

"You are forbidden to remove this until you stand before the Council for judgment," the Master said sternly. "They will send you a summons once the date for a hearing has been decided on, usually within the month. Until then, disobeying the instrumental restriction you're under will be considered rebellion against the Council and will be dealt with severely, regardless of the final judgment concerning your charge." The Master's voice softened. "This restriction was put in place because of the power music has in our society to keep the balance in all things, to effect, for good or ill, the lives of all Bardians. While I have no doubt whatever that your music has never been used to harm anyone, I cannot set the restriction aside. I'm truly sorry, Kaelin. Were there any other option, I would gladly take it." He turned to the Bards. "What has happened here tonight is confidential to our Order and not for open discussion outside of it until the Council has made a final decision on the matter. Is that clear?"

A chorus of assent came from the Bards, who then quietly left, looks of disbelief and pity going to the frozen apprentice as they went. Brent, however, approached Kaelin and laid a gentle hand on his shoulder.

"Whatever happens, I count you my friend, now and always." He grasped Kaelin's arm and shook it firmly, as to one of equal rank. The apprentice looked up, startled, but did not speak. Brent released him, nodded respectfully to Master Talan, and took his leave.

Kaelin, his eyes stinging with unshed tears, knelt down to repack his bag. The Master watched him for a moment, then left for his workshop. His thoughts were almost as miserable as Kaelin's. He could see no way the Council would decide in the boy's favor, for now that the charge had been made, he would have to prove his innocence, and how could he? Talan frowned. To have his instruments and his Master taken away from him forever would be devastating to Kaelin.

Sleep did not come easily to the Master that night. He couldn't help but hear the restless movements in the room next to his, couldn't keep himself from imagining the tears being quietly shed there. His mind alternately defended and accused him.

I did what had to be done. He had the opportunity, and my tuning fork was found in his pack, before witnesses.

That doesn't mean he put it there! He had no reason to do such a thing and a great many reasons not to.

Then who did? Who had a reason?

The Master lay stunned, struck by the realization that if Kaelin was not a thief and a liar, one of his own Bards must be. Then his stricken mind rallied, and the war resumed.

Must we know who did it before we can clear him of something no one saw him do?

Yes! It's Bardic Law.

What kind of law allows an innocent person to be condemned, his life ruined as easily as that?

A law ... that needs to be changed.

He scowled into the darkness. Never before had he doubted Bardic Law. Never before had he thought that the Law governing them could be unjust. When the Bardic Isles had been settled over two hundred cycles ago, Master Cyral had understood the need for a new system of governance. So, the Master had created five Guilds ... for Trades, Crafts, Holders, Merchants, and Shipping. Five Masters would govern the Bardic Order under Bardic Law; five Guildmasters would govern each Guild under their own Guild Law. Any dispute between Guilds would be referred to a Bard serving their territory, and if it couldn't be settled to the satisfaction of all parties, it would be arbitrated by the Master Bard of that island. If it remained in dispute, it would go to the Council, where the decision of all five Masters would be final. The Guilds would pay tribute to the Bardic Order in the form of coppers, goods, or services, freeing the Bards to use their music for the balance of the Isles as a whole and to ensure that their heritage would not be forgotten. It was a system that had worked well for over two hundred cycles.

Or so he had always assumed. Talan reflected uncomfortably that an occasional innocent might well have been unfairly punished under circumstances much like these, but surely no system could be perfect. *That won't be a bit of comfort to Kaelin if he is truly innocent.* Serious charges were very rare in the Bardic Order, and Talan could only recall one charge of theft, a few cycles ago, committed by a Piper of Kestrel. Since the perpetrator had admitted his guilt, Bergid had handled the dispensing of justice himself. Unlike the Guilds, the Bardic Order had never revised Bardic Law. To

Talan's knowledge, there had never been a need. *Surely there is a need now!* Yet he knew that even if all five Masters agreed to change the Law tomorrow, it would not help the shattered apprentice in the next room, whose case would be judged according to Bardic Law in effect at the time of the charge. Conflicting emotions continued to batter the Master until undisturbed silence informed him that Kaelin had finally fallen asleep. As Talan drifted into sleep himself, an even more disturbing thought startled him back to wakefulness.

By all the Bardic stars ... how am I ever going to tell Bergid?

At the same time that Talan was brooding in his bed, a fire was roaring to life in a cabin northwest of Skye. Pacing restlessly before it, Tyrel's thoughts were still spinning with the imagery of the young apprentice's music ... the flame in his fire ... the dark emptiness in the center of it ... *There is a traitor...* He shuddered. Caught up in the apprentice's vision, it had taken every ounce of strength he had to fling his arm out, hoping to connect with the vase on the table next to him. If it hadn't, the apprentice would have heard his reply and known who the flame was speaking to. However young, there was no doubting the power of this apprentice's music, or that it was Druidic in origin. The words of Belek blossomed in his mind. *Look for one who can transport your senses ... and, if he looks directly at you, can gain mastery of your mind.*

And so Kaelin had, Tyrel thought bitterly. *He entered my mind without warning or permission, rifled through my memories and traveled to the one of his choice! Belek's right. This mere boy is an artist in deception. He beguiles everyone with pleasant scenes. They hang on his every note, not knowing what his Druidic arts will do if someone doesn't stop him.* The way the youngster had used his power to invade the privacy of Tyrel's own mind within the span of a few fragments of music turned the Bard's blood cold. Truly, he'd had no choice but to do something about it, however drastic. A flame that spoke was not the only thing he didn't wish discovered in his cabin. Why, then, did he feel guilty? His own mind instantly answered.

Because of how you treated him!

I promised to find him and so I did, he retorted. *I promised to get rid of him and so I have.* Yet the voice in his mind would not be silenced.

What wrong has he done?

Tyrel flinched. *If I hadn't stopped him, he soon would have!*

You have only Belek's word for that. You should have gone to Master Talan and told him what Kaelin did! You know you could have trusted him to do what's right.

Could I? He flared. *Could I trust a Master who would have thrown me off his island if I hadn't apologized to a traitor?*

The dissenting voice grew fainter. *You were in the wrong, not Kaelin, and you know you're in the wrong again.*

It's not wrong to do whatever it takes to save our land and our people! Tyrel insisted. *It's heroic! Didn't Master Cyral himself do the same? He saved us all by causing death to the warriors and destroying their ship! If he hadn't had the courage to do what was necessary, no matter how hard, none of us would have survived. He was the only one who could stop them. And I was the only one who could stop Kaelin.* A whispered protest began to form in his mind, but the Bard cut it summarily off. *He's a danger to our Order ... an Order I'm sworn to protect! And, with that danger removed, nothing will stand in the way of a reunion of the two Bardic Orders, an Order that should never have been sundered!*

Ah ... so your own personal gain has nothing to do with it?

Of course not!

And so Tyrel firmly believed. Nevertheless, it would be gratifying when his father heard of it. His father, who had railed at him for refusing an apprenticeship to the leather Craftmaster when he turned of age and had ridiculed Tyrel for even thinking he had the talent to become a Bard. Well, Tyrel had shown *him,* progressing from apprentice to Piper to Instrumentalist to Bard. And he would show him again, when his success in reuniting the sundered Bardic Order became known. Belek had told him that he could expect to have his silver cord exchanged for one which was half silver, half gold. The prestigious rank of Free Bard had not been bestowed for many cycles and would free him from the irritating constraints of being assigned to one Master after another. It would also earn him a stipend from all five Masters. Such a rank would be for him to enjoy ... and for his father to hear about and choke on. He smiled and stopped pacing.

The cold, dissenting voice in his mind was silent.

The flame of righteous resolve flared.

Chapter 6

The next morning, Kaelin awoke later than usual but emerged from his room to find Master Talan's bedroom door still closed. He walked toward his flute, as he was accustomed to doing, then abruptly stopped. Memories of the night before flooded his mind, and the hands forbidden to play his flute clenched into fists as grief flooded his mind.

He walked stiffly into the kitchen and began to prepare breakfast, wondering what he would do at the end of the month. He was scheduled to sail for Zephyr and had been looking forward to learning from the Master Flutist. Now, however, the thought of meeting Master Marek for the first time with a medallion hanging around his neck filled him with dread. Not that it was very comforting to think of returning to his own Master in such a way. As the room swam before his eyes, he brushed his tears away before they salted the oatcake his shaking hands were shaping. Yesterday morning, everything had been fine, with nothing more serious to worry about than monitoring a soaking drum hide. This morning, his world had utterly changed. What should by all rights have been a nightmare had become cruel reality upon waking, and he was certain that nothing would ever be fine again.

Enough! You cried all your tears last night. Do what you came to do. He had left home with the goal of learning from each Master, and learn he would, with whatever time he had left. Then he remembered Master Talan's assertion that his summons would come within the month, and his shoulders slumped. He would most likely be headed to Elegy, then, to meet all the Masters at once, his own included, and they would all be sitting in judgment of him, an apprentice who had no way to prove his own innocence. The thought was chilling as he finished frying the oatcakes and got out the bottle of blackberry syrup.

He turned to find Master Talan watching him from the table. The apprentice felt his face burn as he silently served this Master he respected so highly. A Master who had reason to think him a thief and liar. He sat down to his own meal and stared sightlessly at it. Master Talan's cheerful voice startled him.

"Will you be finishing your drum this morning?"

Kaelin looked up in surprise. "Why, no, sir. I ... didn't suppose you'd want me to use your workshop again."

The Master regarded him steadily. "Your supposition is incorrect. I've never enjoyed sharing my workshop with anyone as much as I have with you. You will always be welcome to its use."

A fleeting look of gratitude rewarded the Master before the amber eyes lowered once again. "Thank you, sir. I'll finish the drum right after breakfast." The apprentice pushed his oatcake absentmindedly around the plate, the food as appetizing to him as the wood shavings off the Master's workbench. When the Master finished eating, Kaelin rose to clear away the dishes, the medallion swinging against his chest.

The Master cleared his throat. "I'll be away most of the day attending to some business in Skye. When you're finished with your drum, perhaps you wouldn't mind unburdening the creek from a few of its fish for dinner tonight. I'd enjoy the change and thought you might welcome some extra free time today. You may spend as much time there as you like."

A ghost of a smile crossed the apprentice's face. "Even if you end up eating fish for dinner all week, sir?" he murmured.

The Master arched a brow. "That good, are you?"

Kaelin shrugged. "I guess so. My Master complained about growing fins and a—" He broke off and turned abruptly away.

Talan's eyes rested on the slumped, quivering shoulders of the apprentice for a moment. Then the Master quietly left.

Late that afternoon, he returned to find Kaelin in the workshop, carving the frame of his harp. His completed drum stood on the worktable.

"Did you empty the creek of fish so quickly?"

"I thought I ought to leave a few in there for the rest of Skye to enjoy," Kaelin replied.

The Master chuckled, relieved at the apparent upswing in the apprentice's mood, then picked up Kaelin's drum to test the tone and pitch to see that it was evenly distributed over the hide. "This is well done. Are you going to take it with you?"

"No, sir, my instruments are getting to be a heavy load." The apprentice frowned, struck by the thought that his load would be considerably lightened soon. "You may have it and the other instruments I've made here as well," he offered quietly. "If you'll allow me, though, I'd like to keep the Bardic instruments I've made here, especially my pipes."

"Certainly, you may. I can easily find good use for whatever you don't wish to take." The Master turned his attention to Kaelin's harp. "Have you found a symbol for Eyrie?"

Kaelin held the instrument out. Deftly carved into the wood above the symbol for Elegy was a spray of heather with a constellation of stars above it. The Master nodded in silent approval. He turned to leave, then paused on the threshold.

"Incidentally, I've reviewed your progress while staying with me. I'm not at all happy with one aspect of it."

Startled eyes flew to the Master. "How have I failed you, sir?"

"You have not failed me," the Master said quietly. "It is I who have failed you. In the area of my expertise, you've exceeded all my expectations. However, although you've worked well with the ensembles and have willingly performed in the evenings when asked to, your own instrumental progress has been halted for the lack of proper instruction. I've been so pleased to have such an eager student of my craft that I've been remiss with regard to your *playing* of the instruments I so love making." He saw the hope that lit the amber eyes, and his voice became stern. "But no more. From now until you leave, I'll expect you to have your instruments out and ready to be played immediately after breakfast. If you think I've been a hard taskmaster with regard to the intricacies of making instruments, you'll be quite astounded at what a perfectionist I am with regard to the playing of them. Rest assured, apprentice, the time lost will be thoroughly made up."

Kaelin's eyes filled with tears, and it was a moment before he could speak. "I look forward to being schooled by such a Master of playing as you are, sir," he replied unsteadily.

"I expect I'll learn a few things myself," the Master said gently, then took his leave.

Two evenings later, Kaelin was playing a kithara duet with Master Talan when Brent appeared at the open doorway and stood listening with pleasure. When it was finished, he bowed to the Master. "Good evening, sir. I'm sorry I couldn't come yesterday, but you'll be happy to know the dispute between Craftmasters Fanton and Horven has been resolved to the satisfaction of both parties."

"Good work," the Master said approvingly. "That could not have been an easy task."

"No, sir," Brent replied ruefully, "and I'm quite glad it's over. That was an excellent duet, Master Talan. I had no idea Kaelin had advanced to form six on the kithara."

"Being an advanced harpist helps speed the process. He's done equally well on lute and lyre. Come join us."

Kaelin, who had put the stringed instrument down and stood the moment Brent had arrived, bowed as Brent slid his pack from his shoulder. "Bard Brent. It's good to see you, sir." His welcoming smile disappeared at the Bard's frown.

"I believe, when one has accepted an offer of friendship, bows and titles are no longer appropriate," Brent said reprovingly.

Kaelin hesitated. "I wasn't sure if … if it was a momentary kindness, which I much appreciated, sir, or if you intended your gesture to stand."

"Then let me make my intention clear." Brent stepped forward and extended his arm toward Kaelin.

The apprentice made no move to take it. "Sir, you were *here.*"

The Bard did not lower his arm. "Yes, I was. I know what I saw, and I know what I didn't see. I saw you pull the Master's tuning fork out of your pack, but I certainly didn't see you put it in there. And I *know* the apprentice I met during my week of testing at Master Bergid's. After several weeks of seeing him here, I know him even better. Our apprentice is no thief, and I would be honored to call him my friend, now or whenever he is willing to accept it."

Kaelin stood motionless, struggling to control his emotions. Though he had no desire to face them, the fact that the other Bards of Eyrie had not returned to the Master's home since Kaelin had been charged with theft had hurt him more than he'd wanted to admit, especially the three who, like Brent, knew him from their previous rotation on Kestrel. He knew they were probably just as uncomfortable with the situation as he was, but the thought that they might all believe him a thief and liar … *at least I know one who doesn't.* He reached out and grasped Brent's arm firmly. His throat hurt and his eyes stung.

"Brent," he managed to say. "Your friendship, especially right now, means everything to me. Thank you."

"It means every bit as much to me, my friend."

Master Talan cleared his throat. "Well, then," he said, "now that we have such a congenial trio, why don't you get your flute, Kaelin … and Brent, your kithara, please. I'll take harp." Once they were settled, the Master glanced at the apprentice, whose emotion was still visible. "Brent and I are going to play an accompaniment for you, Kaelin, on a basic cadence in E minor. This is not intended to be an ensemble, but rather an accompanied solo. We'll set the mood for you with a four-measure introduction, then you will join us, creating your own melodic line as you wish."

Kaelin drew a quick breath. "My own?" His lessons with the Master, while informative and thoroughly enjoyable, had been restricted to the various forms of each instrument's repertoire. The Master was apparently determined to bring his level of playing on kithara, lute, and lyre up to the level of his other three instruments, though Kaelin often reflected gloomily that there wasn't much point in doing so. The Council would not care what level his playing was when they took his Bardic instruments away.

"Your own," the Master confirmed, as he set a few harp crooks in place.

"Sir?"

The Master quirked a brow.

"My own music … isn't likely to be very pleasant."

"Play it, nevertheless."

Kaelin nodded and lifted his flute, resting it on his shoulder as the Master and Bard began to play. The Master's harp filled the room with a poignant melodic line, and the mellow tones of Brent's kithara moved up and down the arpeggios of the cadence in waves that left Kaelin too filled with anguish to play, and the duo continued on without him. The apprentice forced air deeply into his lungs and joined them, the low tone coming from his instrument as full of agony as his eyes had been.

Never had the listeners heard such pain expressed in a single note before. Throbbing, it finally moved upward in a torrent of raw emotion that ricocheted throughout the room. The listeners, barely able to continue playing, felt time itself had fled, leaving them suspended in an endless moment of loss and confusion. At last, at the very pinnacle of emotion, the suffering sounds began to ease, then wandered slowly down as though the flutist was re-membering what it had once felt like to be free of pain.

With a deep sigh of relief, Kaelin lowered his flute and looked up at his silent instructor. The Master's fingers had fallen from the strings of his harp. His eyes were closed.

"Master Talan?" Kaelin said in concern.

The Master made no reply as he finally roused himself, put his harp aside, and rose to his feet without once looking at the apprentice. "I ... need to check on something in my workshop," he said in a low voice and left.

Kaelin looked at Brent in alarm, but his new friend shook his head and spoke reassuringly. "Master Talan just needs some time. Listening to how you felt ... was not easy for him. He feels respon-sible, even though he had no choice in what he did."

"I shouldn't have—"

"—obeyed the Master?" Brent shook his head. "He told you to play your own music because he knew you needed to. You had no choice but to do as he asked, and his feelings are not your fault, any more than your feelings are his."

Kaelin was silent for a moment. "I guess I've been so focused on myself that I never thought what this must be like for him."

"Well, that's certainly understandable," Brent said with a wry smile. "I think, my friend, this situation is hard enough on you as it is. Don't *you* be hard on yourself, as well." He fell silent, glancing toward the workshop as though wishing he could say the same to the Master.

A few minutes later, Master Talan returned with a smile and motioned for them to take up their instruments again. The room soon resounded with a lively trio from ensemble form nine, and the last traces of sadness seemed to vanish as though they had never existed. Only the brief glances the Master and apprentice traded when the other wasn't looking told Brent otherwise.

Three trios later, the Bard reluctantly rose to leave. "I'd best be going, sir," he said to the Master. "I'll need to get an early start tomorrow if I'm to make it to Loryn before the end of the week. There are several villages along the way I'll need to visit. "

The Master glanced at Kaelin's crestfallen expression and cleared his throat. "I've decided that can wait for now," he told the surprised Bard. "Of more pressing concern is the help I need in my workshop. For the next three weeks, you'll spend the mornings there, making yourself available to help the Bards currently working on instrument repair. Some of them are in need of more help than I have time to give them. I also have several projects which will require your help in the afternoons, including a full inventory of my supplies so I can place an order for items that are getting a bit low."

"Certainly, sir." Brent suppressed a smile. He knew perfectly well the three Bards the Master referred to required little help, and that the Instrument Master knew his own inventory down to the last bolt. The Bard was also aware that Kaelin had three weeks left on Eyrie.

"You're welcome to have your meals with us, of course," the Master added, "and remain for as much of the evening as you wish. In fact," he said, as though it had just occurred to him, "perhaps you'd find it easier to stay here. Apparently, some of the faery folk of Eire made it to the Bardic Isles," he said whimsically, "and one of them inexplicably cleaned out my second guest room, so you'll find it quite in order and more convenient than traipsing back and forth."

The Bard glanced at the apprentice and caught the grateful look he gave the Master. "I'll be more than happy to stay here and help in any way you wish."

❧ 7 ❧

Three weeks later, Kaelin stood with Master Talan and Brent on the wharf at Skye and tried not to think about the medallion that shone conspicuously against his grey robe. He glanced at the ship making ready to sail to Zephyr and nervously chewed his lip.

Master Talan cleared his throat. "If you wish to sail to Kestrel instead," he said quietly, "you may do so. I'm sure Master Marek would understand."

Kaelin thought longingly of his own Master but shook his head. "No, sir," he said. He glanced up and tried to smile. "Apparently Master Marek knows some flute secrets that my Master wants me to discover ... and discreetly bring back to him."

The Instrument Master chuckled. "I see. In that case, don't forget your promise to me. Impress the Masters with your new headjoint platform and tuning crooks, and I'm sure they'll soon have you instructing their Bards in making them. Once word trickles down the Bardic hierarchy, I'm expecting to be inundated with orders."

Kaelin nodded. "I'll do my best."

The Master hesitated a moment before speaking again. "Before you leave, I want you to know..." the Master's eyes looked directly into his. "You *deserve* to know, Kaelin, that I believe every word you told me."

Tears sprang to Kaelin's eyes. "Thank you, sir."

"You'll enjoy your stay with Master Marek, lad. Unlike your first host, he's a quite decent cook."

Kaelin grinned. "You're a pretty decent cook now yourself, sir."

"Yes, well..." The Master's voice was extremely dry. "I don't believe I was given much choice in the matter, now was I?"

Kaelin looked up innocently. "Sir?"

The Master laughed and the apprentice suddenly found

himself enveloped in a hug that took his breath. When he was released, Brent promptly squeezed the breath out of him again. "I'll miss you, my friend," the Bard murmured.

Then the Master and Bard turned to leave, each receding footstep making the apprentice feel more alone and abandoned than he had ever felt before. With a feeling of near panic, Kaelin turned to board the waiting ship, steeling himself for the stares the medallion was sure to arouse. Unbidden, the clear memory of a question he had asked his Master before leaving Kestrel came to him.

"You're not ... sending me away because of what happened last week?"

"Certainly not. You are, however, quite liable to run across others in your travels who do not agree with the Council's acceptance of your apprenticeship. Whether they're members of our Order or not, I expect you to keep your temper and not give them more reason to complain. Even if," the Master added sternly, "their comment is aimed at me."

Remembering his Master's words, Kaelin boarded the waiting ship, keeping his eyes averted from the crew's stares. He had more to endure now than disapproval of his apprenticeship to a Master. Even those who had accepted the Council's decision would be looking at him doubtfully now. His own doubts about his reception on Zephyr increased with every step he took. Would the Master Flutist himself care to teach anything about the instrument he cherished to an apprentice accused of thievery? Discouraged, Kaelin headed below deck to his cabin, where no one would see the medallion of shame he wore.

Master Talan and Brent parted ways when they reached the town, Brent heading west to follow the coast to Loryn. The Master was halfway up the steep incline to his home when he paused for a moment and glanced back. The ship Kaelin was on had just rounded the eastern point of the bay on its way to Zephyr. Above it, a large kestrel circled the ship, then flew slightly northeast, the same direction the ship was headed. The Master watched it thoughtfully for a moment.

"Stay with him," he murmured under his breath. "He will need a friend." Then he turned and continued on his way.

Late that night, Tyrel sat scowling into the flames of his fire. "Didn't I take care of him for you?" he asked resentfully. "He's no longer a threat! Why won't you let me inform the Council so we can move forward with our reunion?"

The answer entered his mind swiftly. *He's only received a medallion, a mere token of suspicion. You made an excellent move against him, but until he's discredited and his Bardic instruments taken away from him, we can't risk making ourselves known to the Council. You're the only one we can trust.*

"I would never betray the trust of the Bards of Eire!"

Guard your tongue! Not even to me must you say such things out loud. The child might overhear you. You need only think your words as you look into the flame, and I'll hear them as clearly as you hear mine.

Tyrel quickly glanced behind him to the bedroll in the far corner of the room, but the small figure lying within it did not stir. "I told you I don't like doing that," he said with a slight shudder. "Hearing your voice in my head is creepy enough. Besides, she's asleep, and what danger could a child of four cycles be? No one even knows she exists. And what I did for you is no trivial thing. I could lose my robe for far less!"

The voice spoke soothingly. *If they knew what a dangerous threat to the Bardic Order Kaelin's Druidic power is, they would applaud your action. And make no mistake ... one day they will.*

Tyrel fell silent.

Is there some other reason you're so upset?

"I just ... don't like what I did. Even if it was necessary. I stole from a Master I respect, then lied to his face so it would be blamed on an apprentice who, as far as I know, has done nothing to deserve it and may not even realize his power is Druidic."

It's a bit late to be having second thoughts now, came the tart observation. *And don't you think that Master Cyral felt the same way after they escaped from the bay of Aille-Mara, and he had time to think of all the death and destruction he had caused? Many of the people harmed that day had done nothing to deserve it, either. Yet he is accounted the greatest hero in Bardic history.*

Tyrel sat back, his qualms of conscience stilled by Belek's words. "So, what do we do now?" he asked.

We wait.

Movement Two

The Master Flutist

Chapter 7

Kaelin remained in his small cabin for the two days it took to sail from Eyrie to Zephyr, preferring the loneliness of his cabin to the curious or judgmental stares of the crew. Two empty, achingly lonely days, reminding him of the first week of his sense-deprivation test. He seldom spoke except to thank the cook's apprentice for bringing him his meals, though Kaelin left most of them untouched. He heard nothing but the sounds of the sea. His eyes turned traitor, inexorably pulling his attention to the corner where his instrument bags lay. He'd been stunned when he felt the tuning fork in his pack ... filled with grief during his remaining days with Master Talan. But now, alone under the decks of a Bardic ship, anger ignited, the flames growing rapidly at the sight of his forbidden instruments. Anger not only at the undeserved charge of theft he was under, but at the Bard he was convinced was responsible for it. Cold reason made a feeble attempt to quench hot certainty.

Except for the Bards from Kestrel, it could have been any one of them.

It could have been. But it wasn't.

Why? Because he treated you badly?

No ... yes ... I don't know! There's just something about him. Something I don't trust.

It was not quite the same apprentice who walked slowly off the ship, lowered his pack and instruments to the ground, and bowed a greeting to the Master Bard of Zephyr. The youngest of the Masters was in his early forties, his blond hair bleached almost white by the midsummer sun. The creases at the corners of his eyes bespoke a keen appreciation of humor. Though Master Marek couldn't possibly have missed the black medallion against Kaelin's chest, its yellow inlays shining in the afternoon sun, he gave no sign of noticing it.

"Welcome to Zephyr, Kaelin," he said warmly.

"Thank you, sir." The apprentice found it difficult to speak clearly and lowered his head, avoiding the Master's gaze.

"I'm afraid you're in for a walk," the Master told him as he snagged Kaelin's pack, slung it over his own shoulder, and began walking toward the town. "I don't live in Oriel, although I do keep a room here available for my use." He glanced back and turned when the apprentice made no move to follow him. "Is there a problem?"

"It's this, sir." Kaelin glanced down at the medallion. "If you'd rather I didn't stay, perhaps you should tell me now, before the ship leaves. It will be stopping at Kestrel before returning to Eyrie."

Master Marek walked back to the humiliated apprentice. "Doesn't that medallion indicate that you have contested the accusation?" he asked quietly.

Kaelin looked up and found no judgment in the blue eyes that were a lighter version of his own Master's. "Yes, sir, I have."

"Then I fail to see any reason why I should object to your presence in my home, unless you yourself do not wish to remain. Outside of the instrumental restriction you are under, our time together need not be affected."

With a sigh of relief, Kaelin shouldered his instruments and followed the Master. Trying to ignore the stares the conspicuous medallion aroused from the dockhands, he focused his attention on the scenery.

Named for the unpredictable winds that buffeted the smallest of the Bardic Isles, Zephyr was strikingly beautiful. Tall cliffs punctuated the coastline. The town of Oriel seemed carved from solid rock, so closely did it nestle against the surrounding cliffs. *If Eyrie is the most accessible island, then Zephyr must be the most inaccessible.* Wherever the Master Flutist lived, there was only one direction it could be. Up.

The Master led the way through the small town, where once again Kaelin's robe and medallion attracted the attention of everyone they passed. Some appeared curious, others openly hostile. The Master gave no indication that he noticed, and though the apprentice did his best to follow suit, he breathed a sigh of relief as they left the town and headed southeast. The path they followed soon twisted above the town and ocean to an alarming height, and when they reached the top, they paused to catch their breath. Kaelin looked around in admiration. The sea stretched to the south, its expanse broken only by the northern coast of Lyra, clearly visible from where they stood. Zephyr's own coast seemed to be a continuous series of cliffs and valleys. A single peak rose to the north, not nearly as tall as those on Kestrel, but all the more striking for standing alone.

"Mount Tiern," the Master said, following his gaze. "Unlike Kestrel, Zephyr lays claim to but a single mountain, lake, and river. What my island lacks in size, however," he added, "it makes up for in beauty. If there's time, we'll take a journey up the Aille River to Loch Lyon, where you'll get a close-up view of the smallest, prettiest mountain in all the Bardic Isles."

After a steady hour's walk along the cliff-side path, they approached the Master's home. Situated near the top of a rocky crag, it commanded a striking view of the southern coast of Zephyr. The Master pointed out a small village nestled far below, which he said was Aiteal, named for the junipers in the vicinity. Kaelin whistled softly to himself; hiking up and down for supplies would be no small feat.

The Master gestured further southeast. "Following that path," he told Kaelin, "will eventually bring you to Elba, a much larger town than Aiteal and more accessible by land and water."

Master Marek opened the door and gestured for Kaelin to enter first. After his introduction to Master Talan's living quarters, Kaelin felt prepared for anything, but nothing could have prepared him for what he found in this Master's home.

Birds! The large, spacious room came alive with birds, flying, chittering, and trilling in delight at the Master's return. Master Marek gave a shrill whistle, and they immediately flew over to his outstretched arm. Kaelin's first impression of a dozen shrank to five. He recognized the largest as a cardinal, its distinctive red plumage and high crest shining as it preened itself above the rest on the Master's shoulder. A wood thrush, rustling its cinnamon-colored feathers, cocked its head disapprovingly upward and scolded the cardinal. The smallest bird was a wren, grey with black bars on its wings and tail. Upset by the squabble, it kept up a running commentary as it paced restlessly from side to side on the Master's arm. The last two birds were a matched pair, pale brown with unremarkable plumage. Ignoring the others, they chirped softly to each other.

"Are those thrushes, sir?" Kaelin asked, indicating the pair.

"Yes, they're thrush nightingales, the only nightingale found this far north. They may look ordinary, but there's nothing ordinary about their singing, particularly the male's. In fact, this whole ensemble could put every Master in the Bardic Isles to shame, including Master Rial. Though," he added with a smile, "I'd suggest keeping that bit of information to yourself."

Kaelin watched the nightingales with interest. "I've heard of nightingales in stories, but I never knew there were any in the Bardic Isles."

"As far as I know, they can only be found on Zephyr. Some say the cliffs attract them, with so many low shrubs and thickets for their nests, but I prefer to think it's the flute music in the vicinity." He indicated a bird house hanging in the corner. "Nightingales have a strong drive to migrate south for the winter, but these two have decided they prefer it here, where they have an accommodating companion to feed them through the cold months. They move outside every spring to nest, although I have yet to discover where. The female has two clutches a cycle, raising four or five chicks until they fledge. I'm expecting to see their second brood flying about here soon."

He walked to the open window and lifted each bird into flight with his finger. Then he opened a container standing on the table, scooped a handful of seeds from it, and scattered it out the window. Kaelin watched entranced as birds flew from every direction, soon covering the ground. The air reverberated with the clash of wings, indignant chirps, and an occasional fight over ownership of the spoils. When the seeds were gone, all of the birds flew away except for the nightingales. Kaelin could see them flitting from branch to branch not far from the house.

Catching the scent of something savory, he turned to find the Master busily preparing a meal in the open kitchen. Kaelin hurried over, his eyes widening in appreciation as he saw what the Master was preparing. What looked to be crab stuffing peeked out from between two sole fillets, a creamy sauce dripping slowly over its edges. Fresh salad greens and vegetables completed the appetizing meal, a mouthwatering contrast to his first meal on Eyrie.

The Master waved away his apology for not having helped. "You can help with meals tomorrow. I prepped everything this morning, so all that was left was to heat it up. Let's take it to the table."

Kaelin wasted no time taking all he could, then went back for the utensils and mugs of blackberry tea. He inhaled deeply as memories of serving his Master his favorite blackberry tea during their trek across Kestrel filled his mind.

"I thoroughly enjoyed watching someone take such pleasure in my birds," Marek said as they took their seats. "They make wonderful companions and are quite tame." He chuckled. "In fact, don't be surprised if you suddenly find yourself with a bird on your head. I keep that window open so they can come and go as they please."

Kaelin laughed, delighted with this unexpected hobby of the Master Flutist, and relaxed for the first time since leaving the ship. He waited for the Master to help himself and begin to eat, then happily did the same. The apprentice looked around as he ate the excellent food, noticing the large, comfortable living room for the first time. No disorderliness here. It was not only clean, but filled with small, personal touches that revealed much about its owner. The Master's instruments hung from pegs carved in the shape of birds. The front of the mantelpiece sported carvings of the seven Bardic instruments, a flute occupying the center spot. The tables were made of polished maple, the tops of the smaller ones cross-sections of the tree, their legs sturdy, crisscrossed branches. A braided rug lay on the floor by the fire, and two chests stood against the wall. Above them were shelves filled with scrolls and music manuscripts.

"You have a wonderful home, sir."

A smile tugged at the corners of the Master's mouth. "I would imagine, after spending three months with our industrious Instrument Master, that *any* home might seem pretty wonderful."

They looked at each other and laughed.

"It was in much better shape when I left it," Kaelin assured him. "All the clutter is cleared away, so there's plenty of room for ensembles. And Master Talan can cook now."

The Master's eyes widened. "You taught Talan how to *cook?*"

Kaelin shook his head, his eyes dancing. "Oh, no, sir. I wouldn't *dream* of instructing a Master," he solemnly said.

"Of course you wouldn't," Marek said dryly. "How, then, did you accomplish this miracle?"

Kaelin cleared his throat. "Well ... I thought there was no harm in reciting exactly what I was doing out loud every time I cooked, like it was the only way I could keep track. After so much repetition..." He shrugged, indicating the Master's helplessness in the matter. "He made a beef stew one night and I heard him muttering all the steps to himself in perfect order. It was a very good stew."

Master Marek laughed. "We are forever in your debt. Every Master will be grateful to find his next trip to Eyrie a more pleasant experience." He glanced at the rapidly fading daylight. "Leave the clean-up for later. Come, fetch your flute and join me." The Master took his own instrument from the stand next to his desk and settled himself near the open window.

Kaelin quickly complied and sat next to him. For a few moments the Master remained motionless and Kaelin wondered what they were waiting for. Then the stillness was broken by the sound of a bird, singing clearly in the growing dusk. Another answered it. *The nightingales.* Master Marek was right. Whatever their appearance, there was nothing ordinary about their songs.

The avian voice spoke again, and the Master lifted his flute and answered. An amazing duet began, bird and flute singing together in free form. Then the Master stopped and signaled for Kaelin to take his place, his eyes alight with interest.

Kaelin hesitated a moment, resting the platform of his head-joint against his lips, and listened. When the clear song of the nightingale came again, he closed his eyes in concentration and briefly answered it. There was a moment of silence, then the nightingale emitted a questioning chirp, as though it knew perfectly well this was no longer the Master Flutist he was speaking with and was wondering who it was. Kaelin smiled and introduced himself with his music. The nightingale joined him, the clear avian voice rising above the improvised flute music in a conversation no less real for its lack of words. When a fluttering of wings announced the little songster's departure, the room was dark. Kaelin sighed with pleasure.

Master Marek rose and lit the fire. "I see you've enjoyed your first lesson with my nightingales."

Kaelin's eyes shone. "I've never had one like that!"

"Understand, then, that it *is* a lesson. Every day at dusk you are to sit here and have a lesson with the nightingales, even if I'm not here." The Master raised his hand at Kaelin's startled look. "You're allowed to play only under instruction by a Bard or Master." He gestured toward the open window. "My nightingales are Masters of the highest order and can teach you things no one else can. Listen to them and to all my other Masters, and let their songs teach you the few things you need to learn."

"Will you teach me, too?" Kaelin ventured to ask.

"I'm hardly going to give the honor of teaching you entirely to my birds."

Honor? The apprentice dropped his eyes, feeling his face grow warm.

"If you did not have a strong desire to learn," the Master said quietly, "you wouldn't have come here. You would have returned to your Master instead of continuing your travels, knowing the knowledge you gain might not be useful to you later."

Kaelin looked up into eyes so like his Master's, and Marek smiled. "I confess I've been quite looking forward to this," the Master continued, "and that medallion has dampened none of my expectations." The Master indicated his flute. "As regards flute technique, there are things I can and will teach you, but as regards musical *imagery,* there is much that I am hoping to learn from you. Perhaps," he added whimsically, "after so much repetition..."

Kaelin's eyes widened. "I haven't any recipe to recite for that. How can I teach something I don't understand myself?"

"The best learning is reciprocal," the Master told him. "A student learns by listening to what his teacher says and demonstrates; a teacher learns by watching his student learn."

Kaelin looked at the Master with respect, deciding in that moment that he would work for this Master as hard as he had ever worked for his own. The Master nodded, as though in acknowledgment of what Kaelin had not said, then cleared his throat. "Now, I can no longer contain my curiosity about that platform on the headjoint of your flute. Has our Instrument Master been up to his usual clever tricks?"

"He has … would you like to see?" Kaelin eagerly showed the Master Flutist what the platform did to the tone of his flute and promised to instruct him in its making. Then the apprentice took out his harp and showed the Master the wooden crooks that enabled him to play in several keys. Master Marek immediately began making plans to rotate the fifteen Bards assigned to Zephyr to his home for a demonstration of both improvements.

"How fortunate that you went to Talan first!" he exclaimed as he sat at his desk to begin working on the rotation schedule. "Otherwise, it might have been months before I found out about these."

Kaelin glanced down at the medallion, fervently wishing he had traveled to anywhere else. With a sigh, he put his instruments away and went to clear the table and clean up. Then, exhausted from the emotions of the day, he excused himself and went to his room.

Sleep, however, proved elusive. The medallion shone in the moonlight that streamed through the window as he lay facing it, and he fingered it pensively. Its weight was a constant reminder of what he stood to lose: his instruments, his robe, and his Master. Anger flared, his face flushed with its heat, and his throat constricted. Tyrel's face floated before him and Kaelin burned with the desire to rearrange every feature on it. *Why did he do this to me? What did I ever do to him? And what wouldn't I do now, if I had half a chance?*

Kaelin thought with envy of the heather on Eyrie that had sprung back after being smashed flat all night. If the Council decided against him, how could he possibly recover? *But I won't rest until I've had the chance to see Tyrel again. If I do nothing else, I'll make him pay for ruining my life!* Kaelin had not seen the Bard again after that night, but he often imagined their next encounter, played out according to the satisfying script he had composed on the way to Zephyr.

The apprentice scowled. If the Council decided against him, he wouldn't be traveling to Eyrie to exact revenge against Tyrel. The Shipping Guild gave their tribute to the Bardic Order in the form of free passage on any ship. Once convicted of theft, Kaelin would no longer be wearing the Bardic robe that would grant him that privilege and would likely be stranded on Elegy with no means of support.

His Master, he knew, would not abandon him. The memory of words his Master had said when they left Elegy together over a cycle ago returned vividly to him.

I will never send you away unless you wish to go.

Never, Kaelin thought bitterly, would he have thought anything could make him decide to leave the Master he loved, but the idea of returning to him, forever bereft of his instruments and rank, was intolerable. He imagined the Bards of Kestrel playing wondrous ensemble music in the Master's home, laughing and talking freely amongst themselves, and his heart twisted with grief. For he knew he could not bear to listen, forbidden to take part, looks of pity directed his way. Or even worse, see his Master refrain from using his own instruments at night, to spare him. And all because of a promise the Master had made to a boy who no longer had any right to his home or the wonderful room he had created for him ... a promise he might well come to regret having ever made. Kaelin couldn't stand the thought of seeing that regret in his Master's eyes.

He could return to his sister, but something in Kaelin rebelled at the idea. Living so close to Kyet, never knowing when suddenly catching a glimpse of the Master would tear his heart asunder again? No. He would be in enough pain inflicted by the Council without torturing himself afterwards. He would stay on Elegy and make his own way in the world. He would try his best to forget being part of the Bardic Order, though he would never forget his Master. Nor, he told himself grimly, would he forget Tyrel.

Kaelin thought of the maps his Master had given him to study. It was a long walk to Tryl, the seaport on Elegy's eastern coast. That left coastal villages, whose small populations would not readily give employment to an underaged boy with no parents or references. Hot tears gathered in his eyes at the thought of being alone, without any means to make his living, and he dashed them angrily away. Perhaps he could sell his compositions, if he stockpiled pen, ink, and manuscript before the Council hearing. No one could forbid him to compose, after all, even if he could only hear the music in his mind. He would compose reams of music, then, until he had enough coin to go to Tryl and pay for his passage to wherever Tyrel was. No matter what, one day he would find the Bard who had done this to him and have a silent conversation with him ... with his fists. No matter that he would likely wind up standing before the Council again to answer for striking a Bard. This time, he would freely—proudly!—admit his guilt to them all, for no punishment could be worse than what they were about to do to him for a crime he was not guilty of.

The weight of his anger seemed suddenly heavier than the medallion. Kaelin shoved the metal disc roughly to his back and tried to focus his thoughts elsewhere. It was a long time before he fell asleep, lulling himself there with the pleasant hope that somehow, his Master would be able to set everything right again.

The following day, Master Marek handed Kaelin a two-page flute solo after breakfast and told him they would have a lesson on it that afternoon. The apprentice reviewed it carefully, finding the piece technically easy enough, but with an unusual structure that baffled him. The first page was practically a dirge, slow and somber; the second page burst without warning into a fast, lively piece that made no sense when paired together with the first. *Who would write a piece like this? It's like someone took pages from two entirely different compositions and spliced them together for no reason.*

That afternoon, Kaelin felt unusually nervous when he sat before the Master to play the piece he'd been given but did not understand. He tried to put his misgivings aside as he began playing, doing his best to make the piece sound like the single composition it was surely supposed to be. He made no errors and handled the technique, dynamics, and articulation without any trouble. When he lowered his flute, however, the Master rose without a word and left the house, closing the door firmly behind him.

Kaelin sat still, his face burning with shame. He couldn't remember feeling so humiliated at a lesson before, not even when he couldn't concentrate on his Master's lessons within sight of Bardic Mountain. Then the door creaked open, a little at a time, and an astounding sight met his eyes. Master Marek was on his hands and knees, dragging himself into the room, looking so much like he had been mortally wounded that Kaelin cried out and ran to help him. But the Master paid him no attention, only crawled slowly around in a circle, then painfully dragged himself back through the open door and pulled it shut behind him. Utterly bewildered, Kaelin went to the window to try to catch sight of him.

Bam! The door slammed open with so much force it nearly rebounded into the Master's face as he leaped across the threshold in an abandonment of joy. He whirled and twirled himself around the room, then leapt back through the door and swooshed it shut behind him.

As Kaelin stared incredulously at the door, it opened a third time, and Master Marek walked in, calmly closed it, and reseated himself.

"Now," he said with quiet expectation, as though awaiting the performance of a lifetime. "Play it like *that*."

The only way Kaelin could have obeyed the Master was if his flute had obligingly risen and played itself. But his mind, way ahead of his stunned emotions, was already replaying the piece in a completely different way, following the vivid imagery of the Master's demonstration. "What kind of piece *is* this?" he asked wonderingly.

"The piece of a composer who suffered from a malady of the mind," Marek told him. "As you might well be wondering about me," he added with a grin. "At times he was so dejected he was hardly able to move himself from one room to the next. At other times, perhaps in order to balance the scales, he was in a frenzy of happiness and boundless energy. As you've already discovered, trying to meld together two states of mind that the composer had every intention of keeping separate doesn't work. He wrote this piece as an expression of what it's like to be *both* ... to never know from one morning to the next which one would hold him in its sway. So, in order to play it well, you must experience both extremes yourself as you play."

The Master was silent for a moment, gazing at the thoughtful apprentice. "You're well accustomed to playing the music of what you hear, Kaelin, from whatever you concentrate on, be it an object or a memory. A piece like this, however, is not your own composition and has no inherent connection to you. You must forge that connection yourself, from your own experiences and your own emotions." The Master reached for his flute. "I'm going to play the first page's ending twice. The first time, I'll pay strict attention to all the dynamics and articulations, and I promise to play my best, but I will *also* be thinking about what I'd like to have for breakfast tomorrow. I'll leave it to you to determine what I'm thinking about the second time I play it."

Kaelin listened intently as the Master raised his flute and

began to play. A beautiful, simple ending to a musical phrase filled the Master's home, flawlessly obeying every marking on the score in Kaelin's hand. The Master paused for a moment, then closed his eyes and played the same phrase, but this time Kaelin forgot the score, for the simple phrase was uttered by an achingly lonely voice that wrung the apprentice's heart and brought tears to his eyes.

"Tell me what you heard," came the Master's quiet voice.

"The first time," Kaelin replied slowly, "I heard a flute, beautifully played. I heard the notes, the dynamics, the articulation ... every perfectly placed measure line."

"And the second time?"

"I heard a voice ... crying out all alone ... as if it wanted more than anything to be with someone, but at the same time, wouldn't allow it."

The Master gave him a startled look.

The apprentice was too lost in thought to notice. "Was it your voice, sir, or the voice of the composer?"

Marek cleared his throat. "I like to think it was both of us. For isn't human suffering common to us all?"

"It made me feel like I used to feel in Vale, before I met my Master."

"So, my loneliness, coming from my own experiences you are not privy to, evoked the same emotion in you, from your own experiences I am not privy to. And because of that, the two of us, performer and listener, are closer to each other and understand each other better than we did a few moments ago. *That* is the true power of music." He indicated Kaelin's flute. "Play the piece again. I don't want to hear the notes, dynamics, articulations, or measure lines. Those things simply give the music a visible structure, but they are *not* the music. I want to hear *your* voice, describing *your* experiences ... and gifting me my own."

Kaelin lifted his flute, suddenly alive with ideas of what he could describe through such music. It wasn't difficult for an apprentice facing the stripping away of his robe, his instruments, and especially his Master, to visualize and project his emotions through his flute. As he began to play, the composer's music became his own, as fully able to translate his emotion as if he had written it himself.

There was a fluttering of wings, and a small weight landed on the end of his flute. A second fluttering, and Kaelin opened his eyes to the startling sight of two nightingales perched on the end of his flute as he played. Master Marek sat staring at them, his eyes glistening with tears. The nightingales made no sound as the flutist continued playing. One of them nuzzled its head against the other's breast. The flutist came to the end of the page, took a deep breath, then launched into the next page of music in a burst of joy that seemed, indeed, to come from nowhere. The two birds launched themselves with it, flying about the room and singing ecstatically, as though they felt themselves personally responsible for the sudden upswing in the flutist's mood.

The listener caught his breath in wonder as his senses were swept away in the joy of a mischievous boy climbing a tree and raining pinecones down upon his friend's unsuspecting head, his happiness in seeing the pleased expression on his Master's face as he silently read through a composition exercise, his astonishment as his Master joined in a village dance, expertly whirling through the dance patterns and laughing merrily.

When the music ended, Marek, his mind filled with the vivid images Kaelin's music had described, found himself laughing, too. The birds flew out the open window.

Marek wiped his eyes and struggled to assemble a serious expression. "When on earth," he managed to ask, "did you see your Master dancing a village dance?"

Kaelin grinned. "When I followed him out of Vale, he let me stay with him for a trial period while he visited the rest of the mountain villages."

"And he ... *danced* his way through them?"

Kaelin nodded. "He's a very good dancer considering his, um ... well, seniority," he finally said. "And the villagers loved it!"

The Master Flutist dissolved in another fit of laughter. When at last he regained his composure, he shook his head. Never, in all his cycles of teaching, had a student so quickly absorbed a lesson and traveled so far with it. "You and I, youngster," he finally said, "are *definitely* going to have a discussion about musical imagery!"

Chapter 8

For the most part, Kaelin's days on Zephyr were pleasant ones. Only the medallion's presence and his own Master's absence weighed upon him. He found Master Marek to be an excellent teacher, unfailingly patient and full of humorous insights that taught him more than dozens of musical exercises could have. They spent a few days hiking up the Aille River to Loch Lyon, where only a glimpse of Mount Tiern could be seen before a torrential downpour drove them into their shelter. The next day they circled the lake, the mountain still wreathed in mist, ghostly tendrils reaching out to the water as well, then headed back to Oriel. Twice a week they traveled down to the small fishing village of Aiteal for supplies. The Master always spent a few hours there, teaching and playing his instruments. In the afternoons or evenings, there were Bards in the Master's home, receiving instructions, talking over problems, or working on the duets and trios that Master Marek apparently loved as much as Masters Bergid and Talan did.

The first evening he spent helping two Bards make platforms and crooks, Kaelin felt self-conscious of the medallion, lowering his eyes whenever one of them glanced his way. After they left, the apprentice thankfully returned to his own work, then glanced up uneasily when he felt the Master's eyes resting on him.

"Have I done something wrong, sir?"

"I don't know," the Master unexpectedly said. "Have you?"

Kaelin, taken aback, made no reply.

"You stood on the docks of Oriel last week," the Master continued, "looking at me with humiliation and shame on your face, just as you've been looking at my Bards this evening. Why?"

Kaelin flushed and glanced at the medallion. "Because of this," he managed to say.

Marek walked over to the disconcerted apprentice and picked up the medallion. "Curious," he remarked as he inspected it. "I see nothing humiliating or shameful about it. It's simply a medallion, made of metal and suspended on a chain. Why does it make you feel ashamed?" He stood holding the medallion, waiting for an answer.

"Because," Kaelin said slowly, "of the reason it was given."

"I see. Was it given because you thieved from Master Talan and refused to admit your guilt?"

"No, sir!" Kaelin exclaimed, stung.

"If it had been, refusing to take responsibility for your thievery would indeed be reason for feeling ashamed. Is refusing to admit to a theft you *didn't* commit a shameful thing?"

The apprentice blinked in surprise. "No, sir, it's not."

"Then why are you ashamed to wear a medallion that proclaims your belief in your own innocence?" The Master released the medallion. "There is no shame in receiving this unless the one it's given to knows he is guilty and refuses to admit it. If he knows he is innocent, then he refused to lie and chose instead to contest a false charge. Can you give me a reason why such a person should feel ashamed?"

Kaelin looked directly into the Master's eyes and shook his head. "No, sir, I can't. But ... well, not everyone sees it like that. Crewmembers on the ships ... people in the villages ... they see the medallion and look at the one wearing it as if he's a criminal. To them, it proclaims his guilt."

"And is this something *he* should be ashamed of? Or should

they?"

Kaelin considered this in silence.

"You are not responsible for how others think and act," the Master said quietly. "You are only responsible for yourself. When you keep your actions in accordance with what you know to be true, which in this case means wearing that medallion as a proclamation of your innocence and refusal to lie, you will find that what others think loses its power to disturb you." He looked keenly at the apprentice. "For a moment, put yourself in the position of one of my Bards that came tonight. What would *you* think if the medallioned apprentice you just met could not meet your eyes and ducked his head in shame?"

Kaelin's eyes widened in startled realization.

"It isn't easy," the Master said gently, "but nothing—"

"—worth the having ever is," Kaelin finished.

Master and apprentice smiled at each other.

"Did he used to say that to you, too?" Kaelin asked curiously.

"Many a time. And I soon discovered, as I'm sure you have, that the Master Bard of Kestrel knows what he's talking about."

"Yes, sir," Kaelin said, looking thoughtfully at the medallion.

The next evening, the Master Flutist was pleased to see Kaelin open the front door, bow to the two Bards who stood there, and give them a warm smile. "Welcome to Master Marek's home, sirs. My name is Kaelin."

The Bards glanced at the medallion and the young apprentice who stood smiling at them, and smiled back.

"It's good to meet you, Kaelin," one of them said with a nod. "I'm Bard Teryn, and this is Bard Fered."

Kaelin spent the evening helping the two Bards make platforms and crooks for their instruments, then joined them in a quartet. He played his harp, as the Master requested, and flushed with pleasure at the Bards' exclamations of admiration at the construction of his harp and his playing of it.

"We've heard rumors of your playing from the Bards of Kestrel and Eyrie," Teryn said. "Particularly when you solo your own compositions on your primary instrument. We were hoping Master Marek would allow you to play one of them before we go."

The Master nodded his permission, and Kaelin gladly fetched his flute. Since receiving the medallion, he had not played his own music for anyone except Master Talan and Brent. He thought of the nightingales he had watched on the cliffs that afternoon and began to play the music of the memory that filled his mind.

The listeners inhaled sharply as their senses were swept outside. They were sitting near the edge of the cliff, the grass rustling against the grey robe tucked under their legs, the wind ruffling their hair. A nightingale flitted in and out of a nearby thicket. Inside, they spied a nest built of grass and leaves just above the ground. The female moved restlessly, as though aware of their scrutiny, and they caught a brief glimpse of pale blue eggs with brown speckles. They watched in breathless wonder as one of the eggs began to hatch, saw the tiny translucent beak emerge, the closed eyes, the glistening head. The male returned, chittered softly for a few moments, then flitted to a nearby juniper and let loose a burst of song.

When the flute music ended, the room was completely silent. Kaelin moved to put his instruments away as the two Bards roused and began excitedly talking to each other about what they had just experienced. Then they rose and took their leave, thanking Kaelin for his performance and promising to see him again soon.

The apprentice closed the door behind them and turned to find the Master shaking his head in wonder.

"I had no idea they'd built their nest there," Marek said, "even though I've walked past that thicket dozens of times. You've just given me a priceless gift, Kaelin, to see that and know where to watch in two weeks when the fledglings take to the air for the first time. I've wanted to see that moment for cycles."

"I happened to sit down in just the right place to spot their nest and thought you might like to see it," Kaelin said. "Especially when that egg hatched. I'd love to see the fledglings take flight!"

The Master smiled. "You and I will watch it together," he promised. He looked at Kaelin thoughtfully. "I'm curious to know how you play a memory. Do you compose the music for it?"

Kaelin shook his head. "Memories have music of their own." His brow furrowed in thought. "I just think about the memory like anyone else would, I suppose. Music comes to me from it, and I just play what I hear ... and if I haven't set a block first, that brings it to life for anyone who hears me, though I don't know how. With no one to explain it to me, I don't know if I ever will."

Marek nodded. "Perhaps understanding will come to you one day as you grow older and gain more experience with your gift."

"Maybe so, sir," Kaelin said, wondering how he could ever gain such experience if the Council took away his instruments.

And so the days passed, filled with lessons, practicing, and evening ensembles. At dusk Kaelin always stopped what he was doing and took his flute to the window to wait for the nightingales to sing. This was by far the happiest time of day for him, his eyes closed to the rest of the world, his spirit soaring as freely as the birds. Even the Bards who disapproved of his apprenticeship sat astounded as Kaelin's music took them to the remote habitat of the birds, whose music blended with his own. Then they would fly back, soaring effortlessly over cliffs and valleys until they could see the home of the Master Flutist far below them. When Kaelin put away his flute, the silent room would fill with the busy sounds of resumed work and whispered comments.

One afternoon before the Bards arrived, a sudden ruckus outside the open window preceded the abrupt appearance of the nightingales and several other birds, who flew around the room in agitation. The Master leaped to his feet and rushed out the door, with Kaelin right behind him. Marek scanned the skies, then stabbed a finger toward a large bird circling above the house.

"That's a white-tailed eagle," he exclaimed in an accusatory voice. "He's been hanging about here for a few weeks now, disturbing my birds, and occasionally catching one." He glared at the offending predator.

"He's beautiful," Kaelin said in awe.

"Yes," the Master conceded, "and with a wingspan larger than the height of a full-grown man. But he's also a voracious bird of prey and isn't above feeding on his smaller cousins, especially if the fishing isn't enough to satisfy his appetite. Look there!" Master Marek pointed to a smaller bird flying straight for the eagle. "A kestrel! I've never seen one here before, and that's an unusually large one. Ha!" The Master was jubilant.

Kaelin, however, was distraught at the sight of the kestrel he thought of as his own flying straight into such danger. "The kestrel is much smaller than the eagle ... why is he confronting it? The eagle will surely kill him!" he cried.

"No, lad, it won't. Size isn't everything. Watch and see." They stood shading their eyes and watched the drama being played out in the skies above. The kestrel continued relentlessly on course for the eagle and let loose a barrage of challenging staccatos. The eagle spied the kestrel, veered sharply and retreated, beating its powerful wings and climbing into the sky until it was just a dark speck above. The kestrel flew to a pine tree and perched itself on a high branch in plain view of the eagle, then preened itself, clearly proud of its prowess in driving off the much larger bird.

Kaelin let loose a breath of relief. "Why didn't the eagle fight?"

"Because it isn't worth the risk," the Master replied. "Kestrels are the only falcons that can hover, and they're extraordinarily fast divers. If an eagle lets one get above him, he knows the kestrel can dive for its back and do a great deal of damage. So, the eagle willingly concedes his hunting territory until the kestrel moves on. Hopefully this kestrel will stay here long enough to convince the eagle to move on instead."

Kaelin frowned. "But aren't kestrels birds of prey, too? Won't they eat smaller birds as well?"

"Not normally, especially when mice and voles are as plentiful as they are now. If I have the choice of an eagle or a kestrel in the neighborhood," the Master said wryly, "I'll happily take the kestrel, even one as large as that."

Kaelin watched the bird for a moment, wondering. He hadn't seen him on the way to Zephyr ... although, he suddenly realized, he hadn't once been on deck. "Why is he following me?" he murmured, unaware that he had spoken out loud.

The Master threw him a keen look. "Following you?"

"Before I met my Master," Kaelin explained, "that kestrel swooped down and stared at me from the branch of a tree, and I stared back at him for a moment. When I began to hear music, I looked away and he flew off. Later that day I played a variation of it, not knowing Master Bergid was camped nearby, and ... well, it's thanks to that kestrel that I met my Master."

"And the same kestrel has been following you ever since?"

The apprentice nodded. "His size and markings are the same. He followed the ship out of the harbor when it left Kyet, and he didn't like that it was leaving. He followed Master Talan and me on our tour of Eyrie, and I guess he followed the ship here, too."

Marek smiled. "Perhaps you weren't the only one who heard music when you looked at that kestrel." He nodded at the bird, whose head was cocked as he looked down upon them. "Perhaps he heard your song as well and has not forgotten."

Kaelin's first month with the Master Flutist passed quickly. Marek often looked thoughtfully at the young apprentice as he played ever more fluently with the nightingales. *Someone with such music as that inside him couldn't possibly be guilty of thievery!* Nor, he was certain, would his mentor have ever been taken in by a deceitful youngster, however talented he might be. Marek had received a report from Talan concerning the incident, along with a request to send back notice of the earliest convenient time for him to attend a special Council hearing at the beginning of autumn, a surprisingly lengthy delay for so serious a charge as theft. Yet Marek had intentionally delayed answering it. He knew that unless evidence arose clearing Kaelin of the charge, a negative verdict was inevitable. The thought of sitting in judgment over this young apprentice, lost in the glory of soaring with the nightingales... The Master pushed the thought forcefully out of his mind.

As for the apprentice, however agreeable the days were, the nights were times of dread. Thanks to Master Marek, he was no longer ashamed of wearing the medallion, but that didn't stop the anger and resentment that had kindled beneath the decks of the ship from growing stronger. The emotions Kaelin kept at bay during the busy daytime hours could not be ignored while he lay in his bed at night. The more he thought about what had happened on Eyrie the angrier he grew. The black medallion seemed to leach every dark emotion into the boy that trembled beneath it until he could feel its taint all through his body. He struggled in vain against his own feelings, wanting to be rid of them, yet unable to free himself. Each night he lay awake for a longer time before falling into a restless sleep.

Master Marek was not unaware of Kaelin's struggles. The strain showed plainly on the young face in eyes increasingly hollow with fatigue. One night, listening to the tossing and turning in the room next to his, the Master rose, fetched his flute and a cloth, and entered the apprentice's room.

Kaelin sat up in surprise as the Master lit the lamp beside his bed. "Is there something I can do for you, sir?"

"No, but there *is* something you can do for yourself," came the Master's quiet reply. He held out his flute. "Play the lowest note."

Wonderingly, Kaelin lifted the Master's instrument and did as instructed. The low, vibrant tone filled the room, then died away. The Master grasped the end of his flute and firmly plugged the open end of it with the cloth. "Play it again."

The apprentice complied, and this time a strangled, stifled groan emerged from the flute. The Master indicated the end of his instrument. "Isn't the quality of the flute's tone dependent on that opening remaining free of obstruction?"

"Yes, sir."

"Wouldn't you say that was a poor way to treat my fine Bardic flute, plugging up the end and forcing the music to back up inside it?" the Master demanded in a scandalized voice.

"Yes, sir."

"Would you treat *your* flute in such a manner?"

"No, sir."

Master Marek frowned in perplexity. "Then why, Kaelin, do you treat yourself so?"

Kaelin stared at the Master in silence. Words that his own Master had once said echoed suddenly in his mind.

You yourself are the most important instrument to master.

The amber eyes filled with torment. "I don't know! I don't know what to do, or how to stop it."

The Master reached over and grasped the cloth, freeing the flute with a firm tug. "You must remove the obstruction."

Kaelin stared at the Master's flute. "I can't!" he abruptly cried. "I can't just reach inside myself and pull my feelings out like that cloth! The best I can do is ignore them or escape from them with the nightingales."

"Then they will grow stronger, until their weight makes ignoring or escaping them impossible. It's already impossible for you at night, isn't it?"

Kaelin reluctantly nodded.

"And soon," the Master continued, "if you haven't already

begun to notice, it will affect your music as well. Nor will it stop there, for when you poison yourself and your music, the effects will soon spill over to all those around you, especially those you care for the most." He watched as the boy's flushed face paled and the hands still holding the Master's flute tightened. It took no Master to know who the apprentice was thinking of.

"Listen to me, Kaelin," Marek continued with quiet authority. "Listen well, and do not forget. No person or event has the power to change who you are, unless you surrender that power yourself." He grasped the medallion and shook it before Kaelin's startled eyes. *"This* does not have the power to change you ... unless you let it. Whatever happened on Eyrie put this chain around your neck," he said strongly. "It may take your instruments away from you, as well as your robe and your Master." He paused, his eyes still locked on the shaken apprentice, and his voice softened. "But what it *can't* do is plug you with anger, resentment, or hatred. Only you can do that. You alone have the power to destroy yourself." The Master gently took his instrument back and rose to his feet. "There is only one way to free the obstruction."

"What is that, sir?" Kaelin asked unsteadily.

"Forgiveness," the Master replied, looking keenly at the disconcerted apprentice, "either of yourself or, as I strongly suspect, of another."

Kaelin's hands clenched into the fists he had so often imagined using on Tyrel. He felt like he might choke on the anger that flooded him at the Master's words. "He doesn't *deserve* to be forgiven!" he said roughly.

"Perhaps not," the Master agreed mildly. "I did not, however, suggest it for his sake, but for your own."

Kaelin's frown deepened. *Forgive Tyrel for my own sake?*

"When someone intentionally hurts another, it forms a bond between them that continues to hurt them both. The assailant tightens that bond with all the negative emotions that caused him to act the way he did, emotions that often have nothing to do with the one he hurt. The victim does the exact same thing with his own negative emotions. The more he dwells on them, the more entangled he gets, until eventually he becomes much like the one who hurt him. And that, Kaelin, would be a far worse crime than the original one. For now, the victim is all too likely to do exactly what was done to him and hurt someone else. You're well on your way to hurting the one you care for the most. For if your Master were here at this moment, he would be far more hurt by what you're doing to yourself than by what was done to you."

The look of devastation that crossed the apprentice's face smote the Master's heart, but he held the golden, pain-filled eyes and continued. "Forgiveness is not a pass for the one who hurt you," he said gently. "Rather, it's a release for yourself ... a letting go of your own destructive emotions that bind you to him. By forgiving, you take back the power to be who you truly are, not who someone else has made you become."

The Master said no more and returned to his bed. He knew that Kaelin would have to absorb the difficult lesson on his own, and that it would take time.

The next morning, the Master Bard of Zephyr sent a message to the Master Bard of Eyrie, regretfully informing him that the earliest he could possibly attend a special Council hearing would be at the end of autumn.

Chapter 9

On a gusty morning in the last month of summer, Master Bergid received a scroll from Eyrie with Master Talan's seal upon it. No sooner had Bergid read the missive than he stormed from his home, slamming the door with such force that the bar within dropped down on its own, locking him out. He strode on without so much as glancing back. None of his instruments rested on his back; indeed, no pack of any kind accompanied the Master's precipitous departure. Those in the streets veered clear of the Master's fury as he strode toward the docks of Kyet. The unfortunate Captain of the cargo ship he chose to board, when asked tersely if he was bound for Eyrie, blanched before the Master's blazing eyes and quickly nodded, though he had in fact been about to sail to Zephyr, in quite the opposite direction.

It was a silent ship that set forth so unexpectedly for Eyrie. The Master Bard did not once emerge from his quarters, and the weather, as though reflecting the Master's mood, became unseasonably stormy. The Captain gave it little heed, grateful for the strong winds that sped them to their destination. The storm cloud brooding beneath his deck was of far greater concern.

As they approached the bay of Skye, the door to the Master's quarters blew open, and the crew stumbled over themselves to clear a path. A full day of seclusion had done nothing to clear the thunder from the Master's brow. He strode to the rail and stood glaring at the seaport. The Captain glanced quickly at the town as though surprised to find it still standing under so fierce a regard. The moment the ship touched dock, the Master leapt off before a single rope could be brought to secure their mooring. The Captain heaved a sigh of relief as he watched the irate figure stride away, then gave the order to come about.

"How convenient," he muttered to himself. "No tie-up, no gangplank, no baggage. All passengers should be so accommodating." He spared a moment's pity for the luckless object of the Master's wrath. Likely Master Talan, the Captain mused, if the rumors about an underaged Bardic apprentice sporting a medallion were true. Then he sighed, not looking forward to explaining to the merchants awaiting his cargo in Zephyr why it had taken three days to sail there. Being commandeered by Master Bergid was not likely to be believed. Far more likely the merchants would accuse the Captain of drinking himself stupid in the inns of Kyet.

A scant half-hour later, the door of Talan's workshop burst open, and the Master Bard of Eyrie looked up from his worktable into the smoldering eyes of the Master Bard of Kestrel. Talan sighed and set down his tools. He glanced at the three Bards who had been working at their stations, but they were already on their way out the door, barely mumbling a farewell as they made good their escape. Talan would have given a handful of silvers to follow them. He pushed aside the cowardly thought and faced his furious colleague.

"Good evening, Bergid."

"It's not going to be good for *you*, Talan!" came the icy reply. Bergid snatched a message scroll from his robe and threw it down on the table, his eyes flashing blue lightning. "What is the meaning of this absurd charge you have made against my apprentice? And why did my notification take so long to arrive? This scroll is dated nearly *two months* ago!" He glared at his colleague. "I would have found out about it much sooner had I strolled along the docks and listened to the gossip coming off the ships!"

"I suppose you could charge me with cowardice in delaying your notification," Talan said dryly, "and with good reason, it seems, but the fact of the matter is that I was thinking of Kaelin. He's been through quite enough without having to bear the brunt of your tempestuous arrival, here or on Zephyr. Better that your next meeting with Kaelin comes after you've had the chance to regain your composure." He glanced at the livid Master before him. "As for the charge of theft, it's anything but absurd, and I did not make it lightly."

"What I demand to know is why you made it at all!"

"I would *not* have made it at all if the evidence had not been found in his possession, before witnesses."

"*Blast* your witnesses to oblivion!" the Master thundered. "You can't possibly have spent three months with that boy and believe him a thief and a liar! Do you *know* what you've done?"

The Instrument Master slapped his palms to the table and surged to his feet. "I know all too well!" He wrenched open a drawer, removed his silver tuning fork, and shook it in his colleague's startled face. "Don't you think I know that this object doesn't begin to compare with the value of that boy?" He slammed the shining instrument down upon the table with enough force to send his tools skittering across its surface. "I would sooner hurl the accursed thing into the sea," he growled. "I can't stand the sight of it. But from the moment it was found in Kaelin's pack, *I ... had ... no ... choice.*" He stared unwaveringly into the icy blue eyes of his colleague. "I can't ignore Bardic Law," he said with quiet emphasis. "And neither, my friend, can you."

"Oh, can't I?" Bergid growled back. "Nothing—I tell you, *nothing*—will take this boy away from me, not even Bardic Law. I swear it by every oath imaginable!"

Talan's own eyes flashed. "Do you think for a moment that you can break Bardic Law with impunity, whatever the reason? And if you did, tell me how it would help Kaelin to watch his Master's own robe and cord cut from him and see him ousted in disgrace from the Bardic Order?"

"I said precisely what I meant and will *not* take it back!" Bergid slammed his fist on Talan's worktable so hard that pegs and dowel pins landed like hail on the floor. "What kind of Law does something like this to an innocent boy? He's done no wrong, yet he must *prove* his innocence or suffer devastating, irreversible consequences? I tell you, either the Law changes, or I'll break it with my own hands!"

Talan refused to back down before his colleague's wrath. "Change it, then!" he said forcefully. "I couldn't agree with you more that the Law needs revising. I'll be the first to second your motion. But doing so won't help Kaelin, and no one knows that better than the Senior Master of the Council!"

It seemed for a moment that the Master Bard of Kestrel might well shoot back to his island without need of a ship, on the sheer energy of his own shaking anger. Silence took on a life of its own, becoming a heavy, brooding presence between them.

It was not dispelled until Bergid abruptly sat down on a work stool and glared at Talan. "I'm quite aware that I owe you an apology," he stated angrily, as if Talan had just demanded one. "But I'm in no mood to deliver it right now!"

"You owe me nothing," Talan said flatly, reclaiming his own seat. "I'd rather this had happened to any one of us, than to such a gifted youngster as Kaelin, with a scant thirteen cycles to his name. We, at any rate, would not have so long to suffer."

"Nor would we suffer as acutely as he will! For someone as gifted as Kaelin to have his instruments taken from him forever ... he will not be able to bear it!" Bergid rose and paced distractedly back and forth, his agitation rising with every step. Clearly the apprentice was not the only one who would be unable to bear it. "I told him his place beside me would always be there, waiting. If no evidence can be found to clear him, do you realize what I'll be forced to do the next time we meet? Strip him of his robe, his instruments, his music, his friends ... his Mas—" His voice broke in anguish.

Tears sprang to Talan's eyes at the transformation of the raging Master to a friend breaking under a strain every bit as great as Kaelin's. "As Senior Master, you can pass that on. Certainly no one would expect you—"

"To Grened?" Bergid's eyes flashed. "I won't do that to Kaelin to spare myself." He closed his eyes. "If his robe must be taken, it will be taken by the hands of someone—" He swallowed hard and did not continue.

—*who loves him,* the Instrument Master silently finished.

Bergid looked up suddenly. "Does he know?"

Talan cleared his throat, suddenly finding it difficult himself to speak. "Yes, of course. I made certain he understood all the implications before he made his decision to admit guilt or not. I even told him he could have time to think it over."

"And?"

"He said he needed no time, that he hadn't spent two cycles with his Master without learning to value the truth." Talan sighed, staring sightlessly at the table. "Though the evidence is against him, I saw his face when he emptied his pack. I know his shock was genuine. I know the words he said to me were true." He glanced up. "I *know* Kaelin is no thief or liar."

"That much," replied the Master Bard grimly, "I have known from the start. So, who else could have done this, then compounded it by implicating Kaelin?"

Talan shrugged helplessly. "There were eight Bards at my home that night. According to their own word, none of them entered my workshop after Kaelin returned from there, and none of them saw anyone else leave the house or return to it."

"Then one of your Bards is a thief and a liar," Bergid growled.

Talan did not dispute it.

"Which of the eight, then, had something against my apprentice?"

Talan frowned. "Two of them, I think, do not agree with the Council's decision regarding Kaelin's apprenticeship, but they both treated him with respect. The only one who didn't was Tyrel, who had an unreasonable grudge against Kaelin right from the start. He acted as though apprentices were inferior to Bards, an attitude I made clear I would not tolerate, giving him the choice to change it or leave my island. He was civil enough after that. If he continued to disrespect Kaelin in my absence, the youngster made no complaint to me about it."

Bergid frowned. "Could the threat of dismissal have caused him to retaliate against Kaelin?"

Talan shrugged. "If he was willing to mend his behavior to keep his position here, why would he risk far worse just to exact revenge?" He held up his hand. "I realize Kaelin had no earthly reason to take my tuning fork either, not only because he's a transparently honest soul, but because I know perfectly well that the boy would do *nothing* to jeopardize his place at your side. I have weighed and measured them both, Bergid, and it is not your apprentice who comes up short."

"What do you know of this Tyrel?" Bergid asked.

"This is his first rotation. He's quite proficient on pipes and has a good voice for someone who hasn't been worked over by Rial yet. He shows no particular affinity for making instruments, though, and does the minimum amount of work possible to get by." Talan paused, considering. "He keeps to himself and hasn't made any friends that I know of. He's currently staying in one of the Bard cabins east of Skye."

"Where is he from?"

"He comes from a small fishing village on Elegy, and I gather that his father has a hard time making ends meet." Talan rubbed his chin thoughtfully. "That might be reason for the theft of a valuable object, but not for placing it in Kaelin's pack." He looked at Bergid helplessly. "So far as I know, aside from his arrogant attitude, he and Kaelin had no argument or reason for enmity between them. As matters stand, he cannot be accused of anything worse than unmitigated rudeness."

Bergid frowned. "He received his robe on Elegy?"

"Yes, and I've just received Grened's response to my query for information concerning Tyrel's time on Elegy, which you're welcome to read for yourself. He says that Tyrel was apprenticed to a Piper, who took him several cycles ago against the strong objections of his father."

"To his son becoming a Bardic apprentice?" Bergid said in surprise. "Most parents would consider that an honor."

Talan gave a nod of agreement. "So one would think. Grened also mentions that some time after Tyrel obtained his Piper's robe, he joined with a girl from one of the coastal villages south of Tryl and moved there a few cycles later. In questioning the villagers, Grened discovered that the girl—Sylva, I believe—was heavy with child at the time."

Bergid looked at him with interest. "Did Sylva and the child come with him to Eyrie?"

"No. Grened says that a record of the child's birth was filed in the village ... a daughter, but there is no name on record. Three cycles later, Sylva's death was recorded, simply listed as being from an unspecified illness."

Bergid frowned. "And the villagers knew nothing more?"

Talan shook his head. "Apparently the family lived away from the others and kept to themselves. In any event, Tyrel went on to receive his Bard's robe a few cycles later and was assigned to me for his first rotation. He's never mentioned his family since coming here. Perhaps both mother and child died of the same illness, and he failed to record the child's death. But none of this explains why

Tyrel might have done such a thing to Kaelin."

"I would like to see this Tyrel before I leave, nevertheless," Bergid said stubbornly.

"Certainly, if you wish." Talan rose wearily. "However, if you're half as tired from your trip as I am from your arrival, you will need to rest first. Help yourself to anything you need, and of course you're welcome to use any of my instruments, since it appears you brought nothing with you but my notification." He frowned at Bergid's haggard face. "When was your last meal?"

Bergid shrugged impatiently. "It scarcely matters."

"Perhaps not to you, my friend, but at the risk of sounding like Grened, I've no time to tend irascible old fools who starve themselves into sickness." Talan led the way to the house and stood back for Bergid to enter first.

The brooding Master came to an abrupt halt on the threshold. The room was open and spacious, with no evidence of its prior clutter. "By the Maker himself, Talan ... what on earth has happened to your home?"

"Kaelin happened to it," came the dry response. "It has not yet recovered. Go wash up and have a seat at the table while I warm up some leftovers for you." It wasn't long before he filled a plate with a generous helping of chicken and dumplings, doused it with a flourish of gravy, then plunked it before his friend with a challenging air.

"Well, I must say this looks good, Talan," Bergid said. Strategically placing his tea close to hand, he steeled himself for the first bite. His eyes widened at once. "Is it my noble hunger, or has your cooking improved as amazingly as your living conditions?"

Talan heaved a sigh of the long-suffering. "Well, certainly not through any fault of my own. That talkative apprentice of yours kept up a running commentary on everything he cooked around here—morning, noon, and night—until not even I could avoid learning a few things. I'm not sure if it was a peculiar habit of his, or if it was done solely for my benefit, but I suspect the latter." He watched in aggrieved silence as Bergid began to chuckle. "Careful, my friend," Talan warned. "I've had serious thoughts about finding an apprentice of my own and sending him over to change *your* lifestyle."

"I suggest you send him to Grened first," Bergid countered. "From what I've heard, that's a lifestyle that could stand some change." He frowned. "I would have expected Kaelin to be summoned immediately, yet you've proposed the first month of autumn for the hearing, three months after the charge."

"Yes, well..." Talan said defensively, "considering the circumstances, I had to give Grened time to find out more about Tyrel, didn't I, and how was I to know how long that would take? Elegy is a large island. I also doubted that anyone would be eager to travel back there so soon after the Spring Council. Rial and Grened responded immediately, both of them indicating they were free at the beginning of autumn, but Marek only recently sent his regrets that he will not be free to join us until the *last* month of autumn. He made no mention of why."

Bergid glanced appreciatively in the direction of Zephyr.

"And since you responded in person at an exemplary tempo," Talan continued dryly, "I'll save myself another missive and ask you now. Will you be able to come to Elegy at the end of autumn?"

Bergid frowned in apparent thought. "I'll need to check my schedule after I return to Kyet," he said. "But don't worry. I'll get back to you with an answer ... eventually."

The two Masters looked at each other in mild amusement. Then a shadow fell over Bergid's face again. "We can buy him some time, perhaps, but what are a few months compared to all the empty cycles to come?"

Chapter 10

Kaelin stole a sidelong glance at the Master Bard of Zephyr as they climbed the steep path toward home. After several trips down to Aiteal, he had an idea why the Master had picked a location for his home that was more convenient to the village than it was to the seaport of Oriel. It had nothing to do with the scenery, either, despite what Kaelin had been led to believe ... at least, not the scenery around the house. The apprentice chuckled softly to himself.

Her name, he had discovered, was Trella. Kaelin knew, from a few stray comments he had overheard from the Bards, that the Master had known her for several cycles. Trella was short and slightly plump, with an open face full of good humor. Her hair, which she wore braided down her back, was the color of sunlit honey. She looked to be about the Master's age and was always on the fringes of the crowd that clustered around the Master as he played. Her eyes never left his face, and Kaelin noticed that the Master's eyes strayed often to hers and were pulled away with effort. The Master Flutist looked for excuses to speak with her and if no opportunity presented itself, would brood half the way home. He was brooding now.

Kaelin cleared his throat. "Why are none of the Masters joined?" he asked. "Is it forbidden them?"

The Master Flutist glanced at him in surprise. "No, it's not forbidden, though I'm of the opinion they shouldn't."

"Shouldn't join? Why not?"

Master Marek frowned. "Bards and Masters seldom make good husbands," he said flatly. "Our lives are spent traveling and teaching, which can only result in a great deal of discontent for their wives and children."

"Aren't any of the Bards or Masters joined, then?"

"Well, yes, about a third of the Bards are," the Master admitted. "Master Rial was also, many cycles ago, but his wife died of fever. He grieved a long time for her. And," he added absentmindedly, "Master Bergid considered a joining once."

"He did?" Kaelin looked up with lively curiosity.

Marek came to an abrupt halt and cleared his throat. "Well, actually, I shouldn't have mentioned that to you. It was many cycles ago, and as things turned out, he didn't end up doing so."

"Do you know why?"

The Master's look of discomfort increased. "He ... found out that the woman he loved had decided to join with someone else." The Master began walking at a fast clip, as though to outpace any further questions.

A flash of intuition struck the apprentice hustling to keep up with him. "Was she someone you knew?"

The Master frowned deeply, and Kaelin hurried to apologize. "I'm sorry, sir. I shouldn't have pried."

"No need to apologize. Your curiosity is quite natural, and I'm the one who aroused it." He walked for a moment in silence before continuing. "Yes, I knew her, though not during the time we're speaking of. She was my mother." He glanced at the apprentice's astonished face. "After she joined with someone else, she left Kestrel. I was born on Elegy. When I was six, my father deserted us and we moved back to Kyet, where she was from. I don't remember much about my father, except how angry I was when he left and never came back."

"No wonder you're against Bards and Masters joining," Kaelin said softly, as if to himself.

Marek looked at him sharply. "What do you mean?"

"Nothing really, sir," the apprentice said hastily. "Just that ... well, you know what it's like to grow up without a father, just like I do. So, since Bards and Masters are often gone ..." He shrugged.

Marek stopped abruptly for a moment, looking surprised by the apprentice's observation. He gave a short nod before walking on. "My mother never knew what became of him," he continued, "but I later discovered that he went to live in a small coastal village in southern Elegy with someone else. When Bergid became the Master Bard of Kestrel soon after we returned to Kyet, he made sure my Mother and I were well provided for. He gave me a flute and secured lessons for me that he paid for himself ... encouraged me to join the Bardic Order. The flute I play today is the one he taught me how to make when I became an apprentice to an Instrumentalist, just as he helped you to make yours."

Marek cleared his throat. "So you see, Kaelin, I understand your feelings for your Master because I share them myself. He has been both Master and father to you, who lost your own at a young age. To me he was the mentor I needed ... the father I always wished I had. Whatever I know and love of music, whatever I believe in strongly and value deeply, I owe to him." The Master slowed his steps. "What I've told you is in strict confidence. Your Master has never spoken to me of his relationship with my mother. If he wanted me to know, he would have told me."

Kaelin vowed utter silence on the matter and the Master nodded, picking up the pace again. The apprentice was quiet for a while, remembering his Master's composition that had produced such a clear image in his mind of a Bard with tears glistening against his cheeks. Could that have been his Master, after all? Had Kaelin seen into his memory through the music the Master had composed that expressed that moment? A vivid image of a flame came unbidden to his mind ... a flame from which a voice spoke of a traitor. He frowned. Was that image also a memory? Tyrel's memory? Deeply disturbed by the thought, Kaelin forced himself back to the present.

"Have *you* ever considered a joining, sir?" he asked casually.

"Well, I thought about it once, but decided it wouldn't be fair to her. I was a Bard at the time and often gone." His voice dropped. "It would be lonely for her..."

"Lonelier than living alone?"

The Master frowned, but before he could reply, another unexpected question flew his way.

"What are these small, twisted trees that grow out of the cliffs? They look like the junipers that grow in the valley."

"They *are* junipers, only they've adapted to the cliffs and grow smaller because there isn't much soil. The village below is named for them because the villagers take pride in having the fortitude necessary to live in such an inhospitable location."

"I like the twisted junipers better than the ones that grow in the valley," Kaelin declared. "They're tough and adaptable, and that makes them more interesting." He walked along for a few minutes in silence. "Do you think, sir, if you took a juniper from the valley it was used to and transplanted it onto a cliff, that it could grow?"

"Well, I suppose so, but it would take time. And it would depend on the plant."

"Why is that?"

The Master glanced at him. "I should think you can understand why it takes time to adapt to new circumstances ... and why not everyone is able to do it."

"Yes, sir," Kaelin agreed readily, "thanks to you. And if *I* can understand that, someone older and wiser and more experienced would understand it even better, wouldn't they? Someone like ... Trella, for instance?"

Marek came to an abrupt halt and narrowed his eyes at the apprentice. "All right then, let's have it," he said sternly. "Are you going to transpose all this or leave me to guess the key signature?"

The apprentice to the Composition Master of the Bardic Isles did not hesitate. "You came to me one night and taught me something important that I never would have figured out on my own. You showed me that, no matter what my circumstances, the only one who could enable me to accept them was myself. You didn't decide I couldn't change and leave me as miserable as I was. You showed me there was a choice and let me make it on my own. It's taking time," he admitted ruefully. "I have to make that choice every day or it overwhelms me again. And I don't always want to make it," he confessed. "It's like part of me *wants* to wallow in anger and think up ways to take revenge for what was done to me ... for what I'm going to lose because of it. But then I think about the junipers on the cliffs here, or the heather on Eyrie that springs back after being crushed, and I can let it go and ... remove the obstruction." He looked steadily at the motionless Master before him. "Thanks to you, I'm adapting to this," he held up the medallion, "like those trees have to the cliffs. And all because you asked me why I was treating myself in a way that I wouldn't think of treating my flute. And so, I've wondered..."

"Go on," the Master said quietly.

Kaelin took a deep breath. "I've wondered why you're treating Trella in a way that you didn't think to treat me." He hurried on at the Master's shocked expression. "You're not giving her the choice to make up her own mind about what she can or can't adapt to, the way you gave it to me. I would never speak like this to you, sir, but I've ... well, I've recently learned the value of time. It shouldn't be wasted, should it? If I don't tell you what I'm thinking while I'm here, I may never have the chance to. And if you don't tell Trella what *you're* thinking, you might never have the chance to, either." A spasm of pain crossed the apprentice's face as he glanced at the medallion. "There's just no knowing, from one day to the next, what might happen."

The Master stood silent, as rooted in place as the junipers on the cliffs below. Kaelin lowered his eyes. "I know I haven't much time left, making me far bolder than I have any right to be to a Master. Especially one who has treated me with kindness and respect since the moment I arrived." He bit worriedly at his lip. "I hope I haven't offended you, sir."

The Master Flutist's frozen demeanor thawed. "I'm not offended," he replied gently. "Stunned, perhaps ... but certainly not offended." He reached out and put his hand on the apprentice's shoulder. "You need never apologize for telling me how you feel about anything. I promise you I will always listen."

Kaelin nodded, struck by the realization that this was one of the vows his own Master had made when he apprenticed him. The rest of the walk home was a silent one.

That night, Marek gave Kaelin no lessons. In fact, he scarcely seemed aware the apprentice was there, so preoccupied was he. And it wasn't Kaelin who tossed restlessly on his bed and finally rose to stare out the window toward the village below.

The next morning, Master Marek brooded over his breakfast for an hour before pushing it aside, uneaten. Then he got up and left the house. The apprentice, busy with cleaning up the kitchen, glanced through the window and saw the Master pacing restlessly back and forth along the cliff's edge. A few moments later, Kaelin grinned as he saw the Master head purposefully toward the path that led down to the village.

It was late afternoon before he reappeared. Kaelin, looking up from his composition, hastily rose to his feet, his greeting dying on his lips at the stern expression on the Master's face.

"Recite to me the six ranks in the Bardic Order," Marek summarily ordered. "Beginning with the lowest."

"Yes, sir," Kaelin quickly replied, wondering what he had done to get into trouble. "The lowest is apprentice. Then Harpist, Flutist, and Piper, which are all the same level in rank. Then Instrumentalist, then Bard, then Free Bard, then Master."

"And which of these are we?" The Master demanded.

"I'm an apprentice, and you're a Master."

"Refresh my memory, then, on which of us is supposed to be giving lessons to the other."

A slight flush spread over Kaelin's face. "The Master is."

The Master Flutist's brow raised. "And what do you think should be done with an apprentice who boldly usurps that role?"

Kaelin lowered his eyes. "The apprentice should apologize on his knees to the Master he offended and accept any punishment the Master sees fit to give him."

"Well," Marek said consideringly, "since this particular apprentice did not offend the Master, he will not be required to apologize. However," he continued sternly, "he must still accept the consequences for daring to teach a Master his own lesson."

The apprentice barely had time to blink before he was enveloped in a hug that squeezed the breath from him. "Thank you," came the heart-felt words above him, "from both of us."

The moment he was released, Kaelin did his best to assemble a shocked expression. "Surely you can't mean ... she said *yes?*"

At that moment, both nightingales flew in through the window to fly around their heads and add their music to the mingled laughter of Master and apprentice.

Two weeks later, the Master Bard of Zephyr was joined to Trella in a quiet ceremony on the bluff in front of the Master's home. The only guests were the Bards of Zephyr and Trella's family. The only music was Kaelin's. The ceremony was held above cliffs blushing in the last rays of the sun. The couple held their right hands toward each other as the village official bound them together with the

Master's gold cord. They spoke their vows and the joining was complete.

The apprentice, however, never played the song he had prepared for the end of the ceremony, for the moment he lifted his flute the clear song of a nightingale was heard. Abandoning his song, Kaelin chose instead to answer it. The joyful music of both nightingale and apprentice twined together for a moment. Then the little songster flew out from behind the Master's home and perched on the end of Kaelin's flute, trilling in pleasure. When the music came to an end, it chirped and flew away. There was no burst of applause ... no sound, in fact, of any kind. Marek looked into Kaelin's eyes for a moment and smiled, then he took Trella in his arms and kissed her. The cliffs echoed with cheers and clapping.

Trella's family moved forward to congratulate the newly joined couple. The Bards spoke to each other in low tones, then approached the apprentice, who had just finished putting away his flute. Bard Teryn spoke for all of them. "Master Marek commanded us to give you a critique on your playing, Kaelin. However, we can find nothing to criticize ... nor, apparently, did the nightingale, a superlative judge of song." He smiled. "It certainly qualifies as a lesson, though. For us." To Kaelin's surprise, he bowed. "Thank you, young apprentice, for all you have done for our Master."

Kaelin's throat tightened as the other Bards followed Teryn's gesture, even the few who had opposed his apprenticeship. Returning the bows made the medallion dance on its chain, but no one paid it any attention and, for the first time, Kaelin did not feel its weight.

Chapter 11

A few days later Kaelin sat outside in the Master's garden, carving his harp frame. He found it a pleasant place to work since Trella had taken over the area. An herb garden had appeared as if by magic, strategically located near the kitchen door. Fresh flowers lined the path, and several rows of seedlings were thriving in the vegetable patch. He could hear Trella singing as she worked in the kitchen. He found it a bit uncomfortable to be living with a newly joined couple, but they would not hear of his leaving two weeks early on their account. Master Marek insisted that if he felt out of place, he had only himself to blame.

The door opened and Trella stood smiling at him, her long golden braid draped over one shoulder. "What are you working on, Kaelin?"

He showed her his harp. "I've decided on a symbol for Zephyr." Intricately carved into the wood was a juniper tree growing from a cliff. Trella peered at the tiny bird perched on one of its branches.

"The nightingale's not quite finished," Kaelin clarified.

"It's beautiful! And so appropriate." She looked at him warmly. "While I have the chance, I want to thank you for helping Marek come to his senses. I thought he never would."

"It was his own lesson." Kaelin grinned mischievously. "I just returned it to him."

"You certainly did," came a dry voice behind them, "and I haven't been the same since."

"Thank the Maker," Trella said, rolling her eyes.

Marek laughed and planted a kiss on top of his wife's head.

He admired Kaelin's new carving, then handed him a bundle of papers. "Would you deliver this to Teryn for me? He's offered to do the majority of my paperwork for me for the next few weeks, and I've decided," he said, with a smile for Trella, "to allow him to do so. If you follow the trail along the cliffs to the east you'll see the Bard's cabin he's currently using, about eight furlongs from here. It's set back from the path, so keep an eye out. If you come to a bridge, you'll need to backtrack a bit."

Kaelin nodded. "I've seen it on my walks. May I take my flute with me? I promise not to play it alone," he continued hurriedly, "but it helps to have the keys to finger when I have new ideas for compositions, and the scenery along the cliffs gives me all sorts of ideas. I'll leave the headjoint with you if you prefer."

"That won't be necessary, Kaelin," came the reply. "Your word is sufficient for me."

Kaelin turned away quickly, unexpected emotion blurring his sight. His word was sufficient for this Master he regarded so highly. It was enough, he thought, for Master Talan, and he knew without question that it was enough for his own Master. Why, then, wouldn't his word avowing his innocence be sufficient to obtain the majority ruling he needed from the Council? How was it right that what satisfied the majority of the Council members would not satisfy the Law? Kaelin was finding it increasingly difficult not to despise this Law these Masters were all sworn to uphold, a law that would judge him guilty by default if he could not prove his own innocence. The apprentice put the manuscript in his pack, wishing he could as easily stow his turbulent feelings, then set off eastward along the cliffs. A half hour's brisk walk brought him to the Bard's cabin, and Teryn soon came to the door and accepted the Master's paperwork from him.

"I see you have your flute with you," the Bard observed with a mischievous glint in his eye. "Obviously hoping for a lesson." He sighed. "Well, since you've come all this way on my account, the least I can do is give you the benefit of my expertise."

Kaelin suppressed a smile. Much like Darryk, Teryn was a superb string player and a decent piper, but his abilities on the flute were notoriously limited. "If I wouldn't be imposing, sir."

"Not at all." The Bard led the way into his home and got out his own flute.

"Would you like me to begin with breathing exercises?" Kaelin suggested helpfully.

"Certainly."

Kaelin began doing basic breathing exercises, each one carefully copied by Teryn. When he saw that the Bard was doing each of them correctly, he picked up his flute. "Do you want me to practice those exercises every day, since my tone depends on it?"

"I *insist* on it."

Kaelin nodded, then placed the flute against his lip, every movement slow and deliberate, watching as Teryn tried to duplicate it. "I seem to be having some trouble with my embouchure. Would this be better?" He demonstrated it correctly.

"You're learning quickly, apprentice." Teryn carefully altered his embouchure.

Kaelin took a deep, controlled breath and produced a clear tone on his flute. He watched as Teryn copied him, the Bard's eyebrows lifting in surprise at his own tone.

"Why, Kaelin, that's much better already!" he said with a pleased expression. "And on the first note, no less." He grinned. "Apparently I'm an amazing teacher!"

They laughed, then worked together for an hour, keeping their roles reversed in humorous rapport. Finally, seeing that his teacher was tiring, Kaelin brought the session to a close.

"Thank you for an instructive lesson, sir. Those breathing and tonal exercises have produced a big improvement, don't you think? Master Marek will be pleased."

The Bard chuckled. "Yes, I should think he will be. And I'd be pleased if you stayed and practiced here for awhile. I would imagine that the more crowded living conditions at Master Marek's are cutting into your practice time."

Kaelin, in the act of putting away his flute, glanced up. "Why, yes, sir ... they are." He'd indeed had scant opportunity to practice in the Master's presence.

"Well, then, I'm happy to provide a place for you to make up that time. I can arrange to be here every afternoon for your practice session on your flute, or whatever instrument you wish to bring. Master Marek has given me a great deal of his paperwork to do for the next few weeks, and I've a few other projects I've been wanting to get to."

Kaelin's eyes lit with mischief. "You can do all that while supervising my practice at the same time?"

"Bards are adept at doing multiple things at once, apprentice," Teryn said loftily. "It's part of our rigorous training."

Kaelin laughed. "In that case, perhaps you would consider giving me a lesson before I practice," he suggested.

"Like the one we just had?"

"I found it very helpful, sir."

The Bard chuckled. "Well, apprentices do need to learn how to teach before they can advance in rank." He nodded his head. "Very well, then ... we'll begin with a session on how to teach a beginning flutist, followed by a lengthy practice session, whenever Master Marek allows you to come. How does that sound?"

"Wonderful! I have sufficient free time in the afternoons to come, and I often go on long walks now, to ... well, to give Master Marek and Trella time to themselves."

An hour later, after a satisfying practice session, Kaelin

walked back along the cliffs, wondering if his own Master found teaching him as tiring as teaching Teryn had been. A sudden surge of loneliness and despair swept over him. *Will I ever have another lesson with him again? Or fall asleep at night to the sound of his playing?*

As Kaelin approached the trailhead down to the village, the sound of agitated voices interrupted his thoughts. He hurried along the trail and came upon a group of villagers peering anxiously over the edge of the cliff. One of the men held a rope over the edge while the woman next to him sobbed hysterically, held back from the cliff by a woman at least twice her age.

The man holding the rope called down, "Lyetta! Grab the rope and put the loop under your arms! Lyetta, *listen* to me!"

Horrified, Kaelin looked over the edge. He could see a small juniper growing from the sheer cliffside, too far below to be reached. A child lay on the twisted trunk, clutching it tightly. The rope dangled next to her, but fear had paralyzed her. Her eyes were tightly shut, and she made no sign that she heard the man's calls, or the frantic cries coming from the other villagers who had gathered.

"Can someone be lowered to her?" Kaelin asked.

"Don't you think we've thought of that?" the older woman demanded. "Be off with you, boy! This is no time to be bothering us with questions!"

The man with the rope glanced at Kaelin, taking in his Bardic robe and shining medallion. "The cliff is too broken here," he said tersely. "We're apt to send one of these rocks down on her. Now go, lad, there's naught you can do to help."

"I can help her grab the rope," Kaelin asserted.

The man barked a short laugh. "Going to fly down there?"

Kaelin looked down at the girl, then at the people shouting advice from the cliff. "I can help her," he repeated stubbornly, "but they must quiet down, so she can hear me."

"And why should we listen to the likes of *you?*" the old woman sneered.

"Now then, Mother, there's no need to—"

"We've no time to be listening to a boy who's committed a crime!" the woman retorted. "Who knows what he's done or might do to my granddaughter!" She tossed her head angrily. "Get you gone, boy. You aren't wanted here."

"Mother!" Even in his distress, the man was shocked at such rudeness. "But truly, lad, there's naught you can do. She's got to grab the rope. There's no other way."

Kaelin took a step forward, ignoring the woman's furious glare. "Then let me help her do that," he said urgently.

"We've tried everything already, I tell you!"

"Then you've nothing to lose."

"Except my daughter!" cried the younger woman.

The clamor of the villagers had waned as the dispute escalated, and now there was complete silence. Taking advantage of it, Kaelin quickly removed his flute from his pack and stepped as close to the edge as he dared. He tried to still the flutter of panic in his chest. Every face turned toward him, some in curiosity, some darkening with suspicion at the sight of the medallion. Ignoring the growing exclamations of outrage, he closed his eyes and thought only of the nightingales. Then he began to play, filling his music with the soaring freedom of flight. The cliffs were suddenly empty of angry voices. Only the clear music of the Bardic flute filled the air.

Far below, the child also listened, her frozen thoughts captured by Kaelin's music, her senses filled with the rapture of being aloft, safely held in the air with invisible wings. Gradually her death grip on the trunk of the juniper relaxed; she took a shuddering breath and opened her eyes to see two nightingales chirping at her from a branch of the tree she clung to. She stared at them in wonder as one, twittering gaily, flew to the rope that swayed close by and perched on the loop, as though inviting her to touch it. To the encouraging music of flute and nightingale, her hand moved slowly toward the rope. The nightingales fluttered around her as she grasped it; one of them hovered and trilled above her head. She slipped the loop over her head and worked her arms through, oblivious to her precarious position, her mind and senses filled only with the music and the nightingales.

Kaelin stopped playing as the girl was lifted to safety and clasped by her joyful parents. He caught sight of the nightingales flying away, beating their wings upward toward the Master's home. *How did they know?*

The apprentice stowed his instrument and took advantage of the throng smothering the girl and her parents to slip quietly away. A short time later, he entered the Master's home, to Trella's cheerful greeting and a somewhat absentminded one from the Master, who was working at his desk. Kaelin took his flute from his pack and approached the Master. He took a deep breath and held out his flute.

"I broke my word to you, sir."

Trella looked up startled from her bread-making. The Master's quill came to a halt on the page. Marek put it aside, then took the flute the apprentice offered him and laid it gently on the table between them. "That is a serious matter," he said gravely. "If I charge you with disobeying the restriction you're under, you will have to answer to the Council for it, and they will not be lenient. Nor will you receive your flute back from me. Now, tell me what happened."

Kaelin nodded and related the events on the cliff. "The nightingales knew somehow," he ended in wonder. "My music must have called them, and they came to help. They knew exactly what I was trying to do."

The Master smiled. "I don't doubt that they did." He picked up Kaelin's flute. "As far as your word to me is concerned and the restriction you're under, the life of that girl was far more important. Only an utter fool would charge you for breaking your word to save her. And, if ever anyone does, I will tell them that *two* Masters were indeed present, for such my nightingales are. My colleagues," he added in a steely voice, "would be well advised not to argue otherwise." He smiled at the relief on Kaelin's face as the apprentice thanked him and gladly received his flute. When the youngster took his harp outside to resume work on its carving, the Master felt Trella's light touch on his arm.

"He never stole that tuning fork from Master Talan." The calm certainty in his wife's voice brought a troubled look to Marek's face, but Trella was not finished. "Didn't you just say Lyetta's life was far more important than his disobedience, which he freely admitted to? Isn't *Kaelin's* life more important than satisfying an unyielding law that would exact a terrible, irrevocable punishment for something he never did? You *can't* believe him a thief and a liar, Marek!"

The Master was silent, struck by her words and the significance of Kaelin's act. *He knew what he risked losing and must have thought Bardic Law would force my hand the way it forced Talan's. He risked losing the instrument he loves and has scant time left to play, not to mention the punishment the Council would certainly have inflicted for his disobedience ... and he didn't hesitate to save that girl's life and come straight to me afterwards.* Any trace of doubt that might have lingered about the boy's guilt vanished forever from the Master's mind.

"No, Kaelin is neither a thief nor a liar." He looked up at Trella's hopeful expression, regretting that he must finish what he had begun. "But that doesn't mean I can overturn the Law, thereby breaking it myself."

"Even when the Law isn't just?" Trella demanded.

"Even when."

Trella's brown eyes sparked with exasperation. "Then at least *tell* him you believe in his innocence. He deserves that much, surely!"

The Master was silent for a moment, then laid his hand over hers. "He does, and thanks to you, I will tell him so."

She gave him an impulsive kiss. "You would have done so before long," she asserted. "You love him."

Marek frowned slightly. "Is it so obvious?"

"Only to me ... and, I suspect, to him as well." She returned to her kneading, leaving Marek staring after her in surprise. Then the Master rose and went outside. Kaelin looked up, his welcoming smile fading at the Master's serious expression. He put down his tools as Marek sat down next to him. When the Master said nothing, Kaelin offered an apology.

"I'm sorry, sir, if I was gone longer than my free time allowed me today."

Marek shook his head. "You ran an errand for me during your own time without complaint, then saved a young girl's life on the way back. I'd say the extra time was well spent." He cleared his throat. "I'm aware that you've been going out of your way to disappear whenever possible, even working on your carving and compositions out here in the garden. We've both appreciated it, but there's no need to continue doing so. Trella and I will have plenty of time together, and I would not see your instrumental progress halted any longer on our account. And," he added ruefully, "Trella will have my head if she doesn't get to hear you play your own music soon. She's only heard your musical flights with the nightingales, which she has dared to say are more wondrous than my own," he added wryly. "But I didn't come out here to discuss your lack of practicing. I came to tell you that I've never enjoyed teaching anyone more than I have you."

Kaelin gave the Master a startled look.

"And that gift of yours, marvelous as it is, has nothing to do with it. You arrived here despondent, self-conscious, ashamed— and I've watched you battle to overcome it, learning what it means to believe in yourself, no matter what. Even more, you've learned what it means to forgive someone who's done an unspeakably horrible thing to you, for I believe—we *both* believe—in your innocence. I tell you, I could not be more proud of you if you were my own son. And," he added, with a glance at the frozen apprentice next to him, "I can also tell you that your Master feels the same way. Since he can't tell you himself in person, I'll take the liberty of telling you for him. Bardic Law," he said grimly, "needs some serious revision, and I will not rest until I see it done. I only wish," he added gently, "that changing the Law could help you, who deserves it most." He briefly squeezed Kaelin's shoulder, then rose to his feet.

"Maybe," Kaelin said unsteadily, "part of the reason I'm going through this is so that others won't have to."

Marek's mouth tightened as he turned toward the house. *That,* the Master thought grimly, *is not reason enough.*

Later, Kaelin entered the house and approached Trella, who was shaping rolls for dinner. She looked up with a smile.

The apprentice sniffed appreciatively. "Mmm. Nothing like the yeasty smell of fresh rolls. By the way," he said conversationally, "I've been told that you'd like to hear me play my own music."

Trella's smile widened. "I would, indeed."

"Well, I don't know ... I wouldn't want anything bad to happen to you," Kaelin said solicitously. "If you were slicing something with a knife when I started playing, for instance, things could get a little ... messy."

Trella's smile disappeared. Marek glanced up from reviewing reports and choked back a laugh.

"But don't worry," the apprentice reassured her. "I'll be sure to set a block, like I have with the nightingales, so nothing bad can happen."

"And what fun would *that* be?" she demanded, brushing flour from her hands so briskly she all but disappeared in a white cloud.

"Marek has told me about these blocks of yours," she said disparagingly. "I want the *full* experience!"

"Really? Well ... I suppose that could be arranged." He looked pensively at the finished rolls. "I like your rolls," he remarked. "They're almost as good as my sister's."

Trella's eyes narrowed. "Almost?"

Kaelin shrugged. "Actually, they're even better. Just don't tell Laena I said so."

Trella's smile reappeared and the Master chuckled.

"I'm sure I'll get to enjoy a couple of them at dinner," the apprentice said, "but that will just whet my appetite. Perhaps we can barter," he suggested idly. "Extra rolls for songs?"

Two fists landed firmly on freshly floured hips. "And what would a Bardic apprentice know of bartering?" she demanded.

Kaelin gave her a sly smile. "Only what a village boy from Vale knows ... that one of my songs is worth ten of your rolls."

"Hmph! Village boys from Vale haven't the sense the Maker gave *most* of us, then, if they value their own music higher than my rolls! One of my light, fluffy, utterly delectable rolls is an even trade for a single song of yours," Trella said loftily, "no matter how entrancing it might be."

"Have you any idea how long it takes to compose a song?" Kaelin countered. "The skill involved, the lessons, the practice time? Perhaps," he added consideringly, "I could be talked down to eight rolls, but no less."

"Eight!" came the scandalized response. "However talented you might be, you're still a mere *apprentice* of your Order. I'm a *Master* of my trade, youngster! I'll hand over no more than three rolls for one of your songs."

"Six."

"Four."

"Five, not counting the ones I get at dinner, and I'll throw in an encore ... a short flight over Aiteal, perhaps."

"Done!"

They grinned at each other and sealed the deal with a floury handshake.

⌁ ⸮ ⌁

Two weeks later, Master Marek, Trella, and Kaelin stood on the larger of Oriel's two docks, near a ship making ready to sail for Lyra. The apprentice looked at Trella, who impulsively threw her arms around him and kissed him soundly.

"You're a lot like Laena," he said, a smile belying his rueful tone of voice.

Trella laughed. "I would like to meet this sister of yours someday," she said frankly. "It sounds like she has more sense than a certain Master I could name," she said with a pointed glance at Marek.

The Master chuckled and laid a hand on Kaelin's shoulder. "Well, lad, you'd best be off then, before she has us acting in a thoroughly undignified manner on the docks of Oriel."

Kaelin shouldered his packs and looked out on the grey expanse of sea that mirrored the cloudy skies above. Unwillingly, his eyes strayed southwest, toward Elegy. "Whatever happens, sir," he said slowly, "at the Council hearing..." He turned toward the Master and took a deep breath. "Whatever you may have to do there doesn't change what you've done for me here, and I don't mean just for my flute playing. I loved your lessons and the nightingales' ones. But it's the lesson you gave me with your flute and a piece of cloth that I needed the most. Thank you for giving me, not just what I wanted, but what I needed."

Still the Master did not speak. Kaelin chewed his bottom lip for a moment, then shrugged in defeat. "I think I'm about to give you a thoroughly undignified hug on the docks of Oriel," he said, by way of apology, then flashed the Master an impish grin. "For surely a Master deserves the consequence of treating an apprentice as well as you have me," he said, in mimicry of the Master's voice.

The Master laughed and opened his arms to receive it.

As the apprentice walked toward the ship, Trella slipped her arm through her husband's. Marek watched as Kaelin confidently boarded, no longer the confused, self-conscious boy that had arrived three months earlier.

My perceptive wife is quite right. If Bergid hadn't already claimed his heart, I would gladly take Kaelin for my son. Perhaps Trella and I will be fortunate enough to have a child of our own like him. He clasped his wife's hand as they turned their steps toward home. *But tonight, my nightingale's song will be a sad one. And for the first time, I won't have the heart to answer.*

Movement Three

The Voice Master

Chapter 12

Although the island of Lyra was clearly visible from Zephyr, the voyage took most of the day, for the ship's destination lay far to the south, on the western coast. The voyage proved far more pleasant for Kaelin than his trip to Zephyr had. Knowing the sight of his forbidden instruments would be painful, he left them in his cabin and sought out the Captain, a rugged, bearded man whose face looked as stern and unyielding as the mast he stood next to.

"I'm not allowed to play my instruments for your crew at the moment, Captain, but I'd appreciate being kept busy. Please feel free to put me to work."

The Captain snorted as he gave Kaelin's robe a brief glance. "I'm not in the habit of commandin' members of the Bardic Order aboard my ship, lad, however young they may be. If ye wish, however, ye can help the crew in any way ye like." He frowned at the medallion. "Ye stand accused of a crime?"

"Yes, sir."

"And what crime would that be?"

"Theft," Kaelin managed to say.

The Captain's frown deepened. "Help any who'll allow it, then, but it's enough weight ye bear on your chest already." His voice hardened. "Don't be addin' to it aboard my ship."

Kaelin felt his face grow warm. Before he could form a reply, the Captain turned and bellowed a command to the crew, who scurried to untie the ship and set sail for the open sea.

The apprentice spent the rest of the day on deck, helping to mend nets in the sun and doing any odd jobs given him. Most of the crew were glad for his help, though some scowled at the medallion and pointedly avoided him.

"You see what comes of a Master takin' on an underaged boy 'prentice," one of them snorted as he and his deck mate repaired a pile of frayed ropes within Kaelin's hearing.

"Well, you can be sure Master Bergid's regrettin' it now," the other said with a pointed glance at the medallion.

Kaelin bit back the angry words demanding release and forced himself to continue mending the net in his hands. *Remember what your Master told you! Don't give them more to complain about.*

Though opinions about their young passenger varied, the entire crew watched with interest his efforts to tame the crow that made his home on board. With a clear whistle, the apprentice could get the ill-tempered bird to perch on his hand and soon had the crow fetching and carrying for him.

Though Kaelin kept an eye out, he was disappointed not to spot his kestrel and wondered if the bird had decided to stay on Zephyr. *At least he'll keep Master Marek's birds safe,* he consoled himself, though not without a pang of loss. He would miss his avian shadow, who didn't care who he was apprenticed to or what was hanging around his neck.

The time passed quickly, and when Kaelin finally took a moment to look up, they were sailing along the western coast of Lyra, past slate-grey cliffs and sandy beaches. The coast was similar to Kestrel's, although the interior of the island was less mountainous and more heavily wooded. Forests of oak, maple, and scattered hemlock splashed bright autumn colors over the hills, in sharp contrast to the sparse evergreens of Zephyr. Kaelin thought of Master Talan's beautiful instruments and wondered if the wood for some of them came from this island.

Near the end of the day, they sailed into the western bay of Lyra and headed for the busy seaport of Lyssa. As the third largest island, Lyra had twenty-one Bards under Master Rial's direction.

And one apprentice. Kaelin took a deep breath and went to get his packs. He hadn't expected to travel here at all, for Master Talan had said his summons to the Council would come within the month, yet over three months had passed with no word.

"Apprentice!" The Captain's commanding voice stopped him as he stepped up to the landing plank.

"Sir?" He turned and steeled himself, wondering if he was about to be told to empty his packs before being allowed to leave.

"It's a fine passenger ye've proven yourself to be. I hope ye can free yerself o' the weight ye bear, as well."

"Thank you, Captain." Breathing a sigh of relief, Kaelin settled his packs against his back and walked onto the dock.

A squawk of outrage preceded a black shape that launched itself from the upper sails of the ship. Scolding him with a raucous voice, the crow landed on Kaelin's head, much to the merriment of the crew. The apprentice removed the agitated bird and spoke soothingly, holding it for a moment against his cheek. The next moment a large kestrel dove from the sky and narrowly missed the crow, who flew from Kaelin's hands in a panicked flight back to the safety of the ship's mast. Kaelin stared at his kestrel, who soared off with a series of victorious staccatos. The apprentice turned to find the Master Bard of Lyra observing him.

"I see you've managed to make friends from all directions," the Voice Master said, glancing disapprovingly at the crow. "That one's vocal expertise, however, leaves much to be desired." He turned a look of mild reproof upon Kaelin that belied the humor in his eyes. "I trust you haven't been taking any lessons from it."

"No, sir." Stifling a laugh, Kaelin set his packs down to bow to the Master. "Master Rial. I'm honored to be here, sir."

The Master inclined his head. "And I to have you," he replied, his bearing as stiffly formal as his words. The Voice Master was an impressive man, solid and barrel-chested, his hair greying at the temples. Except for his white robe, the apprentice could easily see him taking the place of the Captain behind him. The Master's sea-green eyes gazed impassively into Kaelin's for a moment, then he turned his attention to the apprentice's chest. Kaelin's face grew warm as Master Rial appeared to study the medallion for several long moments. Then the Master frowned, abruptly turned, and walked quickly along the dock. The apprentice grabbed his packs and hastened after him.

They were soon moving through the busy streets of Lyssa. The marketplace was alive with the sounds of last-minute bartering, stalls being taken down for the day, and unsold items being loaded onto carts. Curious eyes tracked the unusual sight of a young Bardic apprentice hustling after the Voice Master, some narrowing as they caught sight of the medallion. Kaelin kept his own eyes on the Master and tried unsuccessfully to close his ears to the comments that reached him.

They soon left the seaport behind and headed north up a steep hill. The Master strode along without a word, surprisingly quick for his weight and build, and Kaelin was soon grateful for the conditioning the cliffs of Zephyr had given him. The Master's home was situated at the top of the wooded hillside, commanding a fine view of Lyssa and the northern curvature of the bay. Kaelin looked around with pleasure but was given scant time to enjoy the view. The Master opened the door and entered, gesturing to Kaelin impatiently. The apprentice hurried in and found himself in a large, sparsely furnished room that seemed severe and forbidding after three months in Master Marek's comfortable home. The only furnishings were a large desk with an assortment of scrolls and writing tools, two large worktables, and several chairs. When the Master lit a lamp it revealed walls bare of adornment, even the mantelpiece empty of any personal items. Indeed, there was nothing visible that did not pertain directly to the Master's work. Kaelin set down his bags in the guest room silently indicated to him, then returned to the living room.

"Would you like me to prepare a meal, sir?" he asked tentatively, then hurried to do so when the Master, after appearing to study the medallion for a moment, frowned and nodded.

It was dark when they finished eating, and Kaelin's discomfort from the frowns the Master directed at the medallion, and his inexplicable refusal to use his own vocal cords, was becoming acute. If the Master didn't care to speak to him, would he care enough to teach him, or allow him to use any of his instruments? If not, what would they do together for the next three months?

The Master, seated near the fire, silently watched as Kaelin cleaned up, then pointed meaningfully to the floor in front of him. Kaelin stood before him with a mixture of relief and apprehension. The Master scowled again at the medallion, then reached out to swing it behind the startled apprentice's back.

"For the next three months, that's where it stays. Now, breathe!" The command was sudden and unnerving. Kaelin stared at him, and the Master tapped the armrest of his chair impatiently. "Did you not hear me, lad? *Breathe.*"

With a feeling of panic, Kaelin took a breath and held it.

Master Rial glanced upwards in exasperation. "I am the *Voice* Master," he testily informed the ceiling. He brought a deep frown to bear on the apprentice. "If you can't breathe, we're wasting our time together."

"I apologize, sir! It's just that ... I don't understand how you want me to breathe."

"Hasn't Bergid taught you anything about breath control?" the Master demanded. "Surely a flutist with such an incredible command of his instrument—not to mention his audience and the very wind itself—must understand the basics of breathing."

"Master Bergid did teach me breathing exercises, but only for my flute. He said he would leave my voice for you."

"Indeed! A sensible gift and fortunate for you … though I *have* managed to hector your Master into developing a reasonably decent voice over the cycles. Apparently he knows enough to know he doesn't know enough to train *you*. Demonstrate the exercises you've learned for your flute."

Kaelin, suddenly grateful for the many lessons he had recently given Teryn, dropped his diaphragm, took a deep breath, and went through the exercises proficiently. When he finished, he thought he detected a glint of approval in the Master's eyes.

"Well, it's gratifying to see that you *can* breathe, after all." The Master's brow lifted. "Why, then, haven't I seen a proper breath come out of you since you walked off the ship? Do you think that breathing correctly is only important for your flute?"

Kaelin's eyes widened. Was that what the silent Master had been doing? Studying, not the medallion, but his breathing? Without waiting for the answers to his questions, the Master promptly launched a few more.

"Don't you realize, young man, that your windpipe is a far more flexible tube than the ones you hollowed out of wood over there?" he demanded, stabbing a finger at Kaelin's instrument bags hanging on the wall. "Don't you know that your vocal cords are more delicate and nuanced than the strings of your harp? Have you not yet realized that your voice is capable of finer shades of expression and meaning than all the instruments in Talan's workshop put together?" The Master sat back and crossed his arms challengingly.

Kaelin looked at him steadily. Obviously, there was at least one thing the Master cared about. "No, sir, I hadn't realized any of those things until now. But I would like to learn."

This time there was no mistaking the approval in the Master's eyes.

Kaelin spent the next few days paying close attention to every breath he took. Every syllable he spoke had to be clearly enunciated, every word projected to the far corners of the room. He quickly noticed that the Bards of Lyra, who often dropped by to confer with the Master, spoke with practiced control over their own voices. Obviously, though a Bard might come to Lyra with a thin, reedy, or shy voice, Master Rial was determined that none would leave that way, and the Master's determination was in no way relaxed for his visiting apprentice. The voice, the Master emphatically stated more than once, was the only thing of importance while under *his* instruction. He accepted no excuses; any vocal lapse from one of his Bards was visited with a crystal-clear verbal blistering that rarely needed to be repeated.

If any of the Bards were amused at the significant looks and acidic comments the Master directed toward Kaelin to remind him of his voice or breathing, they gave no sign; they had all received their share at one time or another. No one commented on the medallion that hung against Kaelin's back, either. The Voice Master insisted on being able to clearly see the movements of the apprentice's chest at all times.

In addition to his vocal work, Kaelin spent the late evenings studying the scrolls in Master Rial's impressively large cabinet. He had studied all of the ones Masters Marek and Talan owned and most of the records in Master Bergid's extensive collection, but found Master Rial's to be even larger, comprising the full history and lore of the Bardic Isles. The scrolls were copies, for all the originals were stored in the library of Caer Wynd in the northern part of Lyra. Caer Wynd was the highest center of learning in the Bardic Isles, where those who wished to become Schoolmasters or Adepts in any one of six different fields were trained. Although Caer Wynd stored and protected the original scrolls, copies were readily available throughout the Bardic Isles, dealing with many special interests besides music, such as history, art, writing, and the medicinal use of herbs and roots.

Master Rial told Kaelin that Master Grened had submitted several original scrolls of his own on the making of dyes, ointments, salves, and the classification and uses of much of the flora and fauna of Elegy. The Master Harpist also provided copies of these to the Bardic Order, for, Master Rial said, he was a fine scribe as well. Kaelin found the Voice Master's impressive history collection fascinating. Armed with his exceptional memory, the apprentice eagerly absorbed scroll after scroll.

"Provided you handle them carefully, you may read any of the historical scrolls you like," the Master told him, "and any of the other scrolls of lore in my cabinet. This one drawer, however, you're forbidden to open." He indicated a drawer at the bottom of the cabinet.

That night Kaelin dreamed of the forbidden drawer. He woke up in a panic, his fists clenched, horrified to find himself standing next to Master Rial's cabinet. He lay awake the rest of the night and spoke to the Master during breakfast.

"Sir, there's something I think I should tell you," he began tentatively.

The Master looked up inquiringly while buttering his toast.

"The first night I slept at my Master's home, I dreamed of a harp up in the mountains."

Master Rial's knife paused in its lateral journey. "A harp?"

Kaelin nodded. "A harp that stretched across the sky from one of the peaks to the other. Then it faded away and I thought I had woken up to find myself standing in my Master's living room. He was asleep at his desk, and one of the drawers had ... well, harp music coming out of it. The music pulled me to the desk, and I reached out and opened the drawer. There was a book inside that had a gold cover. The music was coming from it, and it scared me awake for real this time, back in my bed. When I told Master Bergid about it, he said that he kept the songs of Master Cyral in that drawer, in a gold covered book."

"I know the book you're referring to." The Master said brusquely. "Why are you telling me this?"

"Because last night I dreamed about the drawer you forbade me to open, and woke up standing next to your cabinet. I couldn't sleep the rest of the night for worrying that I might dream again and disobey you in my sleep. So, I was wondering if perhaps you could..." his voice trailed away.

"I'll set a lock on the drawer," the Master said. He finished buttering his cold toast as though nothing unusual had been requested of him.

"Thank you, sir. I apologize for the inconvenience." Relieved, Kaelin turned his attention to his own meal, not noticing the thoughtful look the Voice Master turned upon him.

No further dreams about the cabinet drawer disturbed Kaelin's slumber that night. When he awoke refreshed in the morning, he lay there for a few moments, wondering how he was going to keep his promise to Master Talan concerning the harp crooks and flute headjoint platforms. Master Rial seemed to have no intention of allowing him the use of his instruments, hanging unused near the front door, nor did he make any move to play his own. Not even the Bards that came ever took out their instruments. Kaelin looked longingly toward his flute as he emerged from his room. *How can I bear having the Council take away my flute forever?* His other instruments, though he loved them dearly, he could perhaps endure the loss of, but not his flute. Being transplanted into such barren ground as that, he thought gloomily, would stunt him beyond all growth.

Much to Kaelin's surprise, the following morning passed without a single frown from the Voice Master. The apprentice glanced at him uneasily. *Either I've improved my breathing, or he's given up on me altogether.*

As though reading his thoughts, the Master spoke. "Your

breathing and speaking are considerably better. It's time for your second lesson." He ignored the apprentice's hopeful expression and impassively continued. "Before I tell you what it is, I want you to know that I have not been intentionally cruel to you without good reason." He held up a hand, forestalling Kaelin's protest. "I'm aware that you're suffering from the instrumental restriction you're under, and that I could ease that suffering." His brow lifted. "I will indeed ease it, but not in the way you would like me to." He indicated the chain around Kaelin's neck.

"That medallion has nothing to do with my decision. Had you arrived here without it, I would still have forbidden you the use of your instruments and seen to it that no instruments were played here during this time. You will hear no other instrument until you learn to use your voice as one, for it is the first and greatest of all instruments, worthy of your full attention. *That's* the only thing of importance for you to master while you're here ... your voice. I have three cycles to train my Bards and but three months to train you. I'll tolerate *no* interference from any other instrument, Bardic or not. Is that understood?"

Kaelin hurriedly nodded. "Yes, sir!"

"Then let's proceed. From this moment on, you're forbidden to talk. Every word must be *sung,* using the same techniques for controlling your breath that you've been practicing. You'll find they were given to you for good reason. I care not what notes you use, only how you use them. Keep in mind that volume and projection are not the same thing. A projected voice commands attention, regardless of its volume. Do you understand?"

"Yes, sir."

The Master frowned at him, and Kaelin flushed as he realized that he had just disobeyed the stricture of lesson number two. The apprentice straightened his shoulders, held his head high, took a proper breath, and sang his first two notes for the Voice Master. "Yes, sir!" he caroled.

Two sung words were certainly not many, yet they were enough to command the Master's sudden and complete attention. He rose and moved to the other end of the room. "Again, softly."

"Yes, sir." Kaelin quietly sang.

"Which takes more support on your flute, a full forte or the softest pianissimo?"

"The softest pianissimo."

"The voice is no different. Sing it again, with the same support you would give the voice of your flute."

Kaelin thought longingly of his flute and imagined himself playing it. "Yes, sir," he softly sang again.

The Master retreated down the hall and through the open door into his room. "Softer, and do not tie the two words together with the letter they have in common." The quietly spoken instructions carried clearly to the wondering apprentice.

"Yes, sir," came the enunciated response.

"I've been told you have perfect pitch. Using the syllable 'la,' sing a D harmonic minor scale as low as you can, then an octave higher."

This required some thought. Once again imagining himself playing his flute, Kaelin sang the scale lower, which was slightly difficult for him, then higher, which he found easier.

The Master emerged with the trace of a smile on his face that vanished before Kaelin was certain he'd seen it.

"A tenor, I believe," the Master said expressionlessly, then favored the apprentice with a frown. "With much to learn." He returned to his desk and told the apprentice to prepare their lunch. The Master opened a fresh parchment and took up his quill, but it was some time before he put it to use. Though his face remained impassive, his thoughts were jubilant. *So, Bergid left his voice for me, did he? Such a gift is far greater than he could have realized. This youngster has a marvelous, untrained voice! Combined with his gift, Talan is sure to sit up and take notice.* He returned to his work, suppressing the smile fighting to display itself. *Best if the youngster doesn't realize what he possesses, or he might not work as hard to develop it. And he'll need more time than he has with me to prepare for what I have in mind.*

That evening, the Voice Master wrote a message to the Master Bard of Eyrie, expressing his regrets that the end of autumn was going to be far too busy for him to make a trip to Elegy. Regardless of the inconvenience of the season, the middle of winter would have to do.

Never was a house so filled with singing voices as Master Rial's was for the last month of that summer. Not a word was spoken except in song, not even by the Master himself. At first Kaelin thought this was to make him feel less self-conscious, but he soon realized that the Master was teaching him with every word he sang. The first time a Bard came by one evening, Kaelin was disconcerted to greet him in song, but Baryl registered no surprise. He simply returned the greeting in a beautifully controlled baritone and continued speaking in song for the remainder of his stay. Other visiting Bards did likewise, and Kaelin soon forgot his embarrassment. It became a game, to express his words in song through a voice that was growing stronger with every passing day. Though the apprentice was unaware of it, his voice was causing a sensation among the Bards of Lyra. None of them had heard such a powerful, pure tenor from a boy whose voice had only recently changed. What, they wondered, would eventually emerge from the Master's rigorous training?

Nor was Kaelin's vocal training confined to the Master's home. Even on trips to nearby villages every word was sung. Kaelin, to his relief, found that the villagers were quite used to this and occasionally joined in, sometimes skillfully, sometimes so ineptly that both parties burst out laughing. He found these brief trips pleasant, not only because they took him away from the tormenting sight of his unused instruments, but because the woods made him feel closer to Kestrel ... and his Master.

The meadows they walked through were filled with peacock butterflies, a variety found only on Lyra. They had a wingspan as long as his index finger, with vivid purple eyespots on their hind wings that looked like the face of an owl when viewed upside down. Though most butterflies lived for only a few weeks, Master Rial told him that peacock butterflies could live for almost a full cycle and would soon hibernate. Songs swelled within Kaelin, filled with the butterflies' intricate, seemingly random movements, and he longed to take up his flute or harp and play them.

Evening was the best time of all. For then Master Rial would sing songs of lore about their history, filled with words of wisdom and pithy advice, all of which fascinated the listening apprentice. Kaelin learned more than vocal music during these memorable nights. He learned in far more detail what the Bards of Eire had suffered at the hands of a few Druids, whose greed for the Connemara mines had come close to annihilating the Bardic Order. He saw the tragedy it would be if the love of power ever gained a foothold in the Bardic Isles. Unwillingly, he came to deeply respect the Bardic Law Master Rial so often sang of. For the Law did far more good than he had realized. Though he had been taught that it established guidelines for mediating unresolved disputes, he hadn't fully realized what that meant. Unlike the common people of Eire, an individual member of a Guild in the Bardic Isles had the right to dispute what his Guild decreed, and if the Guild could not resolve the matter, it was referred to the Bardic Order for mediation. This kept the Guilds from becoming like the Chieftains of Eire, under which the common people had no say, nor even the right to own their own land or move elsewhere without permission.

The more he learned, the more conflicted Kaelin felt. *How can I respect something that's going to punish me for a crime I didn't commit and take away everything I love?* Nevertheless, Kaelin began to understand the dilemma in which the Masters found themselves. Far from being above the Law, they were the ones most bound by it. Though no one knew better than the medallioned apprentice that the Law was not perfect, it had nevertheless protected them from suffering under far worse imperfections for over two hundred cycles. One did not simply toss such a thing out the window. One carefully revised it.

Though his Master had told him that Master Rial's voice was the finest in the Bardic Isles, Kaelin was unprepared for the actual experience of hearing the Master perform. The first time the Master sang for them one evening, the apprentice listened with such rapt admiration that when the song ended and the Master sang him a question about the verses, he didn't respond, still lost in the detailed imagery the Master's voice had evoked.

"I never realized, sir, that a voice could do that," the apprentice said at last, completely unaware of the Master's question, or that he himself had forgotten to sing his own words. "The Bards and Masters I've met play themselves when they play their instruments, and you *sing* yourself in exactly the same way, only more so." He looked wonderingly into the Master's face. "I think the voice isn't just an instrument," he said earnestly. "It's a *better* instrument. It translates human emotions better, maybe because it's not separate from us, like our other instruments are."

"From the voice of an untrained apprentice to the ears of the Instrument Master of the Bardic Isles," Master Rial murmured under his breath, though it reached every listening ear. The Master made no mention of the apprentice's oblivious disobedience and answered him in a normal speaking voice. "You've learned that the voice is an instrument and have accepted it as such in your mind, but now you know it *here,*" and the Master brought his fist to his chest, "because you've heard it for yourself. Even better will be experiencing it with your *own* voice, the instrument you were given by the Maker to express all that is in you to say ... indeed, all that you are. That is what you're here to do within a very short amount of time. If I'm hard on you—and I will be—understand that this is why."

The apprentice nodded, then spoke with conviction. "I'll do everything you tell me, sir, and work as hard as I can."

"That's good to hear. Perhaps you can begin by obeying my directive to *sing* your words."

The horrified expression on Kaelin's face caused more than one Bard to stifle a laugh. "I'm sor—" At the Master's stern expression, he knelt, took a proper breath, and sang an apology for his disobedience in such a sad, minor mode that even the Master chuckled.

"I'll let your disobedience pass, lad," Master Rial told him, punctuating his words with the strummed, suspenseful notes of a diminished seventh chord. He gave the apprentice a meaningful look as he resolved it to the major. "Just this once!"

The room rang with laughter.

Chapter 13

Two evenings later, Kaelin sat with Bards Baryl and Drin, listening to the Master sing a ballad of the Bardic exodus from Eire. Abruptly, the Master stopped and trained his eye on the younger of the two Bards.

"Drin," he said expressionlessly, speaking in a normal voice, "perhaps you would sing the last stanza for us."

The Bard looked up in alarm. "I'm ... not ready yet, sir."

The sea-green eyes narrowed. "Did I not give this piece to you two days ago?"

"Yes, Master Rial."

"Well, then," the Master said comfortably, "surely you know it by now."

The Bard flushed. "My son was ill, and I..." Drin cut off at the Master's frown. "I promise to learn it thoroughly at the first opportunity. Tonight, if you wish."

"Only if *I* wish it?" The Master's voice hardened. "And do you suppose for a moment that *my* wishes will improve *your* voice a single fraction?"

Silence.

"Were it so easy as that," the Master acidly stated, "I would sit comfortably in my chair and wish marvelous voices upon every last Bard in the Bardic Isles ... indeed, upon every rough-edged tongue in the marketplace and every babe yet unborn."

Silence. Kaelin, glancing sideward at Baryl, found the older Bard engrossed in an intent study of the flames of the fire. The apprentice quickly applied himself to the same occupation.

"Do you wish to complete your rotation here?" the Master demanded.

"Yes, sir."

"I *still* haven't heard anything resembling a voice."

"I do wish to complete it, sir!" came the crisp, clear reply.

"You may demonstrate your commitment to that wish tomorrow morning at dawn. That should give you sufficient time to prepare the ballad if you work the rest of the night on it."

"Yes, sir!"

The Master's inflexible voice continued. "Were I you, I would not allow *anything* to interfere with your vocal progress again. If you hope to pass your rotation on my island, nothing must take precedence over your voice. Is that clear?"

"Yes, Master Rial! It is very clear."

The Master's sharp gaze turned unexpectedly upon the apprentice. "Do you find that a hard thing to understand, Kaelin? You may reply in a normal voice."

Kaelin swallowed hard as he stood and faced the Master. "Yes, sir," he said, taking good care to project his own voice. "But it's not for me to question the Voice Master of the Bardic Isles."

"Ah, the apprentice reminds me of my lofty position." The Master's eyes never left his. "And does that position give me the right to do what I wish with Drin's voice?"

Kaelin hesitated. "You have the right to develop Drin's voice in any way you wish."

"So, if I see fit to insist that Drin concentrate solely upon his voice while he is under my instruction, I may?"

"Yes, sir ... if you wish to."

"May I insist that he put it above all personal considerations of his own?"

"If you wish."

"Such an abundance of wishes," the Master said dryly. "Not even the wee folk of Eire are as generous as this Bardic apprentice." The timbre of his voice intensified. "May I insist that Drin put it above all consideration of others, even his own son?"

"Well ... yes, sir," came the hesitant reply. "If you wish to."

The Master's voice abruptly turned to iron. "And may I insist that he put it above the *Law?*"

Kaelin, taken aback at the Master's change of tone, slowly shook his head. "No, sir, I don't believe you could ... or would."

"No," the Master said emphatically, "For that is one wish I may *not* have. I can choose to treat Drin well, or choose to treat him harshly, and Bardic Law will do nothing to forbid me. But I cannot put *anything* above the Law itself, myself and my personal wishes included, for no Master—" and his eyes commanded the apprentice's full attention as his voice projected flawlessly to every corner of the room "—*no* Master can set the Law aside, for *any* reason whatsoever, and remain a Master of the Bardic Isles."

Kaelin started to agree, then froze as the full import of the Master's statement struck deeply into his mind and lodged there like a painful thorn nothing could ever remove. *No Master can set the Law aside ... no Master ...* He stared sightlessly at the Voice Master, hearing the echo of the unyielding statement resound clearly to the farthest corners of his mind. Master Bergid would do what he had to do at the Council hearing, as would all of them; his Master would no sooner break Bardic Law than he would his own word. With harsh clarity, Kaelin saw before him the moment when they would face each other across the Council table, the moment when he would hear the voice he loved above all others strip away his rank, his instruments ... his Master.

Words his Master had once spoken rang in his mind, glinting blue eyes looking directly into his over a cycle ago in response to

Kaelin's anxious question.

Can they make you send me away?

Nothing could ever make that happen.

The apprentice drew a sharp breath of anguish at the realization that, despite his Master's assertion, there was one thing that could indeed make it happen. Bardic Law. A law his Master would not break, a law that would force his hand to take everything away from his apprentice, himself included. Kaelin's last, barely acknowledged hope, that somehow his Master would be able to save him from the Law, burned to ashes.

The Voice Master's unyielding expression returned to his stunned perceptions, and Kaelin's face twisted in silent protest.

You could have left me my hope, even if it was false!

His mental cry died without voice, the answer to it evident in every chiseled line of the Master's face.

No, I could not.

Kaelin's face paled and he lowered his eyes.

"You thought I was too hard on Drin," the Master said quietly. "I am now going to be much harder on you."

Baryl and Drin watched in trepidation as Master Rial fetched Kaelin's own flute himself, attached the headjoint, and held it out to the stricken apprentice. "Take it and let your fingers play the music you are filled with now, but do not touch it to your lips."

Kaelin looked at his flute, his blood burning with the rawest emotion he had felt since the moment he thought his music had killed his parents. Wasn't it enough for the Master to shatter his last hope, without forcing him to hold the instrument that could alleviate his suffering, yet be forbidden its full use? Not even the Council would be so cruel; when they took his flute, it would be gone forever. He would not be made to stand and hold it, commanded to play it without giving it voice.

With the Voice Master standing but an arm's length away from him, Kaelin reached numbly for his flute and rested it on his shoulder, his trembling fingers taking their well-accustomed positions. Without conscious thought, they moved unerringly over the smooth keys, playing the turbulent music inside him without sound, echoing his suffering without giving release to it. He shuddered and lifted the flute, in the grip of an overwhelming need to play the painful music within him.

The Master took a step closer to him. "Do *not* touch it to your lips!"

Amber eyes flashed with unspoken anger at the Master Bard of Lyra. With a cry of pain, Kaelin forced the flute back down onto his shoulder as his fingers continued their silent dance of agony over the keys. His mind cried out against the implacable Master. *If you won't allow me to play it, then why did you put the headjoint on? Just to torture me?* The pressure within him became unbearable.

"Sir ... *please*," he gasped.

"Now, sing it, Kaelin! *Sing* it!"

The apprentice stared uncomprehendingly at the Master.

"Let your voice release the music your fingers are playing!" Master Rial commanded, his voice ringing with authority. "Obey me *now*, or I will take your flute from you, and you will not see it again until you leave my island!"

For a moment Kaelin stood frozen at the horrific threat, delivered mere inches from his face. His need burning within him, and with no other recourse, he swallowed convulsively, opened his mouth, and began to sing. Tentatively at first, nearly gagging on the necessity of vocalizing his anguish, he forced himself to channel the music raging through his senses through the only instrument allowed him. As he lifted his clear tenor voice in song, his windpipe became one with his flute, turning into an instrument in his mind, one that was fully able to translate the music within him. And indeed, it *was* a better instrument, he realized, for he himself was the instrument, his voice allowing subtle nuances of expression that the keys of his flute could not have embraced.

Pure music rose within him. Pent-up, unexpressed music hammered his senses and demanded release with nearly as much force as Bardic Mountain had over a cycle ago. His voice caught it, and his fingers fell nerveless from the keys as the silent flute, no longer needed, was gently taken away by the Master. The apprentice closed his eyes and gave himself to his own voice, to his overwhelming need to release himself. The music within him soared, and his voice soared with it.

The listeners sat stunned by the impact of the singer's thoughts and emotions, carried by the young but surprisingly powerful voice. For just as Kaelin's instruments had always linked his audience to whatever he was musically describing, so his voice did now. Only this time the link was not to a physical place or scene, but to the vocalist himself. For Kaelin's mind was not occupied with his travels, his memories, or the things surrounding him. His mind was filled with pure emotion, with feelings left almost unexpressed since the moment the black medallion had been placed around his neck.

Loneliness. Such aching loneliness pulsed through the room, carried on the controlled vibrato of Kaelin's voice, that his listeners felt it like a physical blow. This was not the emotion of a performer, separate from his audience. It was their own emotion, raw with loneliness ... and running through it like a strangling cord was outrage at the injustice of it.

Master Rial sat in his own moment of exquisite pain, reliving feelings he had thought long buried. He had been so very careful not to allow such emotions to surface again. He could not afford to let them cloud his thinking and affect his teaching, for teaching was all he had since his Shanna had died so many cycles ago. Loneliness had taken him then, and, like the apprentice standing before him, so had outrage at the injustice of having the one he loved above all others torn from him. He had devoted himself to the one thing that remained, becoming a fiercely demanding teacher, never allowing himself to become emotionally involved with his students. The voice, not the vocalist, was all that mattered.

And then along had come this apprentice of Bergid's, with an incredible gift of music and a splendid, untrained voice. The combination had the potential to prove unequivocally that the voice was a Bardic instrument, something Rial himself had been unable to do in two decades of warring with Talan. Struck by what could be accomplished by this gifted youngster in a single demonstration, the Master had determined to develop Kaelin's voice as quickly as possible. He had soon understood why Bergid cared so much for this youngster, but he himself had maintained his aloof, professional detachment ... until now. The Master sat frozen, unable to stop the outpouring of anguish that flooded through him. For Kaelin's gift held him fast, forcing him past the voice he had so diligently worked with and into the feelings and emotions of the one who owned it. He had been hard on Drin, harder yet on Kaelin, but the apprentice had, on the Master's own command, turned and unknowingly dealt the hardest blow of all. The walls Rial had so carefully built around himself were blasted asunder by the young voice he himself had trained. Apprentice and Master were linked in a moment of shared suffering and unresolved outrage, and the Master knew there was no going back. Never again would he be able to separate voice from vocalist.

The music stopped, the sudden silence heavy with emotion. The young singer stood trembling, looking so fragile he might have fallen in the slightest breeze coming through the windows.

The listeners sat motionless. Then Master Rial, quite unable to prevent himself, reached out and pulled the shaking apprentice close. *No one should have such an understanding of loneliness at the age of thirteen. No one.* He'd been a full forty cycles himself before he had been plunged into the depths of misery Kaelin's voice had just described. At least he had been left with his music, his teaching, his life in the Bardic Order ... what would Kaelin be left with?

After a time, the Master led the exhausted apprentice to his bedroll. Then he returned and shook the shoulders of the two Bards, who still sat motionless, lost in the profound misery Kaelin's music had inspired. They rose and shouldered their packs as though all the woes of humanity were stowed inside. Master Rial followed them outside, thinking deeply.

Drin spoke with difficulty. "Master Rial, how can he ... *do* that? I felt what he felt ... as if I were *him!*"

The Master's brow lifted. "I doubt even Kaelin himself could explain the remarkable gift he has. *I* certainly can't." Rial paused, reflecting on what the youngster had just done without the aid of his flute. "He's accustomed to using his instruments as the outlet for his gift, and now that his voice has become an instrument for him, it will do the same. Proving once and for all," he added with grim satisfaction, "that the voice is as much a Bardic instrument as any Talan has ever tinkered with."

Baryl lifted troubled eyes to the Master. "Someone filled with such music couldn't have committed a theft and then *lied* about it." The Master frowned, but Baryl did not back down. "Sir, I just heard music that made me feel exactly what the performer was feeling ... emotions that couldn't possibly have been faked. One would expect a thief and liar to be filled with regret, guilt, or defiance ... not loneliness and anger at the injustice of it. I do not believe his music is capable of lying, even if he were."

For a long moment, Master Rial stood motionless. "No," he acknowledged at last. "It isn't."

"But the *Council—*"

"The Council," the Master said firmly, "will base its decision solely on Bardic Law."

"Are you saying, sir," Baryl said heatedly, "that I could take something of yours and stuff it in Drin's pack, and provided no one saw me do it, Drin would be charged with theft and punished accordingly?"

"As Bardic Law stands now, yes." the Master replied evenly. "We hold by the same Law that existed in Eire before Master Cyral brought us here. The Master rewrote the Law for the Guilds and gave them the right to revise it as they saw fit, but the Bardic Order has never done so. There's always the possibility of an innocent person suffering under it." He sighed deeply. "I like it no more than you, but regardless of what we believe concerning his guilt or innocence, Kaelin's time in the Bardic Order is likely to be cut short. The Law makes no provision for mercy. It has the power to take his robe, his Master, and his Bardic instruments. But before it does," and the Master's expression hardened, "he will prove, to the satisfaction of *every* Master in the Bardic Isles, that the voice is the equal of any other Bardic instrument!"

Drin's eyes widened. "You're going to have Kaelin convince Master Talan by singing for him?"

"Not by merely singing, no. Even if I had the cycles it would require to develop Kaelin's voice to its full potential, no voice will ever convince Talan. It's the combination of the boy's voice with his *gift* that will. It will demonstrate the undeniable use of the voice *as an instrument,* wielded with the same power he channels through his flute." The Master paused for a moment before continuing. "It takes time for a voice to become an instrument, time that youngster doesn't have. So, I intentionally aroused strong emotion within him and forced him to vocalize it, hoping to make it happen spontaneously." Regret crossed the Master's face. "A cruel thing to do, but remarkably effective. The Masters will be arriving a full day before the Council hearing, giving me time to convince Talan that the voice is a Bardic instrument, with Kaelin as living, irrefutable proof!"

The two Bards stared dumbfounded at each other, realizing

that the Master's plan would likely work. Not even the superlative voice of Master Rial had convinced the Instrument Master. This young apprentice's voice, as able as any of his other instruments to wield a gift unique in all the Bardic Isles, could.

"Come here as often as you can," the Master commanded them, "and tell the others to do the same." He looked at them with grim determination. "Kaelin came here to learn, and learn he will. We're going to give our prime example the workout of his life!"

The Bards nodded and the Master turned his attention to Drin. "I think you, perhaps, should remain with your son, then join us when he's better. Our session can easily be postponed until then." The Bard's eyes widened, and the Master cleared his throat. "Kaelin was quite right. I *was* too hard on you. I used you to make a harsh truth clear to him, and for that I apologize."

Drin found his voice with difficulty. "Thank you, Master Rial," he said.

The Master nodded and turned to leave, for once without comment on the less than perfectly controlled voice he had just heard, then stopped when it continued, strong and clear.

"I'll work up that piece for you, sir! It will be the best ballad I have ever sung."

A smile softened the Master's eyes, though neither Bard could see it. "I'm sure it will be," he said quietly and moved toward the house.

"Master Rial?"

The Master paused again.

"If Master Talan acknowledges the voice as a Bardic instrument before the Council hearing, Kaelin won't be allowed to use it, will he?"

The Master stood for a long moment in silence. "No," he said at last, his voice betraying none of his thoughts. "Its use for music will be denied him, just like all his other Bardic instruments." Without further comment, the Master went inside.

The next morning, as Kaelin cracked eggs and sliced sausage for their breakfast, the Master gave him permission to speak normally during conversations, provided he took good care to breathe correctly and project clearly. "By the way," he added, "what was that little gadget on your flute headjoint?"

The Master frowned when Kaelin explained that it was one of Master Talan's devices. "Hmph!" he muttered disparagingly. "I hope you can find something more to recommend it than that."

"Yes, sir, I can. Would you like me to demonstrate it?"

"Hmph!"

Deciding to interpret this as permission, Kaelin got his flute and showed the Master how the device helped him control the direction of his air and improved his tone. When the Master maintained an aloof indifference, Kaelin casually added that he had another new device on his harp that the Master might be interested in.

"Hmph!"

The apprentice grinned and hurried to get his harp. The Master couldn't quite manage to keep his interest hidden as Kaelin showed him how he could change the pitch of his strings with the harp crooks. The lap harp was an instrument the Master made frequent use of when he sang, and its limited range of key signatures was a constant source of irritation. The Voice Master fingered the little crooks thoughtfully.

"Sir, would you allow me to make you a headjoint platform and a set of crooks for your harp, as a gift?" At the Master's startled look, the apprentice earnestly continued. "You've given me a new instrument. I would like to give you something also, as small as it is in comparison."

"I would like that, Kaelin," came the suddenly gentle reply.

They were interrupted by the arrival of Baryl and two other

Bards. The Master sighed, murmuring something about not having specified the crack of dawn.

"Kaelin, show these eager Bards of mine those gadgets while I serve up our meal. If Talan ever hears that his foolish toys kept me from eating, I'll never hear the end of it!"

Kaelin soon had a rapt audience demanding to be shown how to make platforms and crooks for themselves. The Master said that time could be arranged for it, provided they made themselves useful. One of them could work on platforms and crooks while the other two worked on Kaelin.

The apprentice looked up from his own hasty breakfast in surprise but asked no questions. He had barely finished cleaning up when three more Bards arrived at the Master's door. Master Rial, with his customary swiftness, soon had everyone working with orderly efficiency. After Kaelin demonstrated how to make the instrumental devices, three of the Bards began working on them at the table. The other three took Kaelin over to the corner and sat the bewildered apprentice on a stool.

"I want every item covered thoroughly, from the basics through the second form, by noon," Master Rial said with crisp authority. "Master Bergid has told me of his apprentice's marvelous memory. Let's put it to the test. If anything is missed, I shall personally give each of you a refresher course."

The Bards eyed their alarmed student and began their instruction with determined intensity.

Kaelin had never imagined there was so much to learn about proper voice production. He was drilled thoroughly, step by step, note by note, until the Bards were satisfied. Then he was handed over to the Master for a complete testing, Bardic frowns silently promising him dire things if he should fail in any way. He did not.

Drin arrived in the afternoon, to the Master's inquiring look.

"My son is much better, sir," the Bard said with a smile, "and I would like to help." At the Master's nod, he took his place with a fresh rotation of teachers drilling Kaelin through the third form.

By the time the sun had set, Kaelin was exhausted, his voice hoarse. His head ached from the mountain of information he had memorized. The Master nodded as the apprentice wearily finished answering his questions.

"Well done, Kaelin. To have survived a session like this, under such intimidating instructors, is quite an accomplishment. Tomorrow you will begin putting what you've learned to use on your instrument ... your vocal instrument. The following week my Bards shall introduce you to the intermediate forms."

Kaelin nodded, too tired to trust his vocal projection. His eyes traveled wearily to the kitchen, where the night's cooking awaited him.

Baryl chuckled. "After cramming you so full of information, perhaps you should relax and digest it. We'll take care of dinner."

The apprentice nodded in appreciation, then sat down, leaned back against the wall, and closed his eyes. The sound of approaching footsteps was accompanied by the scandalized voice of the Master.

"Surely you don't think your lessons are *over* for the day..."

Kaelin's eyes flew open to the welcome sight of his flute. His fatigue vanished as he reached for it. "Thank you, Master Rial!"

The Master assumed a deep scowl. "These lazy Bards of mine can take turns instructing you." He waved imperiously. "Drin, come over here and teach this apprentice a thing or two about your primary instrument."

Drin settled himself next to Kaelin. "I understand you've already passed all ten flute forms?" At Kaelin's nod, he continued. "Well, then, you may play whatever you like, provided," he added with a grimace, "its key signature is more pleasant than last night's vocal performance."

Kaelin nodded, then turned to the Master. "I can set a block in my mind to keep those who hear my music from experiencing it, but I don't know how effective it will be when I'm this tired. It takes energy to keep it in place."

"So your Master informed me. I would prefer no block. The rest of you," Rial added, turning to his Bards, "put aside what you're doing and take a seat."

As the surprised Bards did as they were told, Kaelin turned his thoughts to the peacock butterflies. They had all disappeared now, finding sheltered nooks and crannies in which to hibernate, but he had often ached to play their music, filled with intricate movements and feather-light melodies. He let the music of the memory swell within him, then effortlessly released it through the Bardic flute he treasured.

The room expanded in the listener's minds until it opened and transformed into a meadow of grasses, moving like the surface of a mountain lake on a breezy day. The last crop of gently swaying wildflowers sprinkled the meadow with color. Around them, peacock butterflies rose in a sudden wave, as though rising to the music of the flutist. The listeners watched, entranced with the myriad colors and graceful, spontaneous movements. Many reached out a hand, desiring to touch what they were so clearly seeing. The air was filled with the fresh scent of grass and pine. Then the music faded, and the scene vanished.

The Bards opened their eyes slowly, reluctant to return to reality, the wonder of the scene still fresh on their faces. The apprentice sat leaning against the wall. His flute rested in his lap and his eyes were closed.

Master Rial stirred and looked long and thoughtfully at the young apprentice. "Kaelin," he said quietly.

The apprentice looked up. "Sir?"

"I would like you to sing it for me, if you will."

Kaelin's eyes were not the only ones that widened at the unusually gentle request. "Sing what for you, sir?"

"I know you're tired, but I've a desire to see just one more butterfly. Capture its music with your voice and show it to me."

Kaelin nodded, his brow creased with uncertainty. His voice had translated his emotions the previous night ... could it also translate his memories? He thought of one of the butterflies, the one that had soared the highest, and heard the music that came from it. Hesitantly, he began to sing, his voice steadying as the strains of music he heard found a new outlet.

The listeners, caught up in the compelling voice, closed their eyes and found themselves once again standing in an open meadow. A light breeze swept a single butterfly from the flowers as it lifted glistening wings toward the sky. The sun caught each color, flushing the golden wings with a spectrum of light. The dark wing edges gleamed; the purple eyespots blazed with sudden fire. The butterfly circled higher toward the light that revealed its beauty. Then it spiraled downwards, dancing toward the earth in joyful abandon to rest once again on the stem of a wildflower, quivering with music.

The voice faded away, and the Master smiled in deep satisfaction. *His voice is becoming as fluent as his flute ... and far more quickly than I would have thought possible.* He glanced at his motionless Bards, then turned a meaningful gaze toward the incomplete preparations for dinner. The room was soon filled with the sound of their hurried activity and excited, whispered comments about what they had just heard and seen.

The flutist, feeling eyes resting on him, opened his own to discover his instructor standing next to him.

"Thank you, Kaelin," Drin said quietly. "I'll never again walk through a meadow, heedless of the butterflies." He hesitated, then spoke in a clearly controlled, projected voice. Master Rial looked up. All preparations for dinner stopped once again.

"I have thought, Kaelin, that the charge you are under must be deserved, or it would not have been given. I've thought you a gifted actor, ignoring the medallion's presence as though innocent of the charge of thievery laid on you ... until last night and tonight." He looked directly into Kaelin's eyes. "You are as honest and transparent as your music. Please forgive me for thinking as I did. I'll not be so quick to judge by appearances again."

"Sir, I—"

"Not 'sir'." The Bard extended his arm. "Drin ... if you will honor one who doubted you with your friendship, for it is one that I will treasure."

For a long moment, no one moved. Then Kaelin rose to his feet and looked steadily at the Bard before him. He thought of Darryk and Brent. Now Drin, but for how long? *Even if they take away my robe and right to speak to them for a cycle, they will still be my friends. They can't take that, or this moment, away from me.* He grasped the arm before him firmly.

"Thank you, Drin. The honor is mine."

The watching Bards glanced at Master Rial, clearly wondering if the conservative Voice Master would censure such a break with tradition, some frowning slightly as if surprised that he had not put a stop to it the moment Drin extended his arm.

The Master sighed heavily. "I quite envy you, Kaelin," he grumbled testily. "The only honor likely to come *my* way tonight is to serve up my own dinner!"

The Bards laughed, and Baryl hurried to bring the Master his overdue meal.

Chapter 14

The remainder of autumn passed in a whirlwind of activity. There were always Bards in the Voice Master's home, working on "Talan's toys" and on Kaelin, whose voice was schooled with methodical intensity. The Master and Kaelin also spent a few days hiking along the banks of the Wyndle River to Loch Senan and back, the Master teaching the apprentice every step of the way.

"I brought you out here for more than the scenery," the Master told the apprentice. He gestured around the meadow they stood in. "Close your eyes and listen. What do you hear?"

A vivid memory of his sense-deprivation test came to Kaelin, when his hearing had been restored and he had heard the myriad sounds of the woods like a symphony. He closed his eyes and readily answered the Master.

"I hear the chattering of a squirrel in the oak tree in front of us, and the sound his claws make as he climbs ... crescendos as he comes around the front of the trunk, diminuendos as he goes behind. I hear the voices of the tree branches rubbing together in the wind like a groaning bass line, and the high tremolo of their leaves. I hear a kestrel in the spruce next to me, dropping staccatoed questions down on us." Kaelin suppressed a smile at the thought of his kestrel, still faithfully following him around the islands. "I hear the whisper of the wind across the grass," he added. "And I hear your finely controlled breathing, sir, in perfect rhythm with all of it." He opened his eyes to find Master Rial staring at him.

"Apparently your prolonged sense-deprivation test did far more than free your gift."

"Yes, sir."

"Then *sing* it," the Master instructed him. "Sing what you hear, for that is true music, as free as the wind that creates most of it. Follow it with your voice and let it teach you what a voice is truly capable of."

Kaelin closed his eyes, listened for a few moments, then tentatively began to sing what he heard. His voice strengthened as it followed the wind over the grass ... ascended to the rustling leaves ... scampered around the oak tree ... leapt to the spruce.

The Master stood still, listening with his own eyes closed, seeing all of it described in vivid detail by the young apprentice at his side, and he marveled. Then the Master began to sing, his voice spiraling above Kaelin's, as though daring the youngster to follow. The apprentice eagerly did so, harmonizing with the Master as he and Master Talan had done on the hills of Eyrie with flute and harp.

"Do you see, Kaelin," the Master said, his sweeping gesture indicating everything around them, "why Talan's definition of a Bardic instrument—indeed, his definition of an instrument of any kind—is narrow and limited? The voice is just one example of an instrument not built by human hands. What of all the *other* instruments that surround us? The wind produces music through the branches of a tree ... does that not make of the tree an instrument, as much as your wooden flute is when *you* blow through it? You yourself send air through your vocal cords, causing them to vibrate and produce music, just as the vibrating strings of your harp do. Why, then, are flutes and harps considered instruments, yet trees and voices are not?"

Kaelin looked around him appreciatively. "The world is full of instruments, isn't it, sir?"

"Indeed, it is. One must keep one's mind open to them, for just like Marek's birds, they are a wondrous source of music ... one that no one can take away or forbid. They can arouse emotion, and they can also provide solace. Do not forget that."

The Master turned abruptly and strode on through the clearing, the apprentice hastening to follow, his thoughts in sudden turmoil. However wonderful, how could the music of a tree or a butterfly ever provide solace for losing his Master?

From then on, they traveled in joint awareness of the music that surrounded them, the music of the wind, the trees, the wildlife, the river. They listened to all of it and blended their voices with it in exhilarating duets.

Kaelin's vocal lessons continued with unabated intensity upon their return to Lyssa, Bards again filling the Master's home to help tutor the young tenor. Indeed, the only respite Kaelin had was one evening when the Master left to mediate a dispute between the Merchant and Shipping Guilds. Three Bards were critiquing Kaelin's rendition of "The Saga of Master Ryndel, who Singlehandedly Outfoxed the Druids of Connachta, part 12," when Drin, noticing the exhaustion in the eyes of his young friend, waved the session to a halt.

"Enough," he said firmly. "There's only so much one person can absorb, however talented ... and I think that particular person is overdue for a little fun."

"Fun?" Kaelin echoed blankly, as though he had never heard the word before and had no idea what it meant.

"Fun. You know, doing something for the pure pleasure of it ... like sitting back and listening to me sing."

The Bards laughed, and Rayce gave Drin a skeptical look. "You? The youngest Bard on Lyra ... in his *first* rotation?"

"Precisely, and therefore the leading authority on fun," Drin declared. "Unlike my stodgy elders, who've apparently been steeping in Bardic Lore so long they wouldn't know a good time if they stumbled into one."

"Leading authority on fun, are you?" Rayce's silver brows lifted. "Let's see you prove it!"

"Get your pipes and I will. Landryn, your flute, please. I may not have a voice as refined as the rest of you, but by the Maker, I know how to have fun with it!"

"We're supposed to be teaching Kaelin," Landryn said reprovingly.

"And so we are," came the swift rebuttal. "Does he not need to learn how to regale listeners in all walks of life and in all venues? Surely you don't enter an inn or tavern and expect to earn a pint or two with dusty old songs of Bardic Lore, do you?"

"Well..."

"Ha! Your flute, then, and be thinking back—a *long* way back—to when you were young and knew the value of a rollicking good song!" He flashed them a smile and fetched his lap harp.

Chairs were soon arranged for the three musicians. Kaelin sat back and listened with delight to a song he had never heard before.

Oh, once upon a distant time, a long, long time ago,
There was a lonely mountain with a valley far below.
And in that far-off pleasant vale a Flute wrote verse and song.
Her silv'ry voice was lifted high in music all day long.
Oh, hidey, didey, didey-die, in music all day long.

Her life was very peaceful up until the fateful day
A set of Pipes came wand'ring by and chanced to hear her play.
He saw the Flute, then raised his snoot and sneered, "What have
     we here?
If all you do is toot and trill, you're of no use, my dear!"
Oh, oom-pa, oom-pa, oom-pa-pa! "No use at all, my dear!"

The Flute rose up in anger. "Beg your pardon, sir," she said,
"But I suggest you keep a civil mouthpipe in your head!

For I'm a Bardic flute, no less, a fact I'm proud to tell.
And I will play your pipes off if ye fail to treat me well!"
Oh, tootie, tootie, snooty-snoot! "Tis best to treat me well!"

It wasn't long before the valley echoed with the sound
Of silv'ry toots and oom-pa-pas that shook the very ground.
The Pipes bellowed an "Oom-pa-pa!", the Flute a sassy "Toot!"
The Pipes inhaled a mighty breath (gulp!) "Now where's that
    pesky Flute?"
Oh, oom-pa, oom-pa, oom-pa-pa! "Where is that pesky Flute?"

The moral of my tale is this—I'm sure you'll all agree—
If you're a Flute, it's best to toot in graceful harmony.
And if you are a set of Pipes, be careful how you blow!
For you may have to live with her someday, for all you know.
Oh, hidey, didey, didey-die, someday for all you know!

Drin ended with a grandiose bow to his laughing and cheering audience, then froze when he caught sight of the Master standing in the open doorway.

"An interesting lesson," came a sardonic, clearly projected voice that silenced the room. "Perhaps you could explain to me, Kaelin, what you've learned from it."

The apprentice stood up and answered without hesitation. "I've learned, sir, that no one should disparage anyone—or any instrument—for being different."

"And this is news to you? Before our helpful young Bard here gave you this child's lesson, you went around mocking lutes and insulting kitharodes?"

"Well ... no, sir."

"Then tell me something you've *learned*," the Master said pointedly.

The apprentice frowned slightly, chewing on his lip as he

thought. Then he brightened. "I've learned that Bards sing in taverns and get paid in pints!"

The Master's eyes narrowed in Drin's direction, to the accompaniment of suppressed laughter. "I can't speak for the Bards of *other* islands, but I can assure you that *my* Bards do no such thing. *Do* they, Drin?"

"They most certainly don't, Master Rial," the youngest Bard hastily assured him as the others began to laugh outright. "I was about to make that very point, sir!"

The following evening, Master Rial told Kaelin to get his harp out. The apprentice's face lit up and he eagerly fetched it. A new picture adorned its frame, deftly carved during rare moments of leisure, for the Master allowed him but a half hour of free time a day. A peacock butterfly, for the island of Lyra. Next to it a cocoon hung from a graceful branch. Rial reached out and briefly touched the cocoon.

"Beautiful ... but that's not just the butterfly's, I think."

Kaelin gave him a wry smile. "No, sir. Your vocal lessons have spun me 'round and 'round as well."

The Master chuckled. "And with dizzying speed. But I think that cocoon is opening, and the voice inside it is nearly ready to fly on its own. A unique voice, as each and every voice is and should be."

After Kaelin had demonstrated his proficiency on form seven's harp exercises for the Master, the Bards left their work and settled back to listen to dessert, as Drin liked to call it. Every Bard looked at Kaelin with respect, even those who disagreed with his apprenticeship. For it had escaped no one's notice that the Master Bard of Lyra had undergone a subtle change since the young apprentice had come to stay with him. Perhaps only Drin and Baryl knew the moment that change had taken place, but everyone was aware that the Master was no longer the detached teacher he had been. He was still implacably stern and his demands of excellence inflexible, but his pointed comments no longer stung.

Tonight, instead of fetching his flute, Kaelin kept his harp out, deftly strumming F major inversions up and down. Then he set a few harp crooks in place and raised the fifth of the chord by a half step, augmenting it. He ran its inversions upward, then frowned and stopped playing. The easy atmosphere in the room had subtly changed. "Master Rial," he asked, "what became of Master Cyral's Harp?"

The Voice Master lifted a brow. "What makes you ask?"

Kaelin's frown deepened. "I think it's that augmented chord. I don't know why, but whenever I play it, I can't help but wonder about Master Cyral. Sometimes I think, if I only play it long enough, I might see him in my mind and know what he looked like." He looked up, suddenly conscious of the stares directed at him. "I know that sounds crazy," he admitted sheepishly, "but it *is* a strange chord ... and it's hard to play it for long."

Rial regarded him speculatively. "Perhaps for you, Kaelin." He held out his hand and raised an inquiring brow. "May I?"

"Certainly, sir." The apprentice handed over his harp.

The Master ran the same augmented chord skillfully up Kaelin's harp. "A superb instrument," he murmured, then glanced up. "Does that chord bother you the same way when I play it?"

"No, sir."

"Nor, I think, does it strike any of us so. It is one of four augmented chords, the rest being inversions, which only sound unsettling because they do not occur naturally within the parameters of our scale system." He handed Kaelin's harp back to him and indicated the strings with a brief motion. "That is not, however, the case when *you* play it. Do any of the other three augmented chords trouble you?"

"No, sir, just that one."

"Play it again."

The moment Kaelin's fingers ran lightly over the chord, his brow creased with tension. The Bards felt it like a point of pressure building in their minds; many shook their heads as if to rid themselves of the sensation. Kaelin's fingers slowed.

"Keep playing."

Kaelin doggedly continued. The tension in the room grew, pulsing in rhythm to the augmented arpeggio. Kaelin gave an inarticulate cry, and the Master caught his hands between his own, stopping the painful arpeggio. Sighs of relief took its place.

"Besides wondering about Master Cyral, were you thinking of anything in particular while you played?" Rial asked.

"No, sir," came the shaken reply. "I've never been able to play it as long as I just did, because it felt ... like something was being forced open against my will."

The Master observed him for a moment. "Perhaps one day, then, you'll discover what is hidden there." He took the harp from Kaelin's unresisting arms and held it on his own lap.

"As for Master Cyral's Harp," he said with a nod toward his well-stocked shelves and cabinet, "I have all the old tales and songs from cycles past, and while many extol the Harp and mention its disappearance, the only thing we know about its fate is that both it and Master Cyral disappeared from his home not long after he relocated to Bard's Landing. He left behind pages of verses and songs, but only one of them begins with the same augmented chord which so troubles you." His gaze swept the room. "As you all know, most prophetic verses come in stanzas of three, yet this one has but one, written at the bottom of a page. It is thought that the page containing the other two verses was unfortunately lost to us."

He placed his fingers against the strings of Kaelin's harp and glanced at the apprentice, who was watching him intently. Once again the augmented arpeggio filled the room, then resolved to the minor as the Master began to sing. Though his words were few, their impact on the listening apprentice was great.

In time to come of greatest need,
My Bardic Harp will then be freed
From time's embrace, whose rigid bands
Will not be freed by Bardic hands.

Kaelin looked up at the Master, his eyes kindling with excitement. "What does it mean, that the Harp will be freed from time's embrace?"

The Master handed Kaelin's harp back to him. "No one knows, but I can assure you that hundreds of people searched from one end of Elegy to the other. No trace of the Master or his Harp was ever found." He sighed and looked suddenly old and heavily burdened. "May the 'time of greatest need' never come to us. We are not a people prepared for war. Invaders would have little trouble stamping us out and our music with us."

"Surely," Kaelin ventured, "the Druids are not still seeking us after so many cycles."

The Master frowned. "That, Kaelin, is exactly the sentiment that has lulled our people into complacency. Unfortunately, hatred has the tendency to grow, not wither, when watered by time. Its tough roots cling like the weed that it is, its seeds spread rapidly and without reason from father to son. May such a poisonous plant never come to trouble the Bardic Isles!" He stirred from his mood, then said with his customary brusqueness, "Now, then, who is Kaelin's flute teacher tonight?"

Bran rose but had scarcely seated himself next to Kaelin when the apprentice, his eyes closed and a distant look on his face, unexpectedly began to play the harp resting against his shoulder. A shiver went through every listener as the same augmented arpeggio rose from the strings for the third time.

Kaelin, his mind filled with an unbidden image of a desk

strewn with manuscripts, resolved the unsettling chord the same way the Master had, to the minor. Then he began to sing.

Cycles turning, cycles passing,
Need is burning, everlasting
Agony until the day
The sundered sprig can find the way.

Bards and Masters, grieve no longer!
Truth will win, for love is stronger
Than the chains it must endure
'Til song is freed, the land secure.

The sound of the harp died slowly away, and Kaelin sat perplexed at the words he had sung, wondering where they had come from and what they meant.

The Voice Master wondered also. *Could those be the missing verses of Cyral's prophecy? They fit ... fit so very well, but by all the Bardic stars, how could Kaelin possibly know them? And how could he have heard about the sprig? Bergid would certainly not have told him, and I have not allowed him access to any of the prophetic scrolls.* He looked appraisingly at the apprentice as he put away his harp. *Bergid can deny it all he wants, but I believe I'm looking at that sprig right now ... here in my own living room! A sprig about to be sundered and left with nothing.*

Kaelin picked up his flute and began to play a song of the nightingales of Zephyr, keeping his thoughts strictly free of Master Cyral and his Harp. Afterwards, the Bards were so engrossed in discussing the imagery they had experienced that none noticed when the Master rose and quietly left the house. He walked to the bluff overlooking Lyssa and gazed down for a long time without seeing.

❧

At the end of the following week, Kaelin stood on the docks of Lyssa with Master Rial beside him. "I congratulate you on what you've accomplished here in such a short time," the Master said. "You've not only survived the most intense course of vocal instruction ever given to anyone, you've used it to develop your voice into a fine instrument." He smiled with satisfaction. "A Bardic instrument, if ever there was one."

"Thank you, sir. I appreciate what you've done for me."

"You must continue to use what you've worked so hard to gain," the Master warned. "And, just like any other instrument, that requires dedicated practice."

"I will," Kaelin promised, "for as long as I can."

The Master frowned. "Surely you're aware that the voice is not currently considered a Bardic instrument."

Kaelin's eyes lowered. "I know it isn't now ... but I'm sure it will be soon."

The Master looked at him sharply. "What makes you think that?"

The apprentice studied the dock beneath him intently. "I suppose, when you command me to sing for Master Talan the day before the Council hearing, he'll be convinced of it."

The Master was astounded. "You *knew?*"

"I didn't mean to eavesdrop on your conversation, but ... well, the doors *were* open. I didn't hear everything, but enough to understand what you intended to do."

"And, knowing the use I planned to make of your voice, you did your utmost to develop it anyway? Believing it would only be taken away from you for your trouble?"

Kaelin nodded and looked up at the incredulous Master. "I would have done so in obedience to my Master's wish for me to learn from you, but I also did it because I wanted to. The voice *is* a

Bardic instrument, and I promise you I'll sing the best I possibly can for Master Talan."

For a long moment, Rial stood staring silently at this apprentice, who had once again taken him by surprise. "The voice," the Master abruptly quoted himself, "is the only thing of importance while under my instruction?"

"Yes, sir."

"No, Kaelin," the Master said gently. "Not more important than you are." He cleared his throat. "I'll admit that I initially developed your voice in order to demonstrate to Talan what I've argued with him about for the last twenty cycles when I first petitioned the Council to include the voice as a Bardic instrument. For someone convicted of a crime, any instruments under consideration must be voted on summarily. The voice has failed all previous votes, with Talan the only one still standing against it. I realized that if he heard you before the Council hearing, it would most likely pass, and you would lose the use of it. However, I rationalized that a boy convicted of theft didn't deserve to *have* a Bardic instrument left to him, particularly not what I consider to be the foremost of those instruments." He paused for a moment, his brow furrowed.

"But then," the Master resumed, "your voice became the Bardic instrument I knew it would, and the first thing it revealed was *you*. The depth of your pain and the anger you felt at the injustice of it could not have been manufactured for our benefit. It was as real and honest as you yourself are. And then, you see, I had a problem, for how could I intentionally add to that pain by developing your voice into a wonderful instrument and then ruthlessly take it away from you?" He shook his head. "I won't do that. If ever the voice becomes a Bardic instrument, it will not be by forcing you to sacrifice your own."

Kaelin was unable to speak as the enormity of the Master's words sank in. Those not in the Bardic Order might well scoff at the long-standing argument between the two Masters, thinking their disagreement was merely one of semantics, but the apprentice had come to realize it was much more than that. It defined the role the voice played in their Order. Those who wished to join the Bardic Order were not likely to pursue voice as their primary instrument if it were not included on the list of Bardic instruments, the mastery of which would count as they climbed upward in the Bardic hierarchy. He remembered Master Talan's irritation with an instrument that couldn't be designed or taken apart. Such an instrument, the Master had insisted, could never be considered Bardic. And now the Voice Master, who had vehemently fought against this sentiment for cycles, was willing to lose the best chance he'd ever had to win that battle.

For me.

Master Rial laid a reassuring hand on his shoulder. "You now have in your possession an instrument which Talan himself refuses to define as Bardic, one which can translate the gift you have as well or better than any of your other instruments. And," he added with a meaningful glance toward Eyrie, "I have by no means lost this battle. It will only be a matter of time before Talan chances to hear you sing. I will look forward to one day hearing him clamor to put it on the list! Indeed," he added with mischief in his eyes, "I might decide to oppose it myself for a few moments ... just to see the expression on his face."

A wave of emotion swept Kaelin. This Master, who had mercilessly developed his voice and ruthlessly shattered his last hope of escaping the judgment of the Council, had just given him a priceless gift to keep when everything else had been stripped away. Not trusting his voice to project anywhere, he looked up into the Master's eyes, willing him to see what he was unable to say. To his surprise, the Master pulled him close in a brief embrace, then cleared his throat and walked away. The apprentice shouldered his packs and boarded the ship, sternly marshalling his thoughts toward his destination to keep his tears at bay.

Elegy ... and Master Grened. The thought was indeed sobering. Kaelin remembered some of the things he had overheard the Bards say about the Master Bard of Elegy, then did his best to put them out of his mind. As he watched the coastline of Lyra fade into the distance, he wondered how long he would have with the reputedly strict and unyielding Master Harpist. Nearly seven months had passed, and still no summons had come from the Council.

Chapter 15

Master Bergid opened his front door and welcomed the tall Bard shivering on his porch. "Come in, Darryk, and have a seat by the fire. You look like you could use some warming up."

"Thank you, sir. It's apparently been a mild winter here in Kyet, but I think your luck is about to run out," the Bard replied as he hurried inside and closed the door. "It ran out in the Skirling Mountains long ago, and I could swear a few storm clouds were chasing me here." He quickly hung up his cloak and sank gratefully into a chair facing the Master's.

Bergid brought some hot tea and a plate of tarts from the kitchen and placed them on the small table between them. "Thank you for coming so promptly."

"Of course, sir." Darryk picked up the mug, cradled it in his hands, and took a sip. It had taken five days to reach Kyet from the Northwest Territory on horseback, and he had indeed hurried to obey the unusual summons to return to the Master.

The twenty-four Bards of Kestrel were assigned to the six territories of the island on a rotating basis every season, so that every Bard worked each territory twice during his three-cycle rotation to Kestrel. In the spring of the previous cycle, Darryk had been posted to the Southeast Territory, which included Kyet. When Laena's husband had died in early spring, Darryk had promised Kaelin he would look after her, for although Lynd was not in Kyet's territory, it was not too far to walk to. He had willingly kept that promise, and the Master had assigned him to the Southern Territory for the summer rotation, which included Lynd. The Bard had spent the autumn rotation in the Southwest Territory, then been assigned to the Northwest Territory, which encompassed many of the mountain villages, Vale included.

Bergid settled into his chair and picked up a tart. "I've been pleased with the reports I've received from every territory you've served, especially regarding your ability to resolve disputes between the Guilds," he said with an approving glance.

"Thank you, sir. I rather enjoy it."

"Not many do," Bergid said wryly, "which is why I appreciate having a Bard who excels at it."

Darryk gave the Master a shrewd look. "Is there an especially difficult dispute in Kyet you would like me to mediate?"

"Well," the Master conceded, "now that you mention it, I wouldn't mind a bit of help with Holders Laryn and Tellig."

Darryk groaned. "They're at it again? What's the problem?"

"The boundary line between their holdings. The two of them planted their apple orchards right up to the line a few cycles ago. Since then, they constantly fight over the fruit that falls and rolls onto the other side, and the branches that spread their fruit beyond their own property. The Holders Guild has given up arbitrating between them and referred the recurring problem to me." He threw Darryk a challenging look. "What would you do to mediate it?"

Darryk thought for a moment, then chuckled and glanced up at the Master. "After suffering through their complaints, I would give them both notice that before the end of spring, each of them must build a fence fifteen paces from the property line, creating a thirty-pace area between. Any fruit that winds up in that area will be collected by their Guild, who will send ten percent of it to the Bardic Order in tithe and keep the proceeds from the rest for themselves." He shrugged. "Any complaints to the Guild or Council about the ruling will fall on deaf ears, for the Guild will stand to make a nice, easy profit from it. And so will we."

The Master laughed. "And the troublesome Holders will be too busy transplanting their apple trees to squabble with each other over anything else. Judging by the size of the trees, I'd estimate they have no more than two cycles to transplant them before they're too big to manage. And afterwards, they might think twice before infringing on each other's property."

"In the meantime, both Guild and Order will enjoy the peace ... and the apples," Darryk said, glancing appreciatively at his tart.

"No wonder you enjoy mediating disputes," Bergid said dryly. "It appeals to your conniving nature."

Darryk grinned. "I learned from the best, sir. Which begs the question ... what's the real reason you sent for me?"

The Master brushed a few crumbs off his robe. "I have a carting job for you," he said mildly.

The Bard blinked. "A ... carting job?" He'd hustled across the length of Kestrel in mid-winter to cart something for the Master?

"The result of a bit of mediating I've been involved in myself lately. You are aware, of course, that due to my own conniving nature as a Master, I have eyes and ears scattered about my island that provide me with a constant supply of information ... some of it even useful."

Darryk chuckled. "I've surmised as much."

"Word came to me last season that one of the Bards serving my island wishes to join with a young woman from Lynd but has been refused."

All amusement vanished from Darryk's face.

"So," the Master continued, "I visited the woman to ascertain the facts of the matter and discovered that, although she is admittedly in love with this Bard, she refuses to be joined until her brother returns and can attend the ceremony." He picked up his cup of tea and took a deep sip. Darryk did not move.

"Now, *that,*" the Master said, frowning over his cup, "is a problem which concerns me. She and this Bard have spent all last season and half of this one apart, and he will be required to continue rotating every season. He won't return to the only two territories within reasonable distance of Lynd for another half cycle, and there's no telling when, or even if, her brother will return here. My Bard is likely to pine away from the separation, his performance as a Bard will deteriorate, and my island will suffer." Bergid shook his head disapprovingly at his teacup as he returned it to the table. "Which is not something I will allow," he sternly informed it. He glanced up and indicated the plate. "Would you like the last tart?"

Darryk wordlessly shook his head, and the Master scooped it up and took a bite before continuing.

"So, I took it upon myself to offer a solution to the young woman. It occurred to me that either she or her brother might want to relocate to Vale, a notion she readily agreed with. The advantage for her is that the location is adjacent to three territories my Bard will be rotating to." The Master paused, and a shadow of grief crossed his face. "For her brother, it will allow him to use his considerable woodworking skills to support himself, should he not wish to continue living in Kyet. Regardless, it resolves the couple's current dilemma and my future one." The Master punctuated this conclusion with a decisive bite of his tart.

"The only remaining obstacle was that the house she and her brother grew up in was sold when she moved to Lynd. So," the Master said complacently, "I gave the current owners of the house an offer they couldn't refuse and found them another house closer to the village, which they could now afford. I also placed the deed of their former domicile in the names of the young woman of Lynd and her brother as co-owners. I then took the liberty of having the house extended to twice its former size so the two of them can enjoy separate living quarters ... or, if her brother declines to stay there, room for an expanded family, perhaps. She does not yet know this, but either or both of them can move in at any time." Bergid snagged his cup of tea and washed down the last bite of his tart.

Darryk's mouth dropped open. "You ... *bought—*"

The Master cocked a brow. "As an able mediator in your own right, do you think my Bard will have a problem with this solution?" he inquired.

"No, sir," Darryk said faintly. "Your Bard most certainly will not."

"Excellent," the Master said with an approving wave of his cup. Then I shall consider the matter resolved to the satisfaction of both parties."

"And ... the carting job?"

"Yes, well, the young woman can hardly be expected to move her possessions all the way to Vale by herself in the middle of winter," the Master lectured his empty teacup as he placed it on the table. He glanced at Darryk. "I thought the least my Bard could do was give her a hand." He settled back in his chair. For a long moment, only the sounds of the fire disturbed the stillness.

"No one I know," the Bard said softly, "not family, close friend, colleague, or any other Master, would have done something like this. No one. Your Bard, try though he may, can never thank you enough."

The Master frowned. "I'll consider it thanks enough if word of this never gets out. This was a special circumstance, done not for my Bard, but for the welfare of my island ... and for my apprentice and a young woman I consider to be my family, for she is Kaelin's sister and only living relative."

A gleam entered Darryk's eye. "If you consider her your family," he said expressionlessly, "then wouldn't the Bard who joins with her become part of your family as well?"

The Master's stern voice belied the amusement in his eyes. "If so, I would warn my Bard that it will not give him a single special privilege while serving my island."

Darryk chuckled. "Consider him warned, sir."

The Master glanced out the window, framing a wintry fairyland outside. "It looks like one of those storm clouds has indeed caught up with you. Why don't you stay here tonight, instead of at the inn? The ferry will have closed with the snowfall." He tapped his fingers against the arm of the chair and sighed. "One would think that so many Bards coming in and out of here at all hours would make loneliness impossible. Perhaps a good meal and your excellent harp music will ease it."

Darryk was silent for a moment, struck by the depth of feeling that crossed the Master's face. "If you'd like, I'll gladly stay here while making arrangements for the trip and remain until Laena and I leave for Vale."

The Master's rhythmic tapping came to a fermata against the chair arm and the first smile Darryk had seen crossed his face. "I would like that. And perhaps I can return the favor and give you some help on your flute," he added dryly. "I received your letter last month informing me you had passed level three, narrowly avoiding having your harp confiscated until you did. I suggest you waste no time starting level four."

Darryk nodded glumly and hastily changed the subject. "Is there any chance Kaelin could come back before the hearing?"

The Master's smile vanished. "Each of us except Grened has already delayed it and cannot do so a second time. At this point, it will almost certainly be set for just after Kaelin's trip to Elegy ends. So, the answer to your question is no. Not without a miracle, aimed squarely at our good Master Harpist. However," he continued with a brief smile, "with Kaelin, miracles are not necessarily out of the question. I believe both Talan and Marek would agree."

Darryk's grey eyes danced. Rumors about the orderly house and newfound cooking ability of the Instrument Master had reached Kyet months ago, and the equally startling news of the Master Flutist's joining had soon followed. "Has Master Marek told you about his joining yet?"

"After I don't know how many cycles of vehemently objecting to Bards and Masters joining? No, he hasn't. Not a single word." They looked at each other and laughed.

"Didn't Kaelin travel to Elegy today?" Darryk asked. At the Master's nod, the Bard sighed. "If he survives three months with Master Grened, I'll become an ardent believer in miracles."

A week later, a heavy downpour turned the snow to sludge, providing the Master Bard of Kestrel an excellent reason to stay home and catch up on his paperwork. He had barely finished two reports, however, when he caught a glimpse of a familiar face outside his window. "Marek!" he exclaimed, rising to open the door before the youngest Master could reach it.

"Sorry to arrive with no invitation or warning," began the Master Bard of Zephyr in apology as he hurried in out of the rain. "It was a rather sudden decision."

"Warnings and invitations are unneeded between us, as you well know," Bergid told him. "It's good to see you." He cleared his throat. "It's been an unusually long time since the last Council meeting."

"It certainly has," Marek commented dryly as he removed his cloak and seated himself near the fire. "A busy cycle, indeed. Far too busy for traveling."

"Obviously," Bergid said with equal dryness. They exchanged glances and chuckled.

"I appreciate the extra time you gave Kaelin," Bergid said, heading to the kitchen for refreshments.

"He needed it," Marek replied simply.

"So did I."

"Yes, I've recently heard rumors that led me to believe as much ... which is why I've come."

Bergid paused in the midst of filling a platter. "Rumors?"

"Zephyr is a small island, as Grened so loves to remind me, and normally I hear rumors soon after their hatching. This one, however, took a half cycle to reach me. I suspect it's because the merchants of Oriel did not wish to cause trouble between us."

Bergid cast an inquiring glance at his guest. "I can think of nothing that would cause trouble between the two of us. Unless, of course, you have selfishly refused to divulge your flute secrets to my apprentice so that he can bring them back to me."

Marek laughed. "I stuffed every secret I possess into that receptive young head of his." His expression sobered. "A certain Captain has been spreading fearful tales of being commandeered by the wrathful Master Bard of Kestrel last summer and forced to sail to Eyrie when he was bound for Zephyr."

Bergid set a platter of scones on the table, along with a crock of butter, a jar of honey, and a pot of tea. "I'm hardly in the habit of using my rank to commandeer Captains." He said reproachfully, then seated himself and reached for a scone. "I *did* make an unexpected trip to visit Talan near the end of summer. I merely asked the Captain if he was bound for Eyrie." Bergid shrugged innocently and buttered his scone. "He told me he was."

Marek chuckled, imagining Bergid storming onto the ship and furiously demanding to know if it was headed for Eyrie. He reached for a scone. "Well, now that I understand matters, I'll do my best to repair your shattered reputation on my island."

Bergid's expression turned serious. "Thank you. I'll send a letter and some coin with you for the Captain who suffered the displeasure of my company. Perhaps an overdue apology and some remuneration for his trouble will help ease matters." He grimaced. "Thank goodness he wasn't bound for Elegy."

"Yes, I can just imagine Grened's reaction." Marek buttered his own scone and reached for the honey. "Has Talan managed to recover from your visit?"

"It's only been a half-cycle. Give the man some time."

Marek laughed, then leaned forward. "Which brings me to the second reason for my visit. Did you discover anything on Eyrie that would help Kaelin?"

"No," came the terse reply. "And it wasn't for lack of trying." Bergid rapped the arm of his chair impatiently. "I'm convinced of another's guilt, yet I could not produce a shred of evidence." The Master brooded silently for a moment. "It's a thankfully rare thing for someone in our Order to be brought up on charges like this, but I have to wonder if the Law we're sworn to uphold has committed other such injustices before now." Deep blue eyes turned to steel. "I give you fair warning ... I will go up against a Law that mandates such a thing, and I will not rest until I see it changed. What is happening to my apprentice will never happen to another member of the Bardic Order!"

"I'll be right beside you when you do," Marek assured him. "But I would argue that it needn't happen to Kaelin, either. I, for one, will not be manipulated by anyone or anything, including the Law, into voting against someone I know to be innocent. If that's heresy—and I'm sure Rial and Grened at least will insist that it is—so be it."

Silence fell between them for a moment. The eyes resting on Marek shone with an emotion the younger Master could not quite identify.

"So," Bergid said softly, "you came to inform me that, when I stand up against the Council on Kaelin's behalf, I will not be standing alone?"

"I'll gladly stand next to you," Marek said stoutly. "And, if we succeed in persuading Talan as well, we'll have the majority vote Kaelin needs to—" Marek broke off at Bergid's frown.

"Talan is the one who brought the charge against him. He will not willingly go up against the Law he himself invoked."

"But surely he knows that Kaelin is innocent!"

"He knows. And he is a conflicted soul because of it, on a precarious fence between two viewpoints he cannot reconcile."

"Then would he not listen to reason?"

"Reason is just as apt to send him one way as the other. It's best that he comes to his own decision without interference from us." Bergid shook his head to forestall the protest he saw on Marek's face. "Talan is quite willing to break with tradition when it results in the improvement of an instrument, but he's a stickler with regard to the Law ... as demonstrated by the medallion around my apprentice's neck. I don't expect we'll get the majority we need, but if nothing else, we'll give them a fight to remember."

Marek's expression turned grim. "We certainly will."

They sat in comfortable silence for awhile. "I'm glad that, of all the islands, yours was the one Kaelin went to next." Bergid said. "The trip there must have been hard on him, not knowing how you would react to the medallion."

"Yes," Marek agreed. "I think he expected me to toss him bodily off my island at first sight."

"Grened probably would have ... and may have already."

"Oh, I don't think Grened would go that far," replied Marek with a brief smile. "Although it's a shame Kaelin's last three months have to be spent there. Do you think Grened would consider giving him more time?"

"No," Bergid said flatly. "Granting time to young apprentices accused of thievery is not apt to be high on his priority list."

"Then could you not summon Kaelin back?" Marek persisted. "He's only been on Elegy a week. It would give you time—"

"Don't tempt me!" Bergid cut in with unexpected force. "For I would be acting for myself, not Kaelin." He rose abruptly and paced restlessly before the fire. "I know that makes little sense," he muttered distractedly, "but something is keeping me from bringing him back ... or even going to see him. I don't know what it is, but I can't ignore it. I only wish I could."

"Perhaps it's because he needs to learn from this more than he needs comfort from his Master," Marek said quietly, earning a startled look from Bergid. "I think you may not recognize your young apprentice when you next see him. He arrived on my island in turmoil, afraid to look anyone in the face. He left with a smile, his head held high."

The restless pacing stopped. "I've you to thank for that."

Marek shook his head. "No, you've yourself to thank, not me." His mouth quirked wryly at Bergid's look of surprise. "I merely passed along a certain lesson I learned long ago, when I applied to you for my tests to become a Bard. Have you forgotten?"

Bergid chuckled. "Apparently *you* haven't."

"I'll never forget a single word. You told me there was no sense in taking those tests if I did not first rid myself of the anger and hatred I was holding against my father for the way he treated my mother and me. You told me I could not expect to arbitrate fairly between crafts and trades if I was crippled with an emotional reaction to anyone who reminded me of him. You said that, although my feelings were understandable, the Bardic Order did not deserve to be crippled along with me, and so you must reluctantly refuse my request."

"As I recall, you were quite unhappy with me."

Marek snorted. "That's putting it mildly. I was furious! I'd been studying every spare moment for three cycles to take those tests. Never, I'm sure, has any Instrumentalist dared to upbraid a Master the way I did that day. And you just stood there and calmly took my insubordination, letting me rant on about my father not deserving my forgiveness, and your utter gall in requiring me to do so before I could become a Bard. Then I suddenly realized that every word I said was proving you right. For if I could act like that to the one man who'd given me everything good in my life for telling me a truth I did not want to hear, I couldn't be entrusted with the welfare of the Bardic Isles." Marek shook his head ruefully.

"That finally silenced me," he continued, "and you must have known why, because you said nothing of my atrocious behavior. You simply said that forgiveness had very little to do with the one being forgiven. It was something I needed to do for myself, and if I didn't, I would run the risk of becoming like my father, filled with anger I would end up taking out on someone else, just as he had. You told me I would always be welcome in your home, that any help I ever needed was mine for the asking, and that you hoped I would come back to take my tests after I forgave my father ... not for his sake, but for my own, for the Bardic Isles needed me whole and complete, not crippled. And so did you."

"Whereupon you turned around and left."

"Too stunned to even deliver the apology I owed you."

Bergid shook his head. "What I told you was not an easy thing to hear, and I knew it would take you time to absorb it. Returning the following cycle to tell me you'd found Coltran and forgiven him, then requesting permission to take your tests ... that was far better than an apology."

"Nevertheless, I apologize deeply for it now," Marek said quietly. "I would like you to consider what I did for Kaelin to be my very belated thanks for what you did for me that day."

The Master reseated himself with a sigh. "You could not have thanked me better than to have helped Kaelin when he needed it so badly and I couldn't be there for him. I've been so worried..."

"You needn't be," Marek told him. "Kaelin is quite capable of standing on his own."

Bergid nodded slowly, his face still troubled, then looked up in surprise as Marek rose to leave. "Surely you'll stay the night."

"I must get back, and there's a ship leaving with the tide."

"And ... Trella's waiting?" Amusement lifted one of the Master's brows.

Marek flushed. "I suppose you've heard," he murmured.

"From everyone but you," Bergid said mildly.

"Yes, well..." Marek's discomfort grew. "After all the times I've sat in that very chair, reciting long lists of reasons why Bards and Masters should not join..."

"That had occurred to me."

"Well, it's your own fault," Marek said defensively, "sending that apprentice of yours around to us! He has a distressing habit of echoing lessons back to his teacher."

Bergid laughed and rose to clap his young colleague on the back. "My congratulations, Marek. I'm very happy for you both." He went to his desk, taking paper and quill to write out his apology to the Captain, then handed it to Marek with ten silvers, which elicited a look of surprise.

"A generous compensation," the Master Flutist observed.

"He deserves it to recompense his crew and the losses he might well have had on my account. I'm sorry I didn't think to do it sooner." Bergid gave his friend a keen glance. "You went well out of your way by coming in person to remind me."

Marek shrugged. "Missives can go astray, and it was the fastest way to bring the matter to a close before the rumors reach Elegy and Grened learns of it. I would go a great deal further than this to avoid any trouble between the two of you, especially now."

Bergid assumed a shocked expression. "The Master Bard of Kestrel, cause trouble? You, of all people, ought to know—"

"I know you to the last measure," Marek interrupted with a laugh, "and that should explain my trip well enough."

Bergid took down his cloak and opened the door with an injured air. "I believe I'll accompany you to the docks to be sure you leave without spreading such an unflattering opinion of my temperament. And," he added, as Marek began to laugh again, "you have my thanks for keeping my list of grievances against Grened to a bare minimum. Despite frequent disagreements over the finer points of the Law, our friendship has never faltered. But I've been hearing rumors that all is not well on Elegy. Merchants and Sea

Captains fall silent when I mention his name and deflect any probing. Darryk impressed upon Kaelin the need to tread softly around the Master Harpist but would say no more than that. So, I questioned Flynn, whose last rotation was on Elegy and has served there before. He would only say that Elegy's Master was 'perhaps more difficult to please than he used to be'."

Marek frowned, having heard much the same thing from his own Bards, and made a mental note to do some probing of his own upon his return to Zephyr. As the two of them walked toward the docks, he turned the conversation to Kaelin, speaking enthusiastically of his abilities. Then he told Bergid of the boy's affinity with the nightingales and the incident on the cliffs.

"Kaelin came to me immediately afterward, handed me his flute, and told me he'd broken his word not to play it. I'll never forget the look of desolation on his face, Bergid. He did not expect to receive his flute back." The Master Flutist frowned. "As if I would take it away because he used it to save the life of a child! But considering what Bardic Law had already done to him, he probably thought it would force me to charge him with breaking the restriction he is under, whether I wanted to or not. And, expecting full punishment for it, he saved that girl's life in defiance of her family's objections and came directly to me afterwards. Few Bards I know, in the same circumstances, would have acted as honorably as your young apprentice did."

Bergid's face lit with pleasure, perceiving more than the words conveyed. Bergid had known Marek since he was a boy and saw clearly that the young Master's feelings for the apprentice mirrored his own.

"The villagers now count him a hero," Marek continued, "and claim his music is powerful enough to speak in the language of the birds and command their obedience." He glanced whimsically at Bergid as they walked onto one of the docks. "Perhaps it will prove powerful enough to speak to our Master Harpist as well."

Bergid chuckled, but there was no humor in his eyes. "Hopefully so. For if he mistreats Kaelin in any way, the Master Bard of Kestrel shall certainly prove his ability to cause trouble."

They said their farewells, and Marek frowned as he watched his colleague and mentor stride from the dock. The Master Flutist cast a worried glance in the direction of Elegy as he approached the ship about to sail for Zephyr, then noticed another ship being readied to sail with the tide. He stopped abruptly.

"Captain," he called to the man awaiting him. "Where is that ship headed?" He pointed to the vessel whose white sails were billowing in the breeze as the crew made ready to hoist them.

"To Elegy, Master Marek," the Captain replied. "They've a shipment of fine wood carvings on board to deliver to Tryl."

The Master glanced behind him to make sure that Bergid was no longer in sight. "I believe I'll switch ships. I'd appreciate it, Captain, if you would give a message to Trella for me. She'll be awaiting the arrival of your ship in Oriel."

"Well, now, I doubt it's my *ship* she's waitin' to see."

Marek chuckled. "Will you let her know I've been delayed for a day or two and that I'll greet her with, er ... appropriate apologies when I return?"

The Captain laughed and promised he would.

Marek turned and headed toward the ship bound for Elegy, determined to see for himself how a certain young apprentice was faring with Master Grened.

Movement Four

The Master Harpist

Chapter 16

Kaelin's trip from Lyra to Elegy was a short one, taking only half the day with the help of favorable winds. The apprentice spent his time on deck with the crew, trying to keep his mind focused on his work and away from his forthcoming meeting with the Master Harpist. It was impossible not to feel apprehensive after all he had overheard, although he also found it perplexing. After all, hadn't this same Master returned his cord to him and given him a box of his precious dyes? Surely, he thought, there was more to Master Grened than many of the Bards seemed to think. He thought of Darryk's advice.

Many things that your Master takes humorously, as they're intended, Master Grened will see as insolence and punish accordingly. He has no tolerance for mistakes, either, however honest they may be. So please be careful, Kaelin.

The apprentice frowned. Being serious and careful, he realized, wasn't likely to be enough. If the Master had no tolerance for honest mistakes from his Bards, what tolerance would he have for an apprentice sporting a charge of theft around his neck? He glanced toward Elegy and tried to put aside his trepidation. *I'll find out soon enough.*

They reached Tryl by noon. Master Grened strode straight onto the ship as soon as the planks were lowered and stood grimly before the apprentice. The other passengers eyed the Master nervously, skirted around them, and quickly disembarked.

"Did you play your instruments while on board, boy?" he demanded.

"No, sir, I'm forbidden to," Kaelin replied, taken aback at both the question and the Master's accusing tone.

"Captain! Did this apprentice play his instruments while on your ship?"

The Captain, a rugged, clean-shaven man with a scar above his weathered brow, glanced at the flush spreading across his young passenger's face and cleared his throat. "I believe ye just heard the answer to that, Master Grened."

The Master's iron-grey brows shot up. "I believe I asked *you* to answer it," he said sternly, as though addressing an impudent cabin boy.

"I believe I have," the Captain said evenly. "The lad kept himself thoroughly occupied helpin' my crew mend nets ... though no one asked it of him."

The Master frowned and turned a baleful eye upon the apprentice. "Is something wrong, boy?"

"No, sir."

"Perhaps you're not accustomed to having your word doubted?"

"No, sir, I'm not."

Master Grened directed a meaningful glance at the medallion. "A thief and a liar had better *get* used to it," he stated, and abruptly turned to leave. Kaelin stood still, his face burning from the Master's verbal slap.

The Captain stepped forward. "To think I've always thought," he announced to no one in particular, "that 'accused' and 'guilty' meant different things."

The Master stopped. "Did I say they were the same?"

The Captain's voice, though impeccably deferential, had a hard edge to it. "Pardon me, Master Grened, I must have misunderstood ye ... as perhaps the lad did as well."

Master Grened turned, directing a cold eye toward the silent apprentice. "Then let me make myself perfectly clear, boy. The decision of the Council will not be made by either you or your champion here. And if you think your precocious performance last cycle will have any bearing on that decision, I advise you to think again. It will assuredly make no difference to *me*." He turned stiffly and continued on his way.

More humiliated in two minutes with this Master than he had been in nine months with the other three, Kaelin shouldered his packs and followed him off the ship. Master Grened, he stubbornly determined, was not going to shake his new-found confidence. He had paid too high a price to obtain it. He stepped onto the dock, pausing long enough to give the Captain a grateful look, then turned and hurried after the irate Master.

The first mate stepped quietly to the Captain's side. "Do ye think the boy's a thief, then, Cap'n?"

The Captain sighed as he watched Kaelin leave. "Maybe he is and maybe he isn't, but I tell ye plain, Calem, if he's stayin' with Master Grened, he's being well punished, regardless."

～ ⸘ ～

Every Master that Kaelin had stayed with loved the heights, and Master Grened was no exception. His home, situated near the top of a bluff, overlooked Tryl to the southeast. A stream flowed nearby, splashing over the rocks in a series of miniature waterfalls. Its music called to Kaelin, and he longed to take up his flute and answer. To the west, the lesser peak of Bardic Mountain was visible, a smoky wreath of clouds obscuring the topmost pinnacle. Kaelin stared at it, the stream forgotten. Even at this distance, the mountain's pull was far stronger.

The Master strode to the door and waited pointedly for the apprentice to open it for him. Kaelin quickly put down his packs and did so, waiting respectfully as the Master brushed past him. The apprentice picked up his packs and stopped on the threshold to look around the large living area. To his left were two worktables and chairs, the cubicles above them filled with music manuscripts and scrolls. To his right, near the open kitchen, was a large table, which could serve for eating as well as working. To the left of this, situated next to a large window, was the Master's desk, filled with scrolls and writing tools. The wall next to the window was filled with driftwood shelving holding an assortment of collections, including rocks, crystals, and preserved samples of flora. The small table under this displayed a number of jars filled with various inks and dyes.

"Since you seem reluctant to enter my home," the Master said curtly, "leave your packs here and go around the south side of the house to my dye shed. Inside you'll find a leather cinch strap hanging on the wall. Fetch it."

"Yes, sir."

"Touch *nothing* else in my shed!" Grened commanded.

"I won't, sir." Kaelin hurried to do as he was told.

Situated under the shade of two massive oak trees, the Master's dye shed proved to be nearly half as large as Master Talan's workshop and every bit as orderly. Two large worktables were set against the wall on his right, with numerous shelves filled with interesting receptacles on the opposite one. A large cabinet stood centered against the far wall, a smaller cabinet on either side. On the wall next to the door were several hooks filled with an assortment of ropes, strands of hemp, and a leather cinch strap. Kaelin quickly removed it and returned to the house, hesitating once more on the threshold.

"Well, are you coming in or aren't you, boy? Close the door behind you, then hang the strap up on the side of the mantle." The Master fixed a baleful eye on the apprentice. "Behave yourself in my home and take nothing that does not belong to you, and you will have no need to take it back down again."

His face warming once again at the Master's pointed words, Kaelin hung up the strap, then jumped at a terse order to stop wasting time and prepare lunch. The apprentice busied himself making a cottage pie, taking pains to do it as well as possible. He found the kitchen large, the cold pit well stocked, the utensils shining and neatly organized. He made careful note of where everything belonged as he used it, knowing it would not do to misplace a single item. Only the Maker knew what would happen to him if another Master's silver fork went missing.

They ate their noon meal in silence. As Kaelin finished cleaning up, he stole a quick glance at Master Grened, who sat brooding at his desk.

The Master's voice cut across the room. "I seem to remember your interest in dyes, boy. Do you still wish to learn about them?"

"Oh, yes, sir!" Kaelin replied in relief. "I was hoping you would teach me about them during my stay."

"Yes, I imagine you were. It is, after all, the only thing you can *take* from me that will be of any use to you."

Kaelin's face burned yet again, but he did not lower his eyes. "I hope only to take a good deal of learning from you, if you will teach me."

The Master looked dispassionately at him a moment longer, then reached for a thick sheaf of papers. "The making of dyes is a lengthy process, boy. It begins with a thorough understanding of the plants used, their growing cycles and preferred habitats. If enough time remains after you learn this, I will teach you how."

Kaelin nodded and carried the thick manuscript to the small table the Master indicated he should use. The tears stinging his eyes would have to wait until later. For he understood what the Master's barbed comment had implied. The Master Harpist considered him guilty of theft, so there would be no music for him here. What, indeed, would be the use in teaching music to an apprentice whose instruments were about to be taken away from him forever? *But not my voice,* he firmly reminded himself. *Master Rial promised me that!*

Kaelin studied with dogged determination for the remainder of the day. He found the manuscript more interesting than he had thought it would be. The first section was on yellow dyes and contained a long list of plants that could produce the various shades of this color. Every plant was illustrated, with the locations where it grew and how best to cultivate, harvest, and extract its dye explained in detail. He read the section carefully until he was sure he understood it. Then he read it again, committing the information to memory. When dusk fell, he hurried to the kitchen to prepare dinner, and again they ate in silence. The Master returned to his desk, and Kaelin began cleaning up. For the first time, he found himself hoping the Council's summons would arrive. Three months stretched suddenly into as many cycles. As he returned to his studying, the Master's voice startled him.

"Come here, boy. Let's see what you've managed to learn."

Kaelin rose and went to stand apprehensively before him.

"Tell me what you've learned about yellow dyes," the Master commanded.

Kaelin began to steadily recite. If the Master Harpist was impressed with the quantity of information the apprentice had memorized without error, he gave no sign of it.

"Yellow's learned well enough," he conceded gruffly. "What about blue?"

"I was about to begin that section, sir."

"Well, then, get on with it, boy! The production of dyes takes time and I've none to waste." He impatiently waved Kaelin away and returned to his work.

Kaelin spent the rest of the evening learning about blue dyes. He had never been more thankful for his good memory, which was evidently going to get as rigorous a workout under Master Grened as it had under Master Rial. Late that night, he again recited to the Master, who growled "Well enough," and told him to begin the section on red dyes in the morning. Kaelin nodded, then went wearily to his bed and mentally read the memorized letters he had received from his Master. After the letter Kaelin had received on Eyrie, he had received two more, one during his stay on Zephyr and the other on Lyra. Neither mentioned the charge against him, filled instead with interesting stories and news of home. Kaelin had worn all three letters out with his reading.

He sighed deeply and tried to relax. He missed Master Talan's busy workshop, Master Marek's pleasant home with the nightingales, and Master Rial's house filled with singing Bards. He missed Darryk, Laena, and Sean, but more than anything else, he missed his own Master. Lying in the cold guest room of Master Grened's home that first night, Kaelin was overwhelmed by a torrent of homesickness he had not experienced so acutely since watching Kestrel disappear behind the ship.

As if in sympathy, the weather turned to rain that night, a steady drizzle that continued nonstop for three days. Studying was only interrupted by the preparation of silent meals and recitations to the Master. Master Grened made no unnecessary comments, and the monotony was not once broken by the sound of any instrument, save that of the rain against the roof and windows. Kaelin memorized feverishly. Master Grened did not leave the house, though whether by preference or to keep a watchful eye on the young thief he had so unwillingly brought into his home, Kaelin could not say. The Master hadn't allowed him any free time, so the apprentice had no opportunity to practice his new vocal instrument in the privacy of the woods. Nights were increasingly restless with no outlet for his music and no relief from his growing loneliness.

Early one morning, after a particularly restless night, Kaelin decided to study, giving himself more time to prepare for his recitation of the last section of the manual. When he heard the Master stir, he quickly rose to prepare breakfast before being censured for laziness. In his haste, he knocked over the small ink pot. The lid clattered across the table, and ink spread quickly to the Master's manuscript. Kaelin snatched it up, but not fast enough to save three of the pages. His heart pounding, he set the unspoiled pages on the larger table, grabbed a cloth from its peg, and began blotting ink from the three ruined pages and the table.

"I'm sorry, sir," the apprentice said, glancing nervously at the Master, who had emerged from his room and was glaring at him from the doorway. "I rose too quickly and knocked over the ink. I'll recopy the damaged pages and sand the stain from the table..." His voice trailed away at the Master's unnerving silence, and Kaelin quickly turned his attention back to wiping up as much ink as he could. Then he disposed of the cloth and washed the ink from his hands until the water ran clear, though only time would remove the stains.

"Come here, boy." The Master's voice cut across the room.

Kaelin walked in mounting dread to stand before the Master, then swallowed hard and dropped to his knees. "I deeply apologize, sir, for my clumsiness, and beg your forgiveness for the damage it caused. I'll accept any punishment you see fit to give."

"It's gratifying to see you know how to make a proper apology, boy, though I imagine you've had a great deal of practice. Fetch the strap," the Master commanded.

Kaelin rose and forced his feet to move.

The Master accepted the strap from him and indicated the floor. "Remove your robe, boy, then turn and kneel."

Kaelin's mind spun with pleas and protests he dared not give voice to for fear of increasing the number of strokes he was about to receive. He removed his robe with fingers grown suddenly cold, then turned around and knelt once again. His memories of the Schoolmaster's switch across his palm paled with the first stinging blow across his back, his tunic no match for the Master's heavy hand. Kaelin bit his lip as hard as he could but could not prevent his cries of pain as five more punishing blows were dealt him. When the Master was finished, the apprentice crouched trembling, the taste of blood in his mouth. Slowly, he pulled his robe back on, flinching as the strap was dropped next to him. The Master's voice grated on his ears.

"You'll not only sand the table, you'll also recopy the *entire* manuscript before you do anything else, including eating. The illustrations I'll do myself, but I'll be expecting a clean, legible copy of the text, boy, exactly where it's written on each page, with no mistakes."

Words of his own Master echoed in Kaelin's mind. *He is the Master Bard of Elegy and deserving of respect.* He swallowed the angry protest on his lips and schooled his face to meet the Master's stern demeanor without expression.

"Yes, sir." Kaelin rose, returned the strap to its place, then served the Master his breakfast in silence. After cleaning up, the apprentice took the abrasive cloth and small pot of fine sand the Master handed to him and sanded the stain from the table, wincing as sweat stung the welts on his back. Finally, the task finished, he began copying the manuscript, taking care not to let his back or shoulders touch the chair. He looked in despair at the thick sheaf of papers. Only three were damaged, yet he must copy all fifty. *It will be a long time before my next meal.*

He worked until noon, trying to ignore his painful back and the increasing complaints of his empty stomach. It was tedious work, and with every sentence he carefully copied, his mind became more insistent that he should leave here.

Once the manuscript is finished, pack up and go! What's the point of staying?

There isn't one ... but what would happen if I left?

When he finally rose to prepare the Master's lunch, his hand ached and he had only finished ten pages, but the conflict in his mind was resolved.

As he walked stiffly to the kitchen, a loud knock on the door startled him. Not a single person had come to the house since he had arrived. At the Master's nod, he opened it and found himself looking into the smiling face of the Master Flutist.

"Master Marek!" he cried gladly, clasping the Master's hand and nearly pulling him into the room. "It's so good to see you, sir! How are Trella and the nightingales and Bard Teryn's flute playing and…" his words spilled over themselves. With a laugh, the Master raised a hand to stem the torrent, but it was an outraged voice from the other side of the room that silenced it.

"Boy! You will apologize to Master Marek for that disgraceful greeting!" The Master nodded to his guest. "Good day, Marek. I'm just as shocked as you must be to find such a mannerless apprentice in my home. I assure you he will be punished."

Marek, too astonished to reply, saw the color drain from Kaelin's face.

At a pointed look from Master Grened, the apprentice dropped to his knees for the third time that day and bowed his head before Master Marek. "For an apprentice to be discourteous to a Master is inexcusable, sir. I apologize and beg your forgiveness. I will accept any punishment you or Master Grened see fit to give me for my lack of manners."

Marek found his voice with difficulty. "I took no offense to your enthusiastic greeting, Kaelin … nor," he said clearly, turning a steely gaze upon Grened, "do I wish you punished for it."

The two Masters locked wills. The apprentice watched in alarm, helpless to intervene.

"Boy!" Master Grened's voice snapped across the room.

"Yes, sir?" Kaelin glanced at the strap and incautiously bit his sore lip. *Please, not again. Not in front of Master Marek.*

"Replenish our water and prepare lunch," the Master commanded. "Our guest is undoubtedly hungry after his trip." The

Master lifted a hand as Kaelin rose unsteadily to obey him. "You're forbidden to speak to Master Marek during his stay here, except in response to a direct question. Perhaps that will teach you to school your tongue. Is that clearly understood?"

"It is, sir." Kaelin picked up the water bucket and headed toward the door. His legs felt strangely light.

"Carelessness and discourtesy are two things I'll not tolerate in my home, boy. I trust you'll not forget the lessons you've received today."

Kaelin turned on the threshold of the open doorway. "No, sir, I won't forget them." He looked directly into Master Grened's eyes. "But I will forgive them," he quietly added.

No wind ever left the sails of a Bardic ship more suddenly than speech did from Master Grened at that moment. But before he could unleash the tirade this insolent youngster deserved, Kaelin bowed respectfully and left. Turning angrily toward Marek, Grened was arrested by the steady gaze of his colleague.

"I remember a time," Marek said, "many cycles ago, when I had my rotation on Elegy. The Master I served spent a great deal of time helping me on my harp, which I sorely needed. I looked up to that Master with the greatest respect." He paused, holding Grened's astonished eyes with his own. "I am grieved to hear and see that the Master's methods have changed over the cycles. You cannot inspire both respect and fear. If you prefer respect, you can command it again by being the Master and teacher you once were to me." He turned abruptly and left the house.

Marek found the apprentice kneeling by the stream, the empty bucket next to him. Kaelin rose quickly at his approach, hastily brushing tears away.

"I'm sorry my arrival caused you such distress, Kaelin," the Master said gently. "I came to see how you're doing and am not pleased by what I have found. Tell me, have you played any instrument since coming here?"

"No, sir."

The Master frowned. "How, then, have you spent your time?"

"Memorizing Master Grened's manuscript on dyes."

The Master Flutist's frown deepened. "You've been given no musical instruction at all?"

"No, sir."

"Do you know why?"

Kaelin was silent for a moment. "Perhaps," he said at last, "Master Grened feels that giving harp lessons to a thief who is about to have his instruments taken away is a waste of his time."

Marek was shocked. "He told you he believes you guilty?"

"He's made it quite clear to me without saying so." Kaelin looked anxiously at the increasingly upset Master. "I've taken no offense ... truly. He's a Master. And maybe he's teaching me about dyes instead because that's something that will be useful to me after the Council hearing."

Marek surveyed the apprentice for a moment, thinking of the strap he had seen Kaelin glance at. "You have an expressive face," he said, "and I've seen many emotions written on it, but never fear ... until today. Show me your back."

The apprentice dropped his gaze and made no move to obey.

"That wasn't a request," the Master said quietly.

In mute misery, the apprentice turned, untied his cord, and lowered his robe. Marek lifted his tunic and surveyed the vivid welts crisscrossing his shoulders and back. A wave of intense anger swept through him. "What happened?" he asked tersely.

Kaelin carefully pulled his robe back on. "I knocked over a bottle of ink early this morning. It stained the table and three pages of Master Grened's manuscript."

"That punishment was for an *accident?*" Marek asked incredulously.

"Yes, sir."

Marek stood aghast, filled with a fury he had not experienced so acutely since his father had abandoned him. Like Bergid, Marek had heard rumors that there was something amiss on Elegy, but this ... He glared in the direction of Grened's home. Even if Kaelin's act had been deliberate, for a Master to mete out such punishment to a youngster who would not even come of age for a cycle and a half was unthinkable. Marek did not trust what he would do, should he walk back into Grened's home right then. "Is that the only punishment he has inflicted on you?"

"I'm not allowed to eat until I finish copying the manuscript," Kaelin said reluctantly.

"The three damaged pages?"

"The whole manuscript," Kaelin admitted.

"And how many pages is that?" the Master asked icily.

"Fifty."

"Fifty!" The Master Flutist was incensed. "And your last meal was yesterday's dinner?"

"Yes, sir."

"And when do you estimate your *next* one will be?"

Kaelin thought for a moment. "The day after tomorrow, perhaps."

"Perhaps," the Master echoed ominously. "Have you copied the damaged pages yet?"

The apprentice nodded. "I did those first."

"Go fetch my pack and all of your possessions," the Master ordered in a tone that brooked no argument. "If Grened wants the rest of his precious manuscript copied, he can do it himself! If he asks you what you're doing, tell him you're obeying my direct order and that I've forbidden you to tell him anything more. Then return to me here. There's a ship leaving for Zephyr in a few hours and I intend to be on it. With you. Unless you prefer returning to Kestrel, in which case I'll—" The Master stopped at the stubborn expression on Kaelin face. "What is it?"

"I'll fetch your own pack for you, sir, but I can't go with you."

"You certainly can't stay here! I won't allow it." He looked at the silent apprentice in exasperation. "Is the knowledge you might gain here worth the price you're paying to obtain it?"

Kaelin's eyes begged for the Master's understanding. "No, sir. But my Master *is* worth it ... he's worth all of it and more."

Master Marek frowned. "What has Master Bergid to do with this? He, above all others, would want you to leave here."

"Yes, sir," Kaelin agreed, "and then what would he do?"

The Master Flutist was silent. The words that had inspired his impromptu visit echoed in his mind. *If he mistreats Kaelin in any way, the Master Bard of Kestrel shall certainly prove his ability to cause trouble.*

Kaelin, seeing the Master's eyes widen in comprehension, continued. "I can't let that happen. I wanted to leave, but when I thought it over I knew I couldn't. I've spent nine months with three wonderful Masters, and I've learned how ... well, how the Law and the Masters and everything all fit together, how our music keeps our land balanced. My back will heal before long, but if Master rises against Master, how long will it take for the Bardic Isles to heal?" He looked earnestly at Master Marek. "My Master once told me that even the smallest of pebbles can start an avalanche. I will not be that pebble, sir."

The Master Bard of Zephyr looked into the steady eyes of the apprentice before him and hunted vainly for an argument to refute his words. He sighed deeply. "Once again, Kaelin, you have managed to persuade me ... this time against my will and certainly against your Master's. I'll leave you here, then, though if Bergid ever hears of this..." He shuddered at the thought. "Come, I'll return with you so you can't be accused of laziness or any such absurdity." He grimaced. "With luck, word of my visit here won't reach Kestrel, and your Master will never know that I could have taken you out of this situation and did not." He glanced sternly at Kaelin. "Provided *you* take care not to tell him."

"I won't, sir," the apprentice promised. "Thank you for letting me stay."

Marek frowned. "I'm hardly doing you a favor." Then, ignoring the apprentice's protest, he filled the bucket himself and headed for the house.

Grened frowned disapprovingly as Marek entered with the water bucket in hand. The two Masters settled themselves by the fire and discussed a few trade matters. When lunch was ready, they rose and took their places at the table Kaelin had set for them. The apprentice ladled generous portions of lamb stew into their bowls, taking pains not to spill a single drop. Then he brought them thick slabs of fresh bread and a crock of butter.

"I suppose you've heard, Grened, that I've been joined recently?" the Master Flutist asked abruptly.

"Not by you, I haven't." The Master Harpist snorted when Marek made no reply. "Just didn't want to eat your own words, I suppose," he said with a knowing look.

Marek sighed. "If I can survive having my own words fed to me by an apprentice, I can survive eating them for you, as I did for Bergid and will undoubtedly have to for Rial and Talan."

Kaelin turned quickly away and began preparing tea.

"It never fails to amaze me," Marek remarked, "how adaptable people can be. One would think they were junipers."

Grened gave him a baffled look.

"Someone once told me that adapting to difficult circumstances should be each person's own choice, and it's been a pleasant discovery to find it to be true." Marek cleared his throat. "Oh, and speaking of birds..."

"Birds?" Grened repeated in perplexity.

"My nightingales in particular. Surely you remember them," he said, as though scandalized at his colleague's lapse of memory.

"Oh, yes, certainly."

"I'm afraid they had a bad spell a few months ago. Acted most peculiar, flying about every evening and making distressed calls as though they had lost something they valued highly."

Kaelin, in the act of removing the tea from the kitchen hearth, paused.

"I tell you, Grened, not even my best flute music could console them. I was deeply concerned, but you needn't worry. They seem content once again to sing with me."

"Er, yes, that's ... good to hear."

The Master Flutist took no notice of his host's confusion and accepted the cup of tea Kaelin brought him. "Thank you, Kaelin. And I must tell you what happened to one of my Bards, Grened," he said, with his eyes still on Kaelin. "I believe you know Teryn?"

"Why, yes, his last rotation was here," said Grened, trying to keep up with yet another shift in the bizarre conversation as Kaelin quickly turned to bring him his tea.

"Then you recall what a poor flutist he was. Excellent voice and very good on harp after your tutelage, but simply no flair for the flute, you might say." Marek shook his head sadly. "So, I made time this past autumn for consistent lessons with him. Imagine my shock when he sat down at our first session, took out his flute and began to play the fourth form competently, with a vastly improved tone." Marek glanced toward the heavens as though to indicate the obvious occurrence of a miracle. "The *fourth* form, mind you, when the second was beyond his capabilities at the beginning of summer."

Grened, finding himself on conversationally solid ground again, was impressed. "That's remarkable progress. Did he tell you how he accomplished it?"

Marek shrugged. "He just said he'd done some teaching."

Grened snorted. "Teaching? When he could scarcely play the instrument himself? And Bards do not take students!"

"My thoughts exactly. I must say that whoever he taught did us both an enormous favor, however it was accomplished."

Kaelin cleared away the last of the dishes and turned quickly away, not daring to acknowledge the look of approval Master Marek gave him. "An excellent job, Kaelin."

"What was?" asked Grened suspiciously.

Marek indicated the cleared table with a raised brow. "Why, the lunch, of course. Quite excellent."

"Oh … er, yes. It was prepared well enough."

"My pleasure, sir." Though the apprentice spoke directly to Master Grened, his eyes strayed to Master Marek.

Grened frowned, wondering at the sudden emotion he felt. At that moment, he would have given much to have received the look of respectful regard Kaelin had just given Marek.

After the Master Flutist left, the rest of the day passed in silence, Master and apprentice working industriously at their tables until it was time for dinner. Kaelin found it increasingly difficult to cook meals for the Master while his own stomach rumbled with hunger. After the Master finished eating, the apprentice hurried to clean up. Aware of the critical eyes that followed his every move, Kaelin made a thorough job of it, sweeping the floors and hearth and wiping down the mantel and tables for good measure. Then he returned to his tedious copying. The few times the Master left the room, Kaelin put down his quill, cradled his hand, and flexed his fingers to ease their growing ache, fervently wishing he had some of his Master's salve to rub into them. At last Master Grened put away his work, the apprentice thankfully followed suit, and they both went silently to their rooms.

Chapter 17

Despite his exhaustion, Kaelin could not sleep that night. His shoulders and back were hot and swollen, and he thought longingly of the icy stream near the house. He rose, quietly opened his door, and listened, thankful when no sound came from the Master's room. Taking care to make as little noise as possible, he made his way to the front door and left the house, heading for the stream. He did not hear the door open behind him.

Master Grened had not been sleeping. While lying in bed, he customarily planned the next day's activities and tried to ignore the persistent and disquieting notion that the mountain was somehow interfering with his sleep. Tonight, however, his thoughts had centered on the aggravating apprentice in his guest room. Carelessness rated fairly high on his mental list of offenses. Discourtesy scored even higher, especially when it was committed against one of higher rank. For an apprentice to be guilty of both in a single day—against two Masters, no less!—was clearly deserving of punishment.

Yet Grened lay awake, deeply disturbed by his own actions. Accustomed to keeping neat, orderly compartments in his mind for everything, from offenses to dyes, from plants to people, he felt strangely frustrated. This apprentice seemed stubbornly determined not to fit into any of them. Talan himself had charged the boy with theft, yet Kaelin seemed scarcely conscious of what he carried around his neck. This highly offended the Master's sensibilities. Moreover, Grened had endorsed this apprentice at the Council hearing a cycle and a half ago, had wrapped the black apprentice cord around his waist himself. Why, he'd even given the boy a box of precious dyes that he never gave to anyone! How dare the recipient of his gift turn out to be a thief and a liar? Obviously, Bergid had been taken in, with Marek right behind him, and Grened chafed at the thought that he'd almost been taken in himself by this talented shyster.

And, speaking of talent, what *was* the Maker thinking, to bestow the gift of old upon a thieving liar of a boy? Such a precious gift clearly belonged in the hands of someone deserving of it. Equally baffling, the boy had shown no resentment at being denied the use of his instruments. And to top off this list of indignities, that outrageous statement of forgiveness kept echoing relentlessly in the Master's mind. Ruthless honesty forced him to admit the boy's tone hadn't been insolent. Nevertheless ... *forgiveness, indeed! Why, I ought to punish the boy for such ... such...* He scowled. Forgiveness was not on his list of punishable offenses.

Grened found Marek's attitude toward the apprentice equally perplexing. Of course, Marek had always been on familiar terms with his Bards, which Grened did not approve of. Nevertheless, the Master Flutist's obvious rapport with Kaelin aroused a strange envy. He thought back to when Marek had been a Bard, serving his first rotation on Elegy, and was struck by the realization that he and the young Marek had also developed a rapport, laughing during their lessons together, the eager young Bard peppering him with question after question ... *he's right. Things were once different ... but Marek doesn't understand what's happened since then. No one does. No, not even me.*

He heard the guest room door open, then a few moments later, the sound of the front door opening and closing. The Master's reflective mood vanished. *Perhaps he's taking his flute outdoors at night to play! That would explain one thing at least.* Grened rose, wrapped his cloak about him and silently left the house. He had no desire to punish the boy again, but if he was breaking the instrumental restriction Bardic Law had placed him under, the Master would not hesitate to do so.

Spotting Kaelin standing by the stream, the Master moved closer to see if an instrument was in his hands, then stopped short as the apprentice removed his clothing and stood shivering at the water's edge. There was nothing in his hands, but there were vivid welts across his back, visible in the moonlight even from a distance.

Kaelin eased himself into the stream with a sigh of relief. As Grened watched, the boy looked northward through the trees, and a single agonized word broke the stillness.

"Master!"

Though the cry was barely more than a whisper, its intense loneliness seemed to resonate from the earth itself, striking the Master Harpist a bitter blow. This was not the sly, deceitful apprentice he had expected to find. This was a suffering boy. And he, a Master Bard who was sworn to place the good of the people of the Bardic Isles before all consideration of himself, had caused a great deal of that suffering. He stood staring at the young head bowed low over the water, then turned his gaze toward the mountain. The silhouette of the twin peaks, barely visible behind ethereal wisps of clouds limned with moonlight, brought a troubled frown to the Master's face.

His fists clenched as he turned resolutely away and went back to the house, brooding over the welts he had seen on Kaelin's back. He had made the boy fetch a strap and hang it in plain view as a warning, having no intention of using it. He had never strapped a youngster before and could not, for the life of him, understand what had possessed him to do so today. Not that the boy hadn't deserved punishment ... but a strapping? Hard enough to leave welts like those? His own father had been a stern taskmaster, the

Master reflected as he entered his home, but not even he had ever been so harsh.

Behind him, Kaelin looked longingly toward the island of Kestrel. The icy water had effectively numbed his back, but was powerless to reach his heart, which ached unbearably. No summons from the Council had yet arrived, but it surely would before his three months here were over. A heavy depression settled upon Kaelin as he thought of the many weeks ahead with such a difficult Master, followed immediately by the Council hearing, and then what? He could not imagine a life without his Master or instruments.

Maybe I should just leave ... take my instruments and find somewhere the Council summons will never reach me. There's no point in staying here, and I'm going to lose my Master anyway. For a moment the idea had enormous appeal. Then the thought of his Master's disappointment in him banished it. Dark depression reasserted itself with a force that bowed his head again.

Sing it! Let your voice release the music... His spirits lifted a fraction at the sudden memory of the Voice Master's command. *My voice!* He took a deep, controlled breath and began to softly sing. The power that pulsed through the freezing water almost took his breath away. It flowed around him, infusing his body with a measure of warmth and strength, as though the music were an intrinsic part of the element that surrounded him, its source the distant mountain. Kaelin abandoned himself to it, the song without words an inexpressibly sweet release. He kept a tight rein on his volume, having no wish to awaken the Master. He had forgotten that a voice trained by the Voice Master of the Bardic Isles could project far, regardless of its volume.

Nor could he have known that Master Grened was not asleep but was sitting in his chair listening to the quiet singing that carried clearly on the cold night air. Unaccustomed tears stung Grened's eyes. Surrendering to the pull of the lonely melody, the Master closed his eyes, and a small valley unfolded before him, surrounded by cliffs. At one end of the valley a waterfall spilled gracefully down the side of a cliff into a deep pool that emptied into a swiftly running stream. The water flowed toward a narrow break in the cliffs and disappeared from view. Then the singing came to an end and the vision left him. He opened his eyes and frowned. He hadn't recognized the scene, but he knew that mountain ... knew the slopes, the woods, the cliffs of granite. He had grown up in its foothills, isolated from everything except his father and the growing pressure of the mountain. Though it had lessened when he left to pursue his desire to join the Bardic Order, the mountain's shadow had continued to grow in his mind. So long as he was the Master Bard of Elegy, there was no escaping it.

Outside, Kaelin reluctantly climbed the bank, wondering at the clear vision the mountain had apparently sent him through the water that flowed from it. He pulled his clothes on over his shivering body and returned to the house. He opened the door to find the room bright with firelight. The Master regarded him from his chair near the fire.

"Come here, boy."

Kaelin stood paralyzed by the gruff command, trembling now with more than the cold. Though he would have welcomed the fire's warmth, he remained where he was, moving only to close the door firmly behind him. He would take the Master's punishment without complaint for doing something wrong, even if it was accidental and the punishment was severe. He would not take it for doing nothing. He took a deep breath, turned, and looked straight into the Master's eyes.

"No, sir." The thought crossed his mind that Master Rial would have thoroughly approved of his voice. It was clear and steady and projected to every corner of the room.

"What did you say?" Master Grened demanded.

"I said 'no, sir,'" Kaelin replied evenly. "I've done nothing wrong. You can send me away if you wish, but I'll not submit to a second beating when I've done nothing worse than soak myself in the stream to numb the pain of the first one."

The Master's brow lifted. "I would hardly call your singing 'nothing,' boy."

Kaelin paled at the revelation that the Master had heard his singing, which he might well consider intentional disobedience to the Council. "If that's what you want to punish me for, I'm under no restriction not to sing," he said firmly. "The Voice Master of the Bardic Isles told me that the voice is not a Bardic instrument."

The hazel eyes widened. "Master *Rial* told you that?"

"Yes, sir, the day I left to come here."

The Master was silent for a long moment, then roused himself from his reverie and looked sharply at the shivering boy. "I'm not going to punish you again," he growled. "Now, come stand by the fire. No sense in freezing when you don't have to."

Relieved, Kaelin moved toward the welcome warmth.

Master Grened lapsed once more into silence. "So," he said at last, "you would leave if I wished you gone. Back to Kestrel?"

"I won't return to my Master before my back heals. I have enough coppers to pay for a room in Tryl until then."

This gave the Master pause. "Do you wish to go?"

The question caught Kaelin off guard. He thought for a moment and discovered to his own surprise that he did not. "No, sir. I'd prefer to stay and do what my Master sent me here to do. I love my harp, and he told me there is much I can learn from you."

"He said that, did he?" The Master brooded for a few moments, his eyes fixed on the fire. "Has he ever punished you, boy?" he asked abruptly.

"No, sir."

"Indeed! Perhaps that explains the medallion you bear."

Kaelin stiffened. "No, sir!"

"You have a different explanation?"

"I do, but with all respect, there is no point in giving it to a Master who has already judged me guilty."

Master Grened stared at the apprentice. This was not the terrified, cowering boy he had expected to deal with. Nor could he refute the claim that he had already judged the boy guilty. Before he could recover, Kaelin continued, determined to finish what he had started.

"As for my Master, though he has never punished me, he has never hesitated to discipline me when I've needed it, and I'm not afraid to receive it. Discipline teaches, and my Master is an excellent teacher."

The Master's brows arched into iron grey peaks. "You defend him admirably. Continue. What has this discipline of his taught you?"

The apprentice glanced at his medallion. "To value the truth, whatever the cost."

"And this lesson was effective?"

Kaelin's head lifted at the derision in the Master's tone. "If you doubt it, sir, then why question me? There is nothing to be gained from the answers of a liar."

A brief smile crossed the Master's face. "You make an able adversary, boy."

Kaelin shook his head. "I've no desire to be considered one."

The Master Harpist regarded him appraisingly. "Let us say, then, that your Master succeeded in teaching you honesty. What other fault has he cured you of?"

Kaelin's face grew warm under the Master's gaze. "Before I met my Master, I had picked up the habit of cursing."

Grened's brows raised. This was definitely on his list of punishable offenses. "And?"

Kaelin hesitated. "He told me to bring him a switch—"

"Didn't you tell me he's never punished you, boy?" the Master interrupted sternly.

"He didn't use it." Kaelin swallowed hard at the memory he had never shared with anyone. "He made *me* use it on his own hand, hard enough to leave two welts." He looked steadily into the Master's incredulous eyes. "Then he told me that sound is a powerful force, and the human voice is the most powerful sound of all because it has the power to both heal and hurt. He said my words had hurt him worse than the switch and would take longer to heal, though no one could see the welts they left. He told me that such words could not be beaten out of me ... that the decision never to use my voice like that again was my own to make." He lowered his eyes, remembering the pain of that lesson. "Hurting my Master with that switch was the hardest thing I'd ever done," he said softly, "and to think that my words had hurt him even worse—" He broke off and lifted his eyes to the Master. "I've never cursed since that day."

Master Grened abruptly turned his attention back to the flames and asked no further questions. Only once did he move, reaching out to stir the fire to a brighter blaze. Firelight and shadows danced through the silent room until they subsided once again and still Kaelin waited, wondering what the Master would do.

Finally Master Grened rose to his feet. "Follow me, boy, and bring the strap with you." He pulled on his cloak and headed toward the door.

The apprentice hesitated only a moment, then fetched the strap and hurried after him, pulling his own cloak on as he went. The Master headed straight for the stream and stood for a moment on its banks. Then, with a swift motion, he took the strap from Kaelin's hand and flung it far out into the water, which swirled around the sudden obstacle and carried it out of sight.

Without looking at the astonished apprentice, the Master turned and gazed toward the distant silhouette. "Can you hear the mountain from here, boy?"

"Yes, sir," Kaelin replied. "I usually only hear the music of something if I focus intently on it, but with the mountain, it seems to depend on the distance. From here, I only have to look at it. From Bard's Landing, I hear it whether I can see it or not. From the Council Grounds, it's nearly overwhelming, and I can hardly think of anything else."

"Yes, I remember the battle you fought with it."

The apprentice gave him a startled glance. "I thought only my Master knew what was happening before I played." Even as he spoke, he remembered what the Master Harpist had said when he returned his apprentice cord to him.

You went up against the mountain with a flute, boy, and you won ... only the Maker knows how, for the Master of this island most assuredly does not.

"Your Master knew because of his bond with you," Grened said. "I knew because I'm bound to the mountain." A spasm of pain crossed his face. "I would give a great deal not to be."

Kaelin's eyes widened. There was, indeed, more to the Master Harpist than was apparent. *Perhaps he lashes out at other people because he's in pain himself ... from the mountain.* Before he could give the matter further thought, the Master continued.

"I did not expect you to be successful in your battle with it—with dissonance that knocked over the chimes and nearly took us from our chairs!—and yet you somehow managed to break free of it." The Master was silent for a moment, visibly struggling with his next words. "How did you do that, boy?"

Kaelin hesitated, wondering how he could possibly explain the unexplainable. "When I lifted my flute to play for the Council, the mountain's song filled my mind, as if it knew I had an instrument in my hands. It was powerful and dissonant ... and beautiful. I couldn't stop my fingers from playing every note of it. I could only refuse to give it voice, and that was a battle I was losing." He paused, knowing how difficult it would likely be for the Master to believe his next words. "I called out to my Master—just in my mind—and somehow, he heard me. He told me something he couldn't say out loud." He shook his head. "It wasn't me who banished the song of Bardic Mountain from my mind. It was my Master."

Master Grened stared at him. "And what was it that he couldn't—" he began, but the apprentice shook his head again.

"It's not for me to say what my Master can't."

The Master nodded, silently accepting this, and turned his gaze back to the mountain. Both of them stood for a moment, looking at the ever-changing shape of the silhouette through the clouds.

"Can you hear it, too, sir?" Kaelin ventured to ask.

The Master frowned slightly. "Hear the music of it? No. But I can *feel* it, like a ruptured song whose dissonance grows with every passing cycle." The lines in the Master's face seemed to deepen, reflecting the burden he spoke of.

"And ... its dissonance has become your own," the apprentice said softly, as if to himself.

The Master did not dispute this. He turned away from the mountain with effort. "Come along, boy. Let's go home."

～ ⸮ ～

The morning light had moved across his room and out through the open doorway before Kaelin woke the next morning. He tried to move, but the effort made him groan. *Why do I ache so?* He opened his eyes and inhaled sharply, alarmed that the morning was so far advanced and he hadn't prepared breakfast for the Master yet. He tried to rise, but a sharp pain went through his head, and he lay back with a groan.

"Lie still, boy." The Master Harpist was sitting beside him, holding a steaming mug in his hands.

"What's wrong with me?" Kaelin asked hoarsely.

"You've run a fever all night. Hardly surprising after soaking yourself in a freezing stream in the middle of winter like a fool.

Now, drink every drop of this."

Kaelin felt a strong hand lift his head. A spoonful of warm liquid trickled its way into his mouth. He swallowed obediently, grimacing at the taste. Two more bitter spoonfuls followed. *He must have put something—* Before he could finish the thought, he drifted back to sleep.

He woke up again in the afternoon, to the feel of gentle hands rubbing a salve into his back. He flinched and moaned. The hands stopped, and he slept again.

The next time Kaelin awoke, it was to the clear strains of harp music. He lay still, listening to the first music he had heard since leaving Lyra. His head no longer hurt, and the pain across his back had been replaced with a welcome numbness. The soreness of his scribing hand had also disappeared, though he had no memory of the Master rubbing salve into it. It was dark outside his window, but the room beyond his open door flickered with firelight. He sat up and saw the Master sitting by the fire, playing a beautiful Bardic harp. Even from a distance, Kaelin had no difficulty recognizing the loneliness he saw in that unguarded moment. It was etched in the lines of the Master's face and echoed in the minor melodic line the Master so expressively played. Kaelin thought it strange that someone in such a high Bardic position could be so lonely. The other four Masters, he mused, were constantly interacting with their Bards, but not a single Bard had visited Master Grened since Kaelin arrived. *Perhaps he's pushed them away because of the mountain. What an awful thing, to feel its dissonance without being able to hear its beauty.*

Kaelin shuddered at the thought and lay back down to sleep, but it was no use. The Master's music whispered to him, irresistibly pulling him toward it. He pushed aside his blanket and walked unsteadily to the fire. Then, led by an impulse he did not understand and would have refused if he'd had the strength, the apprentice sat on the floor and rested his head against the Master's knee.

Master Grened would have been incapable of describing how he felt at that moment. No one had ever reached out to touch him before. Yet he did not push the youngster who had dared to do so away. Indeed, for the briefest of moments, his hand left the strings of his harp and rested on the young head, then quickly returned to his instrument.

Kaelin stared drowsily into the flames of the fire as the Master continued to play, watching the patterns of light and shadow intermingle. He frowned, wondering at the strange sensation that the Master's music had not just pulled him from his bed, but was pulling him toward the mountain. He gave the music his full attention, and his frown deepened. He knew this music. It was not quite the same, but it was clearly a variation of a theme he had often heard before. And it was pulling him in a way that no one's music but his own had ever done.

Suddenly one of the flames grew higher than the rest. Kaelin caught his breath, the Master's music forgotten. The flame reminded him of the one he had seen at Master Talan's. But this time dark, amber-slashed eyes stared unblinking from the flame's translucent center. The eyes searched, piercing the flame as though trying to see beyond it to the young apprentice staring in frozen fascination from the Master's knee. Kaelin shut his eyes and shuddered. The harp music stopped.

"Is something wrong, boy?" Grened asked.

"I don't know, sir," Kaelin replied shakily. He sat up and glanced warily at the fire, but the eyes were gone. "Your music made me think of Master Cyral and his Harp. Since I've come to Elegy..." he hesitated, "well, my thoughts seem to be drawn to him. And to the mountain." To his relief, the Master registered no skepticism but listened to him gravely. "Just now, in the fire," and his gaze was unwillingly dragged toward it, "I saw eyes, trying to ... to look through one of the flames." He grimaced. "I don't understand it." He glanced up into the keen, appraising regard of the Master.

"Do you, sir?"

The Master was silent, considering the matter. "No ... no, I've seen no eyes in my fire. But I have lived in the shadow of Bardic Mountain too long to dismiss such matters out of hand. That mountain has a life of its own, boy, and it will take more than a Master to understand it. If what you just saw came from the mountain, only the mountain can explain it."

Kaelin was silent. He didn't think the vision had come from the mountain, but if not, then who or what had sent it? He put aside his wondering and leaned back against the Master's knee. The room filled once again with the delicate sounds of the harp, but the fire remained free of visions. He sighed and, lulled by the gentle music, drifted to sleep. He barely roused when the Master shook his shoulder and told him to go back to bed.

"You're playing the mountain's song," Kaelin murmured drowsily as he got to his feet. "That's how you're bound to it. You may not be able to hear it ... but you can play it." Half asleep, he stifled a yawn and moved toward his room.

It was long before the Master went to his own.

Chapter 18

The next morning, Kaelin felt much better, though his back still protested every movement. He resolutely focused on getting breakfast ready before the Master awoke, looking hungrily at every ingredient he used. Then he began copying the rest of the manuscript, trying to ignore the insistent complaints of his empty stomach. He was deep in the section on red dyes when the Master emerged from his room. The apprentice rose and bowed.

"Master Grened. Good morning, sir," he said with a smile.

"Good morning," the Master gruffly replied. He came to the table just as Kaelin set a bowl of cooked oats and dried fruit before him. The apprentice pulled his gaze away from the Master's meal and returned to his copying.

"Have you eaten yet?" the Master abruptly asked.

"No, sir," Kaelin replied, indicating his work. "I have twenty more pages to copy. I'm hoping to finish them by tomorrow."

The Master stabbed an imperative finger toward the kitchen. "Eat, boy, eat!" he ordered curtly. "I can't afford to miss any more sleep tending sick apprentices." He waved impatiently toward the manuscript. "You can finish that on your own time and take it with you when you go. I imagine even *your* memory can suffer a lapse now and then. Put the finished pages on my desk and I'll do the illustrations." He picked up his spoon and shook it in the apprentice's startled face. "See to it that no one—and I mean *no* one—ever lays eyes on that copy!"

"No one will, sir," Kaelin hastily assured him.

"I'll require a copy of those damaged pages, mind."

"I'll put them on your desk right after breakfast." Kaelin wasted no time filling a bowl for himself, then emptied it with such alacrity that the Master snorted.

"Go on, eat your fill, boy. You're going to need your strength back as soon as possible."

Kaelin quickly demolished a second helping. "Are we going to begin making dyes?" he ventured hopefully.

"If you're feeling up to a short walk. Some of the plants I use for my dyes are not far from here. It's hardly the season to harvest them, but you might as well take the opportunity to learn a few things about them." The Master watched in mild amusement as Kaelin's third serving disappeared.

The moment Kaelin placed the copies on the Master's desk, Grened strode to the door, pulled his cloak on and slung his harp over his shoulder. "Time's wasting, boy. These things take time, you know, time and patience. People just don't seem to realize..."

Kaelin grinned, then grabbed his own cloak and followed. To his surprise, the Master set off directly west through the woods. A half hour's walk brought them to a place where the trees thinned and gave way to a secluded meadow. Grened strode across it to where a profusion of healthy, leafy plants grew in orderly rows on a gentle slope. He stabbed a finger at the lowest row. Half of the plants had small clusters of broad leaves; the other half had long woody stems. "Let's see what you've *really* learned thus far, boy. Identify these plants."

Kaelin frowned. "Woad?"

The Master nodded. "What else can you tell me about them?"

"They're biennial," Kaelin replied, "so they'll only grow for two cycles before they die." He pointed to the plants bearing clusters of leaves. "Those are in their first cycle of growth, so you can harvest the leaves this summer to make blue dye. The woad with stems are in their second cycle, so they'll have yellow flowers this summer and produce seeds you can use for your next crop."

The Master folded his arms. "And how will I make the dye?"

"By chopping the leaves and simmering them. Then you'll strain them, add some ash, and stir it till it foams. You'll let it sit for a few hours until the foam evaporates and the pigment settles. Then you'll rinse the blue pigment well and store it."

The Master lifted a brow. "And what are those?" he asked, indicating the rows of plants halfway up the slope.

Kaelin inspected them carefully, noting the long triangular leaves that reminded him of cabbage leaves. "Rhubarb?" At the Master's nod, he continued. "They're perennial, so they'll grow for more than two cycles. You'll dig up the roots and chop them immediately, because once they're dried they're too hard to chop. Then you'll dry the pieces and grind them to make yellow dye."

The Master raised a brow and nodded toward the plants further up the hill. Kaelin moved closer to them, noting their leathery leaves fringed with curved prickles, in whorls of four to six. "Madder root!" he exclaimed. "It's also a perennial and will flower this summer, then it'll have berries that will turn black. The root will make pink and orange, and even red, I think."

"And why do you suppose I planted it higher up the slope?"

"Because it needs more sun and well-drained soil, so you probably added sand to the soil before you planted them, didn't you? I've never seen such healthy plants in the middle of winter."

The Master Harpist observed him silently for a moment. "There's a warm mineral spring on the other side of this hillock," he said at last, "so the ground here never freezes. No one knows of the spring or this grove. No one except you, and I fully expect it to stay that way."

"I'll never tell anyone, sir," Kaelin solemnly promised.

"Not even your Master?" Grened challenged.

"I'll tell him that I've promised to keep your teaching on dyes to myself. He'll not ask me to break my word."

"Very well, then, I'll let you use some of these woad leaves to practice making blue dye. It won't be as bright, but it will serve to teach. There's dried rhubarb and maddock root in my dye shed you can learn how to grind. I've several other plants to introduce you to, here in the grove and near the spring as well. Then I'll show you my secret—and it will *remain* a secret—of using them to stain wood. It's not as simple as you might imagine, and I did *not* write the process down." He glared at Kaelin. "Nor will you."

"No, sir!"

Mollified, the Master nodded. "You've fairly earned the information, boy," he said gruffly. "You've thoroughly absorbed my manuscript when you might have merely skimmed it in the hope of answering a few questions. You've demonstrated a sincere interest, so any questions you may ask me about it will be answered." His voice hardened once again. "That manuscript is my life's work, boy! Fools too lazy to read it can expect no such help. Now, take a single look around the grove. One look only," the Master warned. "Then close your eyes."

Kaelin obediently glanced around once, then shut his eyes.

"Tell me what you saw. In detail."

Kaelin replied without hesitation. "On the east, where we're standing, are your plants for the dyes. To the south there's a creek with a willow tree overhanging it. To the west there are two birch trees and an elm. To the north there's a large oak with wisteria climbing its trunk and several more rows of plants that are different than the ones we're standing by. I couldn't quite see what kind of plants they are, but there are six rows, two for each type. The meadow is mostly grass, though it's probably covered in wildflowers in the spring and summer. The ground gets rocky close to the creek, and there's a pool a short way downstream where there might be good fishing. If you'll allow me," he added hopefully, "I'd be happy to find out." He opened his eyes to find the Master staring at him.

"I know all about the fish there, boy ... and you surprise me yet again. How did you learn to be so observant?"

"During the sense-deprivation test, I spent a lot of time identifying and sorting all kinds of leaves, bark, flowers, feathers, rocks..." he shrugged. "Anything my Master could get his hands on to keep me from boredom, I guess."

The Master snorted. "You guess wrong. He was teaching you more than just useful information. He taught you the difference between *seeing* and *observing*. Thanks to those lessons, you are far more aware of your surroundings than most ever are." The Master began to pace back and forth.

"What do you know about living off the land?" he asked abruptly. "A boy from Vale must know *something* of use."

"Well, we were all taught basic survival skills in school. I can build a fire and a decent shelter, and I know how to forage for edible plants and mushrooms." Kaelin thought for a moment. "My Master taught me a lot about the plants on Kestrel and how to use them, and Master Talan taught me how to use some of the ones that grow only on Eyrie."

"Where would you build a temporary shelter here?" The Master's eyes glinted with challenge.

Kaelin shook his head. "I wouldn't build one here. I'd look for higher ground and hopefully find a cliff face that could serve as a wind break and one of my walls. I'd want trees close by for poles and a nearby water source."

"Where would you position the shelter and fire, and why?"

"The shelter with the opening downwind to keep the weather out. The fire downwind of my shelter so the smoke stays out."

"How would you build the fire?"

"I'd gather long, dry strips of tree bark fiber and dry deadfall for fuel. Then I'd pound the strips with a rock until they were fluffy and use them as tinder to start the fire with my flint, feeding it small twigs until it got going, then larger pieces of wood.”

“How would you start it if you foolishly lost your flint?”

Kaelin frowned slightly. “I don’t know.”

“Can you fish with and without hooks?”

“With them, yes … not without.”

“Set snares? Skin and dress the meat without wasting any?”

“I can set snares, but my sister took care of the rest.”

“And what if you became ill?” the Master demanded. “Do you know what to do for a fever? Blistered hands? Stomach cramps?”

“I don’t know anything about healing.”

The Master frowned. “You’ve much to learn, then, so we’d best get started.” He stabbed an imperative finger at the woad. “After you’ve gathered six handfuls of those leaves to take back with us, how will you carry them so they don’t leave a trail from here to my door that any fool could follow?” The Master glared at him accusingly.

“I … don’t know, sir. I didn’t bring my pack.”

“You won’t always have your pack, boy, but never go *any-where* without your belt knife. Use it to cut two long strips of live bark from the elm, the length of your arm and your handspan in width,” the Master instructed. “Then cut a length of the wisteria twice as long as the length of your arm. Bring me those things, and I’ll teach you what to do with them.”

The apprentice removed his belt knife and hurried to obey. Behind him, he heard the sweet sound of the Master’s harp, and, stealing a glance, he saw Master Grened seated next to his plants, softly playing. Kaelin watched surreptitiously as he cut the bark, and it seemed to him that the plants bent toward the Master as he played, his eyes closed, lost in his own thoughts. The Master’s hand left the strings of his harp and gently touched the broad leaf of a woad plant, then returned to the strings.

Kaelin quickly turned his attention back to his work. *The*

manuscript is just the expression of his life's work. It's this grove that he loves ... every tree and plant of it. And he shared his secret with me. Suddenly feeling honored to be here, he took the required materials to the Master, who put aside his harp and told him to cut holes at the top and bottom of both strips. Then the Master showed him how to crisscross the flexible pieces of bark and bend them into a crude but serviceable basket. Holding it firmly between his knees, Kaelin threaded the wisteria through the four holes and cinched it to make a handle. He slung it over his shoulder and grinned, pleased with his impromptu creation.

"Gather those leaves and let's be off!" the Master brusquely ordered. "Time doesn't stop for fools who waste it."

Kaelin hurried to comply. He soon stood before the Master with a basket of leaves in his arms and a questioning look on his face.

"What is it, boy?"

"I was just wondering how you learned so many interesting things." Expecting to be told to mind his own business, Kaelin was surprised when the Master answered.

"My father was a woodsman, and we lived in the foothills of the mountain. When I was much younger than you, he would take me high up the slopes and leave me with nothing but a belt knife and my own wits to get me home. So, I learned to use them." The Master was silent for a long moment, remembering ...

He'd been twelve the last time his father took him up on Bardic Mountain and left him there ... twelve and full of anger. He'd watched his father head southwest for home, and then the young Grened had bitterly marched off east, toward Tryl, determined never to go home again. Two hours later, his father had come up behind him on the banks of a stream, just as Grened finished threading a catch of fish.

"A bit off course, aren't you, son?"

"I'm going exactly where I want to go, to get what you won't

let me have!"

"Are you, now? It's a three-week trek to Tryl with supplies you haven't got. And how will you support yourself there with winter not far off, much less earn enough to buy what I said 'no' to? No one will hire an underaged boy with no parent to vouch for him."

Grened glared mutinously at his father.

"Come back home with me now, and you'll not be left up on the mountain again ... not that I ever left you. A boy willing to traipse alone to Tryl has learned how to survive on his own."

This gave Grened pause. "I'll only come back if you get me a lap harp," he said stubbornly.

His father frowned. "Why you keep wanting one of those useless things, out here where no one can teach—"

"A lap harp!" Grened insisted. "Or I won't go back."

His father searched his face and sighed. "I suppose you've fairly earned it. I'll get you the materials and instructions you'll need to build yourself one, then. And since we're already two hours closer to Tryl, we'll go from here. We can trap our way there for the coin to pay for your foolish harp and some useful supplies." He nodded toward the trout. "Now, are you going to invite me to lunch, or must I catch my own?"

The Master Harpist returned to the present to find Kaelin looking at him hopefully.

"Are you going to teach me all those things I didn't know?"

"And more besides," the Master affirmed. "You'll need more than a means of support, boy. If you stay on my island, you'll need an affordable place to live, and the woods do not charge their guests. A season or two of saving your earnings from whatever job you find should enable you to board through the winter months." The Master glanced once again at the distant peaks of Bardic Mountain, and a shadow crossed his face. "And if ever you answer the mountain's call, you will need such knowledge."

Kaelin nodded and followed the Master's gaze. They stood for a moment in shared awareness of the power emanating from the distant twin peaks.

"What did you mean," the Master asked abruptly, "when you said that I'm playing the mountain's song ... that it's how I'm bound to it? How can I play something I can't hear?"

"I don't know *how* you're doing it, sir," Kaelin said hesitantly, "but you're playing it, or at least a variation of it. Enough to have created a bond with it and feel its dissonance."

"The music is not dissonant, boy."

"No, sir, the *notes* aren't." Kaelin frowned, searching for the words that would explain what he instinctively knew. "It's as if a composer wrote a beautiful song that so perfectly described what was in his mind that he remained linked to it. But then something happened that created a dissonance in the composer's mind, a dissonance that kept growing with every playing of the song so that now, even though the notes are the same, those who hear them react to the dissonance *behind* them." He shrugged apologetically. "I'm sorry I can't explain it any better."

The Master frowned at the mountain. "I've played that music nearly every night since I built my first lap harp cycles ago. The melody came to me when I was a child and left high up on the mountain to find my own way back. It was ... comforting. Part of the reason I joined the Bardic Order was because I wanted a full-sized Bardic harp to play it on." He grimaced. "Over the cycles, even though the notes are the same, the music has become anything but comforting ... and yet I continue to play it."

Kaelin's eyes widened. Never would he have guessed that he and the difficult Master Harpist had something in common besides their membership in the Bardic Order. *What might I have become if my music had never been freed? If I'd spent cycles being tormented by it the way he has by the mountain's dissonance? I might have begun lashing out at those around me, too, just like he has. I had my Master to help me. Who did Master Grened have?* He gathered his courage.

"Maybe it's like the bonds we have with people," the apprentice tentatively suggested. "The more communication we have with someone, the stronger our bond becomes. The mountain communicates by sending out the music it was created with, and for whatever reason, some of us can hear it more clearly than others. You grew up on its slopes, so would have been affected by it more than most. When you made your harp and played that music, it created a bond between you … a bond that strengthened with repetition." He glanced up and found the hazel eyes regarding him steadily. "I can't imagine," Kaelin said softly, "the pressure you've felt from playing such music as that every night for cycles. If you refuse to play it, it might not break the bond completely, but over time, I think it will greatly lessen it."

The Master nodded and said no more, turning to look thoughtfully at the mountain. When at last he tore his gaze away and turned to go, Grened found himself arrested by clear amber eyes and saw there the respect this apprentice had given Marek. Flustered by the unaccustomed and thoroughly unwelcomed tightness in his throat, he roughly cleared it.

"Think you can find the way home, boy, or must I take you by the hand?"

Kaelin grinned. "I'll be happy to lead the way, sir!" He slung his makeshift basket of leaves over his shoulder and marched unerringly in the direction of the Master's home. Grened chuckled softly to himself and followed.

Late that night the Master Harpist sat by the fire, determined not to play the music he had played every night for cycles, astounded at how difficult it was to resist doing so. He scowled. It was more than just a matter of habit. If it didn't seem like the thinking of an utter fool, he could almost believe his harp was pulling him toward it, insisting that his fingers play the notes they were accustomed to playing … demanding they give voice to the dissonance filling his mind, though the notes themselves were not jarring. He tried to distract himself with one harp solo after the next, then with mindlessly running series of scales and arpeggios … none of it was any use. He even tried to put aside his harp and retire for the night, but inexplicably found himself back in his chair, clutching his harp with shaking hands. His need to play the music was overwhelming, a burning desire that could only be put out by giving in to it. Perhaps, if he played it just once…

The knuckles of his hands whitened against the frame of his harp. *Just once, so I can sleep!*

"Master Grened?"

The Master Harpist's eyes flew open, surprised to find himself breathing as heavily as if he had just sprinted there from the grove. His fingers fell from the strings. He stared at them, not remembering having placed them there.

"Are you all right, sir?" The apprentice stood looking at him in concern, a manuscript in his hand.

"What are you doing up at such an hour, boy?" Grened demanded. "It had better not be to play what's in your hand."

"No, sir," Kaelin hastened to assure him. "I'm sorry I disturbed you, but I didn't realize you were still up. I just finished a solo harp piece and was going to leave it on your desk for you."

"You stayed up composing a harp composition? For me?" The Master's astonished eyes fastened on the apprentice. "Why?"

"I thought perhaps something new that you've never played before might help you sleep. I haven't heard it myself," Kaelin added hurriedly, "but I would love to hear you play it."

"No!" the Master snapped, knowing he dared not touch the strings of his harp right now. "No," he repeated more gently when the apprentice's hopeful expression vanished. "I think I would prefer hearing *you* play it, boy ... or have you foolishly composed something beyond your own harp level?"

Kaelin's face lit. "No, sir, I can play it for you!" Quickly fetching his harp before the Master could change his mind, the apprentice took a seat next to him and removed his harp from its bag for the first time since leaving Lyra.

"So, this is the finished product, is it?" Master Grened set aside his harp and held out his hand. "May I?"

Kaelin handed over his harp. The Master looked first at the pillar, Bardic Mountain beautifully carved into its base. Above this was a spray of heather with a constellation of stars above it, for the island of Eyrie. Then a juniper growing from the side of a cliff, a tiny nightingale perched on one of its branches, for Zephyr. A cocoon hung nearby, a peacock butterfly just above it, for Lyra. Near the top of the pillar was a large kestrel in flight, for its namesake, the island of Kestrel.

The Master's hand traced the carving of the mountain, his expression unreadable. "The dyes you used were well applied, boy, considering you did not know my method," he said brusquely. "Wise of you to use them only to highlight your carvings, not obscure them."

"Thank you, sir."

"My dyes, I believe?"

"I would use only the *best* dyes for my harp," Kaelin stoutly affirmed.

What may have been a smile crossed the Master's features, then he turned his attention to giving the harp a meticulous inspection. "Your Master certainly didn't skimp on the quality of wood he provided you," he said dryly, "and Darryk is apparently a good teacher, though I doubt he had to teach a boy from Vale how to seamlessly fit wood together." He handed the instrument back to the apprentice with a challenging look. "Show me, then, that this boy from Vale is worthy of the harp he has made, and that your

Master did not waste his coin on such fine materials."

As the apprentice began to play without even glancing at the score, the Master was pulled into an experience quite unlike the unforgettable one on the Council Grounds almost two cycles ago. Then, vivid memories of the boy's life—the agony of his inhibited gift and the immense relief of freeing it after following the Master Bard of Kestrel—had silenced all doubts about the apprentice's right to stay at his Master's side. That powerful flute music had been about the boy and his Master. The equally powerful harp music filling Grened's home at this moment was about the Master Harpist himself.

The music began softly, the low, undulating minor arpeggios weaving around the listener, pulling him gently up and out of his home. The notes rose, bearing him on the wings of a rising arpeggio above the trees and to the east, away from the constricting walls behind him. Below, the forest floor could be seen through trees bare of their autumn leaves. Farther east the lower slopes of Bardic Mountain rose, the distant peaks shrouded from view by the ethereal fingers of winter fog.

The music modulated to the major as, between the trees, a clearing came into view. A stream gurgled a twisting path among the rocks at one end. Oak, elm, birch, and willow framed the rest of the clearing's boundaries. Incredulously, the listener looked at the hillside opposite the stream and saw the familiar rows of woad, rhubarb, and madder root. The agony of pressure in his mind lessened as the harp music took him closer, for this was his place, his private retreat where a measure of peace from the mountain could still be found. The music, as if aware of this, swirled about the clearing in a joyful dance, light staccatos brushing one plant after another, one tree after the next. As each was touched, the listener heard its song echoed through the music of the harp. The listener heard ... and understood that he was listening to the incredibly complex, varied music of life itself.

Even now, in midwinter, the song of each plant brought a vision of flow ... of water and nutrients being pulled up through tangled roots, of energy drawn in through the leaves from nothing more, it seemed, than the light and air surrounding them. In it was pulled, and back out it flowed in steady rhythm, as though the leaves themselves were breathing with the music that described them. The listener found himself breathing with them, thrilling to the flow of energy, to the synchronization of his breath with the flora that surrounded him. The music took him up every tree, up into the branches far above the clearing, and he exulted in the flow of life through each of them. The mountain was a powerful force, but life, he saw with crystal clarity, was even more powerful. For Bardic Mountain would slowly diminish over time, worn away by the forces of wind and rain. Yet however fragile the flora seemed by comparison, its seeds would propagate and grow anew, and life would continue, strong and enduring, for the duration of the earth itself.

In a moment of rare abandonment, in the space between the notes, the listener allowed himself to simply be ... to rest in the knowledge that he himself had been created with a variation of this same wondrously creative music, music connected to everything, yet uniquely his own. And for the first time in his life, the listener was awed by an understanding of who he was. Not a boy who had grown up in the shadow of the mountain and been hurt by its growing dissonance. No, nor was he a Master Bard or the Master Harpist of the Bardic Isles, for such things had been left behind, having no part in defining him. He was a being born of the same creative force that thrummed through the fabric of the universe, a being of immense, incalculable value. He gazed at the life around him and thought of the people scattered across his island ... Bards, men of all crafts and trades, women and children. They shone like a myriad of stars in his mind, and he was humbled by the intrinsic connection they all shared, how utterly impossible it would be to hurt one without hurting all. Then the music, as if satisfied that it had revealed far more to him than the young composer could have hoped for or realized himself, swirled through his mind, lifted him up above the clearing, and took him home.

The Master opened his eyes to find the fire burned low before him, banked for what little remained of the night. Kaelin's harp was hung in its travel bag near the door. The apprentice himself was gone, apparently having long since retired to his room. Grened stirred from his reverie and glanced at his own harp, surprised to find that it had also been placed back inside its bag. On top of it was the manuscript of the music he had just experienced. He stared at it for a long moment, understanding the message left there for him, the silent words as clear as those Bergid had sent to Kaelin on the Council Grounds. There, the beleaguered apprentice had turned his attention away from the mountain and focused instead on the Master he loved. He had heard the words his Master could not say, powerful words that had banished the mountain's song dominating the boy's mind. Grened rose, oblivious to the tears that traced a path across his cheeks and nodded to his harp, silently promising it that he also would turn his attention away from the mountain's music. He would play instead the music of what he loved, knowing now that it encompassed far more than the little meadow of peace he had discovered and cultivated. He headed for his bed, his mind at peace for the first time that he could remember, filled with music written by a mere boy ... a boy who had just given him a gift beyond price.

The next morning, the Master rose late and found Kaelin setting breakfast on the table. The apprentice carefully put down the plates and bowed. "Master Grened. Good morning, sir. I hope you slept well."

"Well enough, boy," the Master Harpist said gruffly as he

seated himself. He could not remember having slept so deeply in cycles. "Haven't you eaten yet?"

"An apprentice should not eat before a Master," Kaelin exclaimed, so clearly shocked by the idea that the Master found himself suppressing a chuckle. The apprentice took his seat and waited for the Master to begin eating before he dug in himself. Halfway through their meal, Grened spoke again.

"We might as well have a late lunch as well. That will give me enough time to instruct you in making blue dye from the woad leaves you gathered yesterday."

An exclamation of pleasure accompanied this news as Kaelin happily took another bite of his breakfast.

"And after lunch," the Master continued brusquely, "I'll see to your harp instruction."

The apprentice's fork dropped onto his plate with a clatter.

"Don't think for a moment," the Master said severely as he buttered his scone, "that I didn't hear the uneven execution of the dominant seventh arpeggio you played last night—a simple dominant seventh!" he exclaimed in a scandalized voice, "—not to mention the hesitant resolution to its tonic. There are cures for such ailments." He shook his head disapprovingly. "Someone whom I estimate to be a strong form seven harpist should not be making such basic errors, and I'll have several succinct comments for his Master on the subject when next I see him." The Master finished buttering his scone and looked pointedly at the apprentice's plate. "Perhaps, if you finish your breakfast you'll have strength enough to find your tongue."

For a moment the two of them regarded each other over their meal, the Master's gaze unreadable, the apprentice's filled with hope. "You'll allow me the use of my harp ... and teach me?" Kaelin asked in a hushed voice.

The Master heaved an aggrieved sigh. "I'm afraid I must, since there is no other way to cure you, and on no account will I allow an advanced harpist of *any* age to leave my island making basic blunders that will damage my reputation." He fixed a stern eye on the apprentice. "I'll expect a minimum of four hours of practice every day."

"Gladly!"

"You may have one hour of free time directly after lunch. If you spend it outside the house, you may *not* take any instrument with you ... save that voice of yours, which you are free to use as you wish."

"Thank you, sir!"

"If you are late returning, you will spend the entire evening doing my copy work."

"I'll be on time!" came the fervent promise.

The Master frowned, struggling with his next statement. "Your Master," he finally said, "did not waste his coin on such fine harp materials." He took a bite of his scone, pretending not to see the apprentice's face light with pleasure.

They finished their meal together in comfortable silence. When Kaelin rose to clean up, Grened suddenly spoke again. "And no matter what, don't ever doubt it," he ordered.

Kaelin blinked. "Don't ever doubt what, sir?"

"What your Master can't say." The Master Harpist rose with an air of finality and went to his desk.

Chapter 19

Havalek and Lendin, Bards of Elegy currently assigned to Tryl, were at it again. Though Byron wasn't usually bothered by the two younger Bard's bickering, tonight he looked up with annoyance. "Would you two take your argument outside? I've got to finish this report for Master Grened tonight."

"Well, *our* reports have to be done as well," Havalek retorted.

Byron stared at him. "What on earth has you so ... ah, isn't it your turn to take the reports to Master Grened tomorrow?" He gave Havalek a sympathetic look. No Bard wanted to spend any more time than necessary in the unpredictable Master's presence.

"Yes, it is," replied Lendin, glancing at Havalek's stony expression. "He's been out of tune over it all day. Larad's report still hasn't arrived."

"Oh, I see." Byron sighed. Master Grened preferred not to be bothered by receiving the monthly reports individually from the thirty Bards spread all over his island, so they were sent to the three Bards assigned to Tryl, who took turns delivering the collected batch to the Master. Unfortunately, the Master Harpist was all too prone to blaming the messenger for someone else's failure.

"Well, I wouldn't worry about it," Byron said, giving Havalek a reassuring smile. "He's probably worked himself out on that poor apprentice who's staying with him. Kaelin, isn't it?"

"It *was*," Lendin said with grim humor.

"I can't imagine Master Grened tolerating any apprentice for long, much less one who's been accused of thievery," put in Havalek. "He can barely tolerate *us*."

"True enough," Byron acknowledged. "I'd have wagered the boy wouldn't last longer than a day or two, and here it's been over a fortnight." His brow furrowed. "Perhaps we should go find out if he's all right."

Havalek pounced on the opportunity. "Good idea! The two of you can come with me tomorrow."

"Now, wait a minute," protested Lendin. "That's a risk I'd think twice about taking for a friend, and I don't even *know* this Kaelin."

"You'd do it for Master Bergid, wouldn't you, and this is Master Bergid's apprentice," Byron said pointedly.

"Well..."

"Good!" Havalek said quickly. "Let's get there right after the Master's had his dinner. Here's hoping that poor apprentice is a good cook."

❧ ⸰ ❧

The three Bards approached the Master's home early the following evening and came to an astounded halt outside the door. Clearly audible was the sound of two harps chasing each other up and down a series of arpeggios on parallel inversions. The startling sound of unfamiliar laughter mingled with the musical race. The arpeggios sped faster across the strings, ending with a triumphant flourish. The Master's booming voice startled the three listeners.

"Can't quite keep up with an old man yet, can you, boy?"

"I believe we finished exactly together, wouldn't you say, sir?" The young voice spoke with light amusement.

"Yes, well," the Master gruffly conceded, "we *wouldn't* have, if I hadn't been unfairly distracted by all your laughter." His voice rose imperatively. "Let's see if you can do it *this* time. On the downbeat, boy, and keep your mind on the music!"

The next moment the two harpists were off, no laughter coming from the room now. Outside, the Bards listened spellbound as the undulating arpeggios flew ever faster over the strings. This time they ended with a cry of triumph from the Master.

"Ha! Got you that time, boy."

"Congratulations, sir! I'll do my best to rob you of your victory tomorrow night."

"Hmph! You speak as though the possibility actually exists." The Master's voice rose challengingly. "Cocky enough to put a small stake on the outcome? I shall make breakfast the following morning if you manage to pull off your miracle."

"Yes, sir!" came the delighted response.

"And if you don't, you'll do my copy work for the day."

Not a sound came from the Master's home.

"*All* of your copy work?"

"What's the matter, boy? Not quite so sure of yourself now?"

"Well..."

"Entertaining the thought that you might *lose,* perhaps?"

"The thought had occurred to me."

"How refreshingly humble. Well, boy, do we have a bargain? The barest possibility of a full-scale breakfast, personally made and served by the Master Harpist of the Bardic Isles, against the strong probability of doing *all* the copy work I give you. The amount will depend on how thoroughly I trounce you but will not exceed an hour's work. And I'll change the key signature and add two measures every day, just to keep me interested."

"It's a deal, sir! I'll do my best not to bore you."

Byron, suddenly aware that he and his frozen companions were eavesdropping, shook himself from his immobility and knocked firmly on the door. At the curt command to enter, they walked in, bowed to the Master and chorused a greeting.

"I've brought you the reports, sir," Havalek added nervously.

The Master gestured impatiently. "Put them on my desk."

Havalek hesitated. "Larad's report hasn't come yet."

"When it arrives, return it with instructions for him to deliver it to me in person."

"Yes, sir," came the relieved reply. Havalek spared a moment's pity for his colleague, who would need to trek half the length of Elegy to bring the Master his overdue report.

"I don't believe you've met Master Bergid's apprentice," the Master said, indicating the youngster, who had stood the moment the Bards came through the doorway. "This is Kaelin. Kaelin, these are Bards Byron, Havalek, and ... I've forgotten your name, young man."

"Lendin, Master Grened." The youngest Bard nervously worried the tasseled end of his harp bag.

"Ah, yes ... and Bard Lendin."

Kaelin, somewhat surprised the Master had known the name of his visiting apprentice, bowed. "Bards Byron, Havalek, and Lendin. I'm honored to meet you, sirs."

Byron looked at the young medallioned apprentice, who steadily returned his gaze. "And we to meet you, Kaelin."

Master Grened's voice cut across the room imperiously as he walked toward his desk. "Take out your harps and teach the boy the last duet of form seven while I look over these reports." He glanced at the stunned trio as he took his seat. "Tonight!"

"Yes, sir," Byron replied and quickly removed his harp. Though the arpeggio race had impressed him, memorizing such an advanced duet would surely take several days for an apprentice, however talented he might be. The Master Harpist insisted on using demonstration for teaching, not only to improve ear training, but to commit to memory the material all Bards must have total command of. Byron put aside his misgivings and settled himself next to Kaelin.

"This duet has three sections," he told the attentive apprentice. "I'll demonstrate the first one for you, and when you've mastered it, perhaps Havalek and Lendin will take the other two." The others nodded agreeably, comfortably certain the lesson would never progress that far. Byron began to play the complicated section slowly.

Kaelin watched the Bard's hands intently. When he was finished, the apprentice looked up at him. "Would you demonstrate it once more, sir?"

"Certainly. How many measures would you like to learn first?"

"I ... would like to learn them all, sir."

Byron's brow lifted. "As you wish," he said, then obligingly played the section in its entirety once again. Kaelin silently fingered his own harp as he watched.

"May I try it?" At the Bard's surprised assent, the apprentice began to play, not as Byron had, slowly and carefully in order to teach, but quickly and fluently, drawing incredulous stares from the three Bards. Byron, glancing at Master Grened, thought he saw the corners of the Master's mouth tug in suppressed amusement. The Bard cleared his throat as Kaelin finished the section and looked up at him expectantly.

"That was ... impressive, Kaelin, and learned more quickly than I would have thought possible by anyone ... of any age. Let's play it as a duet now. You'll take the higher primo part that you just learned, and I'll take the lower secondo. We play it first in harmony, then we repeat the melodic line in unison octaves with the secondo part beginning two measures after the first in the style of a round. I'll set the tempo for the first part, then you can take the lead and change it for the round, if you wish. Don't hesitate to slow the tempo if you need to. Hearing the echo of what you're playing can be disconcerting."

Kaelin nodded and Byron began playing, matching Kaelin's previous tempo. The apprentice kept up easily, then took the lead for the round, increasing the tempo considerably. Byron had no time to notice the surprise of his colleagues as he quickly matched Kaelin's pace and played the rest of the round with the enjoyment of playing with a skilled musician.

When they finished, he laid his harp across his knee and gave the young apprentice an approving nod. "I believe we can consider that section thoroughly covered. It's a pleasure to play with you!"

"Thank you, sir. It's an honor to learn from such an excellent harpist as yourself."

Byron smiled, then turned to his alarmed friends. "He's all yours, Lendin."

Lendin frowned. Though an able form eight harpist, he was nowhere near as proficient as Byron, who had long since completed all ten forms of his primary instrument. This was the young Bard's first rotation, and his few lessons with the Master had not been pleasant experiences, though they had improved his playing. He was already embarrassed that the Master hadn't even remembered his name; he certainly had no desire to be further humiliated by this overly talented apprentice in front of his friends and the Master Harpist himself. Reluctantly, Lendin took his harp and began to play the second section slowly and carefully. Kaelin watched his fingers intently, silently fingering his own harp the second time through.

"I think I have it, sir." The apprentice played it by himself once, at the same tempo the Bard had used.

"Well done, Kaelin. The format of this section is the same as the first. I'll take the first lead, then you take it for the round."

Kaelin nodded and Lendin began, playing as fast as he accurately could. Kaelin played fluently with him, and Lendin's heart sank as they approached the round, knowing that if the apprentice increased the tempo at all, he would be forced to stop. As the round began, he glanced up in surprise. Kaelin kept the tempo exactly the same, although the Bard knew he could easily have played it much faster.

He finished the round in relief, then regarded Kaelin thoughtfully. "It isn't often one gets the chance to play with such a ... sensitive young musician."

"Thank you, sir. It isn't often an apprentice gets the chance to play with such fine teachers. I appreciate the opportunity."

There was no doubting the simple earnestness conveyed by the apprentice's words. Lendin chuckled softly. He was going to like this talented youngster, after all.

Kaelin learned the third section from Havalek, again keeping his tempo just within his teacher's capability, which was slightly faster than Lendin's. He thanked the Bard courteously, then turned at the Master's voice.

"Now play all three sections with me, boy, at *my* tempo. You've managed to impress my Bards. Impress *me,* and I just might allow you to begin form eight tomorrow."

The Master indicated for him to take the lead, and the two of them played fluently together, each of them sensitive to the other's part. Byron listened with growing delight. He had not heard such excellent harp playing for a long time. Master Grened did not play with or for his Bards like he used to. *Perhaps because we go out of our way to avoid his presence.*

When the music ended, the Master nodded. "Well enough, boy. You may begin form eight tomorrow."

At the apprentice's soft crow of delight, Byron spoke to Master Grened. "If you would like any help in teaching Kaelin that form, sir, I'd consider it a privilege."

"That would be welcome, Byron," the Master said, "if you don't mind coming here to do it."

"It would be my pleasure," the Bard replied sincerely, wondering what had happened to the world he lived in. Apparently it had been upended by an apprentice.

That night, Kaelin had similar thoughts as he lay down to sleep. Everything had changed, all of it for the better. Mornings were now spent making dyes and practicing survival skills, including learning how to make rudimentary tonics for various ailments from the trees and plants in the Master's grove. Kaelin had boiled the inner bark from an oak branch until it turned brown for the treatment of rashes and other skin ailments. He had learned how to use the inner bark of the wych elm for wounds and had made tea from willow bark to relieve pain.

Afternoons were spent on his harp, sometimes with Byron, most often with the Master. He had found Master Grened to be an excellent teacher, though his methods were strikingly different from the other Masters. Kaelin didn't mind the sudden outbursts or exasperated threats directed into his face from close range. It was a tremendous relief to play an instrument again, with a fine ongoing arpeggio competition with the Master in the evenings. Never knowing which key or mode the Master would choose, the apprentice feverishly practiced them all. So far, the Master had won every competition, handing Kaelin a short stack of copywork that was diminishing in size as the apprentice narrowed the margin between them.

True, he had not been allowed to play any music outside of the harp forms, but this did not disturb him. The undeniable progress he was making was proof the Master knew what he was doing. Every clear afternoon, Grened instructed Kaelin to take his harp and practice next to the stream in sight and hearing of the Master, who stayed comfortably warm in a chair near the window and emerged only when he felt advice was needed.

"Fluency," he had growled, in response to Kaelin's questioning look the first time the apprentice had been told to march into the wintry afternoon with his harp. "Something you could use more of, boy. I could wear out my vocal cords telling you to play with more fluency and likely accomplish little except the fraying of my temper. Or I could tell you to get out there and listen to the master of all fluency as it winds its way from the mountain to the sea and emulate it across the strings of your harp. Since you apparently have an affinity for the stream," he said dryly, "I choose to refer you to it, so take yourself out there and *listen*. If you don't come back playing that piece with greater fluency, I'll see if a good dunking will aid your understanding!"

"But ... wasn't I playing it up to tempo?"

"Tempo is mere speed, boy!" the Master said impatiently. "Fluency is flow, an entirely different thing. You certainly demonstrated an understanding of it on your flute last cycle ... how is it that you do not understand its meaning on your harp?" He stabbed a finger at the stream Kaelin was frowning at. "Don't just stare at the stream ... *study* it, boy! Its tempo changes constantly ... faster in the center where the current is strong, slower by the banks, capriciously changing over boulders and rocks. Yet would you stand there and accuse it of not maintaining a steady beat?"

Kaelin blinked and thoughtfully studied the stream. Words of the Master Flutist awoke in his memory.

I don't want to hear notes. I don't want to notice dynamics, articulations, or measure lines. Those things simply give the music a visible structure, but they are not the music.

"Music doesn't have measure lines ... or a time signature and tempo marking," the apprentice murmured.

"Precisely." The Master regarded the stream appraisingly. "But that's not to say that it doesn't have a *pulsation*. Sometimes, to be sure, that stays steady with the current, and when it does, so must we. When it moves along, faster or slower, we must move with it. But regardless of where it takes us, there is *always* flow, always a sense of forward motion."

When Kaelin wasn't using his free time to compose, or to read and learn the Master's many scrolls, he took a walk and sang to relieve the pressure of the music burning within him. He used his voice as he would have used his flute, diligently practicing the skills the Voice Master had given him. He often saw his kestrel, for the bird had followed him to Elegy and seemed to enjoy pelting him with questioning staccatos from the tree branches above. Kaelin became so accustomed to them that he pretended to understand the avian queries and whimsically answered.

"No, I don't know if I'll be going home before the Council hearing."

"Yes," he replied when the soft staccatos came again, "you can come along with me, wherever I go. We both know perfectly well that you will, anyhow."

Hesitant staccatos questioned him again.

"No, I have no idea what my Master will think of you. You'll just have to be patient and find out. All things come in the fullness of their own measure ... and that, my friend, is something you'd best get used to hearing." He sighed, knowing he would give anything to be able to hear those oft-repeated words again, and headed back to the house.

⌁ ﹖ ⌁

Two mornings later, Kaelin awoke to the sound of clattering pans and the smell of frying salt pork. He stretched luxuriously, enjoying to the full the rare privilege of sleeping an hour longer. He listened to the sounds of the Master Harpist of the Bardic Isles making breakfast and grinned. Beating him by a thin fraction of a beat the night before had been a sweet victory, especially when the Master had taken his loss in good spirits.

The Master Harpist pointedly cleared his throat, and Kaelin hurriedly rose to wash and pull on his robe before seating himself at the table. He looked hungrily at the steaming egg casserole with bits of salt pork and onions inside, cheese lightly lacing the crisp top. His first mouthful was a revelation. "Why, sir ... this is wonderful! You're an even better cook than Darryk!"

"Well, you needn't act so surprised, boy," the Master said dryly. "I've been cooking for myself for many more cycles than you and Darryk put together."

"So has Master Talan," Kaelin said with an impish grin. He gazed appreciatively at his fragrant forkful. "How did you get the eggs so light and fluffy?"

The Master snorted with amusement. "Certainly not by emulating Talan," he said dryly, "though if what I've heard is to be believed, he's recently acquired some new skills in that department." He narrowed his eyes at the apprentice, who immediately busied himself with his breakfast. "What did you do, you young scamp? Recite recipes in your sleep?"

"Just while I was cooking," Kaelin admitted. "After all, I didn't want to *forget* anything."

The thought of his non-culinary colleague being subjected to detailed descriptions of every breakfast, lunch, and dinner for three months brought a rusty chuckle from the Master. "As for the eggs," he said, "I spent a few cycles in Gaul, long ago. The people there know their way around a kitchen." He indicated the casserole. "That dish is more difficult than you might imagine, boy. You can do everything right and still have it fail."

"I'll bet it doesn't fail for *you*," Kaelin said stoutly.

"Hmph ... well, not anymore."

When Kaelin was finished eating, he pushed his plate aside and sighed. "You shouldn't have made such a spectacular breakfast," Kaelin said, looking regretfully at his empty plate. "You've given me a strong incentive to beat you again tonight!"

"And you've just given me a better one," the Master growled. "Such cockiness deserves a sound musical thrashing."

Kaelin laughed and rose to clear away the dishes. The Master inspected the crooks on Kaelin's harp. "Very ingenious. Perhaps, when Byron arrives, you can show us how they're made, then he can help teach the others. Might as well show them that fancy head-joint platform you told me about while you're at it.

Kaelin's face broke into a smile as he went to his pack and removed a small parcel. "I was hoping you'd like them, so I made a platform and a set of crooks for you during my free time at Master Rial's." He offered the parcel to the Master Harpist, who took it in surprise. "Thank you for teaching me."

The Master gave him a curt nod and opened the parcel. "Rosewood?" he inquired as he surveyed its contents.

"I did extra chores for Master Rial to pay for the wood. The Master Harpist of the Bardic Isles deserves the best."

Grened placed the opened parcel on his desk and abruptly changed the subject. "You've nearly finished learning about dyes now, and your lessons on woodlore will take only half the morning, with harp lessons during the other half. Practicing and your free time occupy most of the afternoon, leaving your evenings free. What would you like to do with them?"

"Whatever you wish me to, sir."

"That's no answer, boy."

Kaelin hesitated. "If I can choose ... music?"

The Master frowned. "Your harp lessons are insufficient?"

"Oh, no, sir," Kaelin hastened to explain. "It's just that ... well, the best music isn't a solo, is it? I'd like to play ensembles with as many musicians as possible while I still can." He hurried on before the Master could point out the short amount of time that was likely to be. "The new skills you've given me on my harp may be useless after the Council hearing. That's why I want to use them now. My memories are ... something no one can take."

The Master stared at him for a moment, then turned abruptly and walked to the hearth. He gave the spotlessly clean mantle a thorough inspection before speaking. "So, you'd have me take my Bards away from their work, would you?" he growled.

"Yes, sir."

"Have them underfoot the entire evening, I suppose?"

"Absolutely, sir."

"Force me to turn this pack of fools into tolerable ensembles, is that it?"

"Oh, that sounds *wonderful.*"

"Hmph!" The Master glared. "While they upset my schedule and eat me out of house and home?"

"I'll prepare all the meals ... and I'll do *all* your copy work." The apprentice held his breath.

The Master was silent for an uncomfortably long time. Kaelin jumped as the Master's hand suddenly smacked the stone mantle. "Then that, boy, is exactly what we'll do!"

Kaelin was struck speechless. Then he sprang forward with a glad cry and hugged the astounded Master, dancing him around the room in an excess of joy. "Oh, *thank you,* sir! I'll go get the last batch of mordant ready for the dye right away!" The apprentice dashed out of the house, leaving the Master to drop breathlessly into his chair.

Grened sat there a moment, staring at the open doorway, the cold air streaming in and making the fire pop in protest. Then an amazing transformation came over his face, beginning with a slight softening around his eyes ... a rippling across his cheeks ... an insistent tugging at the corners of his mouth.

The Master Bard of Elegy began to laugh.

"The mind may vacillate,
pulled by the dictates of conscience and convention.
Listen to the soul's essence, which will not lead you astray."
— from Annals of Bardic Lore

Chapter 20

To say that all but eight of the twenty-eight Bards of Elegy were dismayed when suddenly assigned to the Master's home on a rotating basis for the next two months would be an understatement of unprecedented proportions. No reason for the unexpected and thoroughly unwelcome order was given, but it was felt that Master Bergid's apprentice must have something to do with it, and his name was muttered darkly across the length of Elegy. The protestations of all three Bards assigned to Tryl were ignored. Nor was any heed paid to the five Bards who had rotated from Kestrel, who staunchly insisted that if "their apprentice" was the cause of such an order, no Bard had anything to worry about. Those not included in the first rotation waited anxiously for word from their less fortunate colleagues. The reports of constant music and tireless teaching that filtered back were listened to incredulously. Though no one knew the details of this remarkable transformation, credit was instantly laid at Kaelin's door, and the apprentice unknowingly became popular overnight with Bards he had not even met.

Kaelin, for his part, was delighted with the new arrangement. Morning woodlore and harp lessons were followed by lunch and his free time. Then he diligently practiced his harp until the Bards began to arrive for the ensembles, whereupon music and laughter filled the Master's home well into the evening. To Kaelin's relief, the Master didn't pass on his copy work to him or expect him to singlehandedly cook dinner for a passel of Bards every night. Indeed, the Master, despite his grumbling, was squarely in the thick of all the musical and culinary activity filling his home. And although Grened made an impressive effort to hide his enjoyment, he fooled no one. The Bards of Elegy were soon experiencing a closeness to their Master that they would not have believed possible a mere month ago. No one had mentioned the medallion or the charge of theft against the apprentice, and it is doubtful that any Bard of Elegy who spent a single evening at the Master's house gave it a thought. For the transformation of the Master Harpist, they would have unhesitatingly forgiven the theft of half the Bardic Isles.

Kaelin quickly became a favorite among them, not only for the difference in their Master, but for the difference in the music they produced with the apprentice in their midst.

"There's just ... something about him," Havalek mused one evening as he walked back to Tryl with his colleagues.

Lendin nodded. "Something that makes me want to play my best ... not to impress him or anyone else, but to connect with the music the way *he* does." He shrugged in perplexity. "There are no words to explain that. There's just ..."

"Something about him, "Byron finished.

Lendin nodded and the group walked on.

"One of my friends serving on Kestrel wrote to me last week," Bryon said. "He practically ordered me to hear Kaelin play his own music the moment I get the chance. He didn't specify why, and there's been no chance to hear Kaelin play his primary instrument, much less his own music. I've only worked with him on the harp forms and in ensembles, and while he's a young prodigy if ever there was one, I've heard nothing Master Grened couldn't better."

"Or you yourself, I'll wager," Havalek said loyally.

Byron smiled wryly. "For now, perhaps."

"Well, then," Lendin said, "we need to figure out a way to hear him play his own music."

"That won't be easy," Havalek said, shaking his head. "Not even the Bards who rotated here from Kestrel have heard him play yet. Said Kaelin was under his Master's restriction not to."

Byron's brows lifted. "Really? Then Master Bergid must have lifted the restriction after Kaelin played for the Council last cycle."

"Exactly, so we'd better make the most of our chance to hear him before Master Grened rotates us to a new territory."

A few days later, two new Bards arrived to exchange places with Senig and Lendin, who were lingering at the door. The Master's home was bustling with activity, filled with the sounds of harp crooks and flute platforms being constructed on three worktables. Kaelin had just finished playing the final duet of form eight with Byron when a comment was clearly heard from the doorway.

"I suppose everyone checks their packs before they leave?"

The comment, light with humor, fell like a dead weight in the center of the room. Conor, one of the new arrivals, looked around, suddenly aware that his words had not been well received. Byron saw Kaelin's knuckles turn white against his harp frame and a dark flush spread across his face. The others looked toward the Master, who continued his work as though unaware of the scene being enacted in the room. Clearly he was leaving the next move up to the apprentice.

No one spoke. Kaelin glanced at the Master, then set his harp down, took his pack down from its peg near the door and walked over to Conor. The apprentice bowed and held out his pack. "Perhaps, sir, it would be easier to check mine," he said respectfully. "I wouldn't want you to worry that your friends might leave without all of their possessions."

Conor glanced at Senig and Lendin, who crossed their arms

and gazed coldly back at him. "That won't be necessary," he said stiffly.

"As you wish, sir." Kaelin returned his pack to its peg. "My pack will be here," he said clearly, "available to any Bard who might wish to look through it." He turned to the discomfited Bard. "I've heard you're an excellent flutist, sir," he said with a smile. "I look forward to hearing you play, so I can improve my own."

Conor's face darkened. Who did this mere apprentice—this boy accused of *theft*—think he was, to shame him before his colleagues, not to mention Master Grened? "And what would be the point of that?" he asked derisively.

The Master's voice cut across the room, sparing Kaelin the need to reply. "It's a sorry day indeed when an apprentice of Kestrel has more courtesy than a Bard of Elegy." The Master locked eyes with Conor. "The boy may be graciously willing to forgive your rudeness, but *I* am not similarly inclined. Perhaps an evening of doing my copy work will improve your manners. You may begin with this." He indicated the stack on his desk.

"Yes, sir," Conor replied, and hastened to collect it.

"There's a table in the dye shed you can use ... and take your pack with you, since you're so concerned for the safety of its contents. When you've finished the copies, leave them there and return to Tryl. You have just forfeited your evenings here to Lendin."

"Yes, sir. I deeply apologize." The Bard turned, snagged his pack, and left. He did not glance at the apprentice.

Senig nodded approvingly at Kaelin and took his leave. Lendin, grinning broadly, rejoined the Bards, and the apprentice went to help Sten, who was behind the others in the construction of his harp crooks.

Byron approached the Master. "I'm afraid Kaelin might have just made an enemy for himself," he said quietly, "through no fault of his own."

The Master's expression was grave. "I doubt Conor's the first, nor is he likely to be the last. Not every Bard will take easily to the notion of an apprentice being accepted by Bards and Masters and allowed to skip over steps that they themselves had to take."

Byron nodded. "Considering Kaelin's talent, such steps would not have served him, as they did us."

"No," the Master agreed, "and most Bards will understand that. Some, however, will prefer to believe the stigma of the medallion."

"And what do *you* believe, sir?" Byron asked recklessly.

The Master's face tightened. "What I believe is irrelevant, as you well know. Bardic Law will be enforced regardless."

"I know, sir, and it's not my place to be critical of the Council, but ... I hate seeing such talent being lost to the Bardic Order." When the Master made no reply, words began to tumble from the Bard. "I have the utmost respect for the Law, but what it's going to do to him isn't *just*. Kaelin is no thief, nor, I think, could he successfully lie if he wanted to. Sometimes it's hard to remember that he's still just a boy of thirteen, even if he has talent the likes of which I've never seen before."

"The boy plays well enough," Grened acknowledged.

Byron suppressed a smile, knowing that the pronouncement of "well enough" from the Master Harpist was a standing ovation from anyone else. "Exactly, sir, and taking everything from him permanently will devastate him." He regarded Kaelin thoughtfully. "Maybe I can't protect him from the Law," he murmured, "or from the Conors of this world, but there's one thing I *can* give him before I leave for my new assignment at the end of the week." He turned to the Master, who was looking at him in surprise. "I find this apprentice more worthy of friendship than a Bard I've recently observed. Would it displease you if I offered him mine?"

The Master frowned and tapped his quill against the table. He had been outraged at Darryk's friendship with Kaelin over a cycle ago, feeling that it destroyed the proper respect that should be shown to one of higher rank. His brow had lifted when he heard that Brent had done the same thing on Eyrie, and decided that Talan's soft spot for youngsters had overruled his common sense. Then Drin had befriended the boy on Lyra, and Grened had been shocked at the conservative Voice Master accepting such a thing. Yet, as the Master Harpist watched Kaelin respectfully help Sten, he could not find it in himself to deny the boy what Byron was offering. Certainly, this apprentice had no opportunity to have friends of his own age or rank, and the Bards who had offered their friendship would soon be stripped away from him for a full cycle. And longer than that if Kaelin could not bring himself to be around Bardic instruments he was forbidden to play.

"It does not displease me," the Master said, somewhat surprised at his own words, "and I will not forbid it. However," he added sternly, "if you do so, you will not be allowed to leave for your newly assigned territory for another three weeks. You will stay right here and coach the boy through harp form nine. Perhaps that will teach you not to be so quick to break with tradition." He abruptly turned his attention back to his work.

Byron stood looking at the Master for a moment, quite aware that Kaelin had three more weeks left of his stay here. "It will be a pleasure, sir," he said quietly.

The Master made no sign that he had heard. He did not watch Byron walk over to Kaelin, didn't listen to what the Bard said to the apprentice, pretended not to notice the gasps that came from the three worktables. But at the silence that followed, the Master glanced up and found the apprentice regarding him steadily. Byron's arm was extended but had not been taken. Grened gave the apprentice a barely perceptible nod and was rewarded by the smile the boy flashed him as he clasped Byron's arm and called him by name.

Two days later, near the end of a productive evening of ensemble rehearsals, the Master's voice abruptly cut across the room.

"Boy!"

"Yes, sir?" came the startled reply.

"Bring me your flute."

Kaelin was stunned. "My ... flute?"

"Surely you recall what a flute is."

"Yes, sir!" Kaelin left the ensemble he had been playing in and took his flute down from its peg for the first time since arriving on Elegy. His hands trembled slightly as he attached the headjoint. He held it briefly to himself, then turned and walked across the silent room to give it to the Master.

Grened's brows lifted as he took it. "Rosewood again, I see. Fortunate that it went to a boy who knew what to do with wood-working tools." The Master briefly inspected it, then handed the gleaming instrument back to him. "Play it for us. Something of your own ... the music of a memory, perhaps. As I recall, you do that well enough."

"Do you wish me to set a block first, sir?"

"No." The Master glanced at his Bards, who were glancing at each other in confusion. "Those of you with tools or instruments in your hands had best put them down," he advised, then leaned back in his chair.

Kaelin lifted the flute he hadn't touched in over two months. As though the very air surrounding him had brought it, music filled his mind, music he had played once before. Enticing music that had lifted him into the air above Master Talan's home the night the medallion had been placed around his neck. Unable to resist, Kaelin gave in to the sudden, intense desire to take his flute and fly with it. So, fly he did, and his listeners flew with him.

The music spiraled them upward in a flurry of notes, as if the wind itself had been waiting for the chance to reunite with the only one who could hear its music. Within moments they were hovering far above the Master's home. Below them the seaport of Tryl gleamed in the rays of the setting sun. To the east the coast of Lyra was clearly visible, but Kaelin had eyes only for the north, where the faint outline of Kestrel could be seen. The air around him shimmered with colorful paths of music flowing in all directions. Behind him he felt the intense pull of Bardic Mountain, as strong as if he were standing on the Council Grounds. Refusing the urge to turn toward it, he filled his mind with the three words his Master had never spoken, the words he had heard only in his mind. The path heading toward Kestrel brightened, the notes dancing in the air with capricious energy. The music was so exhilarating, his own need so overwhelming, that this time he could not deny its expression. His fingers flew across the keys, eagerly playing what he heard, his intoxicated senses bereft of everything except the need to go where he longed to be.

And then they were flying, straight and true to the north, the waves below skimming by, the two Bardic ships plying the waters below looking like the playthings of a child. Ahead, the seaport of Kyet beckoned, but Kaelin headed straight for the spacious home sitting in lofty solitude on the hill to the north of it. His Master's home ... his home, though his heart ached at the thought that he might never enter it again.

He hovered over it, suddenly uncertain of what he had done. Below them the front door opened. Kaelin caught his breath as his Master emerged and stood there for a long moment, shielding his eyes from the lowering sun. He peered down the path that led to Kyet, a look of hopeful expectation on his face. Kaelin was horrified.

He knows! Somehow he knows I'm here, but he can't see me.

The Master's shoulders slumped slightly as he walked slowly back into his house. With an inner cry of pain, Kaelin wrenched his eyes away and forced himself to leave. His mind berated him as they sped with the wind back to the Master Harpist's home.

You knew it was wrong, and you did it anyway just to see him again. You didn't think of what it might do to him to feel your presence so strongly, yet not be able to see you!

The flutist opened his eyes to find his audience in varying degrees of shock. More exhausted than he had been since playing for the Council, Kaelin filled his mind with the memory of a butterfly-filled meadow on Lyra and played the gentle strains of its music. The peaceful scene of swaying grasses and glistening wings quickly soothed the overstrained senses of everyone in the room ... except for the young performer, whose tears trickled slowly down his cheeks. He brought the brief piece to a close, then lowered his flute and hastily brushed away his tears. The Bards stirred, then erupted in a confusion of excited voices. Byron stood staring at the apprentice, his mouth partially open.

Kaelin did his best to answer the questions the Bards fired his way until the Master Harpist cleared his throat and looked pointedly at the door. The Bards quickly rose, then gathered their things and left, still talking. Kaelin saw them out and closed the door in relief, then took a deep breath and turned to face the Master. Byron had not moved from where he stood.

Grened spoke dryly. "Kind of you to use a meadow to restore us to our senses."

"I'm truly sorry, sir. I should have only played that."

The Master gave a brief nod of agreement. "My Bards believe they saw a memory of Bergid's home, and you did well not to correct their misconception. But that was no memory, was it, boy? Nor, I think, was it a composition of your own."

"No, sir."

"What was it, then?"

Kaelin's brow creased. "I'm not sure. I've only heard that music once before. The notes weren't quite the same, but they belonged together ... like I was hearing a different section of the same piece. And, instead of just lifting me up, the way playing a memory does, this music makes me feel like I *am* the air ... like I can go wherever I want. I didn't try to travel with it when it happened before because it felt like spying." He lowered his head. "This time I didn't think. I just went because I wanted so badly to see him. But it was wrong to give him the hope that I was there when he couldn't see me." He hesitated, then knelt when the Master remained silent.

"I deeply apologize for misusing my gift, sir, and I'll accept your punishment for it." A shiver went through him. The strap was gone, but his belt or the Master's own was readily available. Whatever the punishment, however, Kaelin knew it wasn't the worst thing the Master could do. "I have no right to ask, but please, sir ... please don't take my flute away from me, too. Even if you won't allow me to use it, just knowing it's there, that the possibility of playing it again still exists—"

Still the Master said nothing. Kaelin stood and forced himself to loosen his grip on his flute. He laid it gently down on the Master's desk, knowing he might never touch it again, then fumbled to untie his cord, the traitorous fingers that had just released his flute into the Master's keeping suddenly feeling like they belonged to someone else. Anger flared. Was it so terrible a thing to have done, to have flown with the music of the wind for a brief glimpse of his Master, that he must be beaten for it and lose his flute before the Council took it away from him for a crime he hadn't committed?

The Master abruptly shook his head. "If you had intended to spy on your Master," he said gruffly, "you would hardly have taken a throng of witnesses with you. Nor, I think, has Bergid anything worse to complain of than disappointment. You neither intended nor did any harm to him or to us, so you did not break your vow. You therefore deserve no further punishment than what seeing the look on your Master's face undoubtedly dealt you. And," he added, "if you did deserve it, it would be nothing more dire than a stack of my copy work."

Kaelin let out a breath of relief, not daring to glance at his flute, still in jeopardy on the Master's desk.

"At first," Grened continued, "I kept your instruments from you because I felt you did not deserve to use them. More recently, I thought that it would be easier for you to face the Council if you hadn't played your instruments for some time beforehand, especially your flute. I have revised that opinion." He picked up Kaelin's flute and handed it to him. "You may keep your flute and continue to play it for us after the evening ensembles."

Kaelin's hands trembled slightly as he received his flute.

"See to it, though, that you take better care of how you use your gift," the Master warned. "This time, perhaps, it was inadvertent and therefore excusable. If you do so again, it will not be. No one should fear having their privacy invaded by one who can apparently travel the wind itself."

"I'll be very careful, sir," came the chastened reply. Kaelin bowed his thanks and went to put away his flute.

The Master picked up his quill, then, feeling eyes on him, he glanced up to see Byron regarding him with the same respect Kaelin had given to Marek. The Master cleared his throat.

"Since you'll be staying with us for the next three weeks, you can go over that harp duet with the boy again before you get settled into my second guest room. He rushed the recapitulation, and I expect that to be corrected before you retire for the night. You can fetch your things in the morning."

"I'll do my best to cure him of the impatience of youth, Master Grened," the Bard promised, his voice light with humor.

Kaelin, hanging his flute next to his pack, paused for a moment at the welcome news that Byron would be staying with them, then turned and moved eagerly toward his harp.

Late that night, the Master sat alone before the fire, his mind once again fixed on the youngster in his guest room. The boy's gift was growing, fueled today by his intense desire to see his Master. Its power to take him and a whole roomful of listeners all the way to Kestrel was nothing short of incredible. This was not, however, the only thing occupying the Master Harpist's thoughts.

He knew he had done something he shouldn't have, something he believed I would punish him severely for. He could have easily lied and told me it was just a memory, or that he was unable to stop what happened. Instead, he told me the truth, accepted the severe punishment he thought I would give him and only begged me not to take his flute away as well. This boy would not have stolen Talan's tuning fork ... and if he had, would not have lied about it. The Master frowned, considering.

He wouldn't have risked losing everything for a tuning fork he doesn't need and could never risk anyone ever seeing. His flute alone is far more valuable to him. And if there's one thing that boy values even more than his flute, it's his Master.

Grened sighed and rose to bank the fire and retire for the night. On the way to his room, he passed by his desk and paused, looking at a missive from Talan he had recently received and inexplicably delayed answering. Coming to a sudden decision, he sat at his desk, picked up a quill, and wrote a lengthy reply.

⚬ ⸲ ⚬

Almost three weeks later, the Master handed Byron a list of needed supplies and enough coin to purchase them from the marketplace. Then he seated himself at his desk. The apprentice, surprised he hadn't been the one sent, continued working with alternating rhythms on a complicated run from harp form ten.

A short while later, Kaelin noticed that Master Grened appeared to be having a difficult time concentrating on his work. He picked up his quill, then stared into space for several moments before putting it back down, unused. After repeating this unusual behavior a half dozen times, he abruptly spoke.

"Come here, boy."

"Yes, sir." Kaelin put aside his harp and rose to obey.

"You've done well enough making dyes," the Master said, "so I've decided to give you my permission to come to the grove in the future whenever you need to replenish your supplies. Take only what you need, mind you, and use it well."

Kaelin's eyes widened. "Thank you, sir!"

Master Grened cleared his throat. "It's none of my business what you decide to do with yourself should things go badly for you at the Council hearing, boy, but if you stay on Elegy, your welfare becomes my business." His expression turned stern. "I allow no homeless vagrants who can't support themselves to remain so on my island, and I'll make no exception for you. Therefore, you may build a shelter near here until you have the means to board in Tryl. The ability to make top quality dyes will make any merchant overlook your lack of cycles, though if they insist on a reference, you may refer them to me. A free sample or two and I expect you'll be up to your eyeballs in orders." He picked up his quill.

Kaelin was too stunned for a moment to reply. "You would let me sell your dyes?"

The Master slapped the luckless quill back onto the table. "Certainly not! My dyes are not to be peddled, boy! But what you do with your *own* dyes is your own business."

"Yes, sir."

"I use my dye shed in the mornings," Grened continued nonchalantly, "and if someone were to make use of it at other times, I might not even be aware of it. Especially," he added in a steely voice, "if he took care to keep my tools spotless and where they belong."

Kaelin could scarcely credit his ears. Had this Master, who had thought him a thief and liar upon his arrival, just given him a means of supporting himself after everything else had been stripped from him? "Sir, I—"

The Master frowned and Kaelin clamped his mouth shut.

Grened took up his quill and made a show of rifling through

his paperwork. When the apprentice made no move to return to his practicing, he glanced up. "Well, what is it, boy?"

"I've been meaning to ask you if..." Kaelin began uncertainly. "Well, the first month of spring is nearly over..."

The Master came around from behind his desk and peered through the window as though to check for himself. "No doubt about it, boy."

"I was just wondering if you knew when the Council hearing will be."

Master Grened leaned back against the edge of his desk and leisurely folded his arms. "Well, it seems to have been an unusually busy cycle," he said. "When Talan finally got around to scheduling it for the beginning of autumn, Marek declared that only the end of autumn would do. Then Rial sent word that he couldn't possibly join us until mid-winter, and Bergid made it crystal clear that *any* winter month was a ridiculous suggestion, considering his advanced age." The Master snorted derisively. "An overused excuse of your Master's, at best. Why, he's barely a month older than I am! And right after this absurdity, Talan declared the first month of spring to be his choice for dishing out what he called 'pre-testing' on instrument repair, even though this is *not* a testing cycle. A decision which I'm sure left all the Bards of Eyrie speechless with joy," he added dryly.

Kaelin was stunned. "They did all that ... for me?"

Master Grened shrugged as though there was no telling what had possessed his colleagues to act so foolishly. "Fortunately, each Master is only allowed to delay a session once, so there will be no more unreasonable delays," he said with a satisfied nod.

"Then it will be early next week," Kaelin said dully.

"Have you lost your wits, boy?" the Master demanded. "After catering to the whims of an apprentice for an entire *season*, with hordes of Bards invading my house every evening, what makes you think I have any time next week for such a journey?" He stabbed a finger at the few papers on his desk. "Why, it will take me a month just to catch up on all these reports! Not to mention that the foolish behavior of my colleagues has forced all Council business to be handled by correspondence for nearly a *cycle,* and who is in charge of such correspondence?" he demanded. "*I* am … as if being Master of the largest island in the Bardic Isles doesn't give me enough paperwork to deal with!" He glared as though Kaelin were personally to blame for this. "So, after all these irresponsible delays, I made it clear that they can all wait six *more* weeks until the Spring Council! They have some nerve, the lot of them, and I've no intention of putting up with such—"

The Master's tirade was arrested by a flash of amber joy and a fierce hug. The Master stood motionless for a stunned moment, then he put his arms around the apprentice in an awkward embrace, only the second one Grened had ever received and the first he had ever returned.

"Go to your Master, boy," he said gently. "He'll be glad to see you. And I'll—" The Master Harpist stiffened, thoroughly scandalized at what had almost slipped through his vocal cords.

The arms encircling him tightened. "I'll miss you, too, sir."

A few days later, the Captain of the *Seastar,* bound for the island of Kestrel, shook his head as he approached the motionless youngster gripping the rail of his ship. "Pushin' against its prow won't move my ship any faster, young apprentice."

"No, sir, I don't suppose it will," Kaelin said ruefully. He did not turn to face him, nor did he release his grip.

"You'd best be gettin' yerself a meal, lad. We'll not be sightin' Kestrel for several more hours with this headwind."

A few minutes later, the Captain glanced toward the prow and saw the motionless figure still at his post, still gripping the rail as though he might inexplicably fall into the sea if he let go. Since early dawn the boy had stood there, heedless of time, the need to eat or drink, or the cold salt spray that pelted his face. The Captain shook his head, wondering if the rumors he'd heard were true about the medallioned apprentice traveling the Bardic Isles being Master Bergid's own apprentice. *Masters takin' apprentices ... what's the world comin' to?* he wondered.

Late that afternoon, the ship entered the bay of Kyet and pulled up alongside one of the docks. The crew began to lower the gangplank, one young passenger hovering impatiently as they worked. The moment it was in place, the boy took off across it, his packs bouncing against his back. A short way down the dock, the crazed youngster came to an abrupt halt before an old man in a white robe. All activity on the dock ceased as the Master Bard of Kestrel opened his arms, and the two embraced as though they would never release each other again.

Above them a wild kestrel hovered for a moment, then issued an ecstatic burst of staccatos and flew north. Kaelin smiled and buried his face deeper between the folds of the white robe.

He was home.

Da Capo al Coda

Back to the Beginning

Chapter 21

Kaelin and his Master were nearly inseparable during the six weeks preceding the Council hearing. Indeed, Master Grened would have been surprised and more than a little touched to have known how often his name was silently blessed for giving it to them. They spent the first few days at the Master's home in Kyet, and only once was the harmony between them briefly disturbed.

In spite of the season's chill wind, both still preferred the outdoors, and they lost no time building a bonfire outside the Master's home. There they talked together far into the night. Kaelin related the story of his travels, and the Master listened intently, asking few questions but perceiving far more than his apprentice said in words. *Marek was right. He has indeed grown and can fly on his own. I sent away a boy and am getting back a young man.* The thought was unsettling. *I'm proud of who he's become, but I'll miss the boy ... miss him sorely.*

He noticed that Kaelin didn't speak of his medallion, nor of the events which surrounded it. Nor did it escape Bergid's notice that, unlike the other three islands, Kaelin's account of his trip to Elegy hadn't begun with his arrival there. The Master frowned but did not interrupt Kaelin's enthusiastic description of the music ensembles the Master had hosted.

"It was wonderful playing in ensembles everywhere I went! Almost," he added with an impish look, "as much fun as playing with Master Marek's nightingales."

Bergid's white brows bristled with mock indignation. "Master Marek's nightingales, indeed! I think I've heard quite enough of these feathered Masters of yours. Are you trying to tell me I'm in danger of being replaced?"

"Well, not just yet..." the apprentice said consideringly, then laughed at his Master's exaggerated sigh of relief. "I was glad to hear they're all right now," he continued without thinking. "I was worried about them."

The Master's brow lifted. "How did you hear that? You've just come from Elegy, not Zephyr."

Kaelin glanced up in dismay. "Well, I..." His eyes pleaded with the Master, whose expression did not change. "It doesn't really matter, does it?"

"Perhaps you should let me decide that."

Kaelin's hopeful expression faded at his Master's inflexible tone. "At least I won't have to worry about the Council hearing any longer," he moaned. "Master Marek will kill me first."

"Marek?" the Master exclaimed. "Marek went to Elegy?"

Kaelin nodded miserably.

The Master frowned. "When?" Suspicion threaded its way through his voice like the rumble of distant thunder.

"A week after I did."

Lightning kindled deep in the Master's narrowed eyes.

"Please don't be angry with Master Marek!" Kaelin said in alarm. "It was *my* fault. I couldn't let him tell you!"

"Tell me what?" When his apprentice suddenly found the ground a fascinating study, Bergid remained silent until the amber eyes lifted reluctantly to his. "Marek told me nothing of his little side trip," the Master said, his even voice belying the storm clouds gathering in his eyes. "I strongly advise *you* to leave nothing out."

The apprentice hesitantly began to relate the events of that day, beginning with his accident and subsequent punishment.

Bergid's jaw clenched and one of his bristling brows lifted dangerously. Kaelin nervously continued with Master Marek's arrival and his command at the stream to show him his back. At this, the other bristling brow lifted to match the first, the apprentice's voice faltered, and the Master's wrath erupted.

"Marek left you there? He saw your welted back with his own eyes and *left* you there? Without so much as a word to me?" Incensed, the Master rose to his feet as though to wreak immediate vengeance on the entire island of Zephyr.

"But sir, I haven't finished—"

"Before we next meet," the Master growled, glaring in the direction of Zephyr, "Marek had best learn to fly like those feathered friends of his, for that's the only way he'll escape me!"

"Master, if you'd only—"

"And Grened..."

Kaelin's mouth went dry. After the tirade against Marek, he would have expected the Master Harpist's name to have thundered over the hill and down into Kyet, but it was spoken quietly, with a calmness far more frightening.

For a long moment Bergid stood completely still. Kaelin dared not speak, for his Master's expression as he stared toward Elegy was unyielding ... yet tinged with grief, as though something precious had vanished at the utterance of Grened's name that would not easily be retrieved.

"To think that I ever gave that man my respect and my friendship." The Master's quietly spoken words filled the listening apprentice with dread. "I'll charge him with abuse ... and if the Council won't act on it," he added in a hard voice, "I will."

Kaelin summoned every bit of courage he had. "Sir, please—"

"And you!" the Master whirled suddenly in his direction. "Why on earth did you stay there? Just because Marek lacked the sense to take you with him doesn't mean you couldn't have left on your own. Your robe gives you free passage on any ship, and you well know it!"

"Master, you've just demonstrated—" He broke off as his Master began pacing angrily before the fire, his robe swishing violently with every turn.

"I can't *believe* two Masters would act so ... never in all my cycles have I seen such ... such..." Clearly there was no adjective worthy of describing such unmasterly behavior. Giving up the search, he glared at his apprentice. "Just how long did you plan on keeping this from me?" he demanded.

Kaelin, totally frustrated, glared back. "Until you grew old enough to *deal* with it, sir!"

The two stared at each other, the Master in stunned silence, the apprentice in open-mouthed horror. Then the Master's mouth twitched, and he began to chuckle. Catching a disapproving frown from his apprentice, he erupted in laughter, the hillside echoing with the sounds of his mirth.

"I see nothing funny about insolence to a Master," Kaelin said stiffly, causing a further eruption. The moment it ended, the apprentice apologized. "How could I have spoken like that to you? Please forgive me."

Bergid shook his head. "There's nothing to forgive, for I'm the one who provoked it, and you could not have stopped me otherwise. Do not, however, expect me to forgive Marek just yet," he said darkly. "I intend to have a few choice words with my young colleague first. As for Grened..." The Master's face looked like chiseled stone in the firelight. "Grened I will never forgive. Now," he said sternly, "let's hear the rest of this sordid tale, beginning with Marek's command to show him your back."

Kaelin nodded in wary relief and related the rest of his conversation with Master Marek.

The remainder of Bergid's wrath with the Master Flutist vanished as he listened, perceiving that his earlier thoughts about Kaelin's growth had fallen short of the mark. *I would have been persuaded myself. Kaelin was quite right in knowing what I would have done if he had returned to me with fresh welts across his back.* Anger surged again, his willingness to forgive Marek not extending a single league toward Elegy.

Kaelin looked up anxiously. "So, there's no need to be angry with Master Marek, is there? He only accepted my reason for refusing to leave with him and allowed me to stay, as I wished."

The Master laid a reassuring hand on his shoulder. "Marek did nothing I would not have done in his place," he said, "though I doubt I'll feel any pressing need to inform him of it. Stewing a little will be good for his soul."

"And ... Master Grened?" the apprentice asked hopefully.

The silence that overtook the hillside this time was a long one. "That is asking much of me, Kaelin," the Master finally said. "More, perhaps, than I can give."

"But he wasn't himself, sir!"

Bergid frowned. "Who was he, then?"

"He was ... well, someone who's been affected by the mountain," Kaelin said, wondering how to explain, then abandoned the attempt at his Master's skeptical expression. "He more than made up for it, though ... truly! He taught me how to make his dyes and instructed me through all the rest of the harp forms. He even started doing ensembles for me. And he could have taken away my flute for misusing my gift, but he didn't."

Bergid's brow lifted. "When did you misuse your gift?"

Kaelin flushed. "The first time he let me use my flute to play for the Bards. I remember wishing I could take my flute and fly away with it, and then I heard music coming from nowhere."

"From nowhere? What were you looking at?"

"I'd closed my eyes and wasn't looking at anything. The notes were unpredictable, with constantly changing rhythms. I started to play it, and it took me up into the air. I could still see what was below me, but the air itself looked like a kaleidoscope of colored paths—of music!—that swirled all around me and headed in different directions. I played one of them, even though I knew I shouldn't, and then I was flying."

"Flying? To where?" the Master asked in astonishment.

The apprentice lowered his eyes. "To where I wanted to be."

Only the snapping of the fire filled the clearing. "So," the Master quietly said, "it wasn't just wishful thinking on my part, then, the day I was suddenly convinced you were nearby. You *were* here. You and Grened ... and a roomful of Bards?"

Shame filled the apprentice's face. "I'm sorry, sir. My gift shouldn't be used to spy on anyone, no matter how much I want to see them. As soon as I saw you come outside and realized you knew I was there but couldn't see me, I went straight back and apologized to Master Grened."

"I can understand why it happened," Bergid said gently, "if not how." His face tightened. "And what did Grened say? He didn't take your flute ... did he punish you in any other way?"

"No, he said that if I'd intended to spy, I wouldn't have taken a throng of witnesses with me, and that you and my listeners had come to no harm from it, so I hadn't broken my vow. Then he gave me back my flute and told me I could continue to play it." He looked at his Master's closed expression. "And later, he gave me six weeks to spend with you," Kaelin added softly. "I'd have taken any number of beatings in exchange for that."

Bergid frowned. "I could forgive him hurting me, but regardless of what he did afterwards, for him to have hurt you ... have *you* forgiven him?"

"Yes, sir. I told him so."

The Master's eyes widened, imagining Grened's reaction to being forgiven by a medallioned apprentice. "When you left for Kestrel?"

"I told him the day Master Marek visited me."

"You forgave him the same day he..." The Master's voice failed him.

"I didn't do it for his sake. I did it for my own ... and for yours."

The Master Bard of Kestrel stood silent. The lesson he had struggled to learn himself, then given to Marek so many cycles ago, had come full circle. *I should not have needed the reminder.* Bergid shook himself from his reverie.

"Very well, Kaelin," he said gently. "If you can forgive him for my sake, I can do no less than forgive him for yours." The bands that had tightened around him at the news of his friend's perfidy loosened and dissolved at the look of relief and respect that Kaelin gave him. "Thanks to you, I won't be needing to storm the high seas again."

"Again?" Kaelin searched the Master's face.

"Yes, well ... I was not exactly thrilled with the message Talan finally got around to sending me last summer, and I didn't have an impertinent apprentice handy to cool me off, so," the blue eyes glinted, "I paid a little visit to Eyrie."

Kaelin looked at him in fresh alarm. "But it wasn't Master—"

Bergid held up his hands. "Talan proved quite capable of coping with me all on his own." He paused as Kaelin breathed a sigh of relief. "I spent many days there trying to discover the truth, and though I am convinced of it, I could find no proof." He looked deeply in Kaelin's eyes. "I told you that your place beside me would always be here, waiting. Whatever happens at the Council hearing, whatever I may have to do there, I will find a way to keep my word." Kaelin's eyes filled with tears, and the Master pulled him close. "Heaven knows you've kept yours."

Kaelin let his tears fall. Though he was far from Lyra, the words of the Voice Master still echoed in his mind with perfect clarity.

No Master can set the Law aside, for any reason whatsoever, and remain a Master of the Bardic Isles.

His Master would have no choice.

Two days later, they set out early for Rassek's isolated farm holding, stopping only to order a new pair of boots and a belt for Kaelin and get him measured for new clothes. After making arrangements for having their purchases delivered to the Master's home, they emerged into the bright sunlight, Bergid shaking his head at how much taller his apprentice had grown since the previous spring. Then they headed east, following the coast. Rassek, spotting them from the fields of his holding, waved and began walking toward them. Sean, Kaelin's bonded younger brother, came running to meet them from the barn, his face glowing as he threw himself at Kaelin and hugged him fiercely.

"Ow! You're getting too big to be hugging me *that* hard," the apprentice complained with a laugh. "Aren't you ten whole cycles now?" he teased.

"I turned eleven last autumn and you know it!" Sean said indignantly without releasing him. "I haven't seen you for a whole *cycle,* so you can just stand there and take a whole cycle's worth of hugs at once!" When at last he let Kaelin go, he glanced at the Master and flushed. "Master Bergid. Welcome to our holding, sir!" he said with a hurried bow. "Forgive me for not greeting you first."

The Master chuckled. "You needn't apologize for missing your brother, nor need you greet me with such formality, lad."

Sean gave him a rueful grin. "Father's been working on my manners."

"Good to see you, my friend," said the Holder as he strode up to meet them. "I have indeed been working on my son's manners, and he needs all the practice he can get, so I'll thank you not to sabotage my efforts, Bergid. And it's good to see you as well, Kaelin. Your Master hasn't been the same without you around to keep him halfway human." He turned to his son. "Now *that's* how it's done," he said sternly. "Greetings first, hugs and barbs afterwards. And, speaking of hugs," he added with an indignant glance at Kaelin, "where's mine?"

"Why, Rassek," the Master exclaimed, "I thought you'd never ask!" He gave the astounded Holder a hearty hug, then stood back and joined in with the boys' laughter as Rassek glared at him.

They all headed to the house, talking about everything except the medallion. Sean, after a quick glance at it, kept his gaze studiously averted. The two men took their seats by the fire. Sean, following his father's pointed glance toward the kitchen, hurried to bring their guests mugs of cider and a platter of tarts.

After the refreshments, Kaelin removed his robe, set it on top of his pack, and the boys walked purposefully toward the door. The Holder cleared his throat and his son froze, then turned toward the Master and bowed.

"Master Bergid. Thank you, sir, for coming today and bringing Kaelin with you."

The Master smiled. "My pleasure, Sean. I'll see you later this afternoon ... unless your father refuses to invite us to dinner."

Sean grinned. "Then please accept *my* invitation, Master Bergid. It's sure to taste much better with your company."

"Thank you. I gladly accept your invitation."

Sean joined Kaelin, and the two boys were soon running along the path that led to the sea.

Bergid chuckled. "You're certainly on a mission to instill formal manners into your son," he remarked.

"Hmph! If I were successful, he wouldn't have just insulted my cooking."

The Master laughed. "He needn't be so formally correct with us, surely."

The Holder frowned. "No, but becoming too used to such familiarity won't do him any favors when he meets other members of the Bardic Order. He was raised without any knowledge of the niceties of society and differences in rank, and he certainly isn't going to learn it by observing the two of us. And learn it he must before he comes of age, or he's going to receive a nasty shock the first time he meets someone who will not let his friendly treatment of all people as equals pass."

"I quite agree with Sean's view that all Bardians are equals."

"Says the Master Bard whom nobody treats as an equal ... except his four colleagues and one crusty, incorrigible Holder."

"You're my friend," Bergid said quietly.

"Yes ... because *you* offered it," Rassek raised a hand at Bergid's startled expression. "Don't misunderstand me. Your friendship means the world to me ... indeed, you offered it when no one else would have. But it was yours to offer me, not mine to offer you. How many other Bards or Masters would offer their friendship to a Holder? How many Bards and Masters even *have* friends outside the Bardic Order?"

Bergid frowned.

"Exactly. And how many of your members have friends that are of higher rank than they themselves are? I'd imagine none of them, because that, too, is frowned upon, isn't it?"

"I'll admit I know of no others except Kaelin. He has four of them, all Bards, three ranks above his own."

The Holder's eyes widened. "Does he, now? Good for him! Perhaps there's hope, then, after all."

The Master's frown deepened. "Hope?"

"That the younger generation of the Bardic Order can see past the unwritten barriers that exist between their Order and the Guilds, and within each, the barriers imposed by rank."

"Did we not leave such things behind us when we fled Eire?"

"We hoped to," the Holder replied, looking keenly at his friend. "But did we succeed? I don't think so, though certainly our society is nowhere near as rigid as theirs was and likely still is. I would hate to see it become so, for rigid structures fall the hardest. Your apprentice gives me hope, and yet your Order is about to expel him for no just reason, isn't it?"

The Master's face darkened.

"You haven't mentioned the matter to me, but word of a young medallioned Bardic apprentice traveling the Isles this past cycle spread quickly to Kyet, as did the news that Master Talan had charged him with theft. So, I knew about the medallion long before I saw it today. I didn't tell Sean ... he learned it from the gossip of schoolboys. He came home so furious that half the woodpile was butchered before I came in from the fields."

"I'm sorry I couldn't tell you myself."

Rassek shrugged. "I would hardly expect you to discuss Council matters with me or anyone outside your Order, but *I* am under no such stricture, so will freely speak my mind. For I know perfectly well that Kaelin couldn't commit a theft and *lie* about it if he wanted to! That boy's face is as easy to read as Sean's. Not a particle of guile in either of them." He pushed himself to his feet and began to pace restlessly before the fire. "But that won't matter to the Masters, will it? The rigidity of Bardic Law will condemn him anyhow, and your Order will lose the best thing that's happened to it since Master Cyral discovered this land. And all because of what? An act of spiteful jealousy against an unusually talented apprentice ... for it's a Bard who did this, isn't it?"

The Master gave a terse nod. "There have been a few other unscrupulous members of our Order in the past," he admitted, "but none of them Bards, and they've always been swiftly caught and brought to justice."

"Well," Rassek said with raised brows, "judging from Kaelin's medallion, this Bard has *not* been caught ... and it's been ten months. He's gotten clean away with it! Which means he may have the confidence to thieve again or do something even worse."

The Master's jaw tightened.

"Everyone knows this was not a theft committed in the marketplace of Skye," Rassek went on. "It happened in the home of

Master Talan and was thus either committed by an underaged apprentice or by a Bard of Eyrie. If the Council exonerates Kaelin, I'm not the only one who's going to be wondering which of their Bards is a lying thief that got away with framing an innocent apprentice for a crime he himself committed. Not knowing which Bards were there that night, every Bard currently serving their rotation on Elegy will be viewed with suspicion. And, if the guilty one isn't caught before the next rotation two cycles from now, which island will he travel to next to arbitrate our disagreements ... not to mention collect our tithes?"

Bergid's eyes flashed dangerously and Rassek raised a placating hand. "I'm not for a moment suggesting that the Council condemn an innocent boy! I know you will move heaven and earth to keep that from happening. And I sincerely hope you succeed, for Sean is not the only angry one on this Holding. I'm as angry as if this had happened to my own son, and if I thought butchering wood a viable solution, the woods hereabouts would be a pile of kindling."

For a few moments, only the popping of the fire disturbed the stillness. At last the Master spoke, his voice rough with frustration. "I've tried, Rassek. Talan and the Maker himself know how hard. I spent two weeks on Eyrie trying to ferret out the truth. And though I'm convinced of this Bard's identity, there's not a shred of evidence against him." He sighed. "We can only hope that, overconfident in having succeeded in his move against Kaelin, he makes a mistake. I assure you he is being carefully watched." Bergid fell silent for a few moments and Rassek did not disturb him.

At length the Master looked up. "And you may be right in thinking that our Order and social rankings have become too rigid. I can understand why you felt that our friendship was only mine to offer, but I assure you I never felt that way when I offered it." He returned his gaze to the fire. "Little wonder the position of Master Bard is so often a lonely one, if those who might offer their friendship do not feel free to do so, and our colleagues live on separate islands." He glanced at Rassek. "If ever you wish to break through that barrier you feel between us, know that I would welcome it."

Rassek gave him a startled look. "I didn't mean to imply there was a barrier between us. If I had felt one, I would not have accepted your friendship."

"Even so, I would welcome the privilege of accepting yours."

For a moment the two regarded each other, then Rassek leaned forward in his chair and extended his arm. "With the clear understanding, then, that you will *never* hug me again, I would like you to accept the offer of my friendship," he said, amusement flickering in his eyes.

Bergid laughed and grasped Rassek's arm.

On the beach, in the secret hideout Sean had only ever shared with Kaelin, the two boys sat watching the waves break against the rocky shelf, tossing pebbles into the receding tide.

Kaelin glanced sideways at his younger brother. "So how come you haven't asked me about the medallion?"

Sean glanced at it, then looked quickly away. "Father told me not to mention it unless you did. He said that even brothers are entitled to their privacy sometimes." He glanced at Kaelin. "You don't have to tell me about it if you don't want to."

"But you're dying to know."

"Well, yeah ... but you don't have to."

Kaelin chuckled. "You must have known about it before I got here, or your father wouldn't have said that."

"I know what everyone else does, which isn't much," Sean admitted. "Last autumn some of the kids at school were talking about how Master Bergid's apprentice had, well..." his voice trailed off.

"Been accused of theft."

Sean frowned darkly. "So, I told them my brother would never steal from anyone, and they said he *must* have, or he wouldn't have been accused, and I said they'd better take it back because I knew my own brother better than any of them did. Then the Schoolmaster came out and marched all four of us back into the schoolhouse and gave us a long lecture about the difference between 'accused' and 'guilty' ... which I already *knew,*" he said indignantly. "They kept their mouths shut after that. And good thing they did, or we'd have all gotten switched for fighting, and I'd have had to do nice things for all three of them for weeks!"

"Do nice things?" Kaelin echoed blankly.

"It's how Jared and I became friends," Sean explained. "He kept saying awful things about the Holder when he wasn't my father yet. I finally couldn't take it anymore and gave him the bloody nose he *deserved.* Then he got up and hit me back, and, well ... the Schoolmaster switched both of us and sent us home. I figured the Holder would punish me for getting in trouble, but he didn't." The youngster grimaced. "He did something worse."

"He made you do nice things for Jared?"

"One thing every day for three weeks, but it only took two."

Kaelin grinned. "Sounds like something my Master would've done. And now you and Jared are good friends?"

"Yeah ... but that's not gonna happen with the idiots who were talking about my own *brother* like that!"

"Don't be so hard on them," the apprentice said quietly. "They don't know me like you do."

They were silent for a few moments. "I bet *you'd* like to hit the creep who did this to you," Sean said sturdily.

Kaelin nodded ruefully. "At first that's all I could think about. Master Marek helped me see that I needed to let it go, so that I wouldn't turn myself into a creep just like him."

"Don't tell me you *forgave* him ... he doesn't deserve it!"

"No, he doesn't. But it isn't about what he deserves. It's about what *I* deserve, and the people I care about." Kaelin tossed another pebble into the waves.

Sean frowned, filing this perplexing statement away to think about later. "So, does that mean you're going to forgive the Masters if they vote against you?" he asked, incredulous.

"They'll make their decision according to Bardic Law, which they're sworn to uphold. I won't hold that against them."

"But what they're doing isn't fair!" Sean said angrily. "They haven't any right to treat you this way. If the Masters were standing here right now, I'd give every one of them a bloody nose, and I wouldn't do a single nice thing for them afterwards, either, no matter *what* Father said!"

Kaelin glanced sideways at his simmering little brother. "If you'd like to get an early start, one of them is sitting in your living room right now," he said expressionlessly.

Sean gave him a startled glance. "Oh ... well, I guess I could make an exception," he allowed. "Master Bergid would never vote to throw you out." He frowned darkly. "He'd better *not,* or he won't be invited to any of *our* dinners!"

"Don't throw out the whole Bardic Order because of what one member—" Kaelin began, then abruptly stopped.

"What's wrong?"

"I just remembered something my Master told me a long time ago when I was saying something disparaging about the Druids. He said it was a mistake to think that all the Druids of Eire were bad and all the Bards good. He said that human nature is the same across all professions and times." The apprentice cocked his head, considering this. "I didn't really believe it then, but he was right. After all, the person who did this to me isn't a Druid. He's a Bard, a member of my own Order. But that doesn't make every Bard in the Bardic Isles like him. A few of them will probably be glad to see me thrown out because I'm apprenticed to a Master," he admitted, "but most of them won't. And there isn't a single Master who wants to do what they're going to have to do at the Council hearing, so don't go around giving them bloody noses for it. No Master can break Bardic Law."

Sean scowled. "Then Bardic Law is stupid," he said flatly, hurling a rock into the water for emphasis. "You're coming back afterwards, aren't you?" he asked hopefully.

"I don't think so."

Sean was horrified. "Master Bergid won't just leave you on Elegy!" he exclaimed.

"No, he'll want me to go with him, but I won't do that."

"Why not?" Sean demanded.

For a long moment, Kaelin stared sightlessly at the endless waves lapping against the edge of the shelf. "I could give you a lot of reasons," he said at last. "That I'll lose my robe and have no right to his home anymore. That, even if he's willing to keep me, my Bardic instruments will be taken away forever. That I won't be allowed to speak to him for a whole cycle. That he won't play his own instruments at night anymore, thinking to spare me hearing them, and I ... couldn't stand being the cause of that." He turned and faced his little brother. "All those things are true, but they're not the real reason."

"Then what is?" Sean fell silent at the grim expression on Kaelin's face as he turned and looked south over the waves. "I'm sorry," the youngster said. "I'm just making things worse."

Kaelin shook his head. "Actually, it's a relief to talk about it. I'll come to see you when I can ... I promise. But I won't be able to do it soon because something is pulling me away from here." His voice cracked, and he fought back the sudden tears that sprang to his eyes. "Getting on the ship and *staying* on it to come back here from Tryl took every bit of strength I had, and there was nothing I wanted more than to see my Master again. That's the real reason."

Sean frowned. "You mean..."

"Bardic Mountain is pulling me toward it, and it's gotten so strong I can even feel it from here. I don't think it will let me leave Elegy this time. I have to deal with that before I'm free to go where *I* want to go."

For a long moment, neither of them spoke. Then Sean pulled his knees up to his chest and rested his chin on them. "So, if it's a relief to talk about it, then talk." He glanced at the indecision on Kaelin's face and sighed. "It's simple," he said patiently, as though his older brother were cycles younger. "You start at the beginning, and you don't stop talking until you get to the end."

Kaelin laughed, and it seemed to him that something frozen inside him melted at his brother's words. He took a deep breath and started talking.

Chapter 22

A few days later, the Master and his apprentice collected Poor Oran from the ferryman's boarding stable and headed up the Bronig toward the Master's cabin. Master Bergid refused to answer Kaelin's questions, saying only that someone was waiting for them there. When at last they reached the clearing on the hillside, Kaelin stopped short at the sight of Darryk sitting before a bonfire, his eyes bound and his ears plugged. Bard Fenadal was making hunter's stew over the fire and, judging by the quantity, was expecting them for dinner. He looked up at their arrival with a smile and an exaggerated sigh of relief.

"Master Bergid. Welcome, sir! Good to see you, Kaelin." He glanced at Darryk, who was sitting erect in an attitude of impatient expectation. "Thank heavens you've arrived in time to free him before his last day is over." He sighed in relief. "I swear he's counting the minutes."

The Master chuckled. "Never mind dinner. Let's get the towels heated before we have a berserk Bard on our hands. Before I bound them, the last thing I saw in his eyes was an uneasy suspicion that I might leave him as long as I did Kaelin."

While the two men made preparations, Kaelin knelt beside

Darryk and took his friend's hand in his own. Darryk smiled in anticipation, then froze. Kaelin remained motionless as the Bard reached out and ran his fingers lightly over his face.

The next moment, Kaelin found himself smothered in the silent Bard's powerful embrace. He yelped and pulled himself free with difficulty, but Darryk kept his hand trapped firmly in his own until the Master came with hot towels to loosen the wax in his ears. Then the Master unbound his eyes and sat back, congratulating the Bard on completing his sense-deprivation test, his sight, hearing, and speech denied him for a week.

"Thank you, sir," Darryk said, his voice rough from disuse.

"If you don't need me for anything else, Master Bergid," Fenadal said, "I should leave while I can still catch the ferry. Dinner's ready, and I've already sampled a bowl of it … good stew, that, if I say so myself." He retrieved his packs from the cabin and was on his way, giving Kaelin a cheerful grin as he went.

"Everything's so bright … and loud," Darryk muttered. Squinting against the late afternoon light, Darryk turned to Kaelin and smiled. "But you're a feast for deprived eyes, my friend!" He cleared his throat. "I can't *believe* you endured this for six weeks—eight without hearing, *nine* without speech!—how long did it take before your throat didn't feel like the rough side of a scraping file, and voices didn't boom through your head?"

"A few days," Kaelin replied with a chuckle. "You ought to feel better soon." He froze when Darryk did not ignore the presence of the medallion but picked it up and studied it.

The Bard's knuckles whitened. "If I could bear this for you, I would gladly do so."

Kaelin nodded wordlessly.

Darryk released the medallion. A spasm of anger crossed his face as it fell against Kaelin's chest. The Bard felt the Master's hand gripping his shoulder. "It isn't *right*, Master Bergid!"

"Kaelin is quite aware of that," the Master said gently. "If you cannot bear the medallion yourself as you would like, then do not add to its weight."

Darryk stared at the Master for a moment, then turned to Kaelin. "Forgive me," he said simply. "Perhaps giving you a lesson on your flute—and no, the irony of that has *not* escaped me—would serve to make amends and restore me to my deprived senses at the same time."

Kaelin reached for his flute. "What would you like to hear?"

"Something free," came the quiet reply.

Kaelin inwardly winced. When was the last time, he wondered, that he had felt free? Before the medallion? Or before the mountain had exerted its force in his life? Filled with the desire to free himself from both, Kaelin began playing a variation he had not played since the day before his Master had visited the village of Vale. His music began with a low note, then moved slowly and surely upward, as though searching for something only to be found in the skies above. It hovered on an unresolved note for a spellbinding moment, then swept upwards without restraint.

The listeners' senses were propelled into the sky on the wings of a soaring melodic line. Far below lay their campsite. To the east the Bronig wound its way toward Kyet; to the west the shining river disappeared into the mountains. As they hovered in the air, the distinct feeling of being watched made the listeners look up. In the distant skies above, a dark speck grew as it arrowed swiftly toward them, and a wild kestrel came into view. The bird spread its powerful wings and hovered over them, eyeing the campsite below. The kestrel was over two handspans in length, with graceful, pointed tail feathers and bars of slate-blue on its wings. Its bill was hooked and notched; its feet armed with long, curved talons. Impressive at a distance, the bird was utterly breathtaking at such close proximity in the open air. The flute called from below them, and the kestrel emitted a piercing series of joyful staccatos, then folded its wings and dove toward the listeners, who cried out in alarm. At the moment of impact, however, they felt nothing and looked down with relief to see the bird plummeting toward their campsite in the growing dusk.

The flute music faded and the listeners reluctantly came back to themselves, unwilling to exchange the freedom of the skies for an earth-bound existence. Master Bergid was the first to open his eyes to an amazing scene. Though kestrels were generally smaller than other falcons, the one gripping Kaelin's left arm was the largest one the Master had ever seen. The bird flapped his wings, bringing Darryk from his reverie. The Bard opened his eyes and inhaled sharply.

Kaelin murmured softly to the bird, and the kestrel answered with gentle staccatos. Back and forth the two seemed to converse, for all the world like close friends that had finally reunited after an unbearably long absence. Then Kaelin lifted his arm toward the sky and the kestrel rose into the air with powerful strokes of his wings and disappeared into the darkening sky. The two men stared speechlessly at Kaelin as he sat down, laid his flute on his lap and cradled his arm, grimacing.

Master Bergid moved forward and pushed up the sleeve of Kaelin's robe. There were vivid red marks where the kestrel had gripped him and several bleeding cuts where the sharp talons had pierced his skin.

Darryk quickly brought water and clean cloths from the cabin, and the Master cleaned the cuts and bound Kaelin's arm. He glanced upward with a frown, as though looking for the culprit who had dared to inflict such wounds on his apprentice.

"Brek didn't know he was hurting me," the apprentice said, pulling his sleeve back down over the binding. "If he'd known, he wouldn't have done it. And I hardly even felt it until after he left."

"You've named him?" Darryk looked at him wonderingly.

"No, he came with his own, but I never knew it until now." Kaelin turned toward his Master. "It's the same kestrel! Playing that variation of his song must have made some kind of link between us, because he's been following me ever since I left you."

Bergid's eyes widened. "Is this the same kestrel that hovered over us when I met you on the dock?"

Kaelin nodded. "When I left Kestrel, he circled the ship and flew to the docks twice, like he was trying to get the ship to go back. Then he flew off toward Eyrie. Master Talan was so surprised to see him there that he wanted to know if I had anything to do with it, but I didn't think so then. He followed me to Zephyr and kept an eagle from preying on Master Marek's birds. And when I stepped onto the dock at Lyssa, the ship's crow flew onto my head, and I took it down and held it for a moment. Brek didn't like that. He made an amazing dive and drove it right out of my hands! He stayed in the woods near Master Grened's home, and ... well," the apprentice sheepishly continued, "he seemed to talk to me whenever I walked there, so I started talking back to him as if I understood. Then he followed me here, and at first I just thought he was happy to be back on Kestrel again, but now I know—" Kaelin flushed slightly.

"What do you know?" his Master asked curiously.

"Well, when I played the variation of his song, I could sense his thoughts. He wasn't happy because he was back on Kestrel. He was happy that I was back with *you*. All this time, he was trying to get me to come back to where I belong and looking out for me while I was ... lost." He shrugged helplessly. "Brek thinks I'm your fledgling, sir." He braced himself but, to his surprise, neither of the men laughed.

"And so you are," the Master said softly. "So you are."

"It's okay, then, if I call him to me?" Kaelin asked hopefully.

Bergid gave his apprentice an appraising look. "What is it you need from Brek?"

For a long moment, it seemed that Kaelin was not going to answer. When at last he spoke, his words pierced the Master's heart. "I need someone who won't be taken away from me. Someone who, no matter where I go, will go with me."

"You know that I will not abandon you."

Kaelin nodded wordlessly. *But I might have to abandon you.*

"Call Brek whenever you wish," the Master said gently. "There's some leather scraps in the cabin you can make into a sleeve to protect your arm during his visits."

Though Kaelin nodded and briefly smiled, the shadow was still there, reminding Bergid strongly of the time before the boy's gift had been freed. "You haven't played your own music since you've come back," he noted. "Is there a reason?"

The apprentice frowned. "I just ... never know exactly what's going to happen when I play my own music. I thought that here, with you, it would be like it was before, but I'm not the same and my music isn't, either. Sometimes it shows me what I'm thinking about, or what I'm feeling, like it used to, but sometimes it shows me things or people I've never seen, things I don't understand ... things that scare me," he added in a low voice.

"Show me," the Master said. "Unless your arm hurts too much to play."

"I don't need my flute to show you." He hesitated a moment, his brow creased in thought. Then he closed his eyes and began to sing.

At first, the images that came to life from the surprisingly powerful tenor voice seemed simple enough. A river, threading its way through trees and rocks as the listeners followed it ever higher into the mountains. A series of cliffs, one of them covered with vines that swayed gently in the wind. A grassy shelf with a spectacular view of a small valley below. A waterfall cascading down the mountainside.

Then the music modulated, and the listeners gasped as the waterfall vanished in flames. They blinked in the mesmerizing play of oranges, reds, and yellows, gradually realizing they sat before a fire. The melody leapt from note to note as though dancing with the flames, then hovered on a single note, the seventh of a diminished chord. A single flame stood out against the backdrop of flickering firelight, a flame that did not dance to the singer's music but stood motionless. The listeners felt a chill creep up their spines at the unnatural flame, and their attention was unwillingly drawn to its center. Eyes appeared, regarding them intently, unblinking ... dark eyes slashed with amber.

The singing stopped, and the flames vanished. Master Bergid raised his eyes to find his apprentice's gaze fastened on him, as unblinking as the eyes in the flame.

"What's happening to me, Master?" Kaelin whispered. His shoulders began to tremble.

Bergid pushed his alarm away and pulled his apprentice close, holding him until the trembling stopped. Darryk, catching a look from the Master, rose and went into the cabin.

"How long have you been having these musical visions?" the Master quietly asked.

"Is that what they are?"

"For lack of a better name, we'll call them that."

"I used to have them in Vale," Kaelin admitted. "I often dreamed of a Master who was climbing up a steep slope somewhere in the mountains with a huge harp on his back. The last time I had that dream, he turned and looked at me, and he had amber eyes like mine. The next day, I saw you in the marketplace and followed you. I haven't had that dream since."

"What other dreams have you had?"

"Well, I had that strange dream in your house about the gold-covered book in your desk drawer that was playing harp music. At Master Rial's, I dreamed of a drawer he'd forbidden me to open, and I woke up standing right next to it. I told Master Rial the next morning, and he locked the drawer so I wouldn't disobey him in my sleep.

"What about this vision of eyes in a flame?"

"I've seen the flame twice. The first time, there weren't any eyes in it. The second time was the one you just saw." Kaelin told his Master about both occurrences, and Bergid listened gravely, saying nothing until he was finished.

"What did Master Grened say about it?"

"He said that he didn't understand it, but if the mountain was sending it, then only the mountain could explain it." Kaelin frowned. "But I don't see how the mountain could be sending me visions. Maybe none of it is real. Maybe there's just so much pressure that I'm—" he broke off.

"Your music couldn't show you something that wasn't real," the Master told him. "Regardless of what's causing the visions you've been having, rest assured there's nothing whatever wrong with *you* for simply having them."

The apprentice breathed a sigh of relief.

Late that night the Master sat by the fire, thinking deeply. Kaelin's gift had apparently grown right along with him and was becoming a powerful force just as the time was nearing when the instruments that could channel it would almost certainly be taken away. The Master was quick to see the significance of what Rial had done with Kaelin's voice. Of all the Masters, Rial would be the one most likely to recognize Kaelin's growing loneliness and his deep need to retain an instrument capable of expressing it.

The Master frowned darkly. Visions of Bardic Mountain and gold-covered books were one thing ... flames with eyes in them clearly another. Of all the inexplicable things Kaelin had experienced, a flame that spoke and a flame with eyes disturbed the Master the most. No Bard or Master had such eyes. Who did they belong to, and how were they able to appear in a flame? Were they a vision of the future, or was someone watching Kaelin now? Was his apprentice in danger? What 'traitor' was there to be wary of, and did this have anything to do with the false charge Kaelin was under? Bergid thought back to his conversation with Rassek. Both of them had assumed what seemed obvious, that the Bard who had framed Kaelin had done so out of spiteful jealousy. The idea that he might be aligned with someone who had such power over fire was ludicrous ... wasn't it? The Master had seldom felt so helpless, and brooding another hour by the fire produced nothing but a headache before he finally retired for the night.

The next morning, Kaelin packed Poor Oran with full provisions as he had been told to do, wondering why they would be needed for such a short distance. "Aren't we going home?"

"Actually," the Master replied, "I thought we might take a little trip instead."

"To Lynd?" Kaelin asked hopefully, thinking of Laena.

"I thought you might like to visit Vale."

This was unexpected. Kaelin hadn't visited the village he'd grown up in since the day he followed the Master out of it.

"Your sister has returned to Vale," Bergid told him, "and is eagerly waiting for you and Darryk to arrive."

Kaelin turned wide eyes to his friend. "Me and ... you?"

The tall Bard looked at him uncomfortably. "Yes, well..." he began, suddenly feeling as if he were an erring apprentice and his young friend a Bard awaiting an explanation for misconduct. "You see, Kaelin, I—she—well, the fact is, we—" he glanced at the Master in despair. "I don't know how to tell him!"

The Master, his blue eyes lit with amusement, held up his hands, clearly refusing to aid the flustered Bard.

Kaelin looked from one to the other and frowned. "Are you trying to tell me, Darryk, that you and my sister..."

"Well, yes. That is, we're planning to ... er, join. I hope you're not upset?" The next moment, the Bard was knocked flat on his back and pummeled unmercifully.

"You *scoundrel.*" Kaelin crowed in delight. "I turn my back for a mere *cycle,* and you steal my sister? You deserve a thrashing and I'm big enough now to deliver it!"

Master Bergid chuckled, watching the scuffle turn into a full-fledged wrestling match, both of them laughing as they tumbled over the grass. "When the two of you are finished bonding," he announced dryly, "you can catch up to me. I'll be headed to Vale."

The two wrestlers sat up, still laughing and panting for breath as the Master disappeared down the path. Darryk glanced at the apprentice. "Can I safely assume you're okay with our pending new relationship, then?" he asked.

Kaelin brushed the grass off his robe and grinned. "If I could have chosen a husband for Laena and a brother for myself, it would have been you. And best of all, now you're not just my friend, you're my big brother!" Mischief lit his eyes. "No wonder Sean acts so crazy around me. Being the *little* brother for a change means I get to act as immaturely as I like!" He jumped up, grabbed his pack, and rushed off after the Master. "Last one out of the clearing brings Poor Oran!" he shouted gleefully.

Darryk sat for a moment, chuckling and shaking his head. Then he rose, slung his pack over his shoulder, and took hold of the mule's tether. "Come along, Poor Oran," he said with a sigh. "Looks like you and Poor Darryk had better become acquainted."

Far above the three travelers, Brek cried out, hovered against the wind for a moment, then flew swiftly in the same direction.

"True happiness does not come from the major keys
in the score of our lives.
It comes from the growth the minors provide."
— *Adept Culyn*

Chapter 23

During the next few days of traveling, Kaelin was unusually quiet. His Master, watching him, decided to camp where they were, on the northern shore of Loch Daevon. It seemed to him that each passing day increased the loneliness on Kaelin's face. The apprentice was quick to offer his services in gathering food, from checking the fish trap he had expertly constructed to foraging for roots and herbs. Kaelin called Brek to him often, sometimes with his flute, sometimes by voice alone. He identified with the wild kestrel in a way that wrung the Master's heart. Only with Brek, it seemed, was Kaelin truly at ease. Yet each time he sent the kestrel back into the sky, the loneliness on his face was deeper. He clearly did not wish to discuss it, skillfully deflecting his Master's questions.

The day after they arrived at the lake, Bergid changed his tactics. "Why do you call Brek to you so often?" he asked Kaelin.

The apprentice shrugged. "He knows so many places where people never go. Beautiful, untouched places." He looked up at his Master, who regarded him with quiet expectation. "Brek is so free," he continued, finding it hard to explain his feelings.

"Free of what?"

The apprentice looked uneasily at his Master, as though finding himself suddenly in a trap he wasn't sure he could get out of. "Free of ... problems," he finally replied, turning his eyes away.

"Yes," his Master replied softly, "I *am* a problem, aren't I?"

Darryk, in the act of taking out his harp, slid it back into its travel bag and sat completely still.

The apprentice turned shocked eyes back to his Master but was prevented from protesting by a challenging lift of the Master's brows. He reluctantly nodded.

"And Darryk is a problem," the Master continued in a conversational tone, "not to mention Byron, Drin, Brent, and four other Masters as well." He looked keenly at the silent apprentice. "Brek can take you away from all of us for a while, but he can't take away the pain, can he?"

"Sir, please don't—"

"He can't take it away because he can't share it with you. So, it just keeps growing, doesn't it?"

"Master—"

"Where are you putting it all? It must be a clever hiding place to have eluded friends and Masters for so many months."

Amber eyes flashed. "You told Darryk that if he couldn't bear my medallion, he shouldn't add to its weight," Kaelin said angrily. "So, why are you? Isn't enough going to be done to me without starting now? Maybe Brek can't take away the pain, but he can take me away from it, at least for a while. That's more than any of you can do!" He bit his lip in an effort to stop, but the angry words would not be held back. "Sometimes I wish you'd all just take my robe, my instruments, and yourselves with it," he said bitterly, "and be done with this torture."

"As you wish," the Master said quietly. "I won't confiscate your robe or instruments, but Darryk and I will leave in the morning."

It would have been difficult to say whose face registered the most shock at this statement, Kaelin's or Darryk's.

"You may meet us in Vale, if you wish to see your sister," the Master continued, "or travel west to the coast and await me in Tennyk. I've arranged for our transport from there to Elegy."

The silence in the campsite grew to an unbearable length. Darryk's jaw tightened. Would either of them ever speak again? When at last the silence was broken, Kaelin's voice was so soft, Darryk almost didn't hear it.

"I'm sorry ... I didn't mean it like that."

"I think you meant it *exactly* like that," the Master contradicted. "You have every right to your feelings," he said gently. "Don't deny them. Not to me ... and not to yourself."

"But I don't want you to go!"

"Nor do you want me to stay," the Master replied evenly, his brow uplifted.

Kaelin's brow rose stubbornly back, and Darryk was struck by the similarity between the two. *Surely Kaelin is the son the Master never had.*

"You can fly away with Brek, but he can't share your memories," the Master continued. "You need the release that sharing them with someone will provide. Take me there."

The brows of both remained raised at each other. "Is that a command, sir?" Kaelin abruptly asked.

"No, but I will not stay here and add to your torment if you refuse me."

The apprentice looked silently at his Master. "You made me hurt you once before," he said at last. "It was the hardest lesson you ever gave me. I would rather have been beaten senseless."

"I know."

"Then why are you asking me to hurt you again?"

The blue eyes held his. "You know why."

The apprentice stood still as words from Master Grened suddenly intruded.

And no matter what, don't ever doubt it.

Don't ever doubt what, sir?

What your Master can't say.

"Yes ... I know."

"Then let me share your burden. It's too great for you to bear alone."

After a long, tense moment, Kaelin's shoulders relaxed and he slowly nodded. Master Bergid felt relief flood through him. He did not know how he could have brought himself to leave, had Kaelin refused.

Kaelin's gaze turned to Darryk. "You don't need to share this," he told him. "It won't be pleasant."

"Will it help if I stay?"

The apprentice made no reply.

"Then I will not leave you."

Kaelin's eyes filled with emotion. "Maybe not now, but you will. Bardic Law won't give either of you a choice, any more than it's given me one." The eyes he lifted to his Master were filled with torment.

"Do you really want to know what it was like?" Kaelin abruptly cried. "For months I woke up in dread, wondering if that would be the day the summons would come. I'm grateful for the time I was given with the other Masters and for all they taught me. I know you all did it out of kindness ... but it was cruel, too! It's made everything harder, because I got to know them all. And sometimes I wish I hadn't, because it's given me all the more to lose. Even the progress I've made on my instruments just makes it harder to have them taken away." As if fueled by his emotion, the words began to tumble recklessly from him. "And it's hardest of all now, being with a friend that will soon become a brother I won't be able to speak freely to for a whole cycle ... and a Master I love more than anything, who'll be forced by Bardic Law to do what he said he would never—" His voice broke in anguish. Then he reached for his flute, closed his eyes on threatening tears, and began to play.

The music wandered slowly down, sending chills up the listener's spines, filling the clearing with a tangible loneliness. It moved reluctantly from one note to the next as though pulled from the composer against his will, each phrase of it inexorably lower than the one before.

The listeners were pulled with it, becoming one with the flutist's search for the lowest possible tone, held motionless under the crushing weight of Kaelin's song. Downward they were drawn into a place of pure, raw emotion. Each note a painful memory, each an experience that became their own. They felt the paralyzing shock of finding Master Talan's tuning fork in their bag. They ached with desire to play their instruments and winced at the looks of distrust on a myriad of faces. They felt the stinging bite of Master Grened's strap and gritted their teeth at Conor's barbed comment. They hurt under the weight of the medallion and the awareness of what would be ruthlessly taken from them. Their loneliness grew unbearable. The last note of agony was emptied, and the music faded into silence.

Darryk opened his eyes, surprised to find himself sitting next to Kaelin, holding one of the apprentice's hands tightly with both of his own. He could not remember moving to do so. Deep, wracking sobs came from Kaelin. His Master held him fast, tears running freely down his face. Then Darryk became aware that his own cheeks were wet, astonished at the unfamiliar act. He had not cried since he was a child.

He released Kaelin's hand, intending to leave the two of them alone, but Kaelin would not let go. The Bard willingly stayed, reflecting on what had just happened. He supposed everyone had a place, a private place where they kept certain experiences and feelings locked up tightly, feelings they were unwilling or unable to deal with. Actually entering Kaelin's had made him suddenly conscious of his own. He frowned slightly, remembering things he had thought were long forgotten. Perhaps, like Kaelin's painful notes, they needed to be examined and released. He thought of Laena and saw the importance of sharing these things with each other. *That's part of what love is,* he mused to himself. *And to think that I learned it from a boy of thirteen.*

Kaelin rarely left his Master's side the rest of the day, taking obvious pleasure in his proximity. Not once did he call the kestrel to him. He said little, but asked one question of his Master that made Darryk stop what he was doing and listen to the answer.

"Master, why did sharing my pain with both of you help ease it so much? I thought it would still be there, but only the memory is. The pain is so much less." He shook his head wonderingly.

Bergid looked at him thoughtfully. "What is just one note, standing alone?" he asked. "Is it not the combination of that note with others that makes music? You and I are only single melodic lines, after all, but the score is vast, and I sometimes think the heavens themselves are listening to it. Whenever we try to remove ourselves from that score, we make ourselves miserable."

"Then we have to play the part given to us, don't we?" Kaelin thought of the coming Council hearing and turned abruptly away.

His Master's hand squeezed his shoulder reassuringly. "Yes," he said quietly, "and some of the movements are in minor keys. Don't refuse the minors," he said gently. "They, too, must be developed and heard in their time. And the majors, when they come again, as they surely will, will sound all the sweeter for it."

The apprentice nodded wordlessly, and the Bard returned to his work, devoutly wishing he could take up a quill and change the key signature of the movement the Master and apprentice would all too soon be required to play.

A few days later, the threesome reached Skellig Mountain and began the final climb up to Vale. It was unusually cold, and their breath vaporized in misty clouds before their faces as the slope steepened. Kaelin's eagerness to see Laena grew with every step, as did Darryk's. Indeed, they both began climbing faster without realizing it until the Master's exasperated voice from well behind them brought them to a halt.

"Perhaps the two of you can accelerando your way up to Vale without feeling it, but an old man like me needs a fermata or two along the way. Oh, go on, both of you," he said, when they began to apologize. "I'll get there—"

"—in the fullness of your own measure?" Kaelin deftly inserted.

The Master favored his chuckling apprentice with a stern look. "On second thought, *you'll* be staying with me." Then he glanced at his Bard, who was looking longingly in the direction of Vale. "Be off with you," he said, waving aside the Bard's protest. "And that's an order. I'm quite capable of handling this impudent apprentice on my own. And I'm sure you and Laena would prefer to greet each other without an audience."

Darryk smiled. "Thank you, sir." He hurried off.

The Master redirected a stern look at Kaelin. "Now, then, *you* will accompany your Master at *his* tempo—a strict andante to the last measure, with strategically placed ritardandos and fermati wherever he decides to place them!"

"Whatever the Composition Master of the Bardic Isles desires, sir." With a chuckle, Kaelin adjusted his pack, took Poor Oran's lead and followed his Master.

They passed by Wynd without stopping at the village and continued on as the steep path gradually eased. They made their way at a leisurely walking pace, entering Vale just as dusk fell. Reaching the deserted square, they both paused, gazing at the place where the Master had sat three cycles before, looking into the startled eyes of a village boy.

"That was the best day of my life, Master."

"Mine, too."

They smiled at each other and walked on together in silence, filled with the same memories.

The joining of Darryk and Laena was overseen by the Master Bard of Kestrel himself, to the delight of the village of Vale. Indeed, it was a joining that would be discussed and wondered at for cycles to come. Few there could recognize the youngster of eleven in this self-assured Bardic apprentice of nearly fourteen, especially his friend Erik, who stared at him as if he were a stranger until Kaelin went over and punched his arm to prove otherwise. No one's reaction, however, could equal the flabbergasted expression of the Schoolmaster of Vale.

Aside from the prestige of having the Master Bard himself perform the ceremony, the music played by the Master's apprentice left everyone speechless. Kaelin chose to play his flute, as he had for Master Marek's joining, and waited, a lump in his throat, as Darryk and Laena spoke their vows. Master Bergid wrapped Darryk's silver cord around the couple's hands and spoke the words joining them together as one. When Kaelin set a block and began to play, his song was filled with the freedom and joy of all winged creatures. Within moments, birds of all kinds swooped over the heads of the crowd in an ecstasy of flight. Avian chirps and trills embellished the music coming from the Bardic flute until Kaelin brought the piece to a close and the birds flew off in all directions.

Darryk and Laena came over to him, their faces glowing with happiness. Kaelin gripped Darryk's outstretched arm and hugged his sister, then told her he had something special planned for her. "Do you remember how we used to hike up Skellig to watch the kestrels? You told me you wished you could climb high enough to touch one of them."

Laena smiled. "I remember."

Kaelin glanced at his Master. "May I, sir?" At the Master's nod of permission, he withdrew a leather sleeve from his robe and slipped his left forearm into it. Then he looked up into the sky and emitted a clear whistle.

The crowd gasped as Brek glided over their heads and landed on Kaelin's protected arm. Laena, her eyes shining, reached out at Kaelin's invitation to touch the beautiful wings and stroke the smooth head. Brek, listening intently to Kaelin's murmured words, stood still and allowed the caresses. The crowd was silent, watching the amazing spectacle until Kaelin, with a brisk movement of his arm, sent the kestrel back into the sky.

The next morning, Kaelin and his Master paid a visit to Flutist Torin. They found the old man dozing in his chair. Kaelin lightly touched his arm. "Flutist Torin?"

The Flutist snorted and stared for a moment at the white and grey robes in front of him. He blinked twice, mumbled something about crazy dreams, and closed his eyes.

The apprentice gently shook his arm. "It's Kaelin, sir. I've come to thank you for everything you've done for me ... and I've brought someone who would like to speak with you."

The old man frowned and opened his eyes. "Kaelin? He doesn't come around anymore," he said plaintively. "Haven't seen him in cycles ... grown too big, I suppose, to be hearing the tales of a fumble-fingered—" he peered closely at the grey robe, then at the boy's smiling face. "Kaelin? Is that you, lad? Why, wherever did you get a Bardic *apprentice* robe? You can't just walk around in one of those like you own it, youngster," he lectured sternly. "You have to *earn* the right to—" he caught a glimpse of the white robe and gold cord of the man standing next to Kaelin, and his jaw dropped. "Master Bergid," he managed to whisper.

The Master smiled at him. "It's good to meet you, Flutist Torin," he said. "I can assure you that Kaelin has fully earned the right to walk around in the robe he wears, thanks in great part to you." He shook his head as the old man struggled to rise. "Do not trouble yourself. I came only to thank you for your service to the Bardic Isles as an excellent flute instructor and performer in Caerlach for so many cycles. Many of your students are themselves members of the Bardic Order now because of you. I also came to thank you for all that you did for my apprentice."

"*Your* appren—" The old man's voice failed him.

"What you did for Kaelin helped him become a Master's apprentice, the first one in Bardic Isles history."

"I didn't teach the boy!" Torin protested. "I'm in no shape to be taking students."

"You taught him by playing for him. You gave him the wood to make his own flute. You instilled in him a love of Bardic history. Those are gifts beyond price."

The Flutist stared at him, too flabbergasted to speak.

Kaelin picked up the old man's flute that was lying on the table and glanced at his Master. "Sir, Flutist Torin told me once that, in the hands of a Master, his flute would come to life and would never be the same flute again."

The Master's gaze turned to Torin. "May I?" At the old man's speechless nod, he took the flute from Kaelin's hand and looked at it appraisingly. "The owner of such a well-made and cared-for instrument deserves to have a song composed for the two of them." He lifted the old man's flute and began to play, his eyes resting on Torin's face.

Kaelin sat down at the table and, quickly taking up a quill and piece of manuscript lying there, transcribed the simple, beautiful melody the Master played on the old man's flute, while Torin listened with tears in his eyes.

I thought he would compose something impressively difficult, Kaelin thought, *but instead, he's gifting him a song ... a song of his own that Old Torin can still play. And he'll treasure every note of it because they were written just for him.*

When the Master was finished, he placed Torin's flute in the aged hands, took the quill, and signed his name at the bottom of the composition.

Torin gently stroked his flute and spoke to it wistfully. "We must be dreaming, you and I."

"This is no dream," Kaelin said. "Remember when you told me that there is music trapped in every instrument, music waiting for a Master's hand?"

The old man nodded without looking up. "I remember."

"There was music trapped inside me, too, waiting for a Master's hand. This Master's. Your words gave me the courage to follow him, and this is the flute he helped me make." Kaelin removed his flute from its travel bag and held it out.

Torin reached out and gently stroked the silky rosewood. "This is a Master's flute, lad," he said in a hushed voice, "the finest I have ever touched." He glanced up. "Will you play it for me?"

Kaelin smiled. "Is there somewhere you would like to go, if you could? Someplace or something you would like to see again?"

"I grew up on Eyrie," the old man said softly, his eyes losing focus as he remembered the island of his childhood. "We moved here when I was ten, but I still remember the hills filled with heather ... the sky bursting with stars that were so bright, it seemed like I could almost reach out and touch them. I would like to see them once more before I pass on." He sighed and shook his head. "But that's a wish no one can grant me, lad."

"I've been to those hills," Kaelin told him, "and I've seen those stars. I can show them to you again."

If the old Flutist had suspected he was dreaming before, he was utterly convinced of it now as his senses were taken by the clear voice of the Bardic flute, lifting his awareness gently above his home and speeding him to the island of his birth. He saw the shores of Eyrie beneath him, saw what the island looked like from above ... the grasslands of the interior with rolling hills of heather surrounding them resembling the eyrie of a giant bird. He skimmed over the heather, his eyes wide with delight at the pur-plish blooms swaying in the breeze, his nostrils filled with the scent he had never forgotten. The music slowed, the scene below darkened, and he glanced up to a sky filled from horizon to hori-zon with a brilliance of stars. The constellations his father had pointed out to him stood out like pictures painted from his past. He gasped in the wonder of it, his mind filled with memories, and then the music gently took him home.

Kaelin put away his flute and smiled at his Master. "Thank you, sir," he said. Bergid nodded, and they left the old Flutist peace-fully sleeping, his hands curved around his flute.

Late that afternoon, Torin awoke, his mind filled with a blend of music, heather, and stars, surprised at feeling his flute in his lap. He shook his head. "What a dream," he murmured. "What an amazing, incredible dream!" He carefully placed his flute on the ta-ble, then frowned at a piece of manuscript lying there. He reached out to put it back where it belonged, then, catching sight of notes written on it, paused and took a better look. He gazed in disbelief at the notes he had heard in his dream, played by a Master on the flute he had just placed on the table. Then he saw the signature at the bottom and clutched the music to his chest, his aged face alight with wonder.

～ ¿ ～

The following morning, Kaelin stood outside the cottage with Dar-ryk and Laena, loath to say goodbye. He looked at his friend and barely succeeded in producing a smile. "I can't even begin to trans-pose what I'm feeling right now into words. And there's so much I want to say."

"You don't need to say anything."

Kaelin's eyes filled with tears. "You've been a true friend since the day you greeted a very intimidated apprentice at Bard's Land-ing. I had the best Master in all the world, but no chance of any friendships until you offered me yours. You listened to my darkest memory, taught me how to build my harp, put up with all my impudence. You've always been there for me ... thank you."

"They may take away your freedom to speak to me for a cycle, but they can't take our friendship away for a single moment," Darryk said strongly, "and we are brothers now as well. The addition to our home that your Master provided is yours whenever you want it." At the look of surprise on Kaelin's face, he smiled. "He didn't tell you?"

Kaelin wordlessly shook his head. He had assumed the addition had been Darryk and Laena's doing.

"We couldn't have afforded to buy it back, much less renovate it," Darryk said. "Your Master did both, then put it in Laena's name and yours. So, if you choose not to return to Kyet, come back to your home and family. Laena and I both need you."

Amber eyes and brown rested on each other for a long moment, then Kaelin turned to his sister, whose tears traced shining paths down her cheeks. She hugged him for a long moment. "You *will* come back, won't you?"

He looked at the pain in her eyes and swallowed hard. "Of course I will ... I just don't know when." He stepped back and hoisted his packs.

Darryk and Laena watched him go, their hands entwined, their hearts as heavy as the apprentice's footsteps. Master Bergid had already made his farewell and was waiting at the edge of the woods. Kaelin turned once and waved, managed a fleeting smile, and was gone.

Coda

Passage to a New Beginning

Chapter 24

Kaelin stood at the stern of the ship with his Master, watching the island of Kestrel grow smaller with each passing moment. He sighed. "You can never really go back, can you?"

"Not as the same person, nor to the same place. Time changes both all too quickly."

The apprentice nodded, continuing to stare out over the waves even after the island disappeared from view. Looking back was more comforting than looking forward.

A few hours from Kyet, the crew was shocked to see a large kestrel fly to the apprentice's outstretched arm. He fed the bird and spoke to it gently, then set it on the railing. The kestrel paced restlessly back and forth, allowing no one near it but Kaelin. When the coast of Elegy appeared, the kestrel launched himself into the air and flew toward it, and the apprentice took himself to his quarters. He did not emerge until the ship had anchored off Bard's Landing. Two crewmen rowed them to shore, and as Kaelin stepped onto the beach, he nearly cried out as the mountain's song pulled him with renewed force, stronger than he had ever felt it before. Indeed, it seemed to thrum through the earth itself.

He had barely recovered himself as Bards Byron, Havalek, and Lendin came hurrying toward them. After exchanging greetings, Kaelin gripped arms with his friend.

"I see the three of you are as inseparable as ever!"

Byron chuckled. "We're all assigned to different territories now, but we convinced Master Grened that you couldn't possibly land on Elegy without our personal assistance."

Kaelin assumed a shocked expression. "Sirs! Are you still pestering and inconveniencing the Master Bard of Elegy in the last cycles of his life?"

Havalek's eyes danced merrily at Kaelin's deft mimicry of Master Grened's voice. "We certainly are, you young rascal, and he's loving every minute of it!"

"Not only that," Lendin put in with a challenging air, "but just you wait until I fetch my harp!"

Havalek groaned. "Fair warning, Kaelin. Master Grened has been working him over, and he's positively itching to challenge you to a duel."

Kaelin gave Lendin a grin. "I'll look forward to it."

Byron turned to Master Bergid, who had listened to this exchange with a bemused expression. "We'd like to thank you for sending Kaelin to us, sir. This island is a far better place for it."

Master Bergid smiled. "That I can well believe. Are the other Masters here yet?"

"Yes, sir. They're all settled and will greet you tomorrow morning at your cabin. They instructed me to tell you they'll be armed with their instruments."

Kaelin pumped his fist in delight, and the Bard continued. "They also said to send word if either of you preferred to be left in peace. I believe I already have Kaelin's vote."

"And mine to match it. Let's be on our way, then."

Havalek and Lendin hurried to take the Master's pack and instruments, and Byron insisted on taking Kaelin's. A steady hour's walk brought them to the Master's cabin, located just east of the Council Grounds.

"Where is Kaelin?" Byron asked suddenly. The Bards looked

blankly at each other. The apprentice's pack and three of his instrument bags were hung where Byron had placed them. Kaelin and his harp were gone.

"I think I know where he is," Master Bergid said, moving toward the door. "You're welcome to stay here this evening, if you wish."

"We'd love to stay, sir," Byron said, "but if you prefer to spend the evening with Kaelin alone, we certainly understand."

The Master paused. "Thank you, but I think good food, company, and music would be a welcome distraction for us both tonight." The Master left the cabin and followed the steep path behind it to the top of the hill.

Bardic Mountain's twin peaks rose in shadowed splendor, the sun just beginning to sink behind them. Directly below, the Chyrn cut a silver path through a valley flushed with the last rays of sunlight. Kaelin sat motionless before it, harp in hand, staring at the mountain.

"How can something that looks so beautiful be so frightening?" the apprentice asked softly, as though questioning himself. "How can I want so badly to go there, yet at the same time want to run from it as far as I can get?"

"What frightens you about it?" the Master quietly asked.

"It ... pulls me, and I don't want to be pulled by something I don't understand. Master Grened is right. The mountain wants something, and I think ... it wants it from me." He turned his gaze away from the mountain with effort and stared at his harp as though startled to find it in his hands.

The music seemed to come from nowhere and everywhere, as if it originated from the air itself ... indeed, the listener did not at first realize it came from Kaelin's harp. The young harpist's fingers moved steadily and surely across the strings, the music increasing in power as though amplified by the currents of wind crossing the valley.

The listener's senses were filled with a vision of a much smaller, secluded valley that Kaelin's voice had painted for him once before. A waterfall shone like a satin ribbon against the cliffs. The listener was drawn inexorably toward it, moving faster and faster until he was sure he would be propelled into the icy spray and dashed against the rocks. With heart-stopping suddenness, he was in a dark tunnel, moving with unabated swiftness into the heart of the mountain. He emerged into dazzling sunlight, blinking furiously, to find himself standing on an open, barren ledge. To the right a granite cliff, sheer and formidable, rose into the sky. A mere glimpse. Then the image faded away.

The Master stood staring at his apprentice, who was looking at his own hands as though they belonged to someone else. "Was *that* the mountain's song?" Bergid asked when speech returned to him.

"I don't think so," Kaelin whispered hoarsely. "It was just one phrase of what I heard—I didn't even want to play it!—and that vision came out of nowhere." He seemed to diminish to a boy before the Master's wondering eyes.

Bergid gently took the harp from Kaelin's unresisting hands, and they returned to the cabin and the excellent meal the Bards were preparing. Afterwards, Lendin had his duel with Kaelin and, though he was soundly beaten, was proud of his performance and accepted Kaelin's astonished exclamations with a pleased grin. Then Byron took up his harp and swept his young friend into one duet after another. Master Bergid, unable to resist joining them, soon made it a trio. Songs and laughter filled the cabin until a late hour, when the weary travelers finally gave in to their need for sleep.

The next morning, they awoke to dappled sunlight streaming through the open doorway and Master Marek frowning at them in mock disapproval. "Never have I witnessed Bardic indolence on such a grand scale as this," the Master Flutist said severely. "You can all be thankful Master Grened didn't arrive here before me, or your ears would be ringing with reprimands ... and deservedly so. I've half a mind to fetch him myself." He crossed his arms and watched them struggle out of their bedrolls.

"Hopefully the other half has better sense, then" Bergid growled as he emerged from his room. "Though I've been given reason to doubt it."

Marek glanced startled into Bergid's face and turned accusing eyes upon Kaelin. "You told him!"

The apprentice flushed deeply, ashamed that his thoughtless words had put the friendship of these two Masters at risk. "I'm truly sorry, sir, and hope you can forgive me?" He looked beseechingly into the Master's stony expression.

"I'll consider forgiving you *after* hearing what happened. In detail," Marek said sternly, for all the world like a father taking his erring son to task.

"I was just telling my Master about my travels, and when I got to Elegy I said I was glad to hear your nightingales were all right. He asked me how I could have known that, and then—"

"He effortlessly pried the whole story out of you!"

Kaelin's flush deepened. "I'm very sorry, sir."

"You ought to be, after giving me your word not to tell him! I suppose he shot straight through the roof?"

"We were fortunately outside at the time."

"That's a shame. He might have knocked himself out and forgotten your inexcusable slip of the tongue!" Ignoring a chuckle from Bergid, Marek kept an implacable gaze on the apprentice. "And what," he demanded, "prevented him from commandeering the next ship to Zephyr—never mind if it was bound for Eyrie—in order to murder the unfortunate Master Bard of that island?"

"Well, I tried to stop him, but he wouldn't listen at first."

"Listening is difficult when one is busy making furious comments of their own. What, exactly, did he have to say?"

Kaelin glanced uneasily at his Master. "Perhaps you should ask *him,* sir," he suggested hopefully. "He said a lot of things."

"Don't try to insinuate there were too many for *you* to remember!" the Master warned, ignoring yet another chuckle from Bergid. "I'll hear them from you, since it's *my* life that's hanging in the balance, and *you're* the one who put it at risk!"

"Well, he was … a bit surprised that you didn't tell him about your … side trip."

"A bit surprised, was he?"

"Yes, sir."

"And?"

"And he … mentioned your birds."

The Master Flutist stiffened. "My birds? He insulted my *birds?*" Clearly this was an affront of unprecedented proportions.

"Oh, no, sir!" Kaelin hastened to reply. "He just … thought you might enjoy learning how to fly like them."

The Master Flutist's mouth twitched. "Did he?"

"Yes, sir."

"And then?"

"Well, then he … said a few things about … a friend of his."

"I imagine he said *several* things about that particular friend. And after that?"

"He … had a few things to say about me."

"You?" The Master's brow lifted. "What on earth was he upset with *you* for?"

"For not having the sense to leave."

"I see. What else?"

The apprentice made no reply. When the Master's inflexible expression did not change, he reluctantly answered. "Well, he … wanted to know how long I planned on keeping him from knowing what happened."

"And?" Marek raised an inquiring brow.

Kaelin flushed deeply and looked so uncomfortable that Master Bergid answered for him. "He told me he planned on waiting until I grew old enough to deal with it," he said dryly.

Marek stared at him for a moment, then began to chuckle. "And what was his reaction to that?" the Master Flutist asked Kaelin, making a valiant attempt to regain a serious expression.

The apprentice frowned. "He seemed to find it as amusing as you did, sir," he said disapprovingly.

Catching a droll glance from Bergid, Marek's chuckles turned into outright laughter.

Bergid raised a brow. "I doubt you would laugh if you knew how close you came to being the *late* Master Flutist of the Bardic Isles. Perhaps you'd best forgive the boy, since his impudence put a stop to my wrath long enough for me to hear the full story."

Marek's eyes danced. "Yes, that *is* a point in his favor." He turned to Kaelin. "I'm glad to see that, after needlessly putting my life in danger, you had the good sense to save it." He placed a firm hand on one of the apprentice's shoulders. "I want you to know, Kaelin, that I discreetly sent one of my Bards to Elegy a week after I saw you. The report he brought back not only set my mind at ease about your welfare, it pleased me greatly."

"Thank you, sir."

Marek looked inquiringly at Bergid. "I trust the island of Zephyr is no longer in danger of attack from the island of Kestrel?"

"Not at the moment."

"What a relief! I'll send word that the Bards of Zephyr can stop practicing defensive maneuvers and return to their usual activities." He turned his gaze back to the apprentice. "I'll consider the score settled between us, Kaelin, if you'll join me in a few duets."

Kaelin grinned. "How many will it take to settle it?"

"Hmm ... refresh my memory again. How many levels higher is my rank than yours?"

"Five levels higher."

"Five duets it is, then."

When the duets were finished, the Master put his flute down with a sigh of regret. "I should have demanded ten. No piece of music lasts long enough when you're playing it."

The apprentice smiled. "Thank you, sir."

"Have you had any experiences with feathered songsters since you left Zephyr?"

"Well," Kaelin said consideringly, "he's feathered, all right, but I wouldn't call him a songster. He only knows one note and one articulation. He can use a few different dynamic levels, but fortissimo is his favorite." The apprentice slipped his leather sleeve on, then took the Master outside and called Brek to him. A few moments later the kestrel flew to his arm.

Marek's eyes widened in recognition. "Is that ..."

Kaelin nodded. "Brek is the one who protected your birds from that eagle."

"Well, he has my fervent thanks for it! He disappeared the day you left. Fortunately, the eagle had found himself a new territory and didn't bother us again. Brek followed you?"

"He followed me all the way from Kestrel and back again."

"And you used your voice to call him, instead of your flute," Marek said in wonder.

"Three months on Lyra gave me a different kind of flute."

"I wonder what Talan will think of that," Marek said with a sideward glance at Bergid, who had followed them out.

"For heaven's sake, Marek, don't tell him!" Bergid exclaimed. "We'll never hear the end of it."

"Never hear the end of what?"

All three turned to see the Master Bard of Elegy walking toward them. Marek glanced at Bergid, whose jaw had tightened. Before anyone could say a word, Kaelin lifted his arm, sending Brek into flight. Master Grened stopped short at the sight, and Kaelin promptly surprised him further with a hug. Grened, grumbling pointedly about the mannerless greetings of apprentices, nevertheless took his time about releasing him.

Kaelin stood back and swept him a bow. "Master Grened. It's a pleasure to see you again, sir!"

"Hmph! It's a pleasure to see you regain your senses, boy. Now, what sort of intrigue is afoot? Who isn't supposed to tell what to whom?"

"I believe my voice is not to be discussed with Master Talan."

"I should certainly hope not!" Grened frowned at his colleagues. "If Talan hears that this boy's voice is the equal of any of his Bardic instruments, we'll never accomplish anything for who knows *how* many cycles."

"My point exactly," Bergid agreed. "Do convince Marek of it."

The Master Flutist, smiling in relief at his colleague's mild tone of voice with Grened, raised a hand. "I'm convinced, I'm convinced," he surrendered with a laugh. "He won't hear a word on the subject from me."

"Good," Grened said. "I, however, have a word or two for this apprentice of yours, Bergid, and both of you might as well hear it." He turned to Kaelin. "Traditionally, apprentices do *not* teach Masters, but you seem to be an exception to all rules, boy." He glanced up at Marek's chuckle, then continued. "This island is benefiting from that, and you have my sincere thanks for it. And, I might add, for the additional harp music you somehow found time to write and leave for me. They're ... quite effective."

Kaelin's face lit. "It was my pleasure, sir."

Marek cleared his throat. "I've heard that the Master Harpist I studied under has returned to Elegy," he said, smiling as Grened glanced at him in surprise. "Welcome back."

"And," Bergid chimed in, "you have my sincere thanks for sending Kaelin—"

"I was simply making a well-deserved point!" Grened huffed.

"Of course you were," Bergid said equably. "The unintentional effect of which was much appreciated."

Grened nodded curtly, then unslung a pack from his shoulder and handed it to Kaelin. "This is for you," he said, then scowled at the three Bards standing in the doorway. "So *that's* where they are!" He strode toward them, muttering a disparaging comment about Masters who stole other Master's Bards without a word to anyone. Kaelin stifled a laugh as the other two Masters exchanged droll glances and followed him.

The apprentice lingered outside to open the pack he'd been given. Inside was a net, fishing hooks, coils of thin, lightweight rope, a tinder box, flints, two knives, utensils, a folded oilskin, cloths, a cooking pot with small vials of tonics packed tightly inside, each labeled in the Master's elegant script, tins of salt and garlic, even a small box of dyes to replace those he had been given two cycles before. Tears welled in Kaelin's eyes; it was several moments before he was able to school his expression and enter the cabin. His eyes caught the Master Harpist's as he carefully placed the pack next to his old one. He gave a slight bow, the Master gave the slightest of nods, and that, Kaelin knew, said everything that needed to be said between them.

After a light breakfast, instruments were slid from Bardic travel bags, and music once again filled the cabin. Though Grened made frequent comments lamenting the waste of valuable time, he clearly did not wish to leave. After one such remark, he lifted his harp with a challenging glance at Kaelin.

"Still think you can beat a Master on his own instrument, boy?"

"That depends on the stakes, sir."

"Same as ever."

"Challenge accepted!" Kaelin reached for his harp. "The key?"

"Same as the first time ... D major. Would you prefer the root or first inversion?" the Master Harpist inquired.

"Age should be granted the advantage of the root position," came the deferential reply.

Grened snorted. "Cocky as ever! Marek, if you'll give us the beat, I'll see if I can cure him of it. *You* take the root, boy! Youth needs every advantage it can get."

Kaelin nodded, his eyes dancing. Marek obligingly tapped the beat, and the harpists took off in a whirl of arpeggios, skillfully inverting each before reversing their direction. Both faces set in concentration, they flew ever faster up and down the strings, matching each other note for note at an impossible pace. Just before the end, Grened paused slightly, and Kaelin finished barely a moment before him. He bowed to the cheers of his audience, then looked with narrowed eyes at the Master he had beaten, knowing full well the pause had been deliberate.

"I suppose you'll be returning first thing in the morning, sir?"

"Yes, I'm afraid so," Master Grened said mildly. "My congratulations, boy."

"Would someone care to enlighten Marek and me?" Master Bergid asked plaintively. "What, may I ask, were the stakes?"

"If I lost," Kaelin explained, "I would have to do any copy work he gave me. However, since he lost, he has to make breakfast in the morning."

Bergid and Marek stared at each other, quite aware that the Master Harpist's loss had been intentional.

"I see," Master Bergid finally said, glancing at Grened. "Well, we'll find an extra chair for you, then."

"An extra *two* chairs, Bergid," put in Marek, crossing his arms stubbornly. "If you think I'm missing out on breakfast cooked by the Culinary Master of the Bardic Isles, you're quite mistaken."

"Make that an extra *four*," came an unexpected voice. "I believe Grened's new title requires the *unanimous* vote of the Council before being bestowed." Master Rial stood in the open doorway with Master Talan close behind him.

During the laugh that followed the Voice Master's words, Kaelin put aside his harp and stood to bow, then greeted the Masters in a crystal-clear voice. "Masters Rial and Talan. It's good to see you both, sirs."

Master Rial nodded. "And for the two of us to see you," he said simply. "I would, however, much prefer to hear you use your *instrument* to greet us."

Kaelin swung his medallion over his shoulder to hang against his back. He threw his shoulders back, took a deep, relaxed breath, and sang a greeting in a beautifully controlled voice that quivered with power.

Master Rial smiled. "You have not forgotten."

"I will never forget."

Three Masters glanced at each other, fully expecting Rial to begin one of his interminable debates with Talan on the qualifications of the voice as a Bardic instrument, with Kaelin as the prime example. Rial, however, merely laid a hand on Kaelin's shoulder and went to stand near the fire without another word. Talan's astounded gaze followed him.

Before the Instrument Master could collect himself, Kaelin stood before him. Master Talan looked at him searchingly and smiled. There was no evidence of the boy who had left his island nearly a cycle ago in confusion and shame.

"My workshop hasn't been the same without you, Kaelin," he said warmly. "If the Council's verdict is not in your favor, I would like you to consider coming back with me to Eyrie before returning to Kestrel. No one can forbid me to speak to you, and there is much I can teach you about the making of instruments. And," he added with a defiant look at his colleagues, "there is nothing in Bardic Law forbidding the invention of an instrument that would be permissible for you to play. As it happens, I have the designs for two such instruments in mind. One is stringed and bears a slight resemblance to a Bardic harp, though it is emphatically *not* one." He glared at Grened, who held up a hand and shook his head. Molli-fied, Talan continued.

"The other bears some resemblance to a flute, having keys and rods for a very decent range, but it's larger and is held directly in front of the player." He threw a challenging look at Marek, who produced an excellent imitation of Grened's silent disclaimer.

"You needn't decide now, Kaelin," Talan said gently. "It's an open offer, available to you whenever you wish to take it. You will find that any Captain will grant you free passage to my island and the use of my berth, on my given word to reimburse him."

Kaelin looked at him for a long moment, feeling tears sting his eyes. "Thank you, sir."

The Instrument Master nodded and went to warm his hands at the fire. Master Rial regarded him thoughtfully as he moved over to give him room.

Kaelin glanced at his Master and went outside, Bergid follow-ing. They stood at the edge of the clearing, watching the crescent moon sink below the darkened outline of Bardic Mountain.

"When will it be, Master?"

"Tomorrow afternoon. The Spring Council will commence the day after."

Kaelin silently nodded.

"If the Council decides against you, are you coming back with me to Kestrel? I understand why you might not be willing to stay with me if I have to—" Bergid broke off, unable to say it.

Kaelin shook his head and turned toward him. "That isn't why. I won't hold what you have no choice to do against you ... or any of the others."

"Why, then?"

Kaelin's gaze returned to the mountain. "Because," he finally admitted, "I don't think I'll be able to leave Elegy."

Bergid frowned. "Has the mountain's pull grown so strong?"

"I've been feeling it even on Kestrel. It's much stronger here."

"Why didn't you tell me?"

"I didn't want you worrying about it when there's no way to stop it. If it were up to me," he told his Master, "I'd go with Master Talan, make the two instruments he designed that I could play, and pay him for his time and materials by working in his shop. Then I'd return to you. But until I break free of the mountain's pull," he said bitterly, "I doubt I'll have a choice of which island I prefer to live on." He grimaced. "If I managed to board a ship, I'd have to be restrained from jumping off and swimming back. When I sailed to Kestrel, I had to stay in the prow and keep my focus on you, never looking back. The pull from here is much stronger than it was from Tryl."

Bergid turned abruptly toward the mountain, his eyes fierce, his expression hard. *If you pull my fledgling away from me, know that I will stand against you until you release him.*

"If I can't come back," Kaelin quietly continued, "I won't forget anything you've taught me. Wherever I go, I won't make you ashamed of me."

Bergid did not move.

"You've been far more than a Master to me. Whatever you have to do tomorrow won't ever change that," Kaelin said softly. "You've loved me like a son."

The Master cleared his throat in a valiant effort to speak. "I'm sorry I've ... I've never told—" he began, his voice barely audible, his throat too constricted to continue.

"Haven't you, sir? Since the moment you apprenticed me, there's not a day I've spent with you that you haven't told me."

The Master turned then and pulled Kaelin close, wondering how he would ever find the strength to preside over the coming Council hearing.

When they returned to the cabin, they found the Masters engaged in a lively quartet. Grened was on harp, Marek pipes, Talan kithara, and Rial was singing a rousing song of the exodus from

Eire. Bergid immediately fetched his flute and joined them, the Bards and apprentice ready to spell any player wishing to rest. Song after song they played, far into the night, until weariness overtook them.

Master Bergid took Kaelin's flute and handed it to him. "Perhaps the last song should be reserved for you alone."

Kaelin held his flute, the awareness that this might well be the last time he would ever play it written clearly on his face. He looked at each of the Masters in turn, as though memorizing their features, then lifted the finely crafted Bardic instrument.

As the first phrase of music filled the room, the listeners found themselves speeding northwest toward the island of Eyrie. They swept over hills of grass and heather toward the Instrument Master's workshop. He worked on a harp—a tambour—a lyre, his fingers deft and sure, intense concentration and care put into every detail of his work. He stood on the streets of Skye fixing a broken doll with the same absorbed interest. His hand gently touched the leaves of a wild clary ... swept upward to identify star-studded constellations.

Then the flute's music carried the listeners aloft, moving them eastward across the ocean at breathtaking speed. Far below, they could see the steep cliffs and secluded valleys of the island of Zephyr as they sped toward the Master Flutist's home. He sat alone before an open window, playing a sprightly melody on his flute, birds chirping and trilling in counterpoint. He leapt through a doorway and twirled joyfully around the room. He pulled a cloth out of a Bardic flute. He stood near the edge of a cliff, a gold cord joining his hand with his beloved's.

Once again the listeners were swept upward, rushing with the wind to the island of Lyra and the Voice Master's home. Here the Master shaped and developed voices with the same care Master Talan had exhibited in his workshop. He regaled his listeners with tales and songs of long ago, teaching even as he entertained.

He walked through a field, peacock butterflies rising into the air, his clear voice lifting with them.

Yet again the listeners soared upward with music that sped them toward the island of Elegy and the stream outside the Master Harpist's home. The Master stood on the bank as ripples of water swirled something long and dark out of sight. He played his harp, firelight and shadows flickering and dancing to his music. He directed ensemble groups, demonstrating and balancing the parts. Every face was lit with respect, with the excitement of playing with him and for him.

Then the listeners sped northward toward the island of Kestrel with a thrill of joy that was almost painful in its intensity. On a hillock above Kyet, the Composition Master stood before a bonfire, laughing as though he would never stop. He gifted his music to an old man whose face was lit with wonder. He shared the listener's low notes, filled with painful memories. He enveloped them in his arms and eased an aching, unbearable loneliness.

The music faded away, gently releasing the listeners. For a long moment they sat still, lost in the magic of the experience. When at last they roused, Master Bergid was sitting before the fire, Kaelin curled up against him. No one spoke as Bards and Masters quietly gathered their instruments and left.

The following day had scarcely broken before they returned. Grened lost no time commandeering the small cooking area, armed with extra supplies brought by his Bards. It wasn't long before the air was filled with the fragrance of poached eggs, toasted rusks, and potatoes fried with fresh garlic, wild onions, and dried herbs. Praise was heaped upon the Master Harpist, who frowned and feigned deafness. He maintained his aloof indifference even when Rial stated that, since Grened was ineligible to vote on a matter concerning himself, four affirmative votes were enough to ratify his new title as the Culinary Master of the Bardic Isles. Three other Masters swiftly agreed. A vote was taken, which was unanimous, whereupon Bergid tapped his teacup three times with his fork and pronounced the new title officially bestowed. Cheers and clapping filled the cabin, and though Grened snorted and muttered something about being surrounded by a pack of fools, he couldn't quite hide his smile.

After everyone left, Master and apprentice sat talking together, both of them keeping the conversation focused on light-hearted memories, each trying to make the other laugh, neither of them succeeding. Though the two of them had eaten little of Grened's excellent breakfast, no mention of lunch was made.

"Would you play a song for me, Master?"

The words were spoken so softly that Bergid barely heard them. He silently reached for his flute, wondering how the sudden lump in his throat would allow him to play.

"The first birthday I spent with you, you asked me to choose five notes, and you turned them into a song for me. Do you remember?"

I could never forget. The Master's unspoken words hung between them for a long moment before Bergid found the strength to lift his flute.

Seemingly from nowhere, as though the instrument had given up on the Master and decided to play itself, music filled the air. Faltering just a bit at first, it gained in strength and clarity as the Master played, his eyes never leaving Kaelin's. Utterly convinced that he couldn't have played a note to save his soul, Bergid played regardless, finding the strength to do so in the amber eyes of a boy who meant everything to him. He played, and it seemed to them both that somehow this simple song the Master had improvised from Kaelin's chosen notes twined between the two of them, connecting them as firmly as though the Master's gold cord and the apprentice's black one had wrapped themselves around them. It spoke of all the many experiences they had shared in just a few cycles, of teaching and learning, of heartache and laughter. It spoke

... and said everything words could not. Then the music segued back to the beginning, taking them both back in time to the moment their eyes first met in the village square of Vale.

The last note faded away and the beautiful Bardic flute was laid gently aside. They sat looking at each other for a long moment, and then the Master rose and indicated that it was time.

Kaelin waited for him to step outside before slipping into the bedroom and pushing a folded paper deep inside the bedroll. Then he shouldered his instruments and followed his Master, achingly aware that it would be the last time he would ever do so as a Bardic apprentice.

Chapter 25

Kaelin, following his Master down the many steps to the Council Grounds, paused for a moment and looked with dread at the setting below. The Council table stood in the same position as it had when he had played there two cycles ago, the chimes and mallet at the far end of the table, where an empty chair awaited Master Bergid's arrival. Master Grened sat to its right, with Master Talan next to him; Master Rial to its left, with Master Marek next to him. The place at the open end of the table had no chair, but a high stool stood prominently nearby with a leather strap coiled on top of it, a silent reminder of the punishment meted out to thieves who refused to take responsibility for their actions. Kaelin turned his eyes quickly away as he reached the bottom of the steps. He stood still as Master Bergid seated himself at the head of the table, the other Masters rising as he did so. The Senior Master motioned for them to be seated and indicated the opposite end of the table to Kaelin. The apprentice approached, laid his instruments down beside him, and stood silently before the Council. His chest hurt and he swallowed hard, hoping he wouldn't be required to speak soon. He doubted anything intelligible would come out.

Master Bergid, his emotions tightly reined, noticed Kaelin's intent scrutiny of the Council table and paused, giving the youngster a chance to contain his own turbulent feelings. When the apprentice looked up, the Master reached for the mallet and struck the smallest chime three times.

"This Council hearing is now in session. A charge of theft has been brought against Kaelin, an apprentice of the Bardic Order. Master Talan, would you please explain the circumstances which resulted in this charge?"

Master Talan stood. He stated the relevant events in clear and thorough detail, from the moment he had been unable to find his tuning fork to the bestowing of the medallion, then took his seat.

"Kaelin, do you agree with the summary Master Talan has just given us?" the Senior Master asked.

"Yes, sir."

"You have spent nearly a cycle bearing this medallion, understanding the restrictions placed on you?"

"Yes, sir."

"Master Talan, did this apprentice disobey the Council's restrictions during his time with you by removing the medallion or playing a Bardic instrument when not under instruction by a Bard or Master?"

"No, he did not."

The Senior Master received the same reply from each of the other Masters except the last one.

"Yes, once," Marek said. At the surprised expressions of the others, the Master Flutist continued. "However, it was to save the life of a child trapped on the cliffs, and he freely told me of it the moment he returned. His account was verified by several villagers. I brought no charge against him then, nor do I now. Indeed, I commend his action, which he took believing that he would lose his flute and suffer the punishment of this Council for it."

The Senior Master glanced at the looks of agreement around the table and struck the largest chime. "It is decided by this Council that Master Talan rightfully brought a charge of theft against Kaelin and that the Council's restrictions were not broken." The Master turned his gaze to the apprentice.

"Kaelin, tell us why you accepted the token from Master Talan instead of the usual punishment for theft."

"Because of the first promise I ever made to you, sir, that I would never lie again. To admit stealing from Master Talan would be a lie, and I will not break my word to you."

"You do not wish to change your plea, then? The Council will give you this one chance to do so. It will not be offered again."

"No, sir. I did not steal that tuning fork, or anything else, from Master Talan," Kaelin said firmly.

"Do you know, then, how his silver tuning fork came to be in your pack?"

"I believe Bard Tyrel put it there, but I can bring no charge against him without proof."

"Did Bard Tyrel have any reason to do such a thing?"

"I'm certain I gave him no cause, but something happened earlier that evening that might have. After playing my flute for the Bards, I ran some arpeggios on my harp for a few moments and music came to me that I wanted to play. I set a block, so as not to disturb the conversations in the room, then closed my eyes and played it. It took me up into the air, where I saw what looked like colored paths going in all directions. It startled me, and when I opened my eyes Bard Tyrel was staring right at me. Then the music modulated on its own and showed me something that seemed like a memory ... only it wasn't mine."

More than one Master at the table frowned at this statement.

"Has your music ever shown you an unfamiliar memory before?" Bergid asked him.

"I think it did once," Kaelin said hesitantly, "when I played one of your compositions and saw a Bard with tears in his eyes."

His Master sat completely still for a long moment. "Yes," he quietly verified. "That was a memory of mine. Tell us what you saw at Master Talan's."

"I was inside a cabin, sitting in front of a fireplace, and ... one of the flames didn't dance like the others. It was completely still, with a black center like a hole. And it … spoke."

Talan and Marek looked startled. Rial frowned.

"What did it say?" Bergid asked.

"It said 'There is a traitor,' but then Bard Tyrel knocked a vase off the table and my link to the music was broken."

"Are you saying that he broke the vase deliberately?"

Kaelin shook his head. "I didn't see him break it."

"Did anyone else appear to have traveled with you?"

"No, sir, but I wouldn't have been aware of it if they had."

"Has anyone ever managed to breach a block you've set?"

"Not that I know of."

"Yet you feel that Bard Tyrel did?"

"Not at the time. But thinking back on it, it's possible that when I opened my eyes directly into his, it made a connection that took him through the block."

"You realize feelings and conjectures do not constitute proof and cannot be taken into consideration by Bardic Law?"

"Yes, sir, I do. I'm only relating the experience I had because I think it's something the Council should know about, and … I might not be able to tell you later."

"Is there anything else you think we should know?"

"No, sir."

Master Bergid turned to the Council members. "Does any member of the Council wish to ask Kaelin any further questions?"

When all four Masters replied in the negative, Bergid continued. "All the facts of this case have been brought before you. This session is now open to discussion."

Talan spoke first. "I remember that Tyrel seemed more stunned than one would expect after simply knocking a vase off a table. It seems quite possible that Tyrel *was* linked to Kaelin and deliberately broke the vase, hoping to break the link. Couldn't we test that theory right here, using the five of us as his audience?"

"We could," Rial replied, "but even if it worked, it wouldn't prove that it happened to Tyrel. Indeed, we could sit here and dream up possibilities all afternoon, but it would be pure conjecture with no way to prove any of it. We don't *know* if Tyrel saw anything of Kaelin's vision, or why he would be upset enough by it to frame him for theft, which is all that this Council hearing is concerned with."

"And what about the traitor?" Marek demanded.

Rial shrugged. "That could simply be a dream Kaelin once had that he doesn't remember, or even a dream of Tyrel's. A frightening one, no doubt, but there's no reason to think such a thing is *real*."

"The boy had the same vision of an unusual flame in my home, one with eyes in it," Grened interjected, "and he was not playing an instrument at the time. I was."

Three Masters glanced at him in surprise.

"That would lead me to believe both occurrences were his own dream, then," Rial said. "Regardless, without actual proof, and despite the fact that I would wish it otherwise, none of what Kaelin has told us is admissible as *evidence* to this Council, evidence which would logically result in a charge against Tyrel."

Master Bergid glanced around the table at the reluctant nods of agreement, then forced himself to continue. "Very well, then, the case as presented to you is closed. Should Bardic Law be carried out against this apprentice for an act of thievery? I, for one, will vote that it should not."

All eyes swiveled to the Master of Composition. Kaelin's eyes filled with emotion.

Rial frowned. "On what grounds, Bergid, would you vote against it, outside of the fact that this is your apprentice we're passing judgment on?"

"On the grounds that in this case, Bardic Law is unjust, and I will not support it."

"Then you're breaking it yourself!" Grened accused.

"I'm breaking nothing," Bergid retorted. "Any law is subject to interpretation, and I am well within my rights to vote any way I see fit. *No* law can force me to judge someone guilty whom I know to be innocent."

"But Bardic Law must be upheld, whatever we may personally think," Grened stated emphatically. "I don't like it in this instance any more than you do, but we have an obligation—"

"To condemn an innocent person?" Bergid icily interjected. "I have no such obligation, under Bardic Law or any other."

"I quite agree." Every eye turned to the Master Flutist. Marek looked calmly around the table. "I will also vote not to carry out Bardic Law against this apprentice, on the same grounds. He is innocent of the charge against him."

"Marek!" Rial exclaimed. "I can understand Bergid's position. Kaelin is his apprentice, after all. But *you,* surely—"

"Are you accusing me of favoritism, Rial?" Bergid demanded. "I assure you that, if anyone else whom I knew to be innocent were standing there instead of Kaelin, my vote would remain the same. The fact that he is my apprentice makes it worse for me personally, yes, but it does *not* affect my judgment!"

"Regardless of who he is or why you're doing it, you're setting aside Bardic Law for him!" Rial shot back. "No Master has the right to do that, under *any* circumstance!"

"I must agree with Rial," Grened said. He held up a hand, forestalling Bergid's reply. "Do not misunderstand me! I, too, would like nothing better than to set it aside and let this boy walk out of here with his instruments and his Master, but I have no right to do so, for I cannot do it without breaking my sworn oath! And neither can you."

"Are you saying, then," Bergid asked evenly, "that the evidence against him is sufficient to prove his guilt?" He looked inquiringly at Rial and Grened.

Rial nodded curtly.

"Yes," Grened said decisively. "The tuning fork was found in his possession, before witnesses."

"So, then, you must believe he is a thief and a liar," Bergid said reasonably, "for the evidence, as you have just said, proves him so. Why, then," he continued in a steely voice, "would you like nothing better than to set Bardic Law aside and let him walk out of here? Shouldn't you be eager to toss this young criminal out of our Order and free me from his nefarious presence?"

The Master Harpist frowned darkly at the chimes.

"Your silence," Bergid said quietly, "tells me you believe he is as innocent as I know him to be." He turned to Rial, who refused to meet his eyes. "And what about you? Surely the Voice Master of the Bardic Isles will not hesitate to raise his voice against such a sly and deceitful youngster, who stands there without a trace of shame on his face." White brows lifted sardonically. "But then, apprentices *are* known for their poor memories. I'm sure you discovered as much during his stay with you ... Kaelin!" The voice cracked authoritatively.

"Sir?" came the startled reply.

"Look at Master Rial. He has something to tell you."

Kaelin immediately turned his attention upon the Voice Master, who intently studied the table.

"Well, go on, Rial," Bergid said, gesturing toward Kaelin. "Refresh his memory. Surely the lack of remorse on his face comes from not remembering what this is all about. Look that boy in the eye," he commanded, "and tell him he is a thief and a liar!"

The Voice Master looked briefly into Kaelin's eyes, then turned to the Senior Master. "You know I can't do that."

"No?" Bergid's brow lifted. "So, your reluctance to apply Bardic Law is not in mere sympathy for a young boy's plight, then? You believe in his innocence?" His other brow lifted at Rial's continued silence. "As Senior Master, I must insist that you answer my question. If Kaelin is to be condemned by this Council, he deserves to know it's being done in spite of a unanimous belief in his innocence. I will allow no voting until the three of you who have not yet made that clear to him do so. Do you believe in his innocence, Rial?"

The sea-green eyes looked again into Kaelin's. "Yes."

"Grened?"

The Master Harpist looked directly at the apprentice. "Yes."

"Talan?"

The Instrument Master nodded. "Yes."

Kaelin glanced at his Master. "Thank you," he whispered.

Bergid nodded, then surveyed his colleagues. "Tell me, then, *how* do you know he is innocent? What evidence do you have for that belief?" He looked inquiringly at Rial.

"I know it because I've gotten to know him," the Voice Master replied, "and I don't believe his music could lie, even if he were so inclined."

Bergid turned to Grened.

"I've witnessed the boy's behavior under more than one trying circumstance," the Master Harpist said.

"So ... you both believe Kaelin is innocent because you know his character. Thus, you have a greater well of information to draw upon than Bardic Law, which knows only this one incident and is blind to Kaelin's character."

"The Law *should* be blind!" Rial said emphatically. "People's assessments of character can be flawed and untrustworthy."

"Someone who trusts a blind law and has no faith in his own ability to see clearly isn't fit to uphold that law," Bergid stated.

Grened snorted derisively. "If all leaders were fit, what need would there have been to flee Eire? It's because of imperfect leaders that the Law was created. Even you, Bergid, are human and thus fallible ... surely you see the truth of this."

"I see that there are at least two Masters at this table who do not trust their own judgment!"

It was Rial's turn to snort. "Rather say that there are at least two Masters at this table who understand that the Law was designed to override the fallibility of human nature. Everyone believes their own actions are justified. The Law stands as an impartial judge of those actions, where we cannot be impartial … as, I might add, *you* are demonstrating."

"So, we should put aside our common sense and allow the Law to take over? A Law which holds the evidence against Kaelin sufficient to prove his guilt?" The Senior Master's eyes swept the Council. "How can the evidence against Kaelin possibly prove what none of us believe?" he demanded.

"It can't and doesn't," Marek said flatly, "for anyone could have planted that tuning fork in his pack. The fact that it was there is not proof that *he* put it there. We also believe in his innocence, as you yourselves do. *We* do not stand in a position of contradiction. *You* do."

Bergid nodded agreement. "If the evidence against Kaelin is not sufficient to prove guilt, then clearly Bardic Law should not be carried out against him. If this Council does so anyway, it is a misuse of the Law we are sworn to uphold!"

The Voice Master shook his head. "It is a misuse of Bardic Law to set it aside for our own personal reasons, however you might rationalize it and however much I myself would like to do so!" he insisted.

Bergid reached out and unhooked the largest silver chime from where it hung on the set in front of him. "Such a small thing," he said, giving it a brief inspection as he held it up before them. "About the size of your tuning fork, wouldn't you say, Talan?" At Talan's brief nod of assent, the Senior Master continued. "So easy to slip into a pack. *Your* pack, perhaps," he said, turning a speculative gaze on Rial. "And if I did this simple thing when no one was looking, then complained of it having gone missing during this session, what would happen? As second Senior Master of this Council,

Grened would be obliged to ask us to open our packs ... and there it would be, plain as day, in the pack of the Voice Master of the Bardic Isles."

Rial flushed with outrage, but the Senior Master was not finished. "Never mind that you have no earthly reason to steal the chime, and that it's against your known character to do so. The mere discovery of the chime in your pack, before witnesses, would force Grened to charge you with theft, for under Bardic Law, it would constitute *clear proof of guilt*. And since you could not prove that *I* did it, you would face the choice of lying to this Council and confessing to the charge in the hope that *perhaps* you would be re-admitted to our Order a cycle from now. If, however, you dared to speak the truth and contest the charge, those consequences would become permanent. Which would you, a Master Bard, choose? My *apprentice,*" the Master growled, "chose not to lie!"

Marek stabbed a finger at the inoffensive chime. "And that's how easy it would be to rid our Order of *you,* if one of us were so inclined. Poof! One less Master of the Bardic Isles, all accomplished with the full cooperation of Bardic Law."

"Then *change* the Law," Rial said angrily, slapping the table to emphasize his words. "But until it *is* changed, with the full endorsement of all members of this Council, do not ask us to set it aside and break our oath! Must I remind the two of you of the words you swore? *'I will uphold Bardic Law.'*" He glared at Marek and Bergid. "How, exactly, are you upholding Bardic Law by setting it aside for someone you care for?"

Bergid glared back. "You're ignoring the second part of that oath. 'I will uphold Bardic Law, *as far as it lies within me to do so.*' It does *not* lie within me to condemn an innocent person, whether I care for him or not!" His gaze swept the table. "All laws are written by fallible human beings, which is why none of them are perfect. Upholding *any* law at the expense of justice, which is a principle of the Maker himself, is not within me to do. I have a higher moral obligation to uphold the dictates of my conscience, and it does *not* break Bardic Law, or set it aside, to do so!"

Grened shook his head emphatically. "By such reasoning, you could justify setting aside Bardic Law for anyone you chose, stating that you believe them innocent and then refusing to uphold the Law on the grounds that it's against your conscience!"

"And by *your* reasoning," Marek swiftly countered, "you'll apply Bardic Law even when you know the person charged is innocent! The question is, which is more just in a given case? You can say that applying the Law in Kaelin's case is the correct thing to do. You can say it's necessary. You can say it's all so terribly sad, but oh, well, we have to do it anyway. But you *can't* say it's *just.*"

If glares could kill, only one Master of the Bardic Isles would have been left alive at the table. Talan sat in growing horror at the escalating battle before him, unwilling to join either side, for this was the same battle that had been raging inside him since the moment he hung the medallion around Kaelin's neck. And for the life of him, he still did not know which side of it he belonged on. He glanced at Kaelin, and his heart wrenched. The boy stood forgotten, pale and trembling, tears running freely down his face.

Isn't what we're going to do to him—what I've done to him— bad enough without traumatizing him beforehand?

As the battle between the Masters raged on, Talan quietly rose, walked the few steps to Kaelin, and pulled the unresisting apprentice into his arms. "I'm sorry," he said gently, holding Kaelin to himself tightly. "I'm so sorry. You do not deserve any of this." The words brought unexpected clarity to the Master's mind, and he knew in that moment what his vote would be.

Silence fell over the Council Grounds, the charged atmosphere evaporating. Only Talan heard Kaelin's whispered words against his chest. The Master held the apprentice at arm's length and searched his face for a long moment, then returned silently to his place at the table. No one spoke. The Instrument Master reached past Grened, picked up the mallet and tapped the largest chime with it.

"There's been quite enough discussion," Talan said flatly. "If the three most Senior Masters will not finish this, I will. Should Bardic Law be carried out against this apprentice for an act of thievery?" He glanced at Bergid. "How do you vote?"

"No."

"Grened?"

The Master Harpist's face was filled with grief. "Yes."

"Rial?"

The Voice Master closed his eyes. "Yes."

"Marek?"

"No."

Four Masters looked at Talan, whose eyes turned to Kaelin. The apprentice returned his gaze unflinchingly.

"Yes," the Master gently said.

Had an observer been watching from above, he would have thought that single word had cast a spell upon the Council Grounds, turning every participant to stone. No one moved. Not a sound broke the stillness.

At last Master Bergid rose from his chair, as stiffly as if he had indeed been forced to break through invisible bands of stone to do so.

Kaelin closed his eyes, suddenly sick to his stomach.

"Please give each of your instruments to a Master, to be kept by him or given to anyone of your choosing."

Kaelin bent and picked up two of his travel bags. The first contained his lute, lyre, and kithara, the second bag held his pipes. All four instruments had been made under the Instrument Master's direction. Hearing in his mind the haunting sound of the perfectly matched set of pipes, he walked to Master Talan and held both travel bags out. "I would like you to have these," he said unsteadily. "Perhaps you can find someone who deserves, but can't afford, such fine materials." The Instrument Master stared blindly at the offered instrument bags and silently accepted them.

Kaelin went back to his instruments and picked up his harp. In his mind he could see the carvings he had made for each island, hear the fluent arpeggios coming from its strings. He glanced at Master Grened, but the Master Harpist was intently studying the chimes again and would not meet his eyes. Kaelin approached his Master and held it out. "Would you..." he fought to control his voice. "Would you give this to Darryk for me?"

His Master nodded silently and took the harp from his hands. Turning abruptly away, Kaelin walked back and picked up his flute. Unable to prevent himself, he laid it on the table and undid the tasseled ties. He slid the case out and opened it, then removed the flute and attached its headjoint. He held the instrument closely to himself, struggling to control his emotions. Leaving the case and travel bag behind, he began the longest walk he had ever made. Memories of making the beautiful flute assailed him as he approached his Master. He tried to speak, but his words refused utterance. He tried to hold the precious instrument out, but his arms refused movement. His mind cried out in torment. *Not this! Take anything else, but not this!*

The silence in the Council Grounds remained unbroken. Master Bergid's eyes rested on his apprentice. He made no move to take the flute from him.

The words that came at last from Kaelin were barely a whisper. "You always give me time when I most need it." With all his strength of will, he reached for the Master's hand and, opening it, placed his flute there. Then he turned and walked back, fighting the impulse to turn again, snatch back his beloved instrument, and run with it as far as he could from the Council that had unfairly taken it. He forced himself to stoop and pick up the small flute he had made so long ago in his father's workshop. *Will they take even this from me?*

He stood and turned around. His Bardic flute, case, and travel bag were no longer in view, nor were any of his other instruments. Kaelin choked back a sob, knowing he would never see them again. Once more he walked the length of the table and placed the small instrument gently in his Master's hand.

Master Bergid frowned, then withdrew the flute from its bag and held it out to Master Talan. "Would you define that as a Bardic instrument, Talan?"

The Instrument Master took the flute carefully and inspected it gravely from all angles before handing it back. "Certainly not," he said emphatically. "That was clearly made by the hands of a child, in bare mimicry of a Bardic flute, and without any of the key rings and rods that *all* Bardic flutes are required to have."

Master Bergid placed the small flute back in its bag, then placed it firmly into Kaelin's shaking fingers. He closed his hand over his apprentice's until the trembling stopped. When he removed his hand, Kaelin walked unsteadily back to his pack and placed the small flute inside before facing the Council again.

"Do you have any other instruments?" the Master asked.

"Only ... my voice, sir," came the barely audible reply.

"The voice is currently held under petition for recognition as a Bardic instrument," Master Bergid said gravely, "and must be voted on before I can tell you if you will be allowed its use for music." He glanced around the table. "As you all know, a unanimous vote is required for inclusion, and all previous votes on this matter have resulted in four votes in favor and one vote against. Assuming no one has changed their—"

"Though the timing may seem unfortunate," Talan quietly interrupted, "I have indeed changed my mind and wish to alter my vote."

Four pairs of startled eyes turned to the Instrument Master. Before he could continue, the Voice Master surged to his feet.

"No!"

Heads swiveled to Rial, who was glaring at Talan.

"No?" Talan raised a brow.

"The voice," Rial growled, "is *not—*"

"Don't say it!" Talan shot back. "Do *not* stand there and lie to save a boy who refused to lie to save himself! I'll accept no such lie from any of you!"

"And isn't that precisely what *you* have just done?" Rial challenged. "Though why in the name of the Maker you would want to hurt—" He bit his words off abruptly.

"I would not willingly hurt him more than I already have," Talan said quietly, his eyes turning to Kaelin. "Nor have I lied. For last night I had a dream … that someone came into my room in the middle of the night to give me my own private vocal performance, with only the moonlight coming in through my window as witness."

All eyes flew to Kaelin, whose attention remained fixed on the Instrument Master. Rial fell heavily back into his chair.

"I was certain I must be dreaming," Talan continued, "for he never said a word, made no argument or impassioned appeal. He simply sang, filling my mind with the incredibly detailed images his music evokes from all his other Bardic instruments. I experienced the moment his voice became an instrument in Rial's home. I heard the loneliness in his voice as he called a wild kestrel to him for the first time. I felt the pain of bearing for so long a medallion that I myself laid around his neck, eased by his Master's presence … a presence he is forfeiting this day through no fault of his own. Then he turned and left, having never spoken a word. I lay awake for some time and came to the conclusion that the voice is clearly an exception to my definition and qualifies as a Bardic instrument of the highest order. For," he said gently, "no other instrument has ever moved me as deeply as that voice did … no, not even the Voice Master's himself." He looked around the table at the stupefied faces before him.

"Therefore, I will *insist* that my vote be changed, and the voice added to the list." Talan sat comfortably back in his chair and looked at Bergid, whose expression was unreadable. "As Senior Master of the Council, tell us what Bardic Law says about a vote that has been altered on an issue locked in stalemate."

The reply came without hesitation. "It states that one full day must pass before that vote becomes final, during which time the Master who changed it may change it back again. This caveat was put in place to avoid undue pressure being placed on any one Master by another to influence his vote. It gives him time for reflection, to be certain that his vote is being given from his own conviction."

"Skillfully done," Grened murmured as he glanced at Talan.

The Senior Master picked up the mallet and firmly struck the largest chime twice. "It is hereby decided by this Council that the voice will be included as a full-fledged Bardic instrument, effective tomorrow afternoon, provided Talan doesn't take the opportunity Bardic Law has given him to change his mind."

"I will not," Talan stated, looking directly at Rial.

For a moment the two Masters regarded each other. Then Bergid turned toward Kaelin.

"Now that this sensitive subject has been settled to everyone's satisfaction, I can confirm that you may use your voice for music, for it is not currently on the list of Bardic instruments."

Kaelin closed his eyes briefly in relief, then opened them to find his Master staring at the chimes as though he had been transported far from the Council hearing.

Master Grened spoke in a low voice. "Bergid, you don't have to do this. One of us, perhaps—"

"No!" The single word, torn from the Master's throat, startled everyone. Bergid rose with calm determination. "I would rather hate myself than any one of you," he said. He moved down the length of the table, stood before Kaelin, and looked deeply into the amber eyes.

The apprentice's voice came as a bare whisper. "What you

must do, Master, please do quickly."

Bergid reached out and removed the chained medallion from around Kaelin's neck and hurled it away as though the very feel of it sickened him. It struck the stone floor with a dissonant metallic clang. Then the Master removed his belt knife from its sheath. Knowing he would never forget the stricken look on Kaelin's face, he took firm hold of the black cord around the boy's waist, the cord he had bestowed himself and that had once been laid over his own on the Council table. Slipping the edge of his blade beneath it, he sliced it in two. The cord fell to the ground as though slain by the stroke. Then, with a swift, clean motion, the Master cut through the apprentice's robe from top to hem. It fell away from Kaelin and lay on the ground around his feet.

Amber eyes and blue still held each other motionless. Finally, the Master spoke. Though the words were neither loud nor harsh, they fell with devastating force on the trembling boy before him.

"Your robe and cord are taken from you. You have no Bardic rank and for one cycle may not freely interact with those who do. You are forbidden all Bardic instruments. You have no Bardic Master."

Kaelin stood paralyzed before him, feeling as though the Master's knife had ruthlessly sliced more than just his robe and cord in two. Half of him stood in shock. *This can't be happening. I've done nothing to deserve it!*

The other half stood as an incredulous observer of the first. *You've known all along that this was going to happen. Wasn't nearly a cycle of wearing that medallion long enough to get used to the idea?* He stood stunned by the fact that neither time nor knowledge had made the actual event any easier to bear.

Master Bergid stood in his own moment of bitter agony. *It would have been far easier to use the knife on my own throat.* He motioned toward the stool and forced himself to speak. His voice sounded as though a stranger had the use of it. "You will offer the strap to each Master, beginning with the one who leveled the charge against you. Each has the right to inflict up to five strokes."

Kaelin stepped woodenly from the ruins of his robe and fetched the strap as though in a dream. He held it out to Master Talan, who shook his head emphatically.

"I refuse the right."

Kaelin then offered it in turn to Masters Marek and Rial, both of whom refused it, the Voice Master in a rough tone that would have earned any Bard of Lyra an instant reprimand.

The Master Harpist, however, glanced at the strap before him and said, "I do not refuse the right." Glances of surprise came from his colleagues, but the Master Harpist's eyes lifted only to Kaelin. "I do not *have* the right."

Kaelin nodded silently at the Master's distinction. He turned and offered the strap to Master Bergid, who took it only long enough to hurl it after the medallion. Bergid returned to the head of the table and struck the large chime once again.

"Bardic Law stands fulfilled; the judgment of this Council pronounced. But before this punishment becomes permanent, I would like to enter a plea on Kaelin's behalf."

Yet another ripple of surprise went around the table.

"Bardic Law has condemned Kaelin as a thief and a liar," Bergid continued, "yet not one of us can do so. The Law gave each of us the right to further punish him, but not one of us took it. The Law took away his instruments, lest he should harm anyone with his music, yet there is a young girl of Zephyr who could tell you she owes her life to this *dangerous* music of his." The Master snorted in disgust. "If any of you can recount a single time his music ever hurt anyone, I'll destroy those instruments with my own hands." He looked challengingly around the table, but no one spoke. "By majority vote, the Law has taken away his instruments, his robe, and his Master. I do not dispute the Council's right to inflict this, but when the Law stands in the way of justice, I submit to you that *we must not.*" His fist punctuated the words against the table.

"None of us disagrees with you, Bergid," Rial said quietly. "State your plea."

"Kaelin was barely thirteen cycles of age when the charge was brought against him. He turned fourteen five days ago, thus even at this hearing he is still not of age, the age of fifteen, when he would stand fully responsible under Bardic Law for his actions. Any boy of thirteen, convicted of thieving in the marketplace of Kyet, would not receive the same punishment from any Guild or village Council as one who was of age. Surely the only reason our Order doesn't have a similar distinction is because no one except Kaelin has ever been made a Bardic apprentice before coming of age." He paused as the other Masters nodded in agreement.

"He has already suffered more than he should have," Bergid continued, "bearing the stigma of that medallion nearly as long as if he had lied to Talan and admitted to a theft he did not commit. I submit that what he has already endured, added to yet another cycle of the punishment we have just decreed, is more than sufficient to satisfy Bardic Law. I therefore ask that Kaelin be allowed to return here next cycle when he comes of age and, subject to the unanimous consent of this Council, be restored to his former rank and privileges, including the return of his Bardic instruments."

Kaelin bit his lip so hard in the resulting silence that he tasted blood. He hardly dared to breathe, waiting to hear what the Masters' response would be.

Before anyone could speak, Master Talan rose, lifted a large pack sitting against his chair, and emptied its contents. Dozens of thin scrolls scattered across the stone table. "You're not the only one to so plead, Bergid, and had you not done so, I would have made a similar one myself. For these are pleas from Bards of every island, asking that Kaelin's punishment not be made permanent. They claim that doing so would make us guilty of punishing the entire Bardic Order with him. I quite agree." He withdrew a scroll from his robe, opened it, and surveyed the astonished Council. "And *this* plea, which goes a long step further than simple written support, I will read aloud. For the Council needs to hear it, and Kaelin deserves to." Then the Master began to read.

"I would add my voice to the scrolls that must surely be winging their way to you from every island, asking the Council not to make Kaelin's punishment permanent. We all know he's innocent of the charge laid on him, that he could no more commit a theft and lie about it than he could take wing and fly away from the unjust judgment about to fall on him. I'm grateful for the cycles I have spent as a member of our Order and would prefer to remain and serve the Bardic Isles to the best of my ability. But I will not stay in an Order whose Law would mete out an irreversible punishment upon an innocent person. Nor will I allow my robe to keep my friend and brother from his own sister. Therefore, if Kaelin's punishment becomes permanent, I will resign my membership in the Bardic Order and return my robe and cord to the Council, though I retain my Bardic instruments and my right to their use. Please let Kaelin know that he has, and always will have, a home with us."

Master Talan glanced at Kaelin, who was staring at the scroll in shock. "It is signed 'Bard Darryk, currently serving the island of Kestrel.'" The Master turned back to the astounded members of the Council. "These scrolls are an unsolicited, unprecedented tribute given by the majority of our Bards to an apprentice ... one of whom is willing to forfeit his membership in our Order for him. This is a tribute we should *not* ignore. I, for one, am very willing to add my own plea to both Bergid's and these and restore Kaelin when he comes of age."

"As am I," Marek said strongly. "Perhaps the Law makes no room for mercy on those occasions when it falters, but nowhere does it forbid us the use of it." He glanced at Grened and Rial. "If Kaelin's lack of cycles provides us the opportunity to do so, let's take it without hesitation."

"I agree," Grened and Rial said in instant unison.

The largest chime struck a heartbeat later. "It has been unanimously decided," stated the Senior Master, "that Kaelin's punishment shall last only until he comes of age, when he may reappear before the Council to be restored to his former position, which will require a unanimous decision. During that cycle, he may not play any Bardic instrument, nor may he interact freely with any member of the Bardic Order. Since he has already been closely monitored for a cycle by the Masters he has stayed with, further monitoring will not be required. Does this Council agree?"

"We do," came the Master's chorus.

"Do you understand and agree to abide by the terms of the Council's decision, Kaelin?"

The former apprentice tore his eyes away from Darryk's scroll and looked up with a dazed expression. "Yes, sir."

The Master struck the smallest chime thrice. "This Council hearing is ended. I ask the Council, however, to remain for a short while, as there are a few other matters I wish to discuss."

Kaelin looked for a moment into the eyes of his former Master. Then he turned and walked away. The Masters watched in silence as he climbed to the top of the stairs.

Then he was gone.

Chapter 26

After Kaelin left the Council Grounds, bereft of his instruments, robe, and Master, the Council sat for a long moment in silence. Then the Senior Master, looking as though he had aged ten cycles, turned his eyes upon Talan, who closed his own as though finding his colleague's steady regard unbearable.

"Please don't, Bergid," the Instrument Master said in a low voice. "There's nothing you can say to me that I haven't already said to myself. Believe me, having to live with the blame for this is punishment enough."

"You're not to blame for placing that medallion around Kaelin's neck," Bergid told him. "Nor do I blame anyone for their honest vote."

Talan's eyes flew open.

"The four of us, however, voted as we believed was right. You, I think, did not."

Talan sat frozen in silence.

"What did Kaelin say to you?"

Still no reply came from the Instrument Master.

"Tell me, my friend," Bergid said quietly. "I need to hear it from you."

Talan's face twisted with grief. "He knew. With the four of you stalemated, he knew it would come down to my vote. He ... asked me to vote against him," he said, his voice breaking. "And, may he one day forgive me for it—for I will assuredly not—I did as he asked."

Rial and Grened were thunderstruck. Marek, looking almost as haggard as Bergid, closed his eyes.

"Yes," the Senior Master said softly. "He would do that."

"But why?" Rial exclaimed. "He only needed one more vote in his favor!"

When Bergid made no response, Marek answered for him. "He did it because he was refusing, once again, to be that pebble."

Grened frowned. "Pebble?"

Marek opened his eyes directly into those of the Master Harpist. "The day I followed Kaelin to the stream, I ordered him to leave with me. He refused. He said he would soon heal, but if Master rose against Master, how long would it take for the Bardic Isles to heal? He said his Master once told him that even the smallest of pebbles can start an avalanche. Then he told me that he would not be that pebble. I did as Talan just did. I left him there, as he asked."

Grened stared speechlessly at Marek.

"And now," the Master Flutist continued vehemently, "with four Masters at each other's throats over the Law, he once again refused to be that pebble. He chose to lose *everything,* believing it would be forever, rather than see this Council split in two. *That's* the kind of boy the Law has just condemned. I tell you now, I will not rest until I see it changed!"

Bergid stirred. "Bardic Law is definitely overdue for revision and this Council must do it as soon as possible, preferably before the end of this Spring Council. No innocent person must ever be subjected to what Kaelin just endured on these Council Grounds." He glanced at Talan. "I think, however, that Kaelin had more reason to ask you to vote against him than seeing this Council split in two. Though I made no mention of it to him, I think he understood the consequences to befall the Bards of Eyrie if he were to be acquitted, consequences only one of them would deserve." As shocked realization spread around the Council table, the Senior Master of the Council rose to his feet and reached for the mallet.

The Master Flutist's face drained of color. "Bergid, please—"

"Don't try to stop me, Marek, for I know perfectly well you would do the same for him." He picked up the mallet, gently struck each chime once, then handed it to Grened, who dropped it onto the table and stared at him in shock.

"I resign my position as Senior Master of the Council, Master Bard of Kestrel, and Composition Master of the Bardic Isles," Bergid stated. His eyes held Grened's. "I'm confident the Master I leave in my place as Senior Master will serve the Council well."

In the profound silence that followed, Bergid untied his gold cord and laid it on the table, as he had done once before on Kaelin's behalf.

"I make no further claim of any Bardic rank whatever. Not being guilty or accused of any wrongdoing, I retain my instruments and my right to interact freely with all members of the Bardic Order." He removed his white robe, walked to where Kaelin had so recently stood and gently covered the sliced apprentice robe with his own, as if by so doing it might be made whole again.

"Bergid, you can't do this! It's only for a cycle..." The Master Harpist's voice was filled with grief.

"If I could cut Kaelin's robe from him," Bergid said quietly, "I assure you I'm quite capable of removing my own." He glanced at the stricken faces around the Council table. "His robe, his instruments, and his Master have been torn from him, but *I* will not be taken from him. Not for forever, not for a cycle ... no, not for a single day." Calm certainty rang through every word.

"You'll find that Kestrel has been left in good hands," the former Master continued, "and is well able to manage on its own for as long as it takes you to choose another Master for it. Choose wisely for me. The compositions left in the home of the new Master

Bard of Kestrel I give to him, to be used as he sees fit. My personal items can perhaps be stored by him for me to collect later." Deep emotion crossed the Master's face, as if imagining the moment he would enter the home that was no longer his own to collect items that no longer had a place there. He cleared his throat.

"Thanks to all of you, Kaelin has the right to return here and request reinstatement a cycle from now. I, however, do not, for I am no longer a member of the Bardic Order, and when I leave here, have no right to return. Have I your permission to accompany him here, regardless? This favor I will ask of you, for I would very much like to see the robe and instruments I just took from him returned to their rightful owner." Receiving nods from his former colleagues, he turned to Marek.

"Once Kaelin is reinstated to the Bardic Order, he will need a new Master. If you're willing, I could ask for no better one for him than you."

Marek barely managed a single nod, tears running freely down his face.

"I'll relocate to Oriel at that time, then, to remain available to Kaelin," Bergid said. "I will make no attempt whatever to interfere with your handling of him." The former Master Bard looked for a long moment at each of the Masters. "It's been the greatest privilege of my life to serve the Bardic Isles with all of you," he told them. "Truly I couldn't have asked for more wonderful colleagues and friends. I'll miss you all more than I can say."

Bergid abruptly turned and walked across the Council Grounds without looking back. He paused for a moment as the sound of chairs scraping against stone reached him. As he began climbing the stone steps, only the slight trembling of his shoulders betrayed his emotion at the silent tribute behind him.

The former Master reached the top of the steps and walked slowly back to his cabin, feeling strangely naked clad only in tunic and trousers. *I'll have plenty of time to get used to it.* When he opened the cabin door, however, Kaelin wasn't there, nor were his two packs or his bedroll. With a groan, Bergid slapped his palm against the door, furious with himself for not having anticipated that Kaelin wouldn't wait, wanting to spare both of them any more pain. He quickly gathered his packs and began rolling his bedroll. A crumpling noise made him stop to search it and he withdrew a folded note. Opening it, he began to read, tears soon blurring the words before him.

Don't blame yourself, Master, for what you were forced to do. You told me once that each of us must play the part we're given for the beauty of the full score to be heard. The parts we've been given now are hard ones, in a horribly minor key, but perhaps one day we'll hear the full score and understand the part they played. In case I can never see you again, know that I will always love you. —Kaelin.

Bergid stood staring at the piece of paper. Then he slipped it into his pack, hung Kaelin's flute and harp on the wall next to his own instruments, and hurriedly wrote a note to Byron asking him to care for them. The former Master would sorely miss his instruments, but the less burdened he was, the easier it would be to catch up, and Kaelin didn't need to be reminded of what he had just lost. A cycle might not seem overly long to an old man like himself, but it was an eternity to a boy barely fourteen. Bergid shouldered his pack, then paused for a moment, frowning at his flute. Slowly, reluctantly, he removed it from its peg and held it for a moment. An observer might have thought, by the tension in his face and the trembling of the hand that held the precious instrument away from him, that he was straining to put it back, but could not. He glared at it in exasperation, then slid it into his pack and left.

After leaving the Council Grounds, Kaelin walked randomly for a time, numb with grief. He was grateful for the mercy the Masters had shown him and was vastly relieved that his punishment hadn't been made permanent. He was thankfully free to use his voice but was at a loss to know what to do with himself. A whole cycle stretched in front of him, empty of everyone and everything he cared for. His mind clamored for him to take Master Talan's offer to help him make two instruments he could play, but he would not go there until one Bard in particular left that island. His heart yearned to return to Kestrel with his former Master, no matter how hard the restrictions would be on them both.

Not that either of these choices were options he could consider anyhow. He ground his teeth in anger. From the moment he reached the top of the stairs leading out of the Council Grounds, the mountain's song had strengthened its pull, as though fully aware that the only one who could hear its song was now alone. Until Kaelin found a way to free himself of it, he had no choice but to remain on Elegy. He glanced toward the eastern coast ... it was a long walk to Tryl, likely fighting the pull of the mountain every step of the way. But at least he would have a place of his own there, close to Master Grened's grove, and could support himself by making dyes to sell to the merchants of the seaport. That, he knew, was the most sensible choice available to him. Yet he hesitated.

The former apprentice came to a halt, surprised to find himself on the grassy knoll above his former Master's cabin. He looked uncertainly toward the west. Below him, the Chyrn river flowed from the south through the wooded hills and valleys of Elegy, on its never-ending journey from the mountain to the northern coast. It radiated a sense of peace and privacy that Kaelin yearned for after the trauma he had just endured. Farther west, Bardic Mountain stood, as beautiful as the music that even now pulled him insistently toward it. High overhead, Brek angled toward him, then turned and flew toward the Chyrn, skimming the trees southward along its banks before flying back, then flew toward the river again, his message clear to the watching boy. The mountain's song, strong and vibrant in Kaelin's mind, pulled at him with renewed intensity, as if it flowed with the force of the water, indeed, the very air that came from the distant peak. Strong as it was now, how strong would that pull be a cycle from now? Would he even be able to return to the Council to reclaim his rank and instruments ... to rejoin his Master? Indecision left, replaced by deep anger and a clear, immutable purpose.

You and I, he silently informed the mountain, *have unfinished business. And after that's settled, I'll go wherever I want to go with no more interference from you!* He walked quickly to the cabin, collected some food, strapped his bedroll to his pack, and hoisted it over his shoulders. He grabbed the pack of supplies the Master Harpist had given him, thankful for his many lessons in their use. Keeping his eyes strictly away from his former Master's instruments, Kaelin left the cabin and headed west toward Bardic Mountain. He moved with such skill through the trees that Bergid, though he searched long over the wooded slopes, would find no trace of his passing.

Chapter 27

ℬergid paused and wearily mopped his brow. The faint trail he was following was not often traveled, nor had he any clear indication that Kaelin had used it, but it was the only way to reach the two coastal villages east of Bard's Landing. Since the Council hearing two days before, the former Master had not seen or spoken to anyone except Byron, who had verified that Kaelin had not been to the small cove. Since the mountain apparently would not allow the youngster to leave Elegy for Eyrie, surely the boy's only remaining option was to head for the coastal villages and find someone willing to hire an underaged worker.

Bergid frowned, knowing Kaelin had little in the way of coin, and castigated himself for not having had the foresight to provide him with the funds needed to pay for room and board. But then, he reflected, he had never expected his fledgling to fly off on his own ... had assumed he would be waiting at the cabin. Upon leaving the Council Grounds, Bergid had wanted nothing more in his life than to take Kaelin in his arms and tell him he hadn't lost him, that he would *never* lose him. Instead, his boy was out there somewhere alone, thinking his former Master had turned his attention to the mundane business of conducting Spring Council meetings. Bergid ground his teeth in frustration. He had thoroughly canvassed the area around the Council Grounds in an ever-widening circle, hoping to discover which direction the youngster had headed, but without success. Kaelin, it seemed, did not wish to be found.

Bergid adjusted his pack more comfortably on his back, then paused, struck by the feeling that he was no longer alone. Glancing back, he frowned darkly. Though he had not heard so much as the rustle of a leaf, Grened stood less than two arm-lengths away, regarding him impassively.

"I thought I might find you out here when my Bard assured me you and the boy had not taken ship," the Master Harpist said gruffly. "Have you lost him already?"

"I can hardly lose what I have not yet found … Master Grened," Bergid growled.

"Skip the formalities," the Master growled back. "Rank or no rank, there's no need for such absurdity between us, not since we served our first rotation together as Bards on this very island!"

"In that case," Bergid flared, "go away! I've no time for anything but finding him." He turned to leave but was stopped by the authoritative voice of a Master Bard.

"If you refuse to speak with me as your friend, I'll exert Bardic authority over you and *command* you to stop and listen!"

Bergid turned in unbridled fury. "Do not hinder me or dare to call me your friend if you try! *No* one, not Master, friend, or the mountain itself, will keep me away from Kaelin!"

"The Maker help the poor fool who tries," Grened murmured, his icy expression melting into a grimace. He cleared his throat. "I'm no fool, Bergid. I didn't track you down to prevent you from finding him. I came to help you." He held up a hand, forestalling any response. "You're a decent woodsman, I'll grant you that," he said curtly, "better than any of the other Masters or Bards. But you know perfectly well that the best tracker in the Bardic Isles is standing before you. Let me find his trail for you." At Bergid's look of surprised skepticism, Grened sighed and briefly closed his eyes. "He told you what I did to him."

"He did not do so willingly."

"And yet you have not murdered me in my sleep."

Bergid's jaw tightened. "I assure you, you would not have slept through it! He forgave you ... for his sake and my own. I could do no less."

"Hear me out, then, for I bitterly regret what I did that day. And afterwards, if you wish to lay your belt across my back for it, I'll remove my robe and kneel down without protest, as I made him do." Grened looked into Bergid's astonished face. "There is no excuse for what I did to him," the Master said flatly, "nor for the way I've treated my Bards for the last few cycles, with unreasonable demands and flashes of temper ... but there is a reason. The boy understood, though I did not. He asked me if I could hear the mountain—" The Master broke off.

Bergid frowned slightly, remembering Kaelin's assertion that the Master Harpist hadn't been himself. "You can *hear* it?"

"No!" came the anguished reply. "I think it might be easier if I could. I can't hear its song, but I feel its weight, like a growing dissonance in my mind that perhaps no one but the boy can understand. I've felt it all my life, more and more as the dissonance increases with every passing cycle. The last several cycles have been unbearable. It's the reason I kept myself alone ... drove even my Bards away. I thought I was losing my mind. Wondered if I should step down as Master of this island, but what else did I have?" He clenched his fists. "So, I tried to control it by putting everything and everyone into neat little boxes in my mind so I wouldn't lose the mind that kept them there. And I lashed out at the very people I'm sworn to protect."

Grened paused and his voice softened. "And then that boy of yours came along ... that incredible boy who wouldn't fit into any box at all. A boy I assumed was a thief and a liar and treated—*mistreated*—accordingly. And in spite of what I did to him, he saw and understood. He told me I had unknowingly forged a link with the mountain ... and he told me how to break it. I only needed to stop playing the music that had come to me when I was a boy, music I never realized came from the mountain. So simple!" The Master threw his hands in the air, his expression drawn with remembered pain. "And so impossible! I tell you, Bergid, I thought I possessed considerable willpower, but I could not do it. I sat that night in my chair, shaking with the need to play it, unable to stop my fingers from setting themselves in place on the strings of my harp. And that boy of yours—that boy I had just *strapped* for a mere accident—handed me a harp composition he'd stayed up half the night composing for me." The Master shook his head as though still confounded by the undeserved gift.

"He played it," Grened continued, "and his music took me to a place that's ... special to me. The experience it gave me there was so incredible that I knew I would never look at another person or any living thing in quite the same way again. When I opened my eyes, my harp was put away with his composition on top of it, and I heard the words he never said as clearly as I can hear myself talking now. He told me to turn my focus away from the mountain and toward that which I love."

Bergid's eyes widened, remembering that pivotal moment on the Council Grounds two cycles ago when he and Kaelin had so clearly heard each other speak in their own minds. Kaelin, nearly overcome by the mountain's song, had cried out to him, and with all the force of his being, Bergid had sent the words he had never been able to speak aloud directly into Kaelin's mind. Three words that had banished the mountain's song and freed the youngster to play his own music. Little wonder the apprentice had known what the Master Harpist had needed.

"I play that piece every night," Grened continued, his features relaxing with the wonder of it. "It echoes with the memory of what he showed me and has broken the mountain's hold over my mind. Though I'll never admit this to anyone but you, I owe my sanity to that boy of yours, for I was assuredly losing it." The Master took a shuddering breath and scowled. "I'm not telling you this to gain your sympathy, for I neither want nor deserve it. I'm telling you so you'll believe me when I say that I know where your boy has gone. The weight of the mountain is worse since the Council hearing, as if it's reacting to his proximity, as I believe it did two cycles ago. And that means its song is more insistent, its pull greater than ever. If *I* can feel it, imagine its effect on him! He's not hiking to a coastal village, nor has he any intention of sailing to Eyrie. He's answering the call of the mountain."

Bergid paled. "No! He's not ready! Especially not now, when he's had everything taken from him." Deep creases worried their way across his forehead. "He told me the mountain was exerting more of a pull and that it might prevent him from leaving Elegy. But for him to give in to it and *go* there ... what is he thinking?"

"I would not presume to know what the boy is thinking," Grened said with a snort. "That's *your* field of expertise. But I do know something of the overwhelming force pulling him. And after what he endured on the Council Grounds, he would have left filled with grief and anger, in no mood to be pulled against his will. The boy hasn't given *in* to the mountain ... foolish or not, he's following the music to its source to take it *on.*"

The look Bergid trained upon the mountain was so fierce that Grened nearly took a step back.

"He won't be doing it alone!" the former Master growled, glaring at the lofty peaks. "What do you want of him?"

The Master Harpist glanced at the mountain, half expecting to find it leveled under that grim regard. "I doubt even the boy himself knows," he ventured to say. "Certainly, neither of us do. But if *I* were the mountain and knew you were headed my way, I'd think twice before harming a single hair on that boy's head."

With a final glare, Bergid turned away from the mountain, and the Master continued. "It never occurred to me that he'd leave without you, yet I felt compelled to check. And it's a good thing I did, for instead of coming across both your tracks, I came across yours alone, headed in the wrong direction."

"Well, what are we waiting for?" Bergid demanded.

Grened immediately turned to retrace his steps, Bergid following impatiently on his heels. For over an hour they moved quickly back toward Bard's Landing, then Grened took a narrow trail which led them just south of the Council Grounds. Here he paused, then frowned at something Bergid couldn't see. Without a word, the Master removed his robe, stowed it in the smaller of his two packs, and left the trail, moving slowly south through the scrub brush and brambles. Bergid silently followed, strongly reminded of the days he had spent being tutored in woodlore by Grened when they were first-cycle Bards together. Twice Grened paused, frowning in thought, then continued in a slightly different direction until they were headed almost due west.

"The boy is good," he muttered. "Best keep that in mind," he said more clearly, glancing behind him. "If he doesn't want to be found by *you,* he won't be. Knowing his destination is your only advantage ... and a slim one at that. It's a large mountain, and it's anyone's guess what part of it he's heading for. I doubt the boy knows himself. But I'd wager he'll have sense enough to head for the Chyrn and follow it as far as possible, which would take him to the higher peak."

A short time later they emerged from the trees and stood on an open, grassy knoll. In the west the peaks of Bardic Mountain rose like twin sentinels. Below them the Chyrn wound its way through the valley, flowing toward the northern coast. Grened nodded briefly toward the river. "This is the path he took. Even though it means going quite a way south before heading for the mountain, he'll follow the river for the easy water source and in order to lay in supplies. I doubt the boy's in any shape right now to travel quickly, giving you a chance to catch up." He glanced at the lowering sun.

"You should have time to make camp on its banks before it gets too dark, then head out in the morning."

Bergid frowned. "What if he crossed the river and headed straight for the mountain instead?"

As if in answer, a shrill spate of repeated notes reached them as Brek flew toward them from the south. He circled twice over their heads, then hovered directly above them. Suddenly the kestrel voiced a cry utterly unlike the separated notes typical of its kind. The extended, mournful cry rang across the valley, and the loneliness in it nearly broke Bergid's heart, for it seemed to echo the loneliness of the young traveler he longed to find. He focused on the hovering kestrel and impulsively sent a strong mental command to him.

Stay with him! My fledgling will need you now more than ever before.

Perhaps it was only wishful thinking that his message had been heard, much less understood, but the kestrel startled, then flew strongly toward the Chyrn. He glided south along the glistening river for a while, then arrowed down and disappeared among the distant trees.

"I believe you have your answer ... and another advantage in finding him, since I doubt that bundle of feathers will desert the boy any more than you would," Grened said dryly. He glanced at his friend's troubled expression as he stared in the direction Brek had flown. "Don't worry, your boy can handle himself out there. I've seen to that. He has excellent survival skills and will have little trouble feeding himself, especially at this time of cycle. And the pack I gave him is filled with all the things he'll need to make that an easier task."

"He never told me what was in it, and I forgot to ask. You knew, even then?" Bergid asked in surprise.

"I didn't know *when* he would answer the mountain, no ... but I knew it was inevitable that he someday would. If the boy acted sensibly and refused to answer it after he left the Council Grounds, he would need a way to earn a living for himself. So, I taught him to make my dyes and gave him permission to produce them in my dye shed and sell them. Before he boarded the ship, I mentioned that any compositions coming out of that young head of his and winding up in my shed would be fairly converted into coin. I taught him woodlore so he could live on his own nearby ... or in case he proved *not* to be sensible and went running off to the mountain." His eyes slid away from Bergid. "And, when I was filling his pack," the Master casually informed the river below, "I happened to drop a few silvers in the bottom of it." He cleared his throat. "Clumsy of me. I didn't go to the bother of unpacking everything to fetch them back out. He'll find them the first time he foolishly gets caught in a downpour and has to dry out his pack. There's more than enough to pay for food and lodging through the winter months, and I drilled him well on the location of every village on Elegy. With a memory like his, he won't have forgotten."

Bergid regained his power of speech with difficulty. "I ... don't know what to say."

"Then say nothing," Grened said curtly. "After what I did to him, and what he turned around and did for me, I owed him that much and more." He looked skeptically at the single pack over Bergid's shoulder and unslung the larger of his own two packs. "Here, take this. It's filled with supplies." He shrugged, once again avoiding Bergid's gaze. "Just in case I happened to come across some wandering fool out here who might need them."

Bergid suppressed a smile and took it. "Then this old wandering fool thanks you. And what you've done to help Kaelin ... I will never forget."

Grened nodded briefly and turned to leave. A strong hand grasped his shoulder, and the Master paused without turning.

"I forgave you unwillingly, for Kaelin's sake," came the quiet voice behind him. "I thought I meant it, but in reality it was just a decision to let what you did pass and put aside my burning desire to start a war between us. A war that, to my shame, an apprentice of thirteen cycles understood the ramifications of better than I did. I forgive you willingly now, for all you did afterwards for him, for explaining it to me today in spite of how difficult I know that was ... and for the sake of our friendship, which I was grieved to lose. There is nothing standing between us."

Grened stood motionless. "Not even my vote against him?"

"No. I know you did not do so willingly, any more than Rial did, but only because you sincerely believed you had no choice. Kaelin understands that as well."

The Master Harpist nodded, then turned toward Bergid and stopped short at the sight of the former Master's arm extended toward him. He blinked rapidly a few times as he reached out and grasped it with his own, then spoke with a touch of his usual acerbity. "If you ever tell anyone, including the boy, a word of what I've said to you..."

Bergid chuckled. "In forty cycles, when have either of us ever betrayed the other's confidence?"

Grened gave a curt nod. "And don't think I haven't noticed you're still favoring that left knee of yours," he said brusquely. "You'll find an ointment for it in the pack."

Bergid nodded gratefully, squeezed his friend's arm once more in farewell, then made his way down the wooded slope to the Chyrn, as intent on following Kaelin's footsteps as the apprentice had once been to follow the Master's.

End of Book Two of The Bardic Isles Series

Songs in Minor Mode

If t'were no songs in minor mode,
If sorrow never freely flowed,
If no song spoke of pain, deceit,
Would those in the major sound as sweet?

For into every life, it seems,
Come flowing in these two extremes.
Essential that we taste them both
If we're to come to our full growth.

Enjoy the majors in your life,
The times you're free of pain and strife.
And bless the minor songs you meet,
Or the major ones won't sound as sweet.

I hope you enjoyed your trip to the Bardic Isles!
If you would like to hear the music described in this book, all of
which was composed by the author, you can experience it in a
one-of-a-kind audiobook, available on all major audiobook platforms, including Audible (Amazon), Spotify, Apple Books, Google
Play, Barnes & Noble, Audiobooks.com, Chirp, and Kobo. Samples of the music can also be found on the author's website,
mhimedabooks.com, or scan the QR code below.
See the books … hear the music … experience the wonder!

Glossary of Basic Music Terms

Accent: (>) to play the note(s) with emphasis or stress

Adagio: a slow tempo, between largo and andante

Andante: a moderate, walking tempo

Allegretto: a moderately fast tempo

Allegro: a fast tempo

Arpeggio: the notes of a chord, played consecutively

Articulation: markings on notes that define their smoothness and duration, such as a staccato or accent

Augmented: a major chord with raised top note; has an uneasy or strange sound

Cadence: a series of chords that brings closure

Chord: usually three or four notes played together

Coda: a passage that brings the piece or movement to an end

Counterpoint: the combination of different melodic lines

Crescendo: a gradual increase in volume

Da Capo al Coda: a direction to go back to the beginning, then take the "coda" ending

Descant: the highest melodic line

Diminished: a minor chord with top note lowered; has a suspenseful sound

Diminuendo: a gradual decrease in volume

Dominant 7th, or V7: a chord comprised of a major triad and a minor 7th, such as C-E-G-Bb; has an unresolved sound

Dynamics: the range in volume of a piece

Embellishment: the ornamentation on a note, such as a trill

Fermata: a dot with a curved line over it that prolongs the length of a note or rest, at the discretion of the player

Forte: (f) loud or full in volume

Fortissimo: (ff) very loud or full in volume

Half Step: the closest possible distance between two notes

Interval: the distance between two notes

Inversion: a chord whose main (root) note is not the lowest; thus C-E-G (root) is inverted first as E-G-C, then G-C-E

Key Signature: a series of notes (most often a major or minor scale) that defines the tonality, the sharps and flats of which are usually notated at the beginning of the staff

Legato: to play smoothly connected, usually marked with a slur

Major Chord: the 1st, 3rd, and 5th notes of a major scale, played together; has a feeling of well-being

Marcato: (^) to play the note(s) with strong accentuation

Measure: fixed number of beats between two vertical staff lines

Minor Chord: the 1st, 3rd, and 5th notes of a minor scale, played together; has a feeling of sadness

Piano: (p) soft

Pianissimo: (pp) very soft

Presto: an extremely fast tempo

Scale: a series of notes from which melodies and harmonies can be built, the most common being major and minor

Slur: a curved line connecting two or more notes to be played smoothly connected, or legato

Staccato: a dot above or below a note, played short and light

Tempo: the speed of a piece

Time Signature: convention defining how many beats are in one measure, and what kind of note receives one beat

Tonic: first note of a major or minor scale, or a chord built on it

Tremolo: two notes played rapidly back and forth

Trill: a note played in rapid alternation with one a whole or half step higher

Vivace: a very fast and lively tempo

Whole Step: an interval comprised of two half steps; notes a whole step apart have only one possible note between them

Acknowledgments

This series would still be moldering in my computer were it not for Charis Himeda, who not only badgered me into getting it ready for publication, but provided her expert editing skills, which my readers can all be thankful for! She also continues to lead me though the confusing world of publishing, whose labyrinth I would otherwise have long ago been lost in. And thank you, Dawn Hollison, for providing another set of eagle eyes on this manuscript. I don't think a single participle could dangle its way past the two of you, and if it did, it could only be because I tampered with it after you were done. No author could ask for better editors.

A huge thank you to Jeff Brown, of Jeff Brown Graphics, for once again creating a stunning cover I could lose myself in. Looking at it, I can hear the very music coming from Bardic Mountain ... and understand why Kaelin can't resist its magic. Neither can I.

I would also like to thank Veronica Yager, who created a wonderful new website for my books. And last, but certainly not least, a huge thank you to Will Hahn, for his excellent narration of my audiobooks and his willing incorporation of my compositions. No one could ask for a more supportive narrator, or a better friend to travel the Bardic Isles with.

About the Author

Marla Himeda is an award-winning author and lifelong musician who taught piano and clarinet for eighteen years at Punahou Schools and for over half a century in her own studio. She teaches theory and composition courses, coaches ensemble groups, and is a prolific arranger of chamber music for winds. She has performed in the Seattle Opera House, the Seattle Art Museum, and many concert venues in Hawaii, where she has lived for the past fifty years near Mount Olomana, whose twin peaks sparked the birth of Bardic Mountain. She is a member of the National Music Teachers Association, Opus 5 Winds, and the Honolulu Wind Ensemble.

The Bardic Isles Series began over thirty years ago as a story the author told to her four children. It is now an epic fantasy series featuring music as the sole magical element, and the audiobooks include the music of the Bardic Isles, all of which was composed by the author. The Bardic Isles Series is a merging of two passions—music and writing—and portrays a unique world that the author unabashedly admits loving to escape to. The Bardic Isles Series has won nine international awards, including the 2024 Readers' Favorite Fiction Audiobook Gold Medal Winner, the 2024 IP Awards Outstanding Audiobook Winner, the 2023 IAN Fantasy Book of the Year Winner, the BookFest Audiobook Silver Medal Winner, and the B.R.A.G. Medallion.

Visit her at mhimedabooks.com